Annie Thomas

Theo Leigh

A novel

Annie Thomas

Theo Leigh
A novel

ISBN/EAN: 9783337050450

Printed in Europe, USA, Canada, Australia, Japan

Cover: Foto ©Andreas Hilbeck / pixelio.de

More available books at **www.hansebooks.com**

THEO LEIGH

A Novel.

BY ANNIE THOMAS,

AUTHOR OF

"DENIS DONNE" AND "ON GUARD."

NEW YORK:

HARPER & BROTHERS, PUBLISHERS,

FRANKLIN SQUARE.

1865.

THEO LEIGH.

CHAPTER I.

INTRODUCES THEO.

DOWN on the sea-board of the county of Norfolk, on the verge of a long waste of marsh-land that intervenes between it and the German Ocean, there stands a little village, Houghton by name, semi-agricultural and semi-aquatic by nature.

A hardy little village, as it befits one of such purely Scandinavian traditions to be, scorning to shelter itself from the fierce winds that blow across to it from the hardier north, or from the chilling blasts that whistle shrewishly along from the east. A hardy enduring village, bravely patient of the blasts, and as bravely opposed to the mastery of the sea, whose encroachments it has checked with a deftly-constructed bank of most impervious mud; an artistic village, whose fields are tilled and pasture-lands are cultivated into the semblance of the fairest mosaic; an independent village, that sends its own smacks out to "oyster-sea" and panders unassisted to the bivalve loves of its inhabitants; a gallant little village that guards its own portion of the coast from those ruthless rascals the smugglers, by aid of a naval officer in command of six able-bodied seamen; a little village, that is so superb in its appearance of utter remoteness from and indifference to all that goes on beyond its own confines,—that revolves on its own axis so quietly year after year, suffering the world and all its business to roll on without the let and hindrance of question,—that cares so little whether armies are decimated and countries devastated for an idea,—that prays for the Queen's ministers, but does not care very much to what party they belong,—that is altogether so absorbed in and satisfied with itself, that it is hard to believe that it is only "eight hours (usual speed) from London."

Houghton has its drawbacks. What village is free from them? Owen Meredith has declared in one of his misery-fraught melodies that the "women free from faults have beds beneath the willow." I wish he would give a local habitation and a name to the villages "free from faults." The hordes of discontented ones who are weary of the haunts of men, would be down upon them to their detriment forthwith; and Houghton would not be amongst their number, for Houghton has its drawbacks.

First amongst these shall be reckoned a penitude of the perfumes and a lack of the luxuries that commonly infest sea-side places. With the majority of the winds that blow the odour of marsh-mud is prevalent; and the odour of marsh-mud, though healthy, doubtless, is not delightful. But worse than this is the fact, that unless the "tide serves" (which it never does when you want to go on to the beach), it is impossible, though almost on the brink of it, for Houghton to catch a sight of the German Ocean, by reason of that broad expanse of marsh and mud and many creeks which intervenes.

Houghton has its cockle-strand, and the flavour of those cockles is esteemed in that county-side. They are big, blue, burly. They form a mighty portion of the integral trade of that quiet little village, for "peasant girls with deep blue eyes, and hands that offer" burly cockles, "come smiling o'er this paradise," through all the summer months, with baskets full of the result of their bare-footed labours down on the strand. The way that leads down to this cockle-strand is called by a name that indicates (so Houghton proudly asserts) that it at one time traded more largely and had a quay of its own, for the way is called "Quay-land"—and it is the haunt and lounge of the coastguard and fishermen all the week, and of the whole population on Sundays.

The house in Houghton that stands nearest to, and commands the best view of the sea, is, though one of the only three good houses in the village, known by no name. To strangers, the very few who enter, it is pointed out as the "chief officer's" or the "Leftenant's" house: to the inhabitants it is familiar as "The Leigh's."

It is not particularly interesting from an architectural or artistic point of view, for it is simply a square stone building, with straight sash windows in front,—a shiny sloping slated roof, and an entrance door planted with severe exactitude in the centre. But to the casual passer-by it has an importance by means of adventitious aids. For instance, towering above its shiny slated roof there is a "look-out" of white-painted woodwork which stands out well from the blue tiles; patrolling outside the gate there is always a coastguard-man in naval uniform, with a big "Dollond" under his arm, and a hand that is prompt with the graceful salute of the service to any one who may address him.

It is a sweet old farce to me,. this guarding the coast from nothing. Though we are now at peace with every possible invader, and free-trade is in the ascendant, still, I trust the play that gives a remunerative "part" to so many will never be played out. There is monotony, it is true, in the work that falls to the lot of both officers and men. It is tedious to serve your country by writing down every change in the wind and weather daily from year to year; monotony, in boarding well-meaning vessels in which nothing is ever found, and in perpetually patrolling with a spy-glass under your arm. But still it is not laborious monotony.

Down this lane one fine April day a man walked, and the knot of loungers at the top of the lane who assembled themselves together in the sun on the bench outside the Leighs' garden wall, forthwith fell to wondering curiously who he might be, and what he might be about to do, for he was not a Houghton man.

"He's not a friend of the squire's, for he put up at the Bull last night when he come," one of the women said; "he'd a' been sure to be at the house if the squire knew anything of him."

"And he ain't no friend of Mr. Leigh's," the watchman whom the woman specially addressed replied; "for Mr. Leigh be come out just now, and he says, says he, 'Roberts,' says he, 'have you seen,' he says, 'any one go down that there lane?' says he, 'any stranger,' he says, 'for,' says he, 'a stranger there is at the Bull,' he says, 'who, I hear, has been asking about drawing the beach;'" which prove," Roberts wound up with triumphantly, "that our master knew nothing about him."

"Nights ain't fine enough to draw for much good, are they?" the woman asked, for the words "drawing the beach," at Houghton meant dragging the same with nets to which a horse was attached, by which means mighty draughts of fish were occasionally caught.

"Might be better, and might be worse," Roberts replied, screwing up one eye and looking out of the corner of the other away to the horizon through the glass.

"Well," the woman said sharply, "I only know what my man says, and he knows more about it than all the lot of you put together,"—she was a fine smart-looking woman, with a brisk voice and a clear eye, and a neat figure. Roberts seemed struck with her statement, and gazed at her with a vague eye of wonder.

"All the gentry have to come to my Bob when they want to know anything of that kind," Mrs. Barton went on with a bright laugh; "if that gentleman is wanting to draw the beach, I shall know more about him before the day's over, for he'll have to come to Bob."

Then Mrs. Barton collected her troop of children around her, and prepared to depart while the wound her last arrow had made was still quivering. It was quite true, this vaunt that she had made, and the truth of it awakened the seldom sleeping jealousy the rest of the crew of the coastguard station felt for Bob Barton, whose knowledge of wild-duck shooting and fishing had gained him much popularity, and something more tangible still, from what his wife denominated the sporting gentry round.

But before she could execute her purpose and depart, she was arrested by the slamming of the gate round the corner, the gate of the Leighs' garden, and the next moment Lieutenant Leigh himself, with a young lady hanging on his arm, came in sight.

He was a fine old sailor, erect and vigorous, but neither rugged nor weather-beaten, as it is the fashion to depict naval officers of a by-gone day. A man who had not been handsome in youth, the friends who knew him in it asserted, but who was a most stately and dignified gentleman now that he was old. As thorough a sailor, as good an officer, as dashing and gallant a

man as ever stepped the quarter-deck; but one who never related his own feats of dashing gallantry—who never swore, or used sea-slang —who had known little of the sweet rewards of merit, and who was only a lieutenant now at sixty, and Theo Leigh's father.

The young lady who leaned upon his arm, and whose appearance (for was she not the idol of the "crew?") arrested Roberts' eloquence and Mrs. Barton's departure, was Theo herself.

Theo had been a pet amongst her father's crew for so long! just nineteen years had she lived in the world, and amongst themselves they called her "little Miss" still, that bright young lady in whose woman's form a woman's heart beat strongly! And she knew and cherished and nourished this feeling that the rough sailors and their warm-hearted spouses had for her, and, thoughtless girl as she was, prayed God that, let her be what she might, they might never know or name her as other than "little Miss" and "our Miss Theo."

What was she like, this girl who to the slow music of the slamming of a gate, came round the corner into my story? She was charming! that was all. How can another woman hope to make clear why she was so? She was charming, with none of the bright, blonde, beautiful charm of the North, but with a darker witchery, with a duskier hue, with the deeper, more dangerous, more intense fire of the sleepy, languid, passion-fraught South.

Pick her to pieces, anatomise her thoroughly, and she lacked beauty. But who, in the old days when I knew her first, would have picked to pieces that glowing, brilliant, girlish face, or anatomised thoroughly that well-rounded figure that expressed health in every one of its movements? Who could have done it then? The rounded cheek is fallen now, and the bright, merry eye faded from the light of yore, and Theo is a sylph no longer! But she is Theo still, with the old charm about her that no man (or woman either, for that matter) could resist for long.

For my heroine was not one of those adorable creatures whom women persecute. Many women liked her very much indeed. Saw her faults, and censured them maybe, but liked the girl, their committer, despite them all. She was liked, she was popular, she was thought well of, God knows for what. She was sorely ill-used and sorely tried, God knows why.

But on this day, when I show her to you first, the love and popularity and good thinkings-of had alone been hers; the trials were "nowhere," in turf parlance: and Theo Leigh was very bright and fresh indeed; as bright and fresh as the spring costume she wore.

I will paint her portrait for you, with no background and no accessories. My heart knows her well, my hand will limn her forth quickly. I will brighten the high-lights and deepen the shadows in yet unwritten pages; but the likeness of the girl can be put before you in a paragraph or two. No fairy, yet rather small; no sylph, yet rather slight. Cleanly made as to the head and limbs, in fact, which always adds to the look of "breed," while it detracts from the appearance of size. With an oval, dark, glowing face, and grey, glowing eyes, and a profusion of wavy hair that was half curl and half disorder, hanging in richly brown masses from underneath her turban hat. On the round of each of these tangled curls of hers there was a ruddy tinge when the sun fell on it, and in the dark, glowing face not one feature, save the mouth, was perfect. Her eyes were very deeply grey, and very full of feeling, of fire, of thought, of the wildest merriment, of the weirdest melancholy. Very full indeed of whatever the girl herself felt at the moment; brilliantly intelligent, beautifully expressive and sympathetic; but not the large gazelle eyes that should be a woman's portion. They did not look off to the right and left like a hart's or a sheep's; they glanced out thrillingly at you from very close to her nose on either side. But for all that propinquity and thrill they were not the least bit shrewish or vixenish eyes. I love and admire those shy gazelle orbs very much indeed; but I never felt that Theo Leigh's could have been more beautiful than they were.

Do you remember, reader, what Lancelot says when the lady of Shalot, victim to unrequited love for him, floats by the palace—dead?

Ah me! she has a lovely face;
God in his mercy send her grace,

prays the man who has destroyed her. A similar feeling found utterance in other words when the stranger whose progress down the lane was commented upon awhile ago caught the first glimpse of Theo Leigh.

"I think I should like to have the boat to-day, papa," Theo said, after a minute's conversation with Mrs. Barton, during which that good woman had given a *résumé* of the conjectures which had been formed and to which utterance had been given respecting the stranger.

"The tide won't serve till it will be too late for you to be on the water," her father replied. Theo thereat looked slightly disappointed. Her young heart was always very warmly set on having the boat when circumstances over which no one had any control forbade the boat being available.

"I believe there's water enough in the creek for the little boat, papa. I'll go down the lane and see; and if there is, Barton wouldn't just mind pulling me over, would he?" she continued, addressing Barton's wife, who immediately assured her that "Bob would with all the pleasure in life, if so be he could be spared."

Theo released her father's arm now, and sauntered away down the before-mentioned lane. Sauntered slowly, as one is apt to do when the young spring leaves are bathed in bright April sunshine: sunshine that is warm, soft, and tenderly bright as the touch of a maiden's lips, or the first love-light in her eye. There was something deliciously sympathetic in the atmosphere, in the sunshine, in the hum of recently-born insects, in the fragrance of re-awakening nature, to Theo. She sauntered slowly along down to the marsh-bank that was covered with rushes; and in the beauty of the day, and the contemplation of the dazzling light the sun threw upon the waters, she forgot her purpose, and was utterly regardless of the state of the creek.

The winter had been an iron-bound one, the earliest spring had been one shrill whistling blast from the east. The memory of these things made this sudden summer heat, which had endured now for four or five days, doubly delightful through the mighty power of contrast. Theo en-joyed warmth—the warmth of the sun, not that of a fire. She expanded under its influence, its fervour went into her soul, and lapped it to a slumber in which the sweetest dreams were hers. She thoroughly revelled in doing nothing but think—scarcely that, but feel. The girl did not lack energy, but she lacked that peculiar form of it which expresses itself in bustling activity. She had not been stirred into action yet—for life had gone very easily with Miss Theo Leigh—and her appreciation of the *dolce far niente* was too perfect to be agreeable to her friends. It may be that as the elder daughter of a large family Theo would have been undesirable. But she was not the elder daughter of a large family, happily for herself. She was the sole child of the house and heart of her father, and he saw no wrong in aught that Theo did.

She placed herself on the sunny side of the bank of rushes—the side on which she was sheltered from even the light breeze that was up—and thought of what life must be in the lands where the sun always shone, and the sky was always blue. Of Greece, which she knew by heart, she thought, from Byron's fervid and her father's graphic description; where the cypress and myrtle wafted their odours and the vultures raged over, and the doves cooed forth their approbation of that struggle for liberty which terminated well for Greece, and better for Lord Cochrane than anybody who served under him; of Italy—very much of Italy—for she loved art and olives, and longed for a sight of blue-ridged mountains, and brigands, and all the other things the South alone could show her. In fact she dreamed a tour that should last for ever, and found the travelling most rarely sweet.

The dream was dissolved suddenly, but not unpleasantly. A step close behind her, a voice at her elbow, a low, soft, deep voice, monotonous even in its sweetness to some ears, the soul of melody to hers, saying:

"Pardon me for disturbing you, but is there any possibility of threading the maze of these creeks and gaining the beach?"

The sound cut short the dream, the old familiar dream, that Theo had dreamt so often, and she woke to life with a bound, but not to the life she had known before, no, never again to that old peaceful existence.

"The beach can only be gained by a boat, unless you had mud-boots on, and didn't mind walking three or four miles to reach the only point where it is safe to cross the channel," she said, rising to her feet as she spoke.

Then as she stood before him, speaking, despite the suddenness of his address, despite the surprise she could not but feel, with the self-possession and kindly courtesy of a gentlewoman, he thought that which resembled Lancelot's apostrophe to the Lady of Shalot:

"She has a sweet, bright face: I hope it will never be clouded."

She had dreamt of other things in her life besides classic Greece and art-fraught Italy. She had pictured many a hero, built them up as it were from those who were her favorites in romance, and they were all of the cavalier type. Leicester she had loved, though that was a black business, Theo acknowledged, about Amy Robsart. But about six months since she had stayed at an old grange in Warwickshire, whose walls were covered with Vandycks, and there the grace of Buckingham had made every other kind of masculine beauty seem dull, tame, and unprofitable to her, and Leicester was less well-loved than of yore.

Now before her stood a man who, though he wore a coat of Poole's and a hat of André's, might have walked forth from the canvas Vandyck had covered. No velvet tunic, no clanking sword, were needed to further the illusion. All the Stuart grace was his, and thrice the Stuart beauty. He was the embodiment of that ideal which the portrait of Buckingham had first faintly realized.

This man who dissipated Theo's earliest dreams was no beardless Apollo, on whom the golden glory of youth still hung enraptured. He was a man of forty or more, this first god of her imagination.

That lived still in the man's deep, steel-blue, black-fringed eyes, that was more to a woman than the laughing light of youth. There was that in the contrast between his unstudied address, his steady, deep tones, and the wonderful earnestness of his eyes, that thrilled Theo almost before she was conscious of its existence. She took in all: his age, his well-made clothes, the air of high breeding that there was about him, the perfect beauty of his face, and its rarely-refined expression, an expression in which hauteur habitually had a share, but there was no hauteur in the eyes that were bent on Theo; she took in all these things in the one glance she gave him, as she quietly answered his question. Then, when she had answered it, he removed his hat from the head on which grey curling locks still clustered thickly, and stood bare-headed before her—a dignified, handsome gentleman truly; the very type of some old cavalier family.

"You must allow me to profit by the information you have afforded me," he said, with a certain subdued eagerness in his voice, to which it was rarely pleasant to listen. "I have been hoping for a fair opportunity of introducing myself to Mr. Leigh; on your authority I shall tell him now that the beach is not to be gained save in one of his boats."

"I will introduce you to papa. I am Mr. Leigh's daughter," Theo said animatedly. And then she blushed a little, and laughed a little, and added, "At least, I will tell him your strait, your name I do not know; but I'll introduce your difficulty to him, and he will place a boat at your service, I am sure, as soon as ever there is water enough in the creek."

"Perhaps my name may be familiar to him," the stranger said, handing Theo a card on which was engraved "Mr. Harold Ffrench." "We were in Greece together, but as I was but an amateur your father very possibly never heard of me, or if he did, has forgotten me."

"In Greece with papa!" Theo exclaimed; did you serve with him? did you serve under Lord Cochrane? How could you come to Houghton, and know that papa was here, and not give him the great pleasure of seeing an old comrade at once?"

"I may not lay claim to that distinction, Miss Leigh." Mr. Ffrench conveyed a most delicate compliment to the daughter by that allusion to the sire. Theo kindled to it, kindled vividly, but that, perhaps, she would have done to anything else uttered by that voice, and rendered doubly eloquent by those eyes.

"I may not lay claim to that distinction, Miss Leigh. I knew your father, certainly, knew him well, as did every one else who was concerned for the liberty of Greece, and interested in the organization of her navy; but I was, as I tell you, an amateur, and my very name may have escaped your father's memory: have you ever heard him mention it?"

"Never: did you know the Maid of Athens and Mr. Black?"

"Wasn't Black her husband?"

"Yes; did you know them?"

"I did not, but I remember hearing your father's name in connection with them. He had them on board his frigate, hadn't he?"

"Yes," Theo replied. They were walking up the lane now, but though she was anxious to bring this stranger face to face with her father, she found it very pleasant to be walking and talking with him alone,—walking through the old familiar places which she had known from a child, and talking on that scarcely less familiar theme of which her father never tired.

"Yes, he had them on board the ——, I forget his ship's name, and he was god-father to their eldest son; she was fat when papa knew her, a good deal of her beauty was gone; but still, do you know, I think there must have been a touch of romance in knowing her, Byron's Maid of Athens, at all."

"I think, perhaps, the romance would have stood a better chance of being unimpaired if he, your father, I mean, hadn't known her fat, and no longer young; there were many romantic affairs that sprang out of that song, Miss Leigh. Byron was not the only Englishman who fancied some roe-eyed Greek to be his life and soul for a time."

Then Mr. Ffrench looked down at the bright young girl who walked by his side, glancing up at him occasionally with frank admiring gaze, and as he looked at her, his deep blue eyes grew strangely tender, and he thought, "I hope to God her father has *not* forgotten me."

Bear this recorded aspiration in mind when that which is to follow is recounted. He did devoutly hope that himself and the story of his life might be once known, even if now partially forgotten things, by the father of this girl who had won upon him already, brief as had been their intercourse, by the undefinable charm of a most profound sympathy. Through all the length of that lane which led from the rush-covered marsh-bank up to the garden wall where Mr. Leigh still stood, Harold Ffrench hoped it devoutly. When the gate was gained, and Theo Leigh introduced him eagerly to her father, before the latter had time to express astonishment at the sight of his daughter on these friendly terms with a stranger, that hope died out, and another sprang into being. For in answer to Theo's "Papa, this gentleman was looking for a way over to the beach; he is Mr. Ffrench, and he remembers you in Greece," —in answer to this, there came no light of recognition into the old officer's eyes: "I am heartily glad to renew the acquaintance," he said, courteously; "your name and face have escaped my memory. I am getting an old man, you see; walk in, Mr. Ffrench, you are most cordially welcome."

As Mr. Ffrench took the other's offered hand, he saw that if ever known he was now entirely forgotten.

CHAPTER II.

THE FRUIT OF THE SUN.

IT was only natural that the Houghton Bull should see little of Mr. Ffrench after this. Though personally unknown to Theo's father, he still was thoroughly *au fait* with all that had happened in Greece in '28 and the two following years. "I was just of age when I went to Athens," he said, in the course of conversation with Mr. Leigh, "and the first use I made of my nominally perfect liberty was to be off to the seat of the struggle, for everybody was talking about it just then." When he said that, Theo did a sum on the instant, and the year of my story's opening being that of our first Great Exhibition, arrived at the decision that Mr. Ffrench was forty-four! almost an old man in Theo's estimation. She sighed to think of it.

But soon—before he had been with them an hour—she ceased to think it a matter for sighing. He charmed them all round, and fairly won the welcome that had been so frankly offered. Mrs. Leigh asked him to stay and dine with them—asked him with such an evident desire that he should accept the invitation, that Theo felt at once that her mamma was carried as quickly and successfully as she herself had been. Her father, too, was palpably inclining most kindly to one who listened with understanding to his time-honoured stories.

"Besides, he hasn't the look and manners of a middle-aged man," thought the girl, as she looked at the slight and graceful figure, and the proudly-carried, handsome head of this delightful guest. The time-honoured stories, from which, truth to tell, Theo generally fled, gained a new interest now that they were listened to in his company. She threw herself rashly into the conversation, and fired off a brisk volley of questions, some of which struck her papa as being slightly irrelevant. Her papa, in fact, desired to dwell principally on the naval and political aspects of Greece ; Theo wanted to hear something about those other romances to which Mr. Ffrench had alluded.

At length they quitted the past and came down to the present.

"What finally fixed you in this out-of-the-way place after such a career ?" Mr. Ffrench asked of his host.

"Want of interest to get anything better than a coastguard station, and the necessity to take the first thing that offered, no matter what that thing was. I was struck off the list for some years in consequence of that Greek affair, and when I was reinstated, I was given to understand that promotion was over for me," Mr. Leigh answered.

"That was a bad look-out."

"A bad look-out!—it was a blackguard look-out!" Mr. Leigh cried; he could not endure to hear gentle mention made of his grievances and ill-treatment at the hands of the government; they had been many and very hard to bear, and lenient allusion to them was disgusting to him.

"What was the reason assigned for striking you off the list ?" the visitor asked, politely. He had been looking at and thinking of Theo when her father spoke before. His words, "that was a bad look-out," referred to something vastly different to the old sailor's wrongs. But now he recalled his attention and his eyes from Theo to her father—for he was a well-bred gentleman, and he saw that he was expected to do so.

"The reason—a cursedly unfair one, by the by —was that I, being on half-pay, unable to find employment under my own flag, did what any other young fellow would have done, went off and served without leave under a foreign one. That was their only reason, sir—and by God, though they've reinstated me, I have never been able to get my arrears of half-pay from them up to this day! You'd scarcely credit it, but such is the fact ; they've robbed me of it, and as yet I have found no redress ;" and as Mr. Leigh brought the recital of his wrongs to a conclusion, he gave the table a thump in his excitement, and to Theo's delight some of the same enthusiasm appeared to fire the guest.

"Why don't you memorialize ?" Mr. Ffrench said, warmly ; "it is, as you say, scarcely credible that such a punishment should be awarded for such a venial offence against regulation : why don't you memorialize ? "

"I have done so."

"Yes, that papa has," Theo cried ; "I can testify to that, for I have often had to copy your petitions—and I hate their endings, 'and your memorialist will ever pray ;' it seems so abject. I'd rather let them keep the arrears of half-pay, the mean things! than humbly pray for them to give it to me."

Theo had not been lapped in luxury all her life, certainly, still it was evident enough that she had never known the want of money or aught that money could produce. Had she done so, the stereotype prayer to those in power would not have gone so palpably against the grain.

Strictly speaking, there was very little to amuse the stranger guest in that country household. They could not gild the present by offering him the run of their stables in the hunting season, or the freedom of so many acres in September. He was a middle-aged man, accustomed to club life in London, and they had neither a French cook nor choice wines. He was a gentleman who, though never bored or weary when alone, was very apt to become horridly bored in the society of others ; and yet the prosy stories of the old naval officer, and Theo's naïve comments on the same, were heard by him with a fresher interest than he had accorded to anything for longer than he cared to remember. He had not counted on experiencing this phase of feeling when he entered Houghton idly the day before.

At last—not long before he left them for the night—it occurred to them to ask what had brought him to their remote little village—a stranger, with no apparent call there at all. It was not the right time of year for sport of any kind, and for what other end did men ever come to Houghton ?

"I came for the purpose of resting for a day from the society of some very kind friends of mine who are living at a lovely place about twenty miles from this—that was the real reason of my coming here ; my nominal one was that I wanted to take a sketch of a headland that they call 'The Point,' that will come in well in a picture I'm about."

"Oh! it was that kind of drawing the beach, then—not what you thought, papa, when you said 'what folly, at this season.' Do you paint, Mr. Ffrench, in oils?"

"Yes," he told Theo he did "a little in that way."

"Have you the picture with you at the Bull?"

"Oh no; would you like to see it?" he asked, with a softened inflection of the monotonously sweet voice that was very perceptible to the acute ear of the girl whom he addressed.

"Very much, indeed," she replied, with the hearty interest which, though unseen, unknown, we all—the most indifferent among us as well as those who yearn for appreciation—delight in seeing expressed about our works: "Very much, indeed; do you mind telling me what it is, as I can't see it?"

"But you can see it, and you shall see it, if you will do me so much honour. I have it over at the Grange—that's vague, for every third place in Norfolk seems to be called the Grange; the place I mean is Haversham Grange: I am staying there with a cousin of mine: if you will go over, Mrs. Galton will be delighted to see you, and do the honours of my picture and her own."

"Her own! is she your cousin? does she paint?"

"She is my cousin, and she is obliging enough to think my picture worthy of a copy, which she is making with admirable intentions."

"What is the picture?" Theo asked.

"A description such as I can give will not convey the slightest idea of it to your mind; there is a bay, and a boat in it pulling round a headland which partially conceals a little frigate, that is all; it doesn't sound interesting, does it?"

"What is in the boat?" Theo questioned.

"Three men and a woman," Mr. Ffrench replied, rising as he spoke. "And now," he continued, "having given you such a barren account of it, my self-esteem compels me to try and win your promise to go to Haversham and look at my picture."

Then Theo, though she shook her head in a faintly negative manner, gave the promise with her grey eyes; and the guest departed, glad that she had done so.

"Why not?" he asked himself. Why should he not be glad that a fresh, pretty, intelligent girl, young enough to be his daughter, desired to see a work of art—a work of his? There was no reason against it. Nothing to render such a consummation undesirable. He was a time-hardened man of the world, who had out-lived all feeling such as might be detrimental to Theo's peace. He had all his life experienced a certain pleasure in doing a kind action which he had not to go out of his path to accomplish. It would be doing a kind action to introduce this Miss Leigh, who seemed to have but a dull life of it, to a woman who could render that life much more lively, if it so pleased her, even at twenty miles' distance. "And it will please Kate, to please me," he said with a laugh in his eyes. "So why not do it for the little girl?"

He sat down in the little parlour of the Bull Tavern and wrote a letter, over the composition

of which he laboured more than one would have imagined so cool-mannered, so easy-going a man, would have done. With his look of hauteur, with that air of condensed pride and suppressed passion in his face, he was not the kind of man one would have accused of halting over a form of address to any mortal, or choosing his words and phrases with thought and labour.

But it was written at last, written and directed to "Mrs. Galton, Haversham Grange, Haversham, Norfolk." After that Mr. Ffrench went to bed in a low-pitched room, and dreamt that he was in a boat that was being pulled round a headland by two long-dead friends of his. In his arms a woman was lying, and she wore the Greek costume, and her face was the face of Theo Leigh. This mingling of the real and the ideal discomposed him sorely in his sleep, and finally caused him to wake up with a start and a curse. After remaining intensely wide awake for a time, he got up and destroyed that letter which he had written with so much care and thought, and resolved to leave Houghton to-morrow.

But with the dawning of that morrow came the death of the resolution. The bright clear April air, the appetite which it engendered, the difficulty of finding in broad daylight a reason why he should do so, and above all the habit he had of always doing as he wished, decided him upon remaining yet another day in the village to which he had drifted aimlessly, the village that had shown him that which he had never thought to look upon again—something that had the power to stir him.

He may readily be forgiven for not remaining at the Bull long after breakfast. He stayed just long enough to write another letter to Mrs. Galton, and this time he wrote it in haste, and gave no pains to its composition. Then, when he had given the epistle into the hands of a trusty-looking idler, who made many promises as to its rapid delivery at the post-office, he walked up to the Leighs', for the sake of borrowing the "Dollond" and going upon the look-out.

Had Theo expected him? He almost longed to ask her, there was so full an assurance of what her answer would be in the vivid brightness of her face when he appeared. It was the flush of blissful realisation more than gratified surprise. It was such a flush as a woman can flame out upon the man who moves her in very truth alone. Harold Ffrench was a man, nothing more nor less, and he read it aright.

She was far too open a book, this girl of nineteen, for him not to read, and read aright at a glance. It had been the expectation, the hope of seeing him which had robed her this morning with a grace a woman never can attain until the spirit of love bestows it upon her. There was a seductive softness about the folds of the muslin boddice this day that could come only from the softened touch of the hand that had learnt to tremble at a heart thrill, a very tenderness of treatment about the flow of the skirt that could only be the result of that visual accuracy which is solely her portion who would adorn still more what may perchance seem beautiful already in the eyes of him who is now the world to her. There was all this, and Harold Ffrench saw that there was all this, and still more besides. For on the face of Theo Leigh there had come a light which was a revelation to him of the heart that dwelt in the girl; and he knew that this light beams only once in a life-time, and then for the man who first thoroughly awakens that heart, and causes it to know that it beats for some other purpose than that of mere existence.

The heroines of old romance were always dressed in white muslin at most incongruous times and seasons. White muslin represented purity, poverty, grace, and guilelessness, and they one and all wore it. But we costume in these days with a more rigorous eye and a more correct taste. We go back to the fashion books of the year in which the event we relate occurred, and so in these minor matters are rarely caught tripping. This confession may weaken the interest of those readers who decline to believe that novels are built up bit by bit, and who elect to favour the supposition that they are struck out of nothing in a white heat of inspiration. But those who care for correctness of detail will be glad to learn that when we give a full description of the ball dress of our heroine, we do so on unimpeachable authority.

On this April morning Theo had dressed herself in a muslin that was a muslin of muslins, a very miracle of clearness and fineness. It had a white ground, powdered thickly with black dots that rendered the white ground still clearer and whiter, as does the patch on the cheek of beauty; over and above these black dots there was a violet something that might be a leaf or a beetle, or a mere invention of the designer; and the effect of this, when hung upon Theo Leigh, and tied in round her waist and wrists, was something that muslin might well feel proud of itself for attaining.

There had been a little comment at the breakfast-table on this appearance of Theo when she came down that morning so radiant with joy.

"Why, Theo! how's this?" her mother had said; and her father even had looked up proudly at his darling, and remarked, "Halloa, Theo! how fine you are!" To which Theo had replied, "It is *so* hot, you know,—not too hot at all, but quite warm enough to make me take the coolest dress I had into wear." As the coolest dress was likewise uncommonly becoming, who could say aught against the selection, whatever the cause of it?

They kept early hours at Houghton, and Theo had plenty of time to feel remorse, and cry, Oh, the folly of it! (as to the muslin) before Mr. Ffrench sauntered up to borrow the "Dollond," and beg a view of the German Ocean from their house-top. When he came, remorse and bewailings went by, and Theo gave him that mute vivid welcome of which mention has before been made, right freely, without a distracting thought.

It was a luscious morning, the first summer day that Theo Leigh and Harold Ffrench spent together. What matter the girl being young and the man no longer so? She had the heart of a woman, and he the soul of a connoisseur for whatever was beautiful in nature or art. That summer morning was luscious to them both, the sweetness of it mounted like wine to their brains, and soon it was a silent enjoyment of it that they felt as they sat and rested on the bank of marsh rushes after the prolonged stroll, in the course of which her little hand had more than once found a resting-place and support on his arm.

How came she to be out with this stranger alone? It would have been a breach of etiquette had they been in a town, but in that rugged little village, to defer to etiquette would have been a profanation. He had asked Theo to go down and look at the rising tide with him, and Theo had gone without a word of objection, and remained there in that open familiar solitude without a particle of fear—a shadow of suspicion.

Nor was there cause for either. The most rigid could have been defied to cast a stone at him for what he had said to, and thought of, this girl, as yet. There was no harm done, not a particle that could have been taken hold of, as yet. He had spoken to Theo Leigh of literature, of art, of famous men and foreign places. Theo had listened and thought it passing sweet, that was all. He had said no word of love, he had refrained from the slightest look of it. Through the whole of that bright spring morning he had remembered his own age and her youth, and some far more insurmountable barrier than either to anything but friendship between them.

But guarded as he was, that sunny morning was very sweet to them both.

It was very pleasant to the girl, whose intercourse alike with men and books had been rather limited, to hear him speak of great names, which were but names to her and nothing more. We had no shilling magazines in those days, to keep country people on terms of intimacy with those who give us of their best in monthly parts. Moreover, there were no railway-station libraries, and lieutenants of coastguard stations were not likely to be the possessors of an exhaustless choice of books. Therefore was Theo's reading range a limited one, and her longing for an extension of it proportionately colossal.

But all that she had found to read she had read with understanding. The reading had been desultory and promiscuous, but it had been dear to her, and was consequently well remembered. She was better up in Scott and James, in Bulwer Lytton and Shelley, than Mr. Ffrench himself. She was brimming over with quotations from Shelley, in fact, and some of them in their fiery force fell very strangely from her fresh young mouth. She was wonderfully skilled in the art of separating the moral from the merit, and dwelling entirely on the latter. From her own frank confession he learnt that she had seen little of the world—nothing of "society," according to his acceptation of the word. Yet her perceptive faculty enabled her to coin from the coarser metal which had been around her tangibly, responses that were golden in the perfection of their propriety to all he said, to all he suggested.

Harold Ffrench found himself talking to Theo as he had never talked to a woman before, and yet his intercourse with her sex had been of no restricted order. He had talked about love often, but he had kept what lore was his for the solace of his solitary hours, for the benefit of his few male friends. Never a woman had come into his possession or crossed his path before who had been capable or ambitious—which was it?—of making him feel that she was on a mental equality with himself. They had been satisfied with the manner of his words and the languishing of his eyes, and had lightly regarded his matter and language.

But Theo, clever in her very ignorance, pandered to his vanity unsuspectingly. She showed such deep interest in what he said, that the man could not but feel desirous of saying it well. She kindled so brilliantly, that it was well worth his while to strive to make her kindle still more. He had an artist's soul and an artist's eye, and was always on the look-out for studies from nature. Theo was the fairest that fate had thrown in his path for many a long day.

Nature herself had a share in the evil that was eventually wrought. Had April been herself this year, he would have been chilled maybe into prudence. But she was all smiles, all warm dazzling smiles and early fruit-blossoms and premature roses. All things develop more quickly under the sun. The feeling that would have been long in maturing itself in a dull small room by a fire that would never burn properly by reason of its being suffered to get very low indeed, because it might "come warm in the afternoon,"—the feeling that would have been of slow growth under these circumstances, sprang up speedily in the chequered shade, in the hum of sun-born insects, and the fragrance of sun-born flowers. The day, the hour, were enough for the girl. All joy, all that made her know how sweet a thing life was, pervaded her spirit in his presence, and in her ecstasy of bliss she took no heed of what the morrow might bring forth. And he! Who can tell "what idle dream, what lighter thought, what vanity full dearly bought, joined to her eyes' dark witchcraft," chained him to the village in which Theo Leigh underwent her transformation?

For chained there he was, apparently; he took a sketch of "the Point" the second day of his sojourn at Houghton, and when that was done, there was no good and valid reason why he should have remained there any longer. But still he stayed on yet another day, and yet another, till the days grew into a week, and the week into a fortnight, and at the end of the fortnight he called Miss Leigh "Theo" in a tone that made her love her name.

> The cold in clime are cold in blood,

—their love is scarcely worth the name;—will all my English readers feel disapprovingly towards my heroine because this love of hers was no time-ripened one, but a thing that flooded her soul like a sun-burst in a moment? I own that it was reprehensible not to put out the light for sweet prudence' sake for awhile; but she did not, she could not. The statement is true, and must stand: at the end of a fortnight Harold Ffrench called Miss Leigh "Theo," and Theo rejoiced in his so calling her.

CHAPTER III.

KATE GALTON.

THAT letter—successor to the one whose composition cost Harold Ffrench so much care and thought—which we saw last in the hands of the trusty idler at Houghton, arrived at its destination about ten o'clock on the following morning, and was read by its recipient over her solitary breakfast-table.

"How disgusting of Harold!" was her excla-

mation, as she concluded the perusal of the epistle, which ran as follows:—

> "Houghton, 8th April, 1851.

"DEAR KATE,—The headland will be the very thing for our picture. I shall have to avail myself of the courtesy of the officer in command of the station here in order to get put over to the beach. By the way, he happens curiously enough to have been in Greece with me.

"I wish you would show any civility you can to his wife and daughter. I think they would like to see the Grange, and to know you; and as Mr. Leigh intends taking his little girl to town in May, you might act as her chaperone if you knew her before. Couldn't you call?

> "Yours always,
> "HAROLD FFRENCH."

"How disgusting of Harold! he doesn't say a word about coming back here. No, I won't call on his friends; I'll see them anywhere first."

She was a very pretty woman, this cousin of Mr. Ffrench's, of whom he had said to himself that it would please her to please him. A fair, tall woman of thirty, with loosely arranged nut-brown hair, and liquid blue eyes, and an animated face. A pretty woman and a fascinating one—not the ideal British matron, but still a mighty pleasant one if nothing that was very dear to you was in her keeping.

"Dull as I am here! so heartless of him," she muttered, after once more reading the letter; "men are so horribly selfish." Then a few tears of weariness and spite welled up into her liquid blue eyes, and Mrs. Galton rose up and walked to the window.

It was a French window, and it opened on a flight of steps which led down into a garden, gorgeous even at that early season with the brightest flowers. Beyond the flower beds and the lawn there was an invisible fence and a ha-ha, and away from this a timbered meadow that kept up the park-like and pleasure ground appearance of the place.

By-and-by across that meadow and over the ha-ha and over the lawn and up the steps came a man, whose progress towards her she watched indifferently at first, and then with contemptuous eyes. But as he came near enough to read them, Kate banished the contempt, and reinstated the normal expression of innocence so successfully that Mr. Galton had not the slightest occasion to be dissatisfied with his wife's matutinal welcome.

"I'm sorry I could not get down in time to pour out your coffee, dear," she said, holding up her cheek to be kissed as he entered. He was a tall, well-looking man of five or six and thirty, with a florid, good-tempered face, and close-cropped auburn hair and whiskers.

"Look here: don't pore over your painting to-day," he said, blithely: "Come out with me; I want to go to Norwich to look at a young horse Jack Able has, and I thought I'd drive you and the kid, if you'd go."

"Much too long a ride for that child, John. I'll go with you, of course. As to the painting, I'm sick of it."

"Already?"

She looked up into his eyes and laughed.

"I do tire of most things soon, don't I, dear?"

"As Haversham and I are not amongst them I can't say I care very much." He bent over her and kissed her as he said these words; his brow was wet with the exertion of walking rapidly home over rough fields to tell her of his plan for the day as soon as he had formed it, and the embrace with which he accompanied the kiss was a rough one.

The woman he embraced and kissed so confidingly would have deceived the Father of Deceit himself had he come in her way. John Galton's salute revolted her, but she checked all outward signs of it, and replied,

"Tired of you and of Haversham!—my dear John, tired of heaven and happiness sooner. But listen here. Couldn't we get up something that would amuse that poor cousin of mine? We bored him, dear, evidently, with our conjugalities, for I have had a letter from him this morning, bemoaning, as usual: a plague he is, isn't he?"

"I don't see why you need plague yourself about him."

"No, I needn't, as far as duty goes; for he isn't my brother, though I've always looked upon his as one; but he has always been most affectionate and generous to me, and I should like to see him happy."

"Well, what does he want now?"

"He doesn't 'want'—that is, he doesn't say that he wants anything; but he's evidently bored where he is—at some dirty inn in a dirty village; and he doesn't seem to like to come here, poor fellow, without an excuse. I wish you would give him one, John."

"Pooh! An excuse—what can he want of an excuse for coming to a house where he has always been made welcome?"

"Ah! but that's been by me, and I am his sister—I mean his cousin, you know. You must write and ask him to come back to help you in something, that will make him think that you really want him, and that you don't only tolerate him because you're fond of me."

"I daresay he's happy enough where he is; if he were not, he'd go somewhere else."

"No, he isn't happy, John. His letter (I wish I had not torn it up) is written in such a doleful strain; do get him back here."

"I have nothing more alluring to hold out to him than the prospect of seeing the hay cut by-and-by, and the young horse I'm going to Able about to-day broken."

"You dear old dunderhead! Shall I write then, and put it to him nicely?"

"Yes, do, there's a darling. And I say, Kate, where's the kid? I have not seen her to-day."

"Out in the garden, I hope, this fine morning—in the south garden, dear; if you'll go and look for Bijou I will write to poor Harold, and be ready to go to Norwich with you in half an hour."

Then the husband and wife separated, he to look for his child, she to write to her cousin to whom she would not have written without her husband's sanction—for Kate Galton was very wary.

Wary even in her treatment of the husband upon whom such wariness was thrown away, for it was in his nature to trust blindly and wholly when he loved. Wary in her present conduct to-wards the man who had failed her as cousin, friend, lover, and to whom she had been most unguardedly frank in the past. If experience had not taught this woman anything else, it had taught her to be most wondrously cautious; cautious, that is, about many things—about the majority of her acts and the whole of her correspondence. Of her spoken words she took less heed, provided none other than the one to whom they were specially addressed were by. But in her letters she was careful, very careful.

Fourteen years before, when she was a girl of sixteen, very vain and very impressionable, her cousin Harold Ffrench had come back to England after a prolonged absence, during which he had been a myth to her, so little had his family heard of his doings. But when she was sixteen, Harold came home and took up his residence at her father's house, and devoted himself in a sort of elder-brotherly way to his cousin Kate.

The elder-brotherly manner, admirably as it was designed and carried out, broke down after a period. Kate's cheek did not naturally "grow pale and thinner than was well for one so young," nor did her eye hang with a mute observance on all his motions, but she grew desperately fond of him, and showed it in her own way; and he, being unable either to reciprocate fully or to tear himself from the girl who was developing fresh fascinations every day, tried to cure her with calmness; and he failed.

His habits of intimate intercourse with her had come on so gradually that at the end of three years he was startled to find that others—their relations, mutual friends, the world at large indeed—were deceived into supposing that which he had sedulously refrained from giving the girl herself just cause for supposing. Candid as he had been with her—for up to a certain point he had been very candid with his pretty cousin—he was fain to confess that he had been very injudicious—as injudicious as the girl herself; and that, considering how much she knew, how well she was cautioned, was saying not a little. But this confession to his own heart and to her did not mend matters, for Kate refused to aid him in making it patent that it had been in all fraternal kindness, and nothing more, this intimacy of theirs. Young girl as she was, she was very wary even then; and she thought that the world's opinion might do what her charms had been powerless to effect—namely, coerce him into a course of conduct in which there would be both wrong and risk.

"What is it that makes you eternally swear that you never can be more than a brother to me, Harold?" she asked him once. "I will look over the impertinence, if you will tell me the cause. Is it that you care more for another woman?"

He shook his head.

"Don't tempt me, Kate—for your own sake."

"Not tempt you to tell?—but I will, dear. If you had commenced your cautions at an earlier stage, I might have accepted them and your resolve in silence; but, after letting people think for so long that we are engaged, I think I ought to be told the reason why we cannot be."

"I didn't mean don't tempt me to tell that; but don't tempt me in any other way. My fate is devilish hard as it is, without a girl like yourself showing me constantly how much brighter it might be."

Harold Ffrench had been more winningly handsome and attractive when he said this than at the later date when I introduced him and Theo Leigh to my readers. He might have won the heart of the hardest in these earlier days, had he essayed to do so. His cousin Kate was a vain girl; not one burdened with deep feeling, but she was young and impressionable, and she abominated being baffled. She knew that he liked her, and that he was better looking than any other of her acquaintances she likened him to. So when he pleaded that she should not tempt him, and declared that his fate was hard already, she grew very daring—daring as only an insatiably vain, cool-headed, unimpassioned woman may be with impunity.

"Harold, I could bear anything—I could stand anything for you or from you," she exclaimed; and her looks were more eloquent than her words.

"You don't know what you are saying, Kate," he replied, almost coldly.

"Yes, I do; I know full well what I am saying, and I mean it."

Then, despite the dangerous flattery contained in those words, and that meaning of hers, this man, who was no better and no worse than thousands of his class and age, said words for her good that were very hard to utter to so fair, so winning a woman.

"My dear Kate, how you have deceived yourself and me for four years."

"Deceived you? No."

"Indeed you have, to the extent of making me believe that you really loved me, and almost making yourself believe it too. Accept the tribute of my unbounded astonishment and admiration. I had no idea you were a young lady of such resource." Then he added, fearing that she might press him again on this point, and judging that the cause justified a little bitterness:

"O little Kate, forgive me if I am bitter, but you have shown me what I ought to have known before—that all women are as deceitful as the devil. You might as well have let me think well of you." Then he muttered words to the effect that "women had been his bane, some with the love they bore him, and others with their hate," the sound of which reached Kate's ears.

"Don't trouble yourself to taunt in poetry; that's not necessary for my complete cure," she said in a tone that made Harold exclaim, "Gad! you cold-blooded women have the best of it. Women are as deceitful as the devil. Curse it, you might as well have let me think well of you."

Shortly after this conversation, Harold Ffrench had gone away roaming no one knew whither again, and soon after his departure Kate went down to stay at Newmarket for the race week. She was in rare spirits and high beauty at the time, for Harold's abrupt departure was attributed to her having refused him. This created a fictitious interest in the minds of men about her, and brought her a certain popularity that was as pleasant to her vanity as had been Harold's love. At Newmarket, the chief object of interest was the winner of the "cup," "Beelzebub;" and next in order of the talked-about was "Beelzebub's" owner and breeder, a Mr. Galton, a Norfolk squire who lived on his own estate, and just escaped being a county man.

He was a pleasant, good-tempered, good-looking man, not too intelligent, Kate thought, but not stupid by any means, for he soon made it evident to the young lady herself, and all around, that he admired her very much. Had he not been the chief object of interest in that sporting circle, through being "Beelzebub's" owner, Kate would have turned up her nose at him. As it was, she was gracious and merciful, and fanned the flame which was palpably consuming him. It occurred to her that it would be rather pleasant than otherwise to be the mistress of a house, the owner of which had a name in the sporting world, and bred winning horses. He had a "colt in training for the Derby next year," he told her, and Kate saw herself in an elegantly appointed carriage, receiving the congratulations of all that was fastest and most horsey in the Peerage on that colt's prowess. John Galton looked such a big, amiable fellow, that he would be as easily managed as a Newfoundland dog, she thought. Above all, she did not want Harold Ffrench to come back and find her unmarried.

So she married Mr. Galton, and went down, after her wedding tour, for what she meant to be a brief sojourn at Haversham Grange. But when she mooted the question of leaving it, and going in search of the gaiety and society for which she pined, she found that her husband, though amiable and attached to her, had a will of his own that she could not break. He was well off—well enough off to live like a gentleman upon his own estate, and to indulge in all the sports and pastimes of his county. But he was not a rich man, and he had not the smallest inclination to dissipate what he had in doing what he didn't care to do, namely, going to town in the season, and seeking ingress to the ranks of those amongst whom his wife so much desired to shine.

"Are we to live all the year round at the Grange, dear John?" she had asked.

"Well, I suppose you'll want to keep up your town habits and go to the seaside in August, Kate. We'll go to Cromer next year; Cromer is as nice a place, to my mind, as Brighton."

"Very well, we'll go there," she replied, for in all things she resolved to agree with him verbally. Nevertheless she had her own will about the solitary annual outing. It was to Brighton they always went for the sea air; at Cromer, and indeed every other dull place, Mrs. Galton was invariably at death's door.

It was at Brighton that, some nine years after her marriage, she again met her cousin Harold. They elected to ignore the circumstances that attended their parting, and met as cousins should meet after such a long absence. She was on the pier alone when he saw her first, and he asked for her husband and her child with a promptitude that must have been delightful to her wifely and maternal heart.

"I hear you're married to the best fellow in the world, Kate: where is he? You must introduce me to him and to your little daughter."

"My big daughter, if you please. Katy is eight years old; as to my husband, I shall be delighted to introduce you to his goodness, on which you must excuse me if I don't expatiate further. I have so many opportunities of studying it uninterruptedly at Haversham all the year, that I prefer a change of subject during my month at Brighton. Tell me what you have been about, and where you have been all these years, Harold."

"I can more easily tell you where I have not been; but I am tired of wandering, and having met with unpleasantness in most other places, I have come to the conclusion that 'England, with all thy faults I love thee still,' and that I may as well give my own land a benefit. I see you're looking at me and thinking what an old fellow I have grown, Kate, while you are in a better bloom than when I saw you last. See what it is to be married and happy!"

"About my being married there is no doubt; as to the other thing—well, the less said the better. 'Twas not love made me marry John Galton, as you'll believe when you see him; I speak to you as to a brother, you see."

"And I'll return the compliment and speak to you as I would to a sister. Keep your reasons, whatever they are, to yourself, and make complaints to no man. Is your child pretty?"

"Some people think her lovely," Mrs. Galton answered, glancing at her cousin through her languishing lashes. "Do you remember what I was when you came home the first time, Harold?"

"Perfectly well."

"Katy is very much like what I was then; people say she will never have a something in her manner that I have, but still she is like me—or rather like what I was when you came home the first time."

"Rather a forward little girl of eight to be like you at sixteen. You were an uncommonly grown-up young lady then, Kate. So your friends say she lacks the charm of her mamma's manner. Well, I daresay she will get on very well without it." Then, seeing her look a little chagrined, he added: "You get too many compliments to need them from me; besides, they're not current coin between brother and sister, you know, and such are to be our relations."

After this meeting at Brighton the Galtons saw a good deal of Harold Ffrench. Kate was his sole surviving female relative, and he had a certain tenderness for her very faults which was due to that nameless something in her manner, which little Katy lacked. He liked her husband too, liked him for his good-heartedness and confiding trust in everybody, and his happy habit of seeing the best that can be seen on all occasions. It was true that John Galton was not much of a companion for the travelled, accomplished gentleman, who had cultivated his ear, and eye, and taste assiduously for years, in the best schools for such cultivation that Europe offered, in the hope of deadening his heart. That he had not succeeded in so deadening it utterly was shown in this fact, that he was alive to John Galton's somewhat rough merit. "An honest man's the noblest work of God," he said one day to Kate, pointing out as he spoke the burly form of her good-natured husband, who was turning himself into a beast of burden for his child's amusement. What a pity it is you women never think so."

"I prefer art to honesty. Come in, Harold, and let us get on with our bay. I want you to give my waves a second painting: they won't come right."

"You promised to stay out all the morning with Katy."

"Oh, leave the tiresome brat with her father! I shall get daggers in my head if I stay out here in the sun. And I'm so interested in my picture."

So they went away into Harold's temporary studio together, and her brush went freely over the canvas on which she was reproducing his nearly finished picture.

"Upon my word you've caught my touch wonderfully, Kate," he said, coming up to her easel, and looking at her effort with the admiration one is apt to bestow upon a tolerably accurate copy of one's own original idea; "it's a pity, though, you didn't tackle something higher."

"Something higher?"

"Yes, a Landseer, or a Sir Joshua, or an original picture," he said, suggesting the widely different subjects recklessly. "By Jove! Kate, why not an original picture?"

"I should fail, Harold," Mrs. Galton replied, softly. "I shall never paint, never copy anything but yours."

This took place a day or two before Harold Ffrench went away to Houghton, where he met Theo Leigh. He discovered immediately after it that to give reality to the headland which he desired to introduce into his picture, he must paint from nature and not trust to his imagination; that had run away with him on former occasions, he said, and should never be relied upon again.

Kate was not precisely displeased at his flight—for his departure was of the character of a flight, it was so abrupt, so unexpected. She chose to take it as a confession of weakness on Harold's part; and she liked men to be, and feel, and show themselves weak on her account.

He would soon be back again, she told herself; such flights were never for long; her falcon would come back, and her jesses would be upon him again stronger than before.

Aye, stronger than before, for he had slipped those jesses once, when to wear them would have been no shame to her. Now he had come back and fitted them on himself again, and is not the relapse invariably worse than the first disease? So for a few days the thoughts of him filled her leisure sufficiently, and prevented her finding her husband and child more than ordinarily tedious and boring. But after a few days—after the receipt of that letter, they grew extraordinarily so; and Kate Galton waxed pettish and found as little pleasure in her painting as aught else that Haversham could offer her. But still, though she pined for Harold Ffrench's company, she was such a prudent woman that she would not seem to seek it by obeying his request and going to call on those friends he had made at Houghton. Come what would, wary Mrs. Galton resolved that the surface should show that Harold had always sought her with her husband's permission—never that she had sought Harold, unless requested by John Galton to do so.

So, while she was hourly expecting Harold back the days passed and May came in, and there was commotion up in London about the great Exhibition, and all the wonders it contained, and all the visitors whom those wonders drew to our shores. Mrs. Galton waxed very pettish indeed now, for her husband kept on asking her what day "she'd like to go to town;" and she felt that she would not like to go to town at all until she knew whether Harold would be there with her or not, for London with John Galton alone was not to her taste. There had been no letter from Harold in reply to that one in which she had answered his request by simply entreating him to "come back to Haversham, as John wanted him very much." At length she gave up expecting such letter, and cleverly lured her husband on to asking her to go to Houghton.

"John, do you know that Harold has found some old friends at Houghton, some man he knew abroad somewhere, with a nice wife? I'm so glad of it, I wish he'd bring them here."

"When did you hear this?"

"In that letter I had from him he told me—I've only had that one. There's a daughter in the case, and Harold asks me to be kind to her in London; her father is going to take her up to see the Exhibition."

"That's right," John Galton said heartily: he was always ready to enter into anything of this sort with what his wife termed vulgar avidity. "That's right. Lor! you should have looked them up before now, Kate. Drive over and see them, and ask the young lady over here."

"It's a long drive, John."

"Nothing for your pony; he don't get half exercise enough."

"Very well, dear," Mrs. Galton said meekly; she had determined on going as soon as it became patent to her that Harold was disinclined to come back to her, but she was also determined that her husband should tell her to go. It should appear that he was cognizant of everything, whatever happened. Accordingly, now that he told her to drive over to Houghton, she amiably arrayed herself in a blue bonnet that would have been too decided in colour had all the rest of her dress not been black, and drove over.

CHAPTER IV

"THEO! FORGIVE ME."

CONFIDENTIAL intercourse between Harold Ffrench and Theo Leigh was of less frequent occurrence at this date than it had been a few days previously; for May, as I have said, had come in, and with it the necessity for a re-organization of Theo's wardrobe before she could be pronounced ready to go to London. It rather shaded over the vivid charm Houghton had possessed for him before this exigency arose—but there was no help for it. Theo was very deeply and naturally interested in the fit and make of her new dresses—interested to the point of working upon them herself. The fact was that Miss Leigh was anxious to appear in his eyes better adorned, but that he did not know. Consequently he detested the new dresses, and began to find Houghton dull.

But despite this temporary check to solitary intercourse he lingered on in the place still, and sedulously stifled the conviction that it would be well for him to go. He had come upon this oasis in the desert of his life by accident; he would just for awhile tent upon it, and then, before he had brushed the bloom off its verdure, drift on and be forgotten by her.

"I should be a beast to try and make the girl love me," he would say. The saying this seemed to relieve his conscience, and to be regarded by him as an all-sufficient precaution. For after saying it in the solitude of his chamber at the Bull, he would go up and sit by Theo's side, and suffer the girl to see that she had won his affections; which was not the wisest course to pursue, if he really wished to avoid the other catastrophe—that, namely, of winning her to love him.

He was assisting largely in the pavement of a certain place at this juncture. Daily he made the good resolution to go away and be forgotten by, even if he could not forget, this girl; daily he suffered this good resolution to die away unaccomplished. The middle of May was upon them, and he was at Houghton still.

He had been sitting for an hour or two one morning up in the Leighs' garden, near to the open window by which Mrs. Leigh and Theo sat working—sitting there idly, watching the girl and dreaming of bygone days, and events that had occurred in them. Idly dreaming, and even more idly wishing that those days might be lived over again—when he would have acted differently, ah! how differently.

"Can you put that finery out of your mind for an hour this evening, and take a walk with me, Theo?" he asked, when divers sighs made it manifest to him that the Leighs' dinner hour was approaching. Theo was prompt with her answer that "she would gladly."

"What the deuce did I ask her to go for?" he asked himself as he walked down to the Bull. "What can I say that will be pleasant for her to hear, that I hadn't better leave unsaid?" But still, though he thus questioned himself, he held to his resolve to take that walk with Theo—and to say what should be pleasant to her during it.

There was the unwonted presence of a well-built little pony-phaeton in the inn-yard, but he did not regard it much—he was thinking of other things than that, which caused no small excitement to the usual knot of village idlers lounging round. But he was roused from his meditations about these other things by the landlord coming to meet him with the information that "a lady was a-waitin' for him in the parlour," by the sight of his cousin Kate Galton's boy in buttons, the smart and invariable appendage to her pony-carriage.

"Halloa, Mrs. Galton!—my dear Kate, I am very sorry that you should have had to wait here alone for me," he said as he entered the room where Kate sat on a hard sofa, poking holes in a soft slightly decayed carpet, with her parasol.

"Never mind—as you have come in at last," she replied. There was a good deal of grace in the welcoming gesture she made, and a good deal of affection in the tone she adopted.

"I didn't expect you, you see, Kate, after your note; if I had dreamt of your coming I should have taken the precaution of leaving word where I was going when I went out, in order that I might have been sent for if you came."

"Could you have been sent for? I thought you were mudlarking."

"Not exactly—I was up at the Leighs'."

"I have come to call on your friends, Harold. I refused to come at first on account of the distance solely; but when John said I had better come over and look you up, and persuade you to come back to Haversham, I made up my mind to call on them as well."

"Your husband's very good, and so are you," and then he got up and rang the bell, and asked what she could eat and what they could have for luncheon? Then, on the cessation of the small fuss he himself had made, he continued—

"Very good indeed, Kate, to come over in this way. I wanted to introduce you to them, because Leigh takes his daughter to town soon, and I thought if you were there at the same time you might give her a good deal of pleasure she wouldn't otherwise get, and secure a very agreeable companion for yourself."

"Thank you; I don't find the society of my own Katy so enthralling but what I can dispense with it in London."

"Katy! Katy's a child."

"You called your friend's daughter 'a little girl' in your note, Harold," she said, with a quiet little smile of malicious satisfaction overspreading her face as she spoke. Kate delighted in finding every one out, even Harold Ffrench.

"Ah, well, so she is a little girl to an old buffer like myself; we'll go up there after we have had some luncheon, and then you'll see Theo for yourself. How gets on the painting?"

"Not at all well; it won't come right at all. You must come back with me, Harold, and set me going again."

"I can't go back with you to-day."

"Why not?" she asked impatiently; she had set her mind on taking him back in triumph, and she could ill bear to be baulked. "Why not?"

"It would be hard on the pony."

"If it's only on the pony that it would be hard, your leaving Houghton so suddenly, banish all scruple. Fidget is so full of corn, little beast, that he wants 'a deal taken out of him,' as John says; it won't be a bit too much for the pony."

"But it will be too much for me, to make up my mind and pack and be off in such a way; can't do it, Kate. But I'll be at your service to-morrow in the s̶̶̶ that content you?"

"It must b̶̶̶ answered, rightly continuing t̶̶̶ though she spoke lightly, t̶̶̶ told her that this "little g̶̶̶ old Ffrench had made such co̶̶̶ ar more to do with his unwillin̶̶̶ Houghton than had the presence in t̶̶̶ the man whom he had known in Greece."

"Delectable place t̶̶̶ village seems," she said with a sneer, whe̶̶̶ walking up to the Leighs' after lunch̶̶̶

"I thought you̶̶̶," he replied, carelessly; "the whole of it has turned out in admiration of you and your blue bonnet."

"Does Miss Theo Leigh run about without one then?"

"Oh, no, but hers is of a different order of architecture altogether."

"The cottage, I suppose. Well, Harold, I shall not think much of your consideration for my pleasure if you have lured me on to calling on a rustic who'll grab at the chance of saddling me with her country bumpkin ideas in London."

He laughed.

"You're not likely to admire her, Kate, but I don't think she'll strike you as a country bumpkin."

"Why am I not likely to admire her if she's admirable? Do you?"

"Do you ever admire any other woman than Mrs. John Galton? I admire her, do you ask?

I have given up such things, Kate, or I ought to have given them up. Here we are."

Theo was not a country bumpkin; Mrs. Galton was fain to confess that she was not, as Miss Leigh met half way the kindly courtesy that none knew better than Kate how to evince. She was not a country bumpkin, but she was something else quite as ruffling to Mrs. Galton's feelings;—keenly alive to Harold Ffrench's merit, and most flatteringly unable to resist making it clear to the eye of the beholder that she was what she seemed to be.

Her good looks, or rather that same charm which was commented upon a few chapters ago, did not occur very vividly to Kate Galton. She saw in Theo Leigh a nice lady-like girl enough, nothing more. Lady-like, but unformed in manner, the fascinating Mrs. Galton declared to herself, "too small to be fine, and too dark to be pretty." A very feeble rival, as far as Harold Ffrench was concerned.

For still—married woman, blameless matron, wary wife as she was—she could but think of possible rivalship in connection with any other woman whom Harold knew and liked. His heart in the depths of her own she acknowledged that she had never touched. But his fancy had owned her its cherished queen once, and she desired that it should do so again.

Despite this desire though, she contrived to make herself very agreeable to the Leighs, and especially to Theo, and this as much from the force of that good breeding which was second nature to her, as from the deceit that was second nature also. Theo delighted in her, in her softly spoken words and graceful manners, and the refinement of her fair expressive face, and the elegance and general becomingness of her dress, Mrs. Galton strove to please the girl, as she did to please every one with whom she came in contact for a time. She succeeded. Theo, always enthusiastic, was not only pleased but charmed.

Kate had "a way with her," undoubtedly a way that few had ever withstood at first. She had that sort of insight into character which enables one to detect the most easily worked upon of people's idiosyncrasies, and when she detected one she worked it cleverly when it suited her: flattered the vanity of the vain, and the folly of the fool, and was deferential to the wisdom of those who were wise in their own conceit. Gave her pretty sparkling dross freely in fact, for awhile, in exchange for that special form of it without a profusion of which life would have been odious to her, namely, admiration, real or affected.

She did not make any overtures of an introduction to Haversham and the picture, but that, as Harold Ffrench told Theo afterwards, "was because she takes it so thoroughly for granted that you'll call," but she said several sentences expressive of a wish to see Miss Leigh when they should both be in London together. Theo felt well disposed towards the prospect which savoured of future intimate intercourse with Harold Ffrench's cousin.

"She's a charming woman. So kind of her to say she hopes to have Theo with her a great deal in town; and how affectionately she spoke of her own little girl," Mrs. Leigh observed to her husband when the visit was over, and Theo had walked out to the gate with the visitors.

2

"I don't like the woman," Mr. Leigh replied shortly.

"Not like her! I can't think how you can say so; she has the sweetest manner."

"Beastly sweet, I thought. No, I don't like her, and I don't want Theo to see much of her in London."

"She'll be a most desirable acquaintance for Theo, and after her kindness in coming all this distance, to call on us, we can't do otherwise than be friendly with her."

"You don't suppose that she came to call on you?"

"*Mr.* Leigh!"

"Why she came after Ffrench, to be sure." Mr. Leigh said, laughing. "She came after Ffrench as sure as there's a nose on my face. I can't bear the woman with her smirks, and her leers, and her mincing way of speaking."

As he concluded his denunciation Theo rushed in again, animated, brilliant, happy.

"Isn't she charming? I like her so much. And isn't it kind, papa, to say she'll be civil to me in London, where I don't know anybody, you know?"

"I daresay she's all very well," Mr. Leigh replied; he was more reserved in his expression of opinion on the subject of woman before his daughter than before his wife, naturally. It was only at second-hand that Theo came to a knowledge of his sentiments. "I daresay she's all very well; as to her promises of being civil in town, she'll most likely not keep them, so I would advise you not to count on them."

"Oh, papa, that's horribly suspicious: 'have faith in one another,' as Arthur Manby sings. I shall count on her keeping her promises, of course I shall. How did you like her, mamma?"

"Very much, indeed."

"So did I. And her dress—did you notice her dress? It hadn't half such a deep point as Miss Watson *would* cut those of mine; but there's time to save the silk still; it shall have quite a little point, like hers." Then Theo left the room, still excited, brilliant, and happy, to see about her new silk at once.

"'Like hers,'" her father muttered, as Theo vanished. "There she goes, the same impetuous child she always was. I wonder she isn't calling Mrs. Galton by her Christian name already, as if they had been friends from the cradle; the child takes too strong fancies."

"Ah, my dear, don't forget that she's young," the mother cried; she could not bear that her darling should be censured even by implication. "She's so young, and she sees so few people besides ourselves; it's dull for her, you know, and this promises such a change."

Such a change! Poor Theo!

He came in the evening to call Theo for that walk he had asked her to take in the morning, and there was a something that was different in his manner to what it had been hitherto; something that she could feel, but could not see or define, and the feeling saddened her.

The something had been—as is all mischief—the work of a woman.

"What do you think of the little rustic—eh, Kate?" he had asked of his cousin, when they had parted with Theo at the gate.

"Oh, she's all very well."

"That's wonderful praise from your lips, but it's not of the order to elevate the article spoken about."

"I can't rhapsodise about another woman, Harold. I think her all very well, very nice if you like, and I say so; I'll tell you what else I think about her if you like to hear it."

"Don't I like to hear everything you say?" he asked, with the usual air of gallantry he adopted towards Kate Galton.

"I think, then, that it is a very good thing for Miss Theo Leigh that you have promised to come back to Haversham to-morrow."

"Why?" he asked coldly, but his dark face grew red as he asked it.

"Why? because your friend's daughter has taken one of those likings for her father's friend that are disagreeable and difficult to get over."

"Nonsense, Kate: you forget our respective ages," he began. "She's too young——" but there his cousin interrupted him impatiently.

"Too young! Too young for what, pray? Not too young to love you, Harold, believe me; it's nonsense of you to affect to doubt it. Why, the girl is twenty, if she's a day; and if she were years younger it would be the same. Girls are never too young to have their hearts touched. There's my little Katy already prefers to ride-a-cock-horse-to-to-Banbury-Cross on your knee to performing the same journey on her papa's."

He laughed, but the colour had gone from his face, leaving him very pale now. "Katy is an ungrateful little minx, then," he said. "I thought I understood you once that she wasn't at all like her mamma, but it appears as if she, too, had a low appreciation of the legal and recognized. You're wrong about Leigh's daughter though," he added carelessly. "She has heard of me all along as having been a yo██ man with her father. It has never o████ ███ her that I am in reality very much hi██████ ███er, it don't matter. I shall be ██████ ██u with the painting to-morrow, dear ██nd ██ squeezed Kate's hand; and Kate d██████."

He spoke no word to T██████ ████ng until they had strolled the len██h ██ ██e lane and gained the marsh bank where they first met; then he said—

"Well, Theo, wh██ did you think of my cousin?"

"I liked her so m████ ██" Theo said, warmly.

"I'm glad of that██ ██ you'll continue to do so: Kate's very nice and kind where she takes a fancy, and I think she has taken one to you. I shall often think of you enjoying yourselves together when I am gone away."

"Gone away?"

There was no doubt about the girl's distress being real as she turned round and faced him; it was so real, so deep, that he wished he had gone away before.

"Gone away," she repeated, "are you going?"

"Yes," he murmured softly, "I ought to have gone before."

The flat marsh-land scene swam before her eyes; she grew dizzy, and the warm May evening air came down and nearly choked her; there was a ball of fire in her throat, a sensation of numbness in her lips, a dull, dull aching at her heart. She could not speak. She could only sit still and suffer.

He ought to have gone before! Yes, he felt

that since he must go from her at all, he ought to have gone before this evil, that came from want of thought, not want of heart, was wrought. There was a pain on the girl's pinched temples, pain such as he felt sorry to have caused to one so young and bright as she had been but an hour ago. Pain, a sickening agony that only the young and fresh can feel, it is so vivid and strong.

There was silence between them for some minutes after that last recorded speech of his, silence that was unbroken even by the slightest movement. The girl was fainting in her spirit, and the man was bitterly conscious of the feeling and the cause, and his own inability to satisfactorily assuage the former.

They had placed themselves on the slope of the bank, and away to the west they had a full free view of the sea and the sun dying upon the water in a fiery glory. A full view of it, but for awhile Theo gazed at it with eyes that did not see. Then, the first agony over, the first giddiness past, she blessed the spectacle as a means of conversationally coming round again.

"What glorious colour! Don't you wish you could paint a sunset as it is?"

She made an effort to speak in her usual tone, but her voice was a little husky, a little less sure than was usual, and he marked the effort and harshness with such keen sorrow that he could not attend to the sense of what she said. At any cost he felt that the pain that was curdling her young blood in her veins must be assuaged.

"Theo! dear little Theo!"

He put his hand out as he spoke, and gathered both of hers in his grasp. The change was too much for her, the joy that pervaded her soul flooded her face, and made her glow in a way that nearly maddened him. There was such trust in the little hands' quiescence, such faith in what she thought was to follow in the girl's loving look.

"Oh, Theo, don't turn away, darling. By God I can't stand it!" he cried, suddenly releasing her hand and starting to his feet. And when Theo, pale and trembling again, rose also, she felt that that which she had expected was not coming, and her heart swelled with a bitterness of grief.

"We had better go home," he said presently. "Don't look so miserable, my darling. Heaven, what am I saying? Don't hate me, Theo; I must go away, but think of me sometimes—think of me kindly."

"Must you go?"

She stopped short by his side and looked full up into his face as she asked it. He would as soon have thought of telling a falsehood the moment before he knew he was to enter upon eternity as telling a comforting lie to this girl now.

"I must. Theo, forgive me?"

"I have nothing to forgive," she said with a strong effort. She had made her appeal, poor child, and it had failed, and now her pride prompted her to show him that the failure could be borne. Her pride and a something softer; there was such misery in the man's eyes, that her generous woman's nature urged her not to increase it by showing him how fully it was shared.

"I must go; better I had never come," he muttered, after a short pause.

"Don't say that; it has been a very pleasant time—to me."

"And to me too; too pleasant—far too pleasant. You have been the only bright thing my life has known for years, Theo, and I have clouded the brightness."

He bent his gaze upon her as he spoke, and Theo's face quivered under it.

"Oh, Mr. Ffrench, it has been so pleasant; why must it end?"

"Don't call me 'Mr. Ffrench,' for God's sake,—call me Harold, and don't ask me why it must end."

"I only meant," she replied proudly, "why must your visit to Houghton end so soon, if you find it pleasant?"

"Theo, dear little Theo, don't reproach me. I know what you mean, I know what you can't help meaning, and I can't——"

He stopped suddenly.

"Can't what?" asked Theo timidly; the hearing might be painful, but she would bear it.

"Can't see you suffer, and can't help your doing so. You'll soon forget me, Theo can't hope that you will remember me long. you forget me, darling?" he added passately, in an outburst of tenderness that startled the girl.

"No. Oh, don't speak in way. Oh, Harold, you won't go!"

They had come home during this conversation, for the things spoken had been spoken at intervals and had taken some time to say. Now they were in the little drawing-room alone, and even the twilight was dying out of the sky. Theo's last plaint went straight to his heart, and his heart governed his head for a brief space.

"Theo!" his arm went around her as he spoke, and her head rested upon his breast, and there was such passionate love in the way his hand clasped hers. All the misery and uncertainty of the last hour fled from her mind, and she was deliriously happy. She never doubted what this embrace should result in; she never doubted but that it was the prelude to a never-ending series of the same, on which the world should smile. Very confidingly did she submit to his caresses, very modestly and sweetly did she respond to them. The dream was bright that she dreamt in those moments—bright and pure; and he shrank from the task of awakening her from it, his heart still governing his head in an unaccustomed way.

"Why awaken her from it at all?" he asked himself presently. "Love would be more to her than the world." Thus he thought for a moment or two, and then he did her the justice of repenting him of the thought. Removing her head from his shoulder, he bent down and pressed his lips to her forehead, and pleaded for her pardon for the unuttered wrong.

"Theo, forgive me, forgive me?"

"For what?"

"I'll tell you to-morrow. Let me go now," he added, disengaging himself from her, "I can't stand it, Theo."

"Oh, Harold," she cried passionately, "you try me—you try me. Why not now as well as to-morrow, to-morrow that will be so long in coming?"

"No, it won't, poor child, dear little Theo. It will soon come, and you'll listen, and I shall speak better than now. Let me go, darling; don't turn your face away, Theo, there is no harm in it." When he had so said, he departed, leaving Theo in feverish expectation of that morrow which was to make known to her so much.

CHAPTER V.

KATE'S WAY.

LATE in the afternoon of the day following her visit to Houghton, Mrs. Galton put on her hat and went out by herself for a stroll in the grounds.

They were pretty grounds those around Haversham Grange, especially in the early summer days in which this story opens. Not very large, but well arranged; the glades and vistas were wonderful, when the size of the place was considered. There was one avenue that gave you utterly erroneous notions respecting the extent of the place, until you discovered that it was folded backwards and forwards, so to say, upon itself, and only separated from itself by an insertion of Portugal laurels and laurustinus. This avenue led away to a side-gate that opened upon the high road close to a compact plantation, in which rooks dwelt. It was a turfed avenue—one that was consecrated solely to walking purposes; the approach by which everything on wheels or four legs gained the Grange was straight and broad and open as the day, and not the one affected by Mrs. Galton when she went forth to meet her cousin Harold Ffrench.

At an early hour, immediately after luncheon, in fact, she had commenced expecting him; her expectations led her to request her husband to take "Kate out for a ride; horse exercise was so good for the little dear." Accordingly the husband and "little dear" went out for an indefinite period; and, having thus killed two birds with one stone, Kate Galton proceeded to make further preparations which seemed good to her, and with which their presence would materially have interfered.

The drawing-room at Haversham Grange was as pretty a room, as perfect a one of the kind, to my mind, as I have ever seen. Indifferently as Kate wielded the brush, she understood many of the secrets of the art she was essaying to practice upon Harold. For example, she knew that all light or all shade was bad in a picture, and could not therefore be good in a room; and she brought this knowledge to bear upon the adornment of her special sanctuary, and the result was good. She would not have her drawing-room all heaviness and crimson velvet, or entirely pale blue and frivolity and glare. But she had a happy admixture of shade and high lights—of the substantial and the elegant—and the admixture was eminently successful.

A considerable portion of the success was due to there being no over-crowding. Everything was clearly outlined, and there were not too many ornaments spotted about to break every line and fatigue every eye, as is too often the case. Kate Galton detested a mob—even of Dresden monsters or Sèvres shepherdesses, or reproductions of goddesses in Parian marble. These things were represented, and well represented, but not in sufficient quantity to become wearisome; you had no need to spread a mental chart of Kate Galton's room before entering it, in order to avoid dismay and destruction.

I have said she was a very pretty woman; and that she was so even women who were pretty themselves allowed. A variable beauty hers was—she avowed that it was so herself with engaging frankness. It was wonderfully variable when you came to think about it, for the nut-brown hair came out in golden gleams of surpassing brightness occasionally, and the fair, almost flaxen eyebrows and lashes grew very brown indeed at times. But they were all due, these marvellous transformations, "to the weather," Kate would tell you, for she had an organization very susceptible to external influences. As she probably knew more about it than any one else, her explanation, though not remarkably lucid, must be accepted in default of a better.

The weather had a great effect on her shortly after her husband's departure this day. It brought a most delicate hue into her cheeks, and shot her hair with that golden glory of which we have spoken. When it had achieved this, Kate disposed herself in an attitude on one of the couches in her drawing-room, and rested there, like another Lady Hamilton, awaiting Harold Ffrench.

But the hours passed, and Harold Ffrench did not appear, and she grew tired of playing Sultana to the inanimate objects in the room—even though an Apollo was amongst them. In reality she was an active woman; the sofa and languor were little affected by her when she was alone.

So about five o'clock she disturbed the arrangement she had made of swelling pillow and billowing drapery—of one bare arm from which the sleeve had fallen back, and one delicately shod foot from which the flounces had discreetly retreated—of carefully dishevelled hair and coquettishly adjusted half handkerchief of lace; she disturbed this arrangement, and uttered a graphic incisive denunciation against that offender who had caused it to have been maintained so long for worse than nothing.

"That little monkey! if she has wheedled Harold into staying, she shall crawl on her hands and knees in penitence for it."

Having uttered this amiable sentiment, Mrs. Galton felt better, and put on her hat and went forth, as has been stated, along the turfed avenue, in the hopes of seeing her cousin coming along the highroad and intercepting him at the side gate.

They had no lime-trees at Haversham; but the want of the fragrant linden was not felt in that avenue, it was so thickly studded between the trunks of its forest trees with lilacs and with hawthorn bushes in their sweetest, earliest bloom.

And if their odour caused the absence of the linden blossoms to pass unremarked, so did the verdure of the elm-trees leave little room for wishing for the linden's lovely green. Of just the same fair pale hue, with just the same indescribable air of freshness and grace about them, the colour of those leaves brought to her mind a day long passed by, when she, a girl, had listened to Harold Ffrench's stories of lazy hours he had known Unter der Linden in Berlin.

Hours that he had passed there and not

alone. But with whom, or whether happily or not, she could never gather, though in these minor matters she was much in his confidence in those days. Walking there, some of the old curiosity as to what this man's secret was arose in her mind, and a new one that had relation to Theo Leigh grew more poignant still.

"Past five," she muttered as she gained the gate and rested her arms upon it; "if he's coming at all he will come soon;" and she looked anxiously along the dusty road that was rendered unpicturesque by reason of its hedges being clipped to the smallest proportions for the furtherance of agriculture.

He came at last. She, still leaning on the gate, hailed him as he was passing, and the trap was stopped and Harold Ffrench descended from it to join his cousin. It was a hired trap, ill hung, and it had jolted heavily over the roads, and the horse had been a trial also, for it was slow in pace and by no means sensitive to the whip. Altogether he was rather glad than otherwise to descend and join his cousin at the outlet to the shady odoriferous avenue.

"You know the way up to the house? Oh, you don't; well, never mind, you cannot miss it; go on and wait in the yard till I see you," he said to the boy who was let out with the trap. "I wish I had come with you yesterday, Kate," he continued as he took Mrs. Galton's hand and placed it on his arm. "I have had a terrible time of it with that horse; he's accustomed to considerate people, who get out to relieve him at every hill and dip, and whenever the road is rucky and he 'pears to flag,' and under sundry other circumstances that make travelling with him unpleasant."

"And it is a long way from Houghton," Mrs. Galton replied sympathetically. Now that she had Harold back with her, she did not desire to travel Houghton-wards again. "I thought I should never have reached home yesterday; going it was different, I had something to look forward to—but coming home——"

She paused, and Harold made no answer. What was there to say to a woman—a pretty woman too—who implied that it was returning to a blank when she came to her home and her husband and her child! There was nothing to say—so Harold Ffrench said nothing.

"I have been expecting you all the afternoon, Harold," she went on presently; "and the afternoon has seemed so long; it always does when one is expecting an uncertainty."

"What do you mean by expecting an uncertainty?"

"I did not feel sure that you would come. I suppose my heart was very much set upon it, and that made me fear; Harold, you don't know what it is to me to have you here."

"Rather a bore, I should say, if Mrs. Galton were not far too well-bred a woman to suffer any guest to perceive that he bored her."

She laughed. "Ah! Harold, a bore? Well, think that you bore me if you like; perhaps it is as well that you should think so."

"What the devil's she driving at?" he thought. Then a faint idea of the truth dawned upon him —she was trying to drive Theo Leigh out of his head.

"Woman, thy name is—Kate; you can't resist attempting to be pleasant, even though you're quite pleasant enough without the attempt. Where is Galton? when do you dine?"

"John is on his farm—where else does he care to be? He's particularly entertaining at this present time; his crops are in his mouth morning, noon, and night."

"I'm glad to hear you say that you derive entertainment from the discussion of the source of your husband's property; some women are weak enough to affect to despise it," he replied, as gravely as if her speech had been made in all good faith.

"The bullocks were absorbing in the winter, and the pigs will come on in the autumn; you will be glad to hear of my prospects of salvation from stagnation."

She said it in a slightly piqued tone, and a temporary flush, that was of an entirely different shade to the permanent one, dyed her cheeks for a moment. He noticed neither the tone nor the flush, but after a few moments' pause he went on as if she had not spoken.

"For there's nothing more disheartening to a fellow than to find that his wife does not care about his pursuits, whatever they may be."

"Fortunately, John is not so easily disheartened; he has inoculated Bijou with a taste for his hobbies; the little monkey talks quite learnedly on various farm-yard topics."

"Katy's a dear little thing, by Jove! In a few years she will be growing up, and you'll be living your old triumphs over again in your daughter; Kate, you'll have plenty to interest you then."

"I am not quite old enough to take comfort for many things in the thoughts of dowager delights yet, thank you, Harold; and in the meantime, until my daughter is of an age to give me six months' trouble and anxiety perhaps, and then marry and be less to me than ever, you will permit me to remark that my 'lot is not too brilliant,' without giving me a veiled lecture. It's very hard indeed," Mrs. Galton continued, bringing the tears into her eyes for an instant, and then banishing them abruptly as she reflected on the susceptibility of her lashes, "very hard indeed that the only one to whom I have dared to speak as I feel since my marriage should deem me unreasonable, and chill me by cut-and-dried speeches."

"I am oppressed with remorse. Though I don't know what I have done, still I feel that I'm in the wrong."

"Let us sit down here," Mrs. Galton hurriedly exclaimed; and then she planted herself on a mound at the base of a tree, and he stretched himself along on the turf at her feet.

"Harold!" she said softly, drooping her head towards him, "nine years ago you ought to have felt remorse."

He took her hand and brushed his moustache across its firm, rosy, dimpled palm, but he uttered no word of inquiry, or compliment, or refutation.

"Do you ever think of those days, Harold!"

"Occasionally. They were uncommonly pleasant ones: good cook your father had then, to be sure."

"Is it only the cook who lives in your memory as an element of the pleasure you derived from your residence with us? Thank you, Harold."

"No, I have a kindly recollection of the wine also, of which he had good store; what else do you want me to say, Kate? You don't want compliments from me, you don't want me to tell you such truisms as that you are remembered by me, do you? How the deuce should you be forgotten?"

"They were my happiest days—and I dwell on them far too often for my peace of mind," she said rising. "Come, Harold, let us go to dinner." Then she heaved a sigh, and looked resigned and very pretty.

"What do you want me to say?" he asked, as they went on towards the house: and he drew her hand more closely within his arm and pressed it with as much tenderness as he had pressed Theo's but yesterday. "You put strange fancies in my head, my cousin, *mine* no more; you make me feel that it is well that I should do as I have resolved, and leave Haversham to-morrow."

She had looked forward to a period of uninterrupted intercourse and semi-friendly semi-sentimental flirtation with him. He was an adept in the art of saying the things she loved to hear,—namely, that she was fair and fascinating. Her husband never complimented her on her good looks, on her grace, or her seductive bearing. John was affectionate, generous, trusting, and considerate to her—nothing more. She wanted to inspire a *grande passion* and see some one very miserable,—some one who would be the victim of the first, and exhibit the latter in good style. This resolve of Harold's to leave Haversham so soon was extremely disappointing to her.

"Why go, Harold? You were to stay and go up to town with us; can't you wait for a few days? I shall be quite ready to start in a few days."

"I have other engagements, engagements that I can't avoid—unfortunately."

"But you'll be with us in town?"

"No, Kate, I cannot."

"Oh, Harold, why? I shall be hideously dull in London with——"

She paused, and portrayed confusion at having been led as by irresistible impulse to the brink of the confession of finding it dull with her husband. Harold Ffrench's determination to leave Norfolk as soon as possible was a fixed one, and had nothing whatever to do with Mrs. Galton. But he knew that it would be soothing to her fancy, or at any rate to be told that she had the power to move him in any way. So he soothed her.

"Why? Total abstinence is easier than moderation; that's why."

Then Kate Galton enacted modest embarrassment in a way that was infinitely amusing to the man who knew she did not feel it; and felt but one regret, which was, that for her own credit's sake she dared not tell of this confession of weakness which Harold Ffrench had made.

"Don't forget to show any attention you may be able to show to Miss Leigh, Kate," said Harold Ffrench the next day, as he was standing before Mrs. Galton's easel correcting the touches she had given to her picture during his absence. He wanted to win some kind of promise from her that she would show kindness to this girl, to whom he had been aught but kind, when he was gone.

"Forget! Am I likely to forget any request of yours?"

"She took an immense liking to you, fell in love with your beauty, and your 'way,' as she called it. You will be kind to her, won't you?" and then he felt a certain awkwardness when he reflected how indignant Theo would be, if she could but know that he had pleaded to any one to show her kindness.

"Girls of that age are generally bores," Mrs. Galton replied, coolly. "I'll be as civil as the distance will allow."

"She is not a bore." He could not say any more; he dared not trust himself to utter a defence of Theo to his cousin.

"Oh, isn't she? How I shall hate the sight of my tubes and brushes and easel when you are gone, Harold?"

"Get Miss Leigh over here and give her some lessons, you're quite capable of doing it."

"I am getting weary of Miss Leigh before I know her. No, Harold, I couldn't desecrate the taste *you* have developed in me by turning it to account in that way. I will be kind to Miss Leigh in a way that a chit of a girl will appreciate far more fully. I will ask her here, and invite some good *parti* to meet and fall in love with her."

The brush trembled in his hand. It was horrible to him to hear Theo spoken about in such a way, and yet what right had he to feel or resent aught on her account?

"Don't make jokes of that sort. You do injustice to your own delicacy as well as Miss Leigh's by the suggestion."

"Do you think Miss Leigh's delicacy would revolt at a good marriage, Harold? Poor fellow! how completely your flower of the wilderness has deceived you. Trust me, if I bring her out and give her the chance, I shall have a nice little list of her conquests to forward you in six months."

"Then in God's name don't bring her out. I can't paint any more this morning," he exclaimed abruptly. He left the room with a darkened brow and an ill-tempered haste, and Mrs. Galton resolved that the chance should be given Theo ere long, for the mention of it moved Harold more than was becoming in her, "Kate's" vassal.

He was to leave the Grange by the three o'clock train; and as he sat at lunch with his host and hostess, John Galton commenced laying amiable plans for further communion in town.

"I'm sorry you wouldn't wait and go off with us, Ffrench. Kate will want you in town, for I'm not much good at knowing where it's best to go."

"Where shall I address you, Harold, when we *do* go up?" Kate asked.

"The old address."

"The —— Club?"

"Yes."

"Why never at your lodgings? you must have lodgings in town."

"Because I am apt to change them."

"What part of town are you in now?"

"Belgravia."

"That's sketchy. What street?"

"I have not decided yet. I shall look about to-morrow; to-night I shall put up at a hotel; so you see that I can give you none other than the club address," Harold said hastily to John Galton, though it was John Galton's wife, and not John himself, who had asked for another address than the usual one.

"And your engagements? Are you going to stay with any one, or to travel with any one, or what are you going to do?"

"Nothing. Some people I knew on the Continent are coming over to the raree-show, and I have promised to meet them in town; that is all."

"Nice people?"

He shrugged his shoulders. "Nice enough."

"Then introduce them to me, and I'll do the honours of our great metropolis to them, and save you the trouble."

"You are very kind. I will see about it."

"And, Harold, get us an opera-box next Saturday; if you can I will go up on Friday."

"You shall have your opera-box on Saturday. By the way, some time or other, I wish you would take Miss Leigh to the Opera, she's passionately fond of music."

"Girls of that age always are 'passionately fond' of whatever may be mentioned. However, I will take her to the Opera; when do they go up?"

"Next week."

She darted a keen glance at him, which asked as plain as possible, "Are you going to meet them."

He shook his head.

"I shall be too fully occupied to pay the Leighs attention: you do it for me, Kate. They have been very kind to me, and you can requite it far better than I can."

"I fancied from what Kate said that you were going to requite it in the best way, if she's a nice girl," John Galton observed.

"Did Kate expect such infatuation on my part?" Harold Ffrench asked. And Kate blushed slightly as her husband answered,

"Well, I don't know that she did, only she wants to see you married, and so, I suppose, suspects you to be infatuated before you are."

"I must be off; I shall only just catch the train. Good-bye, Galton, good-bye, Kate. Don't plot for me." He whispered the last words as he bent over his cousin's hand, and discreet Mrs. Galton answered aloud:—

"No, no, John is wrong. I don't venture to suspect you of infatuation, Harold, any more. I made a mistake once. Good-bye."

"What mistake did you ever make about your cousin, Kate?" John Galton asked of his wife when he came back into her presence after seeing his guest off. "Did you ever think he cared for anybody?"

"Yes, it was long ago, dear, when I was a mere child: he seemed to admire a fashionable girl whose name was—but what matters? you are not interested in fashionable girls, nor am I any more (till our Bijou is grown up); but it passed off."

"Oh, did it?" John Galton replied, thoughtfully, and then he took both her slender white hands in his and drew her towards him. "Do you know, for half a minute I thought you meant yourself, Kate. I am glad you didn't."

CHAPTER VI.

LOVE'S YOUNG DREAM.

THEO remained in the room alone where he had left her after bestowing upon her that one impassioned kiss in which he had declared there was no harm; remained there alone for an hour after his departure, trying to think, and feeling too happy to accomplish it.

She heard Harold Ffrench's voice out in the garden, and she knew that he had joined her father and mother, who were strolling about in the soft evening air. But she judged him to be her own more especially now, and she could not bear to share him with others, even with them, just yet. So she sat still on the couch upon which he had placed her when he was bidding her adieu, and wondered why he had found her fair, and how this marvel had come to pass.

Her heart was throbbing audibly, but there was no pain in the flutter; it came from a very fulness of joy, and was a commentary on the tidings that she would not venture to tell to another, that she was not ill pleased to hear. He had told her he loved her! he had shown her that he loved her! and he had said that he would come to-morrow when the rest would be told, and would see it too, and the joy would be a secret no longer, though not one whit less sweet.

It never occurred to the girl to give forth the story at once in either a vaunting or an affectedly indifferent spirit. She had lived a very quiet life, and had not been lightly won and lightly lost half a dozen times in the course of it. Lively and light-hearted, and daring as none but a country-bred girl and only daughter can be, she was subdued and gentled and rendered diffident at once by the truth, the reality, and almost solemnity of the feeling that had grown up in her heart for this stranger. Her first love was a genuine one, and Theo blushed at the influence it had already gained over her, and wondered at the vastness of the chasm it had reft at once between the past and the present.

She had no very definite ideas as to what might be expected to take place to-morrow. She only felt that he would come and say something which would entitle him to hold her hand in his own through all time if he liked, and leave her free to call him "Harold." Then she murmured his name, first taking the precaution to bury her head in the sofa-cushion, in order that no one might by any chance hear what would sound "so silly." She pictured him at his easel while she read poetry to him through endless summer days, never thinking, poor child, that it can be aught but pleasant for a man to listen to metrical effusions from the lips of his wife while he is endeavouring to compose a picture.

The hours passed quickly in the indulgence of these happy visions, and then she was summoned to supper, and she went in half shrinking from the light, and strangely tremulous in eye and lip, all happy as she was. Her happiness was as the down on the butterfly's wing to her; she dreaded touching upon it lest one particle might be destroyed. It was so new, so fresh, so delicate—so unlike anything that she had known before.

Despite the wealth of womanly feeling that had been aroused in her recently, she was more of a child than ever in her manner to her parents that night. Perhaps it was the knowledge that she was longing to try her wings abroad that made her fold them so softly now. She sat at her father's feet and rested her loving head on his knee, and held his hand between those two which had known for the first time this day the pressure of another love than his. Her mother, sitting opposite, marked the brilliant colour in her face, and marvelled that Theo should so soon have recovered from that absolute fatigue which Harold Ffrench mentioned as the cause of her not joining them in the garden.

"You don't look tired now, Theo."

"No, ma, I am not a bit tired."

"Ah, I thought the reason you didn't come was that you were gone to see after Miss Watson, instead of being 'knocked up' as Mr. Ffrench said, when your father asked why you didn't come out."

"Did he say that? No, I didn't go near Miss Watson; she gets on better without me."

"She will have to get on better than she does if your things are to be ready by Tuesday; this is Wednesday evening, and Saturday she can't come to me. I wish a later day had been fixed for your going."

"Have you asked for leave, papa?"

"Yes, and got it," he replied.

"Oh dear; do you know, after all, I don't much care about going up," said Theo, throwing her head back against her father's arm. She was thinking how pleasant it would be to meander about those marshes with Harold Ffrench in the glorious summer days that were coming. "If you had not written for leave, papa, I believe I should say, don't go."

"The child's crazy," Mrs. Leigh said, rising and beginning to put away her work.

"No, she's not; she's only showing how magnanimous she can be when her magnanimity can't be accepted," her father said, kissing her. "Good night, my child; Ffrench is going in the morning; did you know it?"

"Yes; that is, he told me he was going, but I don't think he will go," Theo answered; and then she went off to bed, and prayed for and dreamt of Harold Ffrench, while her father and mother pondered over how much money might in prudence be drawn from his agents to expend in giving Theo a taste of relaxation in London.

This going to London, which had been a dream of delight for some time past, sank now into absolute unimportance by the side of this new delight which had arisen. She did not care an atom any longer about those specimens of the arts and sciences which were collected by the enterprising and shown to the curious in Hyde Park. It would be pleasant to look at them with Harold Ffrench; but the dead level of the salt marshes would be equally agreeable objects of contemplation in such companionship; therefore the tedious journey might be saved. Then she remembered that the leave had been asked for and granted, and that some of her father's brother officers might be put to inconvenience as to their own contemplated absences, if he did not take his when he could have it, and come back at the appointed time. She also remembered that the giving this pleasure to her would be the best pleasure her father had known for a long time. So, remembering these things, she resolved to go with all the glee she could muster, and show gratitude for the plan, and gratification in realising it, whatever fate might hold in store for her of far brighter things.

"Dear papa, he means me to enjoy it, and he shall see that I do enjoy it thoroughly," she murmured to herself in her latest moments of coherency that night. On that resolution she fell asleep and dreamed away the hours till the dawn broke—the dawn of the day that was to hear said those words whose promise had been given to her heart already.

It was not an easy thing to behave as if nothing had happened or was going to happen the following morning. She knew that the hour or two which would probably elapse before Mr. Ffrench, in accordance with his usual practice, found his way up from the Bull would appear interminable if she was not employed. She knew this, and yet she was incapable of originating any employment of an absorbing nature, or indeed of doing anything save look out of the window and wonder when he would come.

"There are those frills to be hemmed for the blue muslin, Theo," her mother said to her once when she came into the room and found Theo at that occupation which I have just described.

"Yes, mamma."

"But you don't do them."

"I will presently, mamma—this evening."

"This evening you will be wanting to go out, and then the frills will be forgotten; they wouldn't take you an hour, you lazy child, and when they were hemmed I would put them on, and the blue muslin would be finished."

"Bother the blue muslin," Theo thought; but she only said, "Yes, mamma, I'll get them directly! I am busy just now."

"What are you looking at?" Mrs. Leigh asked, coming to the window.

"An energetic fly dodging a spider," Theo replied, promptly pointing out the spectacle she described in the crevice of some rock-work.

"You may see dozens of them any day," Mrs. Leigh rejoined.

Then, Theo's day-dream being dispelled, she went in search of the frills for peace' sake.

He had said that he would come, and it never occurred to Theo to doubt him; and this, not so much that she was dominated by her passion for him, as that it would have seemed incredible to her that a gentleman should lie. That men break every spoken and implied vow, and still hold their honour stainless; and that women transfer their hearts and caresses from one lover to another, and still consider themselves chaste, she had yet to learn. The majority of young girls believe what is said to them: it is their virtue and their fault. Extreme caution comes only from experience, and it is not desirable that girls of twenty should possess it.

So she sat through the morning hours, hemming her muslin frills, excited and nervous truly, but never doubtful for an instant that the man who had pressed his lips to hers, and told her that in that impassioned salute there "was no harm," would come to her this day as he had promised. She would have been as likely to suspect her father of committing petty larceny as to suspect this man (who had kissed her with a kiss that seemed to make her his own, it was so warm and wild) of lying. Thus, with her strength unimpaired, her soul unshaken by a doubt, she came to a knowledge of the wounding truth at once, and bore it.

"Ffrench has left, I find," Mr. Leigh remarked, as Theo seated herself, still excited but still happy, at the dinner-table.

"I think he might have come up to say good-bye," Mrs. Leigh replied; and Theo felt that her mother was looking keenly and anxiously at her.

"*They* mustn't be made unhappy," the poor child thought; "I'll speak at once."

"What took him away so suddenly, papa? he ought to have said good-bye to us, we have been so friendly."

She thought of that passionate kiss, and those impassioned words which had passed between them the previous night, as she spoke, and her brain reeled with the remembrance, and her proud young heart seemed as though it would burst with the sense of the indignity that had been put upon it. But still she spoke clearly; and she was rewarded for the effort she had made by seeing the anxious look pass from her mother's face.

"We shall miss him very much. I wonder whether he will ever come back, or if we shall ever see him again," Mrs. Leigh said briskly. The words were kind to the departed stranger, but the tone in which they were spoken told of the hope which she felt on the subject.

"Ever see him again?" Yes, it had come to this, that it was more than improbable that she would ever see him again—this man who had won from and shown to her such signs of love as she could never exhibit to another. His kiss was burning on her lips still; her heart had not ceased those quickened bounding pulsations to which his own had responded when he clasped her to his breast last night! He had set his mark upon her, and she could never again be as she had been before; she felt this with a burning brow in the midst of her agony at losing him at all. But even as this feeling was stinging, this agony stultifying her, she resolved that she would make no sign of her sorrow, for the sake of sparing those whose only joy was in her.

"Give me a little bit of the brown, papa? Thank you, that's just the bit I wanted," Theo said resolutely. Then she ate her bit of brown meat resolutely, with apparent appetite, though the eating it at all was a terrible task.

"I dare say Mr. Ffrench will call on you in town," Mrs. Leigh remarked presently. "He said so much last night about the kindness we had shown him; it's little enough, I'm sure, after all, but I don't think he's one to forget even trifling kindnesses."

"I don't think he is," Theo replied; she would not shirk the subject, but had she not been placed with her back to the light they would have seen that, steady as were the words, the lips that uttered them were quivering.

"Ffrench seems to have known many of the men I knew in Greece; it's odd I can't recall his name at all," Mr. Leigh observed, thoughtfully, after a short pause. "There was a young Englishman, whose name,—by-the-by, what was his name? I shall forget my own next,—who joined the expedition in a casual sort of way; but I never met him, and I remember now his name was Linley, so it couldn't have been Ffrench."

"Mr. Ffrench"—her tongue felt as if it had a mountain of alum upon it as she said his name—"must have been too young for you to think about in those days, papa; being a young man yourself, I have no doubt that you despised boys."

"We must have come athwart one another too," her father rejoined, "for he was speaking last night of Mavrocordato and Church,—speaking of things that occurred in connection with them at the very time I was with them; odd I shouldn't remember his name."

"Very odd indeed," Theo thought, considering what a spell that name held for her, but she said nothing. Determined as she was not to shirk the subject, she was not capable yet of being an active agent in its continuance.

In the afternoon of that same day, while a consultation was being held as to the proper position which the frills were to occupy upon the blue muslin dress and mantle, Mrs. Leigh returned to the charge, and Theo was nearly asking for quarter.

"Do you know, Theo, I really can't help thinking it somewhat extraordinary that Mr. Ffrench should have gone off in that way."

"In what way, mamma?"

"Without coming near us to say good-bye; don't you?"

"Oh, I don't know."

"Well, I do; he has plenty of external polish, but if he were as innately gentlemanly and refined as he appears he would not so palpably pick up and drop people just to suit his own convenience."

Theo winced, but said nothing.

"And (it was absurd in a man of his age—for a child like yourself, of course), but I did think he admired you, Theo."

"Oh, mamma!"

"I did really; and I'm not like some mothers: I don't fancy that there is something directly a man looks at my daughter."

"No, mamma."

"But I suppose I was mistaken, otherwise he wouldn't have gone off in that manner; and I'm glad, as I was mistaken, that I didn't say anything to you about it while he remained."

"So am I, very glad."

"And I do think that it was very impolite of him to go away without saying good-bye to us; why, child, how you're trembling!"

"Yes, ma. I have just got a woeful prick; the needle has slipped under my nail. Ah—ah!" (impatiently), "I can't work any more; I'll go and get papa to go down on the marsh with me."

So she went and secured her father's company in that her first visit after Harold Ffrench's departure to the spot on which he had made love manifest to her. For about Miss Theo there was no maudlin sentimentality; she was resolved upon abstaining from the luxury of making these haunts sacred and private.

But still it was hard to walk there and be all a daughter, nothing more, so soon, so very soon! She did it, however, with how much pain and difficulty may not be known, since she never told. She even spoke brightly of that approaching visit to London, which now she would rather have died than have been compelled to pay.

Through all the intervening days she kept up with that proud resolve which this kind of trial is almost sure to develop in a proud woman's breast. Many a chance allusion nearly broke her down, and many a kindly word all but overpowered her. But she was strong, and young, and generous, and would neither be broken down nor overpowered before those who would most sorely have grieved to see her so.

Harold Ffrench had been very tender to her —tender in a way that no very young man could be; and the remembrance of this tenderness would come upon her with a rush sometimes, but never before others. It was only when the girl was alone that she bent before the memory of it, and blushed and turned pale in quick succession at the thought of how warmly he had seemed to love, and how well he had deceived her.

Before others, though, she would neither repine nor repent: there "would have been weakness in doing either," she told herself; besides, repining and repentance on her part might have paved the way to others blaming him—her love, her demi-god, her vitalised Vandyck. There had been miserable misapprehension of his meaning on her part, or foul trickery on his; she could not bear that comment should be made on either. So she suffered in silence, and would not permit her appetite to flag; in which last there was, I think, the truest heroism, it being an awful thing to eat when one is ill in mind or body, and an equally awful thing for all such as dwell in the tents with one to witness the daily increasing disinclination to do so.

So she ate and drank, and made merry in the old way, and was to all outward seeming the same Theo she had been before this stranger came, and saw, and loved, and left her. But her father's frequent assertion, that she "was like a young bear, in that all her troubles were before her," grated harshly on her ears now. She knew that a something was gone from her mind which could never come back to it; a blot made on the surface of her life which no after happiness could eradicate.

She did not set herself to the task of solving the problem of his enforced semi-declaration and sudden exit from the scene. There was a something which he had taught her to desire, but what that something was, God knew—she did not question.

The result would be just the same; the cause was of little worth in comparison. That there had been something insurmountable she did not doubt; for she did not degrade her love, and insult her own heart, by deeming that it had been sought, gained, and rejected as a summer day's pastime by a motiveless trifler.

It was a sharp, deep cut, that she had received; but she resolutely covered it up, and kept the air of observation from it, and would not suffer it to fester. Sharp and deep as it was, it was a healthy wound, and she knew that it would heal perfectly in time, and leave no pain even though a scar remained.

While the wound was young, and before the efficacy of this mode of treatment could be said to be an ascertained thing, the day of departure arrived, and Theo Leigh went up to London with her father without so much as a hope now of even holding intercourse with his cousin, for the charming Mrs. Galton had made no sign.

CHAPTER VII.

WOMAN'S FRIENDSHIP.

It has been said that Kate Galton was an active woman, little disposed toward reclining even in the most graceful of attitudes when there were none near to see her. With a wider scope in the world, and as the wife of an utterly different husband, this activity of hers might have been turned to good account. As it was, the arena of ambition was closed to her, for she was simply the wife of a country gentleman whose name was unknown beyond the limits of his own parish, and whose fame rested solely on "Beelzebub" and his invariably early crops.

Kate told herself and Harold Ffrench that she "had missed her vocation" in marrying John Galton. She thought that she had a diplomatic mind, and that she would have been a charming repository for any man's state and political secrets. "I'm so sympathetic, you see," she would say in her not unfrequent moments of confidence with her cousin, "and I can always expand to the occasion. I ought to be other than I am, in fact."

"There I heartily agree with you," he would reply, leaving Kate in a state of uncertainty as to whether he agreed with the spirit or the letter merely of her statement respecting herself.

"I seem to have nothing to live for; it's impossible to stir John up to do anything."

"What should he do, save breed another two-year-old to run for the Two Thousand? Let John alone, Kate; when country gentlemen get stirred up, as you call it, they develop into pragmatic, egotistical, twaddling prigs. You wouldn't have him go about and adorn country-town platforms with his flowers of ungrammatical oratory, and his honest, stupid face, would you? And what other vent would his enthusiasm find if you did stir him up to feel any?"

"There is the sting; his orations would be ungrammatical, and his face is honest, but stupid. If he were other than he is, I should not be so anxious for him to prove himself something higher than he seems."

"Why can't you take him as he is, and be content?" Harold Ffrench would say; but despite this affected toleration towards his cousin's husband, he was far from unpleasantly conscious that her complaint of John was an implied acknowledgment of his (Harold Ffrench's) superiority, and this consciousness rendered him not by any means intolerant to the complainer. Harold was aware that, were his own deeds brought to light, and his life carefully analysed, he would be found to have done less good in his generation than even John Galton. But he felt that there was no need to impress this fact upon his cousin, since she had not displayed sufficient acumen to discover it for herself. Therefore he was compassionately tolerant to John Galton's ignominious career, and satisfaction in the same, and sublimely resigned to having honours thrust upon him that he did not at all deserve.

In a measure, he sympathised with and understood Kate's vain-glorious desire to be a something, not better and higher, but more talked about, more before the world, than she was. For in his own lazy way be, too, had had his hopes and ambitions, and he had girded fiercely at fate when they had failed. But, after all, a woman's ambition must ever be a poor, small thing, he judged; and, therefore, whether it were realized, or whether it failed, was of little consequence: it could do no lasting harm.

Really in Kate's case he had good reason for supposing this; for Mrs. Galton had ambitions whose name was legion, and they failed her continually, and she bloomed while the memory of them was green just as if nothing had happened. Harold, himself, was a permanent disappointment to her, and he knew it. Yet not even the vanity, of which she possessed an average share, could make him believe that he was thought of by Mrs. Galton as aught but a possible cause of sensation of some sort in the future ten minutes after his exit from her presence, if another agreeable man appeared.

Just now, however, he was the cause of indignation vexing her soul continually, for she was up in lodgings in Piccadilly with her husband, and Harold Ffrench was aware of the fact, and still he abstained from seeking her presence. It was hard on her, cruelly hard on her; for Mr. Galton insisted on patronising the local tailor, a man who lived in the market-town nearest to Haversham, and his coats, one and all, had a ruck in the back that was horribly suggestive of the country and all its abominations to her. It was good broad-cloth that John Galton wore, but the cut of it was a maddening thing to the woman who bore his name, and leant upon his arm, in the haunts of fashionable men in that year of grace. He marred the effect of her own exquisite toilettes, and made her miserable. He took the edge off the Great Exhibition, and made her doubt, for the first time in her life, whether the many stares which were directed toward her were of unmixed admiration or not. After three or four days' endurance of this agony, she could bear it no longer.

"I will write to Harold Ffrench," she said to herself on the impulse of the moment, but she thought better of that presently. Mr. Galton had not suggested that she should write to her cousin, even about that opera-box of which mention had been made.

"I will take you there, Kate; never mind bothering your cousin; he seemed to me to want to shake us off. Country cousins, you know, are not always agreeable, are they?"

"I hope Harold does not look upon me as a country cousin," Kate had retorted indignantly; but still she had said no more about writing to Harold, for John Galton was one who would foist his society on no man, and he would not make the suggestion without which Kate was too wary to write. "I will get that Miss Theo Leigh here," she said to herself one morning when she was languidly adorning herself for a sacrificial saunter under conjugal auspices, "and then, John is always so good-natured, and such a fool, that he will soon propose bringing them together again."

Rather than not have the society of the man

at all, she would have used Venus herself to lure him into her presence. Mrs. Galton's scruples about abolishing Venus as soon as she ceased to be necessary as a lure would have been few, as may be supposed. So now she resolved to bribe Harold to come to her by promising him a sight of Theo, little caring what came to Theo through the means.

Theo, meanwhile, had been struggling very hard to live in the present, and think alone of the future, and forget as much as might be forgotten of the past. She had her reward in finding the present slightly fatiguing, but pleasantly so, and the future not a blank by any means; the wound that she had received was deep, but it was, as has been said, a clean cut, and the edges did not fester and fret her constantly.

Nevertheless, sensible girl and dutiful daughter as she was, she did occasionally feel that other companionship than her father's would have been desirable. He exerted himself much to give her pleasure, wearied himself daily for hours in that fairy palace in Hyde Park, and nightly at the theatres where he distracted Theo by comparing modern actors to the Siddons, Kembles, and Kean, to the invariable disadvantage of the former. Then for a rest he took her to Greenwich, and showed her the hospital (for an appointment to which he yearned), and partook of luncheon with an old comrade who was eloquent on the delights of the place, and the advantages derivable from a residence in it. He was a plethoric old gentleman, this late comrade of her papa's, who grunted and swore a great deal more than was necessary, Theo thought; but he appeared to be admirably contented with his position, which Theo's experience of old naval officers taught her was a remarkable thing.

"No place like it for a man with a family, sir, —no place like it; to live rent-free in a palace is something after knocking about all one's life, eh, Miss Leigh?"

"I don't think that it's too much, after knocking about all one's life," Theo replied, dubiously.

"You don't, eh? you don't. My dear young lady, let me tell you that it is the highest reward the Service offers us, an appointment here, and that a man doesn't get it for nothing, I can tell you."

In her heart Theo thought that no man had seen so much service or done such doughty deeds as her father. His old comrade's satisfaction in the boon bestowed savoured, she thought, of disparagement to her father's claim to it. The young lady had yet to learn that the old gentleman who grunted and swore held a different tone to outsiders to that which those within the gates were accustomed to hear from his lips. She did not know this, so she only said,

"I suppose papa will have it then."

"You'll find the society here delightful," one of the daughters of the house observed with animation. Theo had mentioned that she lived in a dull little village; it was pleasant to the daughter of the house to point out the difference in the places in which they were running the best years of their respective careers. She then went on to give Theo a list of the names and number of the families resident at the time, and

Theo remarked that there seemed "to be a great many ladies."

The daughter of the house tried to look as if she had never thought this fact a drawback to the delights of the place before.

"There *are* a good many; yes, certainly, there are a good many; of course if you don't like ladies' society, you won't think such a number of girls in the place any recommendation."

"Ladies' society in moderation I like, but such a number! Papa, you mustn't come here. I should feel ashamed of myself for adding to such a heavy brigade," Theo said laughingly to Mr. Leigh, whose heart was heavy at the thought of not being there already, living in "rooms in a palace rent-free, and having as many barrels of small beer as he liked at cost-price." He was making up his mind to "memorialise" again for the next vacancy, and looking at his old comrade attentively, in order to detect whether there were any signs of dissolution about that hale but aged man, who fathomed the motive of the attentive gaze, and resented it by being baler and heartier than before out of sheer opposition.

They made the tour of the place after luncheon, went into the Chapel, and were brought up by the rope before the viper and bundle of sticks, and into the Painted Hall, where they duly dislocated their necks and got headaches in the cause of art, and into the wards and kitchens.

These latter places deepened Mr. Leigh's admiration for the "*mag*-nificent scale" on which everything was done, for he was in an admiring mood, and thoroughly believed that the height of naval bliss was to be found here. But aged seamen feeding are pleasanter on canvas than in real life. Theo was quite ready to believe in the place also, but the gastronomic odours on this hot June day did not increase her faith in this paradise to which she, fate and the Admiralty willing, was to be consigned.

But there is a great charm about this place after all,—at least there soon was to Theo. It is utterly unlike every other place; and this characteristic of singularity always will tell in the end. The library and the librarian; the feudal observances of banging a gong at sunset, and barring out visitors at nine; the solemn sorry state that is maintained; the pertinacity with which certain benches are guarded from the contaminating touch of those who "don't belong to the place,"—all these things struck her, and caused her to experience a throb of the same sort of feeling that made her father linger in the machinery department at the Exhibition; for, as that modern sage Dundreary says, human nature "likes to wonder."

She did wonder; wonder greatly about many things that she saw and heard. Amongst other things she wondered whether Queen Mary looked down and smiled upon her work, and whether William was as well satisfied with it as he has cause to be with the majority of the acts of his reign? At least, I am not sure that the wonderings took the form of those precise words at the time, but she did afterwards, when the habit of Greenwich Hospital was no longer upon her.

She had other cause for wonderment when she reached her temporary home in the lodgings in Great George Street, Westminster, that night, for on the table in the drawing-room she found the card of "Mrs. John Galton." The unsolved problem of how Mrs. Galton, *his* cousin, had found her out, kept Theo awake the whole night, and ill prepared her for bearing the burden and heat of the following day.

With the nine-o'clock post that day came an explanation in the form of an epistle from Mrs. Leigh, acquainting her daughter with the gratifying fact of the kindest letter having been received by her from Mrs. Galton, asking so particularly for Theo's address in town, and wishing so much to see her. "I answered it at once," the mother wrote, "and I should not be surprised to hear that she has been to call upon you already; she seems to be a very sweet-tempered domestic woman; she says she wishes that Houghton and Haversham were nearer to each other, in which case she should ask me to have an eye to her dear little daughter during her absence. As a mother," she feelingly remarks, "I can enter into the continual anxiety she experiences while away from the dear child. It is not often," Mrs. Leigh sagaciously added, "that a young and beautiful woman such as Mrs. Galton, is so devoted a mother as she appears to be." (Some few weeks after this, Theo showed her mamma's letter to her fascinating friend in a moment of blind admiration and unlimited confidence, and the fascinating friend performed a mental *pas* of pleasure at having "so successfully hoodwinked the old lady.")

On Mrs. Galton's card was a pencilled statement of an intention to call on Miss Leigh at three o'clock on the following day. Before that hour came, Theo had woven a vision of Harold Ffrench accompanying his cousin; indeed his figure was the prominent one in the pattern, and Mrs. Galton fell into position as merely an accessory, the cause of an effect which should banish thoughts of all beside itself.

She inducted herself into the blue muslin for the first time this day. The sight of the frills had been painful to her hitherto; they had been hemmed that day when she got her "woeful prick," poor child, and they possessed the balsamic quality of making the wound smart. So just in this one thing she had been indulgent to her weakness, and she congratulated herself on this indulgence now, when she put it on in all its freshness towards solemnising with all due splendour the advent of her expected guests, and saw that she looked very well in it.

She would not go out at all this day. When she had deemed that it was all over, and that she should never see him again, she had been most wisely patient, most bravely determined on doing just as she had ever done. But this sudden revulsion, this relighting of the torch of hope, upset her philosophy, and though she resolved to meet and greet him as a friend,—nothing more, never anything more,—still till the time of such meeting came she could but let agitation reign supreme.

It was a long dull morning that Theo passed in the drawing-room of their lodgings. It would have been better for her had she gone to the Admiralty with her father, as he had invited her to do; but she had refused this slight diversion, fearing that three o'clock would come upon her like a thief in the night, and that they would come and go and miss her, and make no further attempt. Such a catastrophe was of too horrible a nature to be lightly brought upon herself, therefore she suffered her papa to go off to a possible interview with the First Lord alone.

It was not a hopeful room to contemplate, with the prospect before you of spending several hours in it by yourself, that drawing-room in the house in Great George Street. Everything in it was for show and not for use, and the show was not fair to look upon. There was an undesirable carpet on the floor, a dark-green ground with branches of red trees strewed all over it, and those branches stood out so well from the green that one involuntarily stepped high in order to avoid catching in and tripping over them; there were *papier mâché* stands sprinkled with a lavish hand about the apartment, and these supported busts of Byron, and Scott, and Shakespeare (the latter with an evident predisposition to water on the brain), and glass shades full of wax fruit and flowers. The chairs, too, were of an order from which one would turn with loathing and disgust when fatigued mentally or bodily, for they were heavy hot velvet; and if one deposited one's self upon one of them with anything like velocity, clouds of dust arose and rendered all things obscure for many minutes. When to this is added the fact, that the French clock on the mantel-piece was addicted to loud ticking, and being always an hour too slow or four hours too fast by reason of its purposeless minute perpetually catching in a feeble kind of way in its stumpy hour-hand, it will readily be believed that the room was not hopeful—that it was, on the contrary, decidedly disheartening. It was not at all a room in a corner or portion of which Theo could enshrine herself and becomingly await the arrival of possible devotees.

It never occurred to Theo to seek relief from the tedium by taking up woman's universal panacea, work. She was not one who could find partial oblivion in a thimble, and alleviation for much in the wielding of that useful little weapon, by aid of which many women keep *ennui*, even despair, at bay. The girl was far from being muscular or coarse in her tastes or appearance; still a needle never looked quite at home in her slender restless hand; she had no liking for the most customary of all feminine occupations.

Cut off, therefore, by habit from this resource; cut off by circumstances from others that were more congenial; Theo sat all the morning in idleness, and though Satan did not find some mischief for her idle hands to do, the fiend Imagination had a rare time of it, waved on by the recently relighted torch of Hope.

She had tutored herself into the belief that she should not be very impatient even if three o'clock passed and they came not. But the schooling was unnecessary, for with the striking of the hour mingled the sound of a resolutely plied knocker, and presently Mrs. Galton alone came into the room.

"I am very punctual, am I not?" Mrs. Galton asked, as she was shaking hands. "I always keep my word." And so, to do her justice, she did in some things; she never broke small promises to casual acquaintances; when Kate Galton ruptured a faith it was a fine big one invariably.

"It is very kind of you to have taken the trouble to find me out," Theo replied; her knees were trembling with excitement and disappointment, and despite her efforts, her eyes rolled towards the door and rested there lingeringly. Kate Galton quite understood why they did so, and resolved to punish this folly lightly in some way or other. Theo Leigh conceiving a genuine passion for a man she (Kate) had elected to honour with an elastic regard, was a person to be abased when she had served the contemplated purpose.

"Ah, I see you looking; but little Katy is not with me, nor is my husband, for a marvel."

"Oh, I know that you did not bring your little girl up; I was not looking for her," Theo said honestly; and Mrs. Galton's brow clouded ever so slightly as she weighed the probabilities of Theo having heard thus much from Harold Ffrench.

"Have you seen my cousin, then, lately?" she asked.

Theo shook her head and said "No."

"Ah, I thought it most extraordinarily negligent of him, if he had seen you, not to have told me, knowing, as he does, how anxious I am to see a great deal of you while in town, and in the country too, I hope; but Harold is so forgetful that, after all, I ought not to have been surprised if it had escaped his memory."

This speech was designed to show Theo how absolutely unimportant a thing she was in Harold Ffrench's eyes, and also that Mrs. Galton's intercourse with her cousin was incessant and familiar. It failed in achieving the first object, for Theo did not believe that she was forgotten by or utterly unimportant to the man who had seemed to love her so warmly but the other day. But the latter and equally natural implication she firmly credited. Why should she have doubted it, indeed? It seemed to her to be in the order of things that Mrs. Galton and her cousin Harold should be much together. Theo had not begun to fear that there was either sin or shame in the combination, or to suspect it of being other than right proper, highly desirable, and extremely natural.

"And what have you been doing?" Mrs. Galton asked, after a few desultory remarks, that did not bear upon anything in particular, and shall therefore be suffered to pass unrecorded. "I suppose you have seen the principal things that are going on; isn't it a wonderful season?"

"It is my first experience of one; of course it is wonderful to me; but I am not in the vortex, you know."

"Ah, how should you be in the vortex with no chaperone save your papa? I forgot that when I asked you what you had been doing. I have ebbed away from London society since my marriage, but I do know some people still, and it would give me great pleasure to take you wherever I go myself."

Theo thanked Mrs. Galton for the kindly disposition evinced, but it was all she could do, for she was beginning to develop the idea that a little more was said than was meant on all occasions. It is unpleasant to accept warmly a conditional invitation, and then to discover that the inviter did not intend to go quite so far in the matter as you in your innocence imagined from the manner.

"It would really give me great pleasure to have you with me, Miss Leigh; do you think you could persuade your papa to leave you with me when he returns?"

Theo tried to say that she thought she "ought to go home with papa" firmly, and she failed. The thought that she would surely see Harold Ffrench at his cousin's house would arise, and it caused her resolution to totter. Mrs. Galton felt persuaded of Theo's acquiescence in the proposed scheme, despite that young lady's gentle indication of a wish to sacrifice inclination to duty; and Mrs. Galton fathomed the cause of this acquiescence, and again resented it in the innermost recesses of her mind.

"Little fool! to nurse hopes of Harold in such a way," Kate thought, even while she was saying:—

"Let us leave the decision to your mamma. I will write to her about it, and if she will trust you with me, you need have no scruples about staying. Mr. Galton will be obliged to return to Haversham, but we shall never lack an escort with my cousin Mr. Ffrench in town. I do not like to think of your going back after only three weeks' experience of this exceptional year."

Theo glowed at the prospect.

"It is very kind of you, very kind indeed, to a stranger such as I am. I shall enjoy staying with you above everything, but it does seem a great thing for you to do for such a recent acquaintance."

"Not at all. I have no sisters, no cousins, no grown-up daughters" (she tinkled out a little laugh here at the preposterousness of the notion of her having grown-up daughters). "Perhaps when Katy's of a fit and proper age to be given her chance, I shall be disinclined for society, and shall be glad of some friend doing for her what I am going to do for you." Then Kate rose up to go, and added, "Mind, Miss Leigh, that you reward me by marrying brilliantly at the end of the season; my protegée's glories will be mine, remember."

"Papa, papa!" Theo cried, when her father came home from that interview with a suave First Lord, who made him happy even while refusing him all he asked,—"Mrs. Galton has asked me to stay with her; she is going to remain entirely on my account, and take me everywhere, though Mr. Galton won't be able to,—that is to say, Mr. Ffrench will, you know, instead. Will you let me go?"

"I don't quite understand the case. When do you want to go to her?"

"Not while you can stay here with me, papa; not till you go back, dear; but then I thought—that is, she thought that you would let me go and stay with her and see a little more of what is going on; and she would take me to parties, she says."

"I know so little of the woman, and what I do know I don't like."

"That's mere prejudice, papa; she's the sweetest, kindest woman; I wish you could have seen her to-day, you wouldn't have been able to help liking her; even if you can't let me go to her, don't say a word against her, please."

"We will hear what your mother says," Mr.

Leigh said, meditatively; he was in a difficulty—a difficulty that frequently oppresses parents. He could not bear to deprive the child of one jot or tittle of pleasure which might be hers. But at the same time he sorely distrusted this woman who was offering to give it to her.

CHAPTER VIII.

KATE GALTON MEANS SO KINDLY.

KATE had secured the bait! She knew that she had done so as soon as she saw that the girl's desire pointed to remaining with her, for she had fathomed that Theo was a pet daughter who could move her parents to consent to any plan. The sole difficulty now was to win her husband's consent to the retention of the cage in which the bait was to be placed. For rooms in Piccadilly let at their full value in 1851, and John Galton was a man who gave thought as to the disbursement of his cash.

It was not alone for the sake of luring Harold Ffrench into her net that the pretty spider with the nut-brown hair made use of the fresh young country fly. Mrs. Galton wanted an excuse, a fair and valid excuse with which neither man nor woman could quarrel, for remaining in London and enjoying herself as much as was seemly; therefore she converted herself into a chaperone, and appealed to John Galton's good-heartedness on behalf of her interesting young friend.

"I have been to call on that pretty Miss Leigh this morning, John," she said to her husband while they were at dinner on the evening of the day on which Hope told a flattering tale to Theo. "Poor child! she looked so doleful at the idea of going back to Houghton so soon that I couldn't help asking her to come and stay with us here when her father goes back."

"When is he going back?"

"In five or six days."

"We shall not be long after him; in ten days at the latest I shall go back; I don't like leaving the place for longer: things get neglected when the master is away."

"John! that's awkward in the extreme: I have asked her, and she has accepted the invitation."

"Take her down to the Grange with you, then."

"She won't thank me for that alteration in the programme; really it's very awkward."

Mrs. Galton put down her knife and fork, and rested her elbow on the table and her head on her hand, in very weariness and vexation of spirit.

"Very awkward, indeed," she repeated. "I forgot when I was talking to her that I had virtually done with London life. I remembered the days when I was a young girl myself, and I tried to show her the sort of kindness I used to appreciate most highly myself."

"It's impossible that I can stay more than ten days longer, Kate," John Galton said, in a vexed tone.

"And it would be miserable without you," his wife replied, calmly.

"It would be miserable for me, dear. But if

you have set your heart on giving this young lady a treat, you shall stay—if you care to stay here without me."

"I should renew a good many acquaintances, for Aunt Glaskill is in town—she may be very useful to my daughter when she is grown up," Mrs. Galton replied pensively, but promptly.

"Haversham will seem duller than ever to you after such a taste of your old life."

She opened her eyes with a little stare of inquiry and astonishment.

"Haversham dull to me?"

"There, I didn't mean to say it, Kate. I don't think that you find it dull, dear, and it would be confoundedly hard," he continued, defending her against himself as it were, "if you, who are not much more than a girl yourself, mightn't want a change sometimes: you shall stay here and enjoy yourself with Miss Theo Leigh, and as soon as I have set things going on the land, I'll come back to you."

He got up and kissed her as he said it, but I fear that the promise contained in his last sentence robbed her response of a little of its warmth.

"I haven't said much about my own connections heretofore, John," she said, virtuously, "but I often think that it is almost a pity that we should drift away from them altogether. Aunt Glaskill's countenance will be a good thing for Katy when she is grown up, and Aunt Glaskill won't be ill pleased at my taking a pretty girl like Theo Leigh to her house."

"Take her by all means and please Lady Glaskill, but my daughter won't want the countenance of an old paint-pot when she's grown up, thank God!"

"Then you really think that I had better remain?"

"Certainly, if you wish to do so."

"Not unless you wish it too, John: I had rather be made downright rude to a dozen Miss Leighs than displease you."

"I would not have my wife rude to anybody; no, Kate, you have asked this young lady to stay with you, and you must not disappoint her. Katy and I will try to get on without you, but it will be dull work."

"As you will; of course, if you think it right that I should stay, I will do so; and John——"

"Well, what is it now?"

"About a brougham? It won't do to risk Miss Leigh's evening dresses in common cabs, you know."

"Oh, won't it? well, dear, as I shall not be here, you can please yourself as to where you like to send when you want a carriage for the night."

"With a young lady on my hands—a young lady towards whom my fastidious cousin Harold inclines most kindly,—I shall want a carriage for other things besides night-work."

"Do you think there is anything in that quarter with Ffrench, then? He denied it when I chaffed him."

"Of course he denied it, and you must not 'chaff him,' as you call it; how can I tell whether or not there is anything in it yet? That remains to be seen. I think that there is a very fair chance of Theo Leigh marrying if she is brought out properly; marrying well, even if she does not marry Harold, which is more than probable."

"It would be different if you had a town house and town connection, Kate. However, you mean it so kindly that I hope your plan will succeed, though I don't think much of it myself. You can't do much for a girl when you're living in lodgings and don't entertain."

"My friends can do a great deal for her. Lady Glaskill (I was under her auspices when I met you, remember, John) is always very kind to aspirants in anything, and she sees a great many people. But about the brougham?"

"You must have it, I suppose."

"And will you see about it, dear?"

"Yes; a single one will do, won't it?"

"No, John, no; were I alone concerned I should infinitely prefer a single one, because—because I do infinitely prefer it; but supposing we are invited to any party at Richmond or Greenwich, and asked to give any one a lift home, my inability to do so might stop an offer. No, there must be room for a third in the brougham, and it must be very dark, and the horse I should like to be black or grey and a very high stepper. Of course you'll send up Rogers and Williams, so that I shall have my own liveries."

"Why, you're regularly going in for a town establishment, Kate; but you mean it so kindly, little woman, that you shall have your own way about it. I hope Ffrench won't disappoint you after all."

"I hope he will not," she said dryly.

"Or the girl herself, for that matter. Is she a beauty?"

"No: too dark; but there is something attractive about her, something very attractive indeed; otherwise I shouldn't take all this trouble to cultivate Harold's possible fancy. I shall call on Lady Glaskill to-morrow and secure her co-operation."

"Is she bent on marrying Harold off also?"

"Oh, no; doesn't care for him a bit; believes him to be all bad, an utterly irreclaimable selfish man, who is rightly dealt with in being wifeless and homeless. She isn't his aunt, you know; she was my mother's sister, no relation to Harold at all."

"Where has your aunt pitched her tent this year? I didn't know she was in town."

"In Wilton Place; but we won't speak about it any more; for when I remember that you won't be with me, all the edge of the pleasure I should otherwise feel is taken off."

"I will run up as often as I can," John Galton said, heartily; "in fact, when I have set things going I may as well come up altogether."

Which promise of happiness struck Mrs. Galton speechless for a minute or two; but after a time her powers of eloquence returned, and she enlarged with a wifely interest on the short-comings of his farm-bailiff—a man whom she "never trusted further than she could see," she said—and on the general and proverbial dishonesty and laziness of the Haversham labourers. It was an unfortunate topic to have chosen, if she desired to have her husband's society in town. The upshot of it was, that he declared the fact to be "that they were not to be trusted, unless they knew they were liable to the inspection of the master every hour of the day; farming won't do itself, and of course I have more interest in seeing it well done than any one else. Ah! well, I shan't give them such another spell of their own way for some time to come."

It was a most unfortunate topic to have chosen,

this one which had terminated in such a decision. And so Kate thought, it is to be hoped.

The days passed quickly, and the call was made on Lady Glaskill, and a rapturous consent to Theo's going to Mrs. Galton came up from Mrs. Leigh, and the brougham was placed at Mrs. Galton's absolute disposal; and the happy husband went home to superintend the ripening of his crops and other things appertaining to his occupation—and the young fly walked confidingly into the spider's net, which was in process of renovation, almost of reconstruction; and still Harold Ffrench kept out of the way.

The apartments which Mrs. Galton occupied in Piccadilly were situate opposite to the Green Park. They were spacious and lofty, as became their position in the world, but they were not all that seemed desirable to her: they were furnished after a grim and heavy fashion that was repulsive to her, although the furniture itself was good. The people to whom the house belonged, before letting it for the season and decamping for economic reasons, had carefully denuded their rooms of everything that could by any possibility be broken or easily carried away; and this precaution had imparted an air of rigidity and general dreariness to the rooms, which it now became Mrs. Galton's task to modify.

The task was one upon which she entered with an avidity which only a pretty woman desirous of worthily enshrining herself and rendering the casket deserving of so fair a jewel as she feels herself to be can experience. She resolved upon having a share in the glories that were going. She had always sighed for a fashionable life, and here was an opportunity of leading one, for a brief space at any rate. Old friends should be looked up and new ones formed through their means, and a lion or two caught and persuaded to roar in her rooms—all for Theo's sake, of course. The utmost triumph she could attain would be in a small way; but these were better than none at all, she told herself. Indeed her vanity led her to believe, that once seen and known and spoken about, but a very small effort would be necessary to make her rooms the resort of all that was most brilliant: it would be a second Gore House, and she rather an improvement on Lady Blessington by right of her youth.

If John Galton imagined the rooms in which he left his wife to be already furnished, it was a pity he could not have been shown the upholstery bill which was run up the day of his departure, and learnt his mistake. "There is no extravagance in it," Kate said, when her aunt, Lady Glaskill, reproached her with extravagance in a tone of jocularity. "There is no extravagance in it, for all these things will do for Haversham Grange by-and-by, when I am forced to go back; at all events you must acknowledge the things are very pretty."

They were that, undoubtedly. The rooms seemed to Theo when she saw them first to be such a combination of fragrance and beauty as she had believed existed only in the "Arabian Nights' Entertainments." There were hanging baskets of ferns and orchids, and creeping things innumerable, and vases of rare roses and pyramids of hot-house flowers of every hue, and sweeping curtains of green velvet and filmy muslin dividing one portion of the apartment from another, and seductive couches, and beauty-fraught statuettes, and a few pictures (all historical) very warm in colouring, and mirrors and tall pier-glasses on every side reflecting all these things.

"It was hardly worth while to get them up in this way for the short time you'll be allowed to stay, my dear," Lady Glaskill observed, when she had marked and approved of her niece's renovated web.

"I don't mean it to be for a short time; I have a plan in my head."

"You always had, if I remember, my dear, a good many plans in your head, and some of them came to nothing."

Lady Glaskill was one of those pleasant old ladies who never neglect an opportunity of saying a possibly disagreeable thing to another woman. She was a little old lady, slightly deformed, but she declared herself to have been a fairy, a sylph, an ethereal beauty in the days of her youth; and as no one could remember those days, she was never contradicted. She was an active restless little woman even now, agile and kittenish and gushing, and full of false enthusiasm and sham brilliancy and fearfully high spirits; a ghastly old coquette who believed in herself and her love-winning properties long after every one who knew her had come to the conclusion that the only things real about her were her bones: for the skin was enamel and the colour was paint, and the teeth and hair were constantly renewed and extremely variable, and the heart and sentiments were falser than everything else. She was a nice old lady! a very nice old lady indeed was Lady Glaskill; and the people frequented her house largely when she was in town, and only speculated as to whether she had really poisoned her husband for threatening to tell that he had been forced to marry her at the point of her papa's sword when she was away.

Lady Glaskill's hair was a great joke amongst her acquaintances; she was always imagining herself to be like some heroine of romance or history, and investing in new hair that might further the illusion. On one day in a long long past year she had fancied a resemblance in herself to Cleopatra, and forthwith she organized a Richmond party and went up the river in a boat under a flame-coloured canopy with black locks streaming wildly around her, a sandalled foot in full view, and a fancy Egyptian garment of scanty proportion over her skinny little person, to the scandal of so much of the world as thronged the banks to look at Lady Glaskill's current folly. Shortly after this she had costumed as "Corinne," and crowned herself with a wreath of bays on the strength of having written a volume of very immoral and unmetrical poetry, which she read aloud with passion and emphasis at several of her evening parties. She had been robed to the chin and she had been desperately décolletée in rapid succession for a longer series of years than one would care to enumerate. She had gained a name for foolish vanity beyond every one of her foolishly vain compeers; her name had been called in question (mainly through her own vain-glorious boasts), and her stories had been refuted a thousand times. Yet still she kept her place in the world, and the denizens of it flocked around her tattered mud-bespattered old standard wheresoever she erected it and called attention to the fact.

She was not a good, a worthy, or a respected woman, but she was a popular and very well-known woman; and she struggled hard to remain this latter thing, and never faded away from any one's mind through lack of continually stirring that mind up with a hint of her existence. She had married Sir Archibald Glaskill by force, and fought her way into society like the enterprising woman she was, and she had held her place hardly but warily, and won for herself a name with which every one, who was any one at least, was acquainted. This was something, all must allow, even if they do not rate the honour as highly as Lady Glaskill did; to her it was as the breath of her nostrils; and Kate Galton had been in the way of this breath passing over her very often when she was a girl.

But Lady Glaskill was a clever fool only, and Kate was something a trifle higher in the scale. The former told her eccentric, enthusiastic, purposeless lies only for the sake of being stared at and called "so very peculiar, you know;" the latter told her better modulated ones for an end always. Kate liked to be stared at, but not to be stared at solely on account of her peculiarities. Her aunt—wizened, ruddled old Lady Glaskill—was happy and content in the assertion that every unmarried man she had ever met had loved and proposed to her, and every married one had lost his head and heart and honour. Lady Glaskill was happy and content with the mere assertion of these things; but Kate was not satisfied unless such things were. The shadow was enough for the voracious vanity of the old woman, but the substance alone sufficed for the not less voracious vanity of the younger one.

It was at Lady Glaskill's house in Wilton Place that Theo Leigh made her entrance into London society. Lady Glaskill had issued cards for a conversazione, and it promised to be brilliantly attended, for she audaciously asked, or caused her friends to ask, every one whose name sounded that year, and her audacity was well rewarded.

"That little girl you have taken up shall be noticeable, my dear, for I won't have too many other women," Lady Glaskill had said to her niece Mrs. Galton, with the rarest magnanimity, or rather with what would have sounded like the rarest magnanimity if her niece had not been fully aware of the fact that "too many women" were not wont to grace her aunt's reunions. So when Miss Leigh and her chaperone floated into the crowded rooms in Wilton Place, it was through a lane hedged almost entirely by men that Theo walked unconsciously to meet her fate.

CHAPTER IX.

THE SHADOW BEGINS TO FALL.

THERE was a man at Lady Glaskill's that night who had written a successful novel. No personality is intended; hundreds of men wrote novels that were successful or the reverse in 1851; and there was also a political martyr, and an African explorer, and a scientific man who had poisoned his wife by accident, and found himself the centre of attraction in the fashionable world ever since the catastrophe. Around these revolved the usual throng that one meets at such places. In their midst rose the fez of an Oriental ambassador, who had been inveigled into gracing the rooms for a few minutes.

The successful novelist and the scientific murderer faded into insignificance, and paled into nothing before the light of Osmanli Effendi, around whom all the women were crowding, basking unctuously in the oily refulgence of the smiles of the child of the sun, who was gazing calmly at their long English throats bared for the occasion, and thinking that not one of them was worthy to be compared with the least lovely of the lights of his far-off harem, and of how many pounds of Rahat La Koum it would take to improve their appearance.

The rooms were very full; people stood thick as ears of corn in a well-grown field, and the buzz confused Theo as she advanced up that aforesaid lane, hedged in by masculine humanity on either side, in the wake of her chaperone, who made straight, with the rush of an adept, towards her hostess. Mrs. Galton never faltered when she entered a room, or undulated up and down like an elastic female figure in cork—she just floated on, cool, quiet, erect, and fair towards her goal. But her advent always made a sensation.

She had the art of entering at the right moment. I do not know whether she lurked in the doorway until such a time as those whose gaze would guide the rest began to yawn, and look as if they needed something new. But at all events, this was the juncture at which she almost invariably appeared, and this night she made no exception to her usual rule.

Her heart beat quickly at finding herself once more amidst scenes from which she had blindly gone at twenty to grace a country Grange. She was radiant in her white robes—in the thick sheeny silk and cloudy *tulle* that became her fair loveliness so well. She was marked as a married woman by the head-dress of downy plumes, fastened by a diamond aigrette, which she wore.

The girl, following in her wake, led the eye off from this beautiful woman very pleasingly, for Theo Leigh was all alight with excitement,—excitement that was partly due to the novelty, but still more to the fact of Mrs. Galton's having imparted to her the probability "of their meeting Harold there." Now this probability had been alluded to by Mrs. Galton in what Mr. Leigh would have termed a "mincing manner," for she had spoken of it softly, and with one of the blushes she could call up at will. But Theo had marked neither manner nor blush in the joy consequent on this announcement. She was going to see him again!—to see him once more, and that was enough.

The hour of dressing had not been one of unmixed satisfaction to Theo, for Mrs. Galton was one of those sweet women who are specially skilful in the sticking in of small mental pins to another woman. She had left it till the day of the party to question Theo as to what she meant to wear. When Theo told her what, and "hoped it would do," Mrs. Galton did not exactly say that it was not fitting and proper, but she damned it with the faintest praise, and Theo felt uncomfortable.

Not that Mrs. Galton in reality disapproved of her young friend's choice of toilette, but it was a point of conscience with her never to let an opportunity pass of putting a sister out of conceit with her appearance, and she was rigorous in attending to the demands of her conscience on this point.

"It's very nice, but do you think it's becoming?" she had asked when Theo had told her that she was going to wear pale blue net over white muslin skirts. When Theo said she "thought blue generally suited her," Mrs. Galton replied,

"Oh, if you think it does, it's all right," in a tone which implied that she (Mrs. Galton) did not think that it did become Theo by any means. Kate then went on to inquire about the wreath Theo designed to wear, and to opine that "forget-me-nots were pretty, but affectedly simple, didn't Theo think, as a rule; only becoming, in fact, to very fair women with little colour."

However, Theo inducted herself into both dress and wreath perforce—she had none other to wear. As she caught a glimpse of herself in the pier-glass she felt that if Mrs. John Galton were dissatisfied with her appearance, then was Mrs. John Galton a difficult woman to please. Theo had yet to learn that it is not invariably excess of affection which renders our friends hypercritical about us. "I will consult her beforehand another time, and get her to order my dress for me," the unsophisticated Miss Leigh thought, as she stepped into the carriage after her chaperone.

It was very exciting to her and very brilliant, she thought, this new scene in which she found herself, but it had not the power to absorb her sufficiently to make her forget the hope that had brightened her journey thither. Even as her hostess was introducing her to His Excellency, Theo's eyes wandered away in search of Harold Ffrench.

"Aunt Glaskill is making a terrible goose of herself to-night," Mrs. Galton whispered contemptuously to Theo after the expiration of a few minutes, during which Lady Glaskill had succeeded in attracting all attention to herself by being ecstatic about the "Orient," to the neglect and partial oblivion of her niece. When Lady Glaskill's follies led attention away from Kate, Kate was as intolerant to them as the wisest could desire. "She's boring that poor man insufferably," Mrs. Galton continued; "any one can see that he wants to talk to me; but Lady Glaskill does hold on so pertinaciously when she once gains a man's ear."

The fact was that the majority of those who stood within speaking range of Mrs. Galton were strangers to her; she would, therefore, have been condemned to a silence which it is always painful to maintain perforce in a gay throng of talkers and laughers. No wonder that she thought Lady Glaskill in a turban and ecstasies was making a goose of herself by engrossing that which Kate herself sighed for—the attention of the mightiest in the room.

The crowd broke up into portions and readjusted itself presently, when ices were brought in and handed round, and then Mrs. Galton found herself drafted on into the immediate circle of which the ineffably bored Oriental was the centre. The opportunity was one which she would not suffer to pass; mental molestation from her would, she rightly judged, be preferable to the same from her aunt, therefore she smiled and spoke with all the fascination of which she was mistress. To this his Mightiness listened with calm courtesy, and replied with solemn stupidity; but that he did listen and reply was enough for Mrs. Galton.

She entirely baffled all Lady Glaskill's innocent attempts to win him solely and wholly to herself again. The younger, prettier woman had the will to take and the power to hold, and Lady Glaskill retired routed—ignominiously routed by one of her own allies. She was put out by her defeat for a brief time, but although an insatiably vain, she was a good-natured woman; therefore the sole revenge she took on her audacious niece was couched in these words, which she uttered in no very low tone when the Oriental 'vantage-ground that Kate had gained departed:—

"Well, my dear, I'm sorry that you have so soon lost the opportunity of making yourself conspicuous; now, perhaps, you will be good enough to come here and let me introduce some of my particular friends to you. I suppose you are disappointed that it isn't a dance, you're looking so blank," she continued, turning sharply to Theo; "never allow dancing in my house, my dear; wear out your tongues as much as you like, but not my carpets."

Which sally was rewarded by a brace of sycophants observing audibly that "Lady Glaskill was as astonishingly vivacious as ever," which remark caused Lady Glaskill to suppose that they were hoping to be invited to her next entertainment, and to decide that they should be disappointed. Flattery, if she fathomed it, was wont to receive mild punishment from her.

Among the particular friends whom Lady Glaskill specially selected to honour with an introduction to the handsome niece of whom she was slightly jealous, was the successful novelist, whose light had been put under a bushel while the Oriental remained. Mrs. Galton, whose object it was to make a party of her own before she quarrelled with her aunt, which past experience taught her she was liable to do at any moment after a week's intercourse—Mrs. Galton, knowing this, made the man of letters her own adroitly in a very short time.

Not by praising his new novel; she was no such bungler as to seek her end by using such clumsy means. She did not open a heavy fire of her opinions respecting it upon him, reducing him to the verge of imbecility by declaring his book to be "so delightful," and herself "so much interested in it," and the heroine to be "a dear," and the end "delicious" or "dreadful," as the case might be. But she anatomised it; spoke of it as a whole as no one who did not know it thoroughly could speak, he told himself; judiciously extracted from him a statement of what he considered to be the finest passages, and then spoke with great feeling and sympathy of those very passages, in a way that was more subtly flattering than any open praise would have been. Men, even successful novelists, are but mortal. Mr. Linley was not ill pleased to find that a work of his was deemed so profound by a woman who was "far from shallow," so he phrased it in his mind. Theo Leigh, standing by, wondered greatly that Mrs. Galton should so rashly venture upon the discussion of a book which she only knew through the medium of reviews, with its author, and still more whether this Linley was the one of whom her father had spoken—the man who had been a young Englishman in Greece contemporaneously with Harold Ffrench.

But speculation on any subject ceased to occupy her mind almost immediately, for a man made his way very quietly to her side and addressed her, and took her hand in his as though they had parted on the most ordinary terms. His coldness cooled her, and his steadiness steadied her, and though she was disappointed—wisely as she had resolved—at this casual-acquaintance manner which Mr. Ffrench adopted towards her, she still could but feel glad that it so immediately reacted upon her own.

"I was very glad to hear from Mrs. Galton that you and she are going to enjoy yourselves together; it was the most sensible plan I ever knew her to form. Is your father in town still? —how is he?"

"Papa is gone home—he is very well."

"What is the move?—oh! going down to supper; my experience of this sort of thing teaches me that it is well to go down at once if you want to get anything; the hindermost are overtaken by evil and hunger; shall we go down?"

He held out his arm for her to take as he spoke, and she placed her hand upon it, and would not suffer her hand to tremble. But she kept her face partially averted from him, and he marked that she did so.

"Theo!" he exclaimed suddenly, as they came to a compulsory pause upon the staircase, "I am very glad to see you again."

"And I am glad to see you," she said frankly; and as she said it she made one of the many efforts to be brave and non-emotional that women situated in her position are compelled to make; she looked him in the face and met his gaze unflinchingly.

"Glad to see me? very quietly 'glad;' well, no matter, what can I expect but a very sober satisfaction to be yours at sight of me. You see many other people now. I ought to have known that I should probably merely bore you, yet I could not resist coming to meet you to-night."

"You know very well that you could never bore me; how can you be so unkind as to pretend to think it?" she cried. Then she was afraid that she had said too much, and said it too warmly, and her hand began to tremble on his arm.

"Theo," he whispered softly, "have you forgiven me?"

"I have nothing to forgive, Mr. Ffrench," she replied proudly, for there was the same tender inflection in his voice that had been in it on that night when he had told her his love for her, and won her to show hers in return. She remembered this, and the remembrance stung her.

"Nothing to forgive! I wish to heaven you had not anything to forgive," he muttered.

Then he went to get her a glass of wine; and Theo marked him as he walked away, and thought what a grand gentleman he looked amongst them all, and how no young man in the room could compete with this one, who carried his forty years so gracefully.

"You have not been long with Kate?" he asked when he came back to her; and when she had said "No," he went on to ask her how long, and where she had been, and whom had she seen; he was very particular on this last point.

"This is my first party; I have been to the Academy several times."

"With whom?"

"Mrs. Galton."

"Without Galton?—had you no gentleman with you?"

"Mr. Galton is down at Haversham," Theo replied; she did not know that Harold Ffrench was very indifferent as to John Galton's whereabouts, and only anxious to learn whether they had been to the Academy unescorted, in order that he might find out if Kate were fulfilling her threat of introducing some desirable parti to Theo.

"It's not much use your going to the Academy with Mrs. Galton alone; she knows nothing at all about pictures; when I can speak to her I will make an appointment to accompany you there to-morrow—she appears to be very deeply interested just now," he continued with a laugh, as Kate sailed into the supper-room on Mr. Linley's arm, and then (it was a supper that people took in a sketchy manner, standing up,) posed herself against the wall, and continued to converse enthusiastically.

"I think she is very much interested in his book," Theo replied.

"What is his book about?"

"I don't know; ask Mrs. Galton, she knows though she hasn't read it," Theo said laughing; "it's a novel, and it's a success."

"What is his name?"

"Linley—I was wondering——"

"Oh! Linley—oh, ah! I have heard something about his novel; one of the reviews said that it was the work of 'a mighty mind accustomed to profound reflections,' and another that it was 'full of clearly defined thoughts of a hard thinker,'—it struck me that it must be rather dull."

"But it's not dull at all; I should think, from what they were saying, that it must be very amusing; but I was going to say I was wondering whether he could be the same Mr. Linley who, papa says, was in Greece at the same time you were there; did you know him? do you remember him?"

It happened that as Theo asked this of Harold Ffrench that Mrs. Galton and her cavalier were advancing towards them. The men were face to face, and were naturally looking directly at one another.

"I do not know him," Harold Ffrench replied to Theo's question in a tone loud enough, Theo thought, to reach the ears of the man who was spoken about. But the next instant Harold Ffrench did know him, for Mrs. Galton introduced her cousin to her new friend with effusion.

The supper-room was rather crowded now, consequently the drawing-room, to which the quadrilateral with whom my story has to do presently returned, was comparatively deserted and free. When they regained it, Kate began to tell Harold how that they had had a specimen of "the land of the east and the clime of the sun" there earlier in the evening, and to lament that he had not seen the same.

"And do you know he appeared to be very prosaic, not to say stupid and common-place, despite his turban and his wonderful costume," she continued.

Then the author, who did not appear to like the probability of lapsing into obscurity again, said that if she liked he would give them a specimen of eastern story-telling, and endeavour to bring the Orient more vividly before them than Osmanli Effendi had succeeded in doing.

"What? will you sit cross-legged on some cushions and tell us a story?" Kate asked; and Mr. Linley said, "Yea, if she pleased—a story with plenty of thrill in it," and forthwith deposited himself in the position she described, and commenced:—

"It does not matter whether it was one, or ten, or forty years ago that two Franks, two Giaours, two infidels, wandering about the streets of an eastern city, saw a face at the grating of a well-secured window that struck them both as being lovely as that of the young Häidee; the loveliest, in fact, that, they had ever seen. Both men—they were Englishmen—thought that face beautiful as that of Venus herself can be, but the younger and warmer-natured man loved it on the instant.

"It will give a greater air of reality to my story, and save a confusion of ideas respecting which of the men I mean, if I give names both to them and to the place; you agree with me?" he continued, throwing a questioning glance around. "Any names will do; help me to some, Mrs. Galton, for I am in the novelist's usual difficulty; any names will do, my own for one (just to avoid confusion) and yours for the other."

"Thank you"—Harold Ffrench had been the one addressed, and Harold Ffrench was now the speaker—"but I had rather that you kept my name out of the story."

"As you will," Mr. Linley replied carelessly, "it was only to avoid confusion. Well, I will call them Stinton and Forbes then. The elder of the two," he went on rapidly, dashing into his story again with velocity, "the elder of the two men thought that face beautiful as that of Venus herself—the younger, warmer-natured man, loved it on the instant.

"I will say that the city was Constantinople; can you help me to a description of Constantinople—a photographic description, a description such as will bring the city itself before these ladies?" he asked, pulling himself up abruptly in his narrative, and addressing Harold Ffrench.

"I regret that I cannot assist you, for I never saw Constantinople," Harold replied, and Theo fancied that he looked annoyed at the attempt to draw him into this "drawing-room entertainment."

"You can't assist me?—good," the man of letters went on glibly. "Briefly, then, the tale of the mosques and minarets has been better told before, so I will spare you the recital; but the window of the house at which this face appeared must be described.

"It was a broad, high, thickly-grated window, and from immediately beneath it projected a huge drawer. This drawer revolved, the two men discovered, on a nearer inspection, and was used as a sort of bazaar. That is to say, the females of the house placed therein articles of their own handiwork; then spun the drawer round, and passers-by took these articles away, leaving money in exchange. Forbes, the younger man, had learnt the Turkish language; he could speak it well, and write it indifferently. But the other language that is familiar as their mother-tongue to the women of Stamboul—the language of flowers—he was an adept in. And soon single sprigs and deftly arranged bouquets were laid constantly in that revolving drawer, and the girl came oftener to the grating without her yashmak on.

"It was a brother and two sisters who dwelt in that house; the brother had been impoverished by the revolution, and the sisters' fate, despite the beauty of the elder one, was not ordained to be bright. She was to go to the seraglio of a small pasha, an old man against whom she revolted; the younger girl's fate was harder and more horrible still,—she was to be immured for life amongst other women whom no man would buy.

"Forbes was as handsome a young fellow as the sun ever shone upon; a well-born, well-bred Englishman; and the Moslem girl with the glorious face soon owned him, not lord of her soul, for Moslem girls are not supposed to possess any, and Leila didn't presume to set herself up above her sisters—but of her heart. And then the solitary sprigs and well-arranged bouquets went on thicker than before. And finally Forbes told Stinton one day that he must assist in carrying Leila off.

"In the dead hour of the night, Leila placed herself in the revolving drawer, which was then slowly turned round by the sister who was left, and whose sobs sounded mournfully in the ears of the two men who were rescuing the beauty. The drawer moved heavily and uneasily; in fact, the eastern houri was of rather substantial proportions, and though she shrank into a marvellously small space under the influence of fear, she was pulled through with difficulty, and not without slight detriment to her back, which got grazed in the passage even through the folds of muslin.

"He was a chivalrous young Englishman; the act was foolishly romantic, but foolish romance was the worst of his offences. The girl he had abduced he resolved to make his wife according to the laws of the church and land to which he belonged. So, with his friend Stinton—the lady still being closely veiled—Forbes took his Leila away without delay, and put her on board an English man-of-war, the chaplain of which married the Ottoman lady to the hope of an English house.

"The romance is generally over when the ring is on and the service read. In this case, though, the romance began at this juncture. I have said that Leila, now Mrs. Forbes, had remained closely veiled all the while, but now that she was his wife, and under the protection of the English flag, the ardent husband tore down the yashmak and saw—not Leila, but her younger sister.

"She fell upon her knees, and he did not kill or curse her, as I think I should have done in the like case. He took her away to Europe, and did not hear what his friend Stinton, who remained in the city, learnt the following day; namely, that Leila, who had sacrificed her lover and herself to her selfish little sister—who, in addition to her other sins, was as ugly as the devil —that Leila expiated her offence against the heaven-born passion, love, in the dark blue waters of the Bosphorus."

CHAPTER X.

MRS. GALTON IS A LITTLE MISTAKEN.

"A VERY good story, with a great air of reality about it. I feel sorry that it isn't true," Kate Galton said, as Mr. Linley brought his narration to a close and rose to his feet.

"And I feel glad," Theo exclaimed. "I was miserable for Forbes for a minute, when it came to pulling down her veil and finding he had married the wrong sister. I couldn't help feeling how wretched he would be all his life; didn't you pity him?" she continued, looking up at Harold, who had retained her hand on his arm all the while Mr. Linley had been amusing them.

"I did," he replied; "the story does great credit to your powers of invention," he went on, looking at the successful novelist.

"My powers of invention were not very severely taxed. I am glad you liked it so well."

"I should have liked it better if you had given us a sketch of Forbes's wretched after-career—for of course it was wretched," Mrs. Galton remarked. "Couldn't you come to my house some evening, and give us a second part,—a sequel to the story? that would be delightful."

Harold Ffrench turned away impatiently, drawing Theo with him.

"What a humbug Kate is, to be sure," he muttered; "the stuff was all very well just to listen to it, as we listen now; but to set about having more of it in cold blood in this way is a little too much. Don't you agree with me?"

"Yes," Theo replied; "besides, I can't think that the 'wretched after-career' will be pleasant to hear about."

"No, it cannot be," Harold Ffrench said. And then the pair seated themselves on a couch, and Theo said:—

"The misery of not alone marrying the wrong sister, but being the cause of the death of the one he loved."

"It was misery."

"He told it very well, or we shouldn't speak of it as if it might be true; didn't he?" Theo asked. "I shouldn't have thought much of it, I think, if I had read it; but he told it in a way that brought it home—didn't he?"

"Yes, he brought it home to one."

"I suppose that's a trick he has gained from writing?"

"I suppose it is, at least I thought he told it very badly; and if it is a specimen of the amusement Lady Glaskill and that mocking-bird, my cousin, mean to provide for their guests, I shall not trouble them very often. I hope you won't follow in Kate's footsteps, and flatter that egotis-

tical fool's vanity by striking up a great friendship with him, Theo."

"Oh dear, no. How should I do so? he a great author; but don't you like him?"

"Like him! I don't know him?"

"Don't you like him even well enough to come to your cousin's house if he comes much?"

"While you are there I shall come, if you care to see me."

She choked back a passionate sigh. "I shall always be glad to see you."

"You are a very tender, sweet woman, Theo; you felt genuine pity for the imaginary man whose life was cursed and blasted by a foul trick."

"Who could have helped feeling pity for him?"

"I declare," he said, "if you take fiction so seriously, I shall be inclined to try my hand at it. I cannot originate, but I can follow up the path Kate and that man have chalked out. What do you say, Theo? would you continue to feel a kindly interest in Forbes if I went on with his history? or must it be from Linley's lips alone?"

"Oh, no; I shall believe in him equally, I am sure, if you undertook him. Take him up from the lifting of the veil," she continued eagerly, "and tell me what he said to his wife, and what she said to him, poor thing!"

"And how in after years, when his love for Leila was a long-dead thing, he met another woman whom he did not dare at first to tell he loved because of Leila's sister, his wife? and how afterwards he forgot everything and lived only for this woman, who lost the world for and forgave him?"

"Yes," she cried eagerly, "tell me."

"I have told you already," he said, jumping up. "Come back to your conscientious chaperone, who has left you to cater for your own amusement the whole night. No, Theo! Forbes hangs fire in my hands; I am not equal to the task of galvanizing him; I must leave that pleasant office to Mr. Linley, whose vocation in life it is to tell lies euphoniously. How about the Academy to-morrow? will you care to go?"

By the time she had told him that she "should care to go very much indeed," and he had spoken to and obtained Kate's assent to the plan, Lady Glaskill's first reunion gave signs of fast-approaching dissolution. Soon the guests were "fled, the garlands shed," the banquet halls were deserted, and Mrs. Galton and Theo were on their way home.

"I can give you a seat if you are lodging at any place within a reasonable distance," Mrs. Galton had said to her cousin when he was handing her into the brougham, and Harold had thanked her, but explained that he was not lodging within a reasonable distance, and would not, therefore, trouble her.

"Queer of Harold," Kate had said to her companion as they drove off; "he never will say where he is living. I should never inquire too particularly into the extent of his establishment. I'm not going to marry him!"

"What difference would it make if you were?" Theo asked.

"Oh, you innocent! Well, he might have a difficulty in answering, my dear; that's all I can say. How cross he was to-night at my talking so much to that delightful Mr. Linley. I could see that he was nearly rabid as he walked about with you."

"Could you?" Theo asked, and a sudden new pang assailed her.

"Oh, yes; it's too absurd of him. But Harold is such a dear creature that I have forgiven his absurdities, and so he imposes on good nature. I felt sorry for him, for he looked quite dull and wretched, and utterly different to the Harold he is to me. You can have no idea, Theo, how agreeable that man can make himself when he likes; if you once saw him in one of his best and brightest moods—in one of the moods in which he is most familiar to me—you would fall in love with him."

"I am glad we are at home," Theo said, the carriage drawing up at the moment. "I am very much tired." So she was, tired and confused and unhappy, about she knew not what exactly, but she had a dim idea that it was because Harold Ffrench (so his cousin told her) had been dull and wretched and rabid with jealousy even while she (Theo) had been leaning on his arm.

Mr. Linley called on Mrs. Galton the following day and found his book lying on a little table by the side of the couch on which Kate was seated.

"This is my constant companion," she said, gently indicating it with the left while she extended the right hand to meet his; and the successful novelist went through the little farce with which he was now familiar, of first appearing not to recognize the book, and then to be gently surprised at seeing it there, and then to deprecate anything like admiration being felt for a work which had been "thrown off carelessly in his leisure hours." It is a difficult thing to speak gracefully of your own literary performances. If you censure them, people are apt to ask, why, in the name of common sense, did you foist that of which you thought so meanly upon the reading public? If you triumph ever so weakly in them, you are naturally and very properly dubbed disgustingly conceited by the unsympathetic masses. But of all the little barriers against overwhelming confusion which you erect, the one of affected indifference is that which breaks down most surely and swiftly.

David Linley had a face that his admirers declared to be expressive of vast power; those who were not his admirers, or those who were capable of separating the man from his works, held it to be unconditionally ugly. He had a rugged nose, a grim chasm for a mouth, and beetle brows. But his eyes were wonderful: large, black, penetrating, they rarely failed in causing the obliteration of his other features from your mind as you met and quailed under them.

For they were eyes under whose gaze the many quailed. The man was a genial observer of men and manners and women (especially the latter) in his works. His characters had just that happy admixture of good and evil, of wisdom and folly, which distinguishes the denizens of the world in which we dwell. Yet for all that they were romantic novels; very romantic novels indeed. Only you felt in perusing them that not only everything that he recounted

might have been, but that it *had* been; and he knew it.

But in the flesh David Linley was far from being genial; on the contrary, he was given to the utterance of cynical truths concerning men and things—and women too, very often. He was not too careful as to whether those of whom he spoke heard him utter these things or not. However, it was well for those who met him if he adopted this view at first, for the case of those whom he won to love him was a cruel one. He stung his foes surely and painfully, but he stung his friends, men said, with a still more fatal poison.

Just on the surface of society, if you met him there and there alone, he could be agreeable, and was agreeable enough. This year, as has been said, he was a lion, and more sought after than usual, despite some doubtful things, which again could never be well authenticated, that were whispered about him. But even now it was seen that he was more popular with women than with men. The latter shunned him instinctively, but the women flocked to his standard and declared it to be that of a true hero, and appeared to find a sort of fascination in that ugliness on which he presumed, as it were,— he took so little care to adorn or set his person off to the best advantage.

Kate Galton would verily have flirted at the veiled prophet himself, had he come in her way and been of any mark in the circle in which she moved. She merely saw in David Linley's ugliness a something which, taken in conjunction with his talent, rendered him the more remarkable. He had shown her his fairest aspect at Lady Glaskill's; he was prepared to go on doing so while this pretty woman pleased him. But those who knew him best said that, if ever the holy bond got broken, Mrs. Galton would smart for the honours she was now enjoying.

He scarcely noticed Theo Leigh when he came into Mrs. Galton's drawing-room this day; he merely recognized her presence by a slight bow, and uttered no word which could break the train of her thoughts. Of this Theo was rather glad than otherwise, for she was thinking of Harold Ffrench, and wondering when he would come to take them to the Academy, and whether she would not be a wise girl to go back to Houghton before the frequent sight of him had caused her a relapse.

Still she was a little disappointed and most unwisely sorry when she heard Mr. Linley, in reply to Mrs. Galton's request that he should do so, decline to accompany them to the Academy. It might not be well for her that she should be free to hear all that Harold Ffrench might care to say to her. It might not be well, it might even be dangerous. Still Theo could but prefer the possible ill and danger to the dismal certainty of his being entirely monopolised by Mrs. Galton, as he would be assuredly, were he the only man. Kate's assertion that Harold had been rabid with jealousy and wearily savage had obtained with Theo during the night; but now, in the brighter, truer light of day, she saw its fallacy and began to doubt it.

Mr. Linley's visit was brief, but highly satisfactory, to judge from Mrs. Galton's manner when it was over. That it was paid at all was a triumph in its way, for he was wont to make himself difficult of access to a remarkable degree; but in her case she could but feel that he was most flatteringly tractable, for when his call came to a conclusion he asked permission to come again.

Before he went he said something which renewed Theo's interest in him, and made her hope that he would come again and recur to the subject.

"By the way, Mrs. Galton, where is your cousin, Mr. Ffrench, living now? I think we have met in former days, and I should like to renew the acquaintance."

"I hardly know where he lives; at an hotel generally; his address is the —— Club."

"He does not keep up a town establishment, then?"

"Oh, dear, no; and he is rather apt to vary his bachelor quarters frequently. You will be sure to meet him here."

"His bachelor quarters! he is not the man I thought, then; the Ffrench I knew was a married man," he continued, turning round and looking at Theo, who flushed scarlet under the look in a way that caused Mr. Linley's eyes to flash smiles that were not pleasant. Then he went away, and Mrs. Galton and Theo had only just time, between his departure and Harold's arrival, to put on their bonnets.

"We have had Mr. Linley with us all the morning, Harold; he wanted your address: he seemed to think that he had known you somewhere at some time or other, till I told him you were a bachelor: the Ffrench he knew was a married man."

"It's not very flattering to be confounded with another fellow, is it?" Harold rejoined. "Now, no one is likely to make such a mistake with regard to Linley himself; you would have a difficulty in finding a face that would remind you of his, wouldn't you, Theo?"

"Yes," Theo replied. It will be seen that Miss Leigh was rather addicted to agreeing with Mr. Ffrench on all subjects.

"I don't think it at all a disagreeable face," Kate said warmly; "it's exceedingly intellectual, and has a—a—something about it that appeals to me more than a merely handsome face ever would have the power to do."

Kate was annoyed with Harold for addressing his reply to Theo instead of to herself, therefore she extolled Linley's ugliness, to the implied disparagement of Harold's mere masculine beauty.

"I believe," she continued, "that were he only younger he could carry the day with any woman against the handsomest man in the world, if he only set himself to try. I am not sure that he could not do it now."

"I have not the slightest desire to dispute or deny his attractions; I have no doubt you are right; the majority of women have a twist in their minds: they like something fiendish, and they find it in Linley."

The brougham drew up at the steps of the National Gallery as he spoke. As he was handing Theo out he pressed her hand, hardly for an instant, and whispered suddenly:—

"For God's sake, Theo, don't you get smitten with that plague of liking Linley. I have heard a good deal about him, and I believe him

to be as fatal as the disease I have likened him to."

"He will never be fatal to me," Theo replied, but Harold Ffrench repeated his caution more emphatically than before, adding,

"He is false in every relation of life; hold no intercourse with him, Theo, keep him at arm's length. I shall write to Galton, and inform him of the character of the man his wife has picked up."

Kate had marked the confidental manner with which her cousin had said these things to Theo, though she had been unable to hear the words, and she was annoyed thereat, and consequently very cross. She had not remained in London for this at all, she told herself; and she felt hardly used, and really thought that Theo was acting with wicked ingratitude in being the passive recipient of those little attentions which Harold was wont to bestow upon herself.

"It's too warm, much too warm to look at a single picture in comfort—the rooms are stifling," she said crossly. "I shall sit down; you can go round with Mr. Ffrench, if you like to go without me, Theo."

"As she came for the purpose of seeing the pictures, and does not object to the heat, I think she had better do as you propose," Harold Ffrench said quietly.

"If she does not care for being liable to the remark being made that she is without a chaperone. I shall be rested presently," Mrs. Galton observed pettishly; she could not find it in her heart to see Harold and Theo go off without her to look at the pictures.

"Make up your mind as to what you will do, Kate,—if you want to see the pictures at all."

"Of course I want to see them—with you—I came for that purpose," she said, regaining her amiability with a little struggle. Then she rose up and made him "tell her the pictures" from his catalogue, and Theo Leigh had no further private word from him that day.

When Mr. Ffrench was about to take leave of his cousin, he repeated that caution to her which he had already given to Theo.

"Kate," he said, "however you take it, I must give you a word of advice. You'll believe that I can have but one object."

"Well?" she interrupted.

"See as little as possible of that man who called on you to-day. It may be impossible for you to avoid meeting him in society; I know that he has the freedom of your injudicious old aunt's house; but don't be carried away by his popularity into giving him the run of your own."

"Ridiculous, Harold! Why not?"

"I can't tell you my full reason, but this much I will tell you, his character is worse than worthless; he is a man who without scruple would sacrifice his nearest, and I was going to say dearest, but nothing could he truly dear to that cold calculating heart; he is not a man whose hand I can bear you to touch: and as your husband is not here I will act as he would act did he know the character of this man—warn you against him."

"Very kind towards me, and chivalrous towards John, but, excuse me, rather mean towards Mr. Linley, to simply denounce him in this way: abuse proves nothing."

"Kate, ask yourself, what motive can I have

but regard for you and your husband in this matter? I am not at liberty to say what I know concerning this man; but this I do know that he should never touch an honest woman if I could prevent his doing it. Will you not be guided by me? will you persist in suffering an intimacy to spring up between that man and yourself and the young girl whom you have undertaken to protect?"

His allusion to Theo was unfortunate: Kate could not mark his interest in her *protégée* and be calm.

"That young girl is not so extraordinarily attractive that I need be always on the *qui vive* about her; and as to being cool to Mr. Linley, really, Harold, I would do a great deal to please you, but you ask a little too much. His character may not be all that is desirable, but if I am to look into the hearts and morals of all my friends and recoil from those in whom I find a flaw, I shall be friendless; what *is* there against the man more than there is against the majority?"

"You refuse to be guided by my judgment, which I could not exercise if I had not a great affection for you, Kate?"

"I will be a lamb in everything else, dear Harold, but *everybody* asks and makes much of Linley just now. And

> If he be but fair to me,
> What care I how false he be?"

"I might have known that you wouldn't listen to reason," he said. Then he went away, and Kate looked at herself in the glass and thought, "Jealous at last."

CHAPTER XI.

HAROLD FFRENCH CALLS HIMSELF TO ACCOUNT

It was not a wise thing to do, but as soon as Harold Ffrench reached home that night he sat down and wrote to John Galton. It was a very foolish thing to do, but he was annoyed with Kate at the time, and it is always an unsafe thing to write to or about a person when you are angry with that person. The spur of the moment in such case is very liable to prick you into evil. However, Harold Ffrench was very earnestly set upon putting an end to all communion between Mr. Linley and the present tenants of those rooms in Piccadilly. Therefore, as the one course of "speaking to Kate about it" had failed, he took the other and surer course of writing to Kate's husband.

"Circumstances have come to my knowledge respecting him," he wrote, "which convince me that he is no fit companion for your wife. Because he is the fashion and not found out, Kate declines to admit of my interference; perhaps she is right to submit to no dictation save yours: but I should be untrue to the regard I have always had for her if I did not caution you on the point; he is not a man to be admitted to terms of intimacy with any woman of reputation." When he had thus written, Harold Ffrench walked out in the cool night air, and did away with the possibility of repenting availingly of anything he had said in that letter, by posting it at once.

Then he went home and took himself to task;

but before I relate what about, I will describe the home to which he returned, in order that the reader may feel that he had nothing concealed in it which could make the secret of its locality one of vital importance.

He had been occupying, since the date of his return from Norfolk, a suite of three rooms in a house in one of those severely respectable squares which bear a strong family likeness to one another, and bewilder the uninitiated who confound the ducal title with the family name. It was quite true, that assertion that he had made to Kate Galton when she asked him to give her his address at his lodgings; "he was very apt to change them,"—for sheer love of change, as it seemed, and certainly without any reason that seemed valid to his various landladies. He wearied of every place very quickly. He was a man who could not make to himself a home upon the earth. He had more than once striven to attach himself to places and things. But there was invariably a great hollow in the place that he could not fill, and a barrenness about his surroundings that even his taste could not beautify. So, after two or three repeated failures, he gave up the game, and subsided into habits of restlessness.

The room to which he returned after posting that well-meaning letter to John Galton had little enough in it to indicate its present inhabitant's tastes. It was the usual drawing-room of the average lodging-house, nothing more. He had seated himself in it for the express purpose of thinking over some eventualities which possibly might—more than that—which probably would arise. It seemed to him that it would be better to do this in a room in which were no disturbing elements, than in one that held some few things that were still dear to him in life, as did the little room adjoining.

Had he done well, he asked himself, in bringing about this intimacy between Theo Leigh and his cousin Kate? The question would arise, therefore he deemed that he might as well argue it with his conscience, and settle it at once. His intention had been good; he had simply sought to introduce a diversity that he had deemed would be harmless enough into a very dull young life. But, in the first place it had been the means of renewing his intercourse with Theo, and this he could not feel to be well for her: and, in the second place, through Kate's obstinacy, Theo would be subjected to the scarcely less dangerous ordeal of intercourse with Mr. Linley—a man of whom Harold Ffrench had his own well-grounded reasons for thinking very badly.

"I'm sorry I did it; they were wrong to suffer her to come," he said to himself at last. By "they" he meant Theo's parents, on whom he was more than half inclined now to shift the charge of imprudence. He almost resolved to put it to Theo's reason that it would be well for her to curtail her visit to Mrs. Galton, "by which two good ends would be gained, for Kate couldn't stay on in London without her husband or a lady companion—she would have no excuse for doing so," he thought, and by so thinking he did scanty justice to Mrs. Galton's powers of resource; she was well prepared with another reason for remaining in London for awhile when Theo failed her. This resolution was of so exalted an order that he entertained it for some considerable time, and thought how, though it would be painful both for the girl and himself to part again so soon, that it would be wiser and better in every way that they should do so. Then he went away into the other and more congenial room, where were his books and papers and easel, and he turned an unfinished portrait that was upon the latter towards him, and leant back in an easy-chair, with a cigar between his lips; and as he looked and smoked the resolution floated away in fragrant vapour, and Harold Ffrench thought that he had much better "let things alone."

It was a selfish resolution at the best, and, looked at from the most tolerant point of view, it was a very selfish resolution that one to which Harold Ffrench had come after that brief self-examination. He knew it to be selfish, and scarcely worthy of his manliness, and still he held to it. It is always easier to let things alone than to endeavour to alter them. Now this unheroic Harold, who occupies the space usually allotted to a hero, was much given to consulting his own immediate ease.

Besides, in what language could he couch a caution which should be at the same time efficacious and not painful to Theo, not subversive of that easily aroused self-respect which in her was so near akin to tender pride? No, he had been cruelly unguarded once for a moment; but for the future his impulses should be ironbound, and so Theo would be safe from him at least. While from the other man, from this Linley, he, Harold himself, would guard her as the friend he strove to be.

On his uncertainty and final determination the portrait on the easel looked approvingly; at least he came, after meeting its eyes for a long time, to fancy that it did, and to half pity it for doing so. For the face painted from memory, and all unfinished as it was, was Theo Leigh's face as it looked to him; other people would perhaps have deemed it highly idealized. He had in truth limned forth a very lovely face, but he had simply painted that which he had seen; when the glamour is on, the loved is always lovely.

The solitary man sat there for hours, smoking and looking at the picture and thinking. Thinking of how in a few years old age would be upon him, and would find him friendless, homeless, objectless, as he was now, and as he had been all along. "It's a cursed fate," he muttered; "life was very bright to me when I entered it, and everything has gone wrong. I haven't even been suffered to go to the devil my own way."

The pleasures of retrospection assuredly are not for the many. The chosen few may find bliss in meandering about in the paths of the past, but I doubt whether the majority do not find that said paths lead them into the society of blue-devils. Still, I trust that few look back with such remorseful pain upon a not-to-be-recalled career as Harold Ffrench was experiencing now.

The sharpest sting that struck home to his heart in this and similar solitary hours, was the reflection that he had done nothing to mark him from the brainless fool and the man of stolidly stupid mind. For aught he had ever shown to the contrary he might have been as these. He had achieved nothing, he had attempted nothing. He had been supine in an active age. He had been an idle man, and now the curse was come upon him of a full consciousness of how thoroughly, how inexcusably, he had wasted his life.

And this was owing to a romantic blunder committed at the very outset of what would otherwise have been a career. A blunder which left him with the false conviction that because one thing had failed, nought else was worth seeking. A blunder that did not harden his heart—to the last, he was a very tender-hearted man—or make him distrust or hate his fellow-men, but that weighted him so heavily that he never thought it possible to be anywhere near the post when the finish came in the race that is always being run. It was true, and he felt it bitterly, that, for all he had ever shown men to the contrary, he had been as the brainless fool or the stolidly stupid.

And this for want of a motive power.

Hitherto, however, he had been but idle and useless in his generation—nothing worse. He had been what is termed a greater foe to himself than to any one else. No man or woman had been injured by his neglect of many opportunities and his lax cultivation of his natural talents and advantages. He had been a lazy, a purposeless, but never a harmful man. What though he had wasted the best years of his life in roaming up and down the picture galleries of the world, in dreamy admiration of those works which they contained, gaining nothing from them, after all, save a superficial knowledge, for a mastery of the art in which he dabbled was a thing for which he had no motive for striving to attain. Such lotus-eating had injured no one, save himself a little perhaps.

But now that he had come back to England, it seemed as if the influence of the land of action was upon him at once. He had already ceased to be a passive mistake: he had become an active error the instant he had endeavored to brighten the path of that solitary young creature away down in the country who had flung an affluence of gratitude at his feet that bade fair to leave her poor indeed. Feeling the full force of his mistake, he still could not rouse himself sufficiently to rectify it before it proceeded still further and assumed a darker hue. The sole effort he made was this compromise with his conscience,—"I will keep near her only so long as she is liable to danger from Linley: once safe from him, I will leave her."

According to the plans that were formed during the days immediately following this by Lady Glaskill and Kate Galton, Theo was not likely to be freed from Linley's influence just yet, if he chose to exert it. But up to the present he had betrayed no desire to attack either her heart or her peace of mind. He was a frequent visitor, certainly, but it was to his fair hostess that he devoted himself. As Harold was wont on such occasions to sit by silent and moody, Kate fairly glowed with pleasure at such satisfactory evidence of the author's devotion and the cousin's jealousy.

It had occurred to Lady Glaskill that, since her niece was so fully determined upon sharing in such delights of the season as she (Lady Glaskill) could command, it would be well to come to an amicable understanding: both would benefit by it. The clever old lady found herself compelled to share the honours; this being the case, she resolved that the costs should devolve entirely upon the usurper. If she was to pipe up recruits to Mrs. Galton's standard, Mrs. Galton should pay for the piping.

"You will be some time working your way, my dear, I'm afraid," she said to her niece one morning when she came in and found Kate looking over a list of names and cudgelling her brains to decide with how many she was sufficiently intimate to ask them to a "quiet evening with a little music."

"I don't know: Linley has promised to bring several of his friends."

Lady Glaskill laughed.

"Linley will bring a brace of boobies, perhaps, as a foil to himself, but none of his *friends*, my dear, to a house and a hostess that are not known; shall I be magnanimous, my dear?"

"If you can, aunt."

"Judge for yourself, Kate. I wouldn't do such a thing for any one else, with the reputation I have of doing such things well, but for my dead sister's child." Here Lady Glaskill's utterance became obstructed by emotion, in which Kate, knowing that her ladyship had not seen her dead sister since the latter was fourteen, declined to sympathise.

"Well, what is it, aunt? You're capable, for your dead sister's sake, of coming to me yourself on the occasion, I suppose?"

"More than that, my dear Kate, more than that," the old lady rejoined briskly. "I have arranged to have a party on the 30th; Gunter is to supply the supper. Now, if you like, I will transfer it to you."

"Let it be my party at your house, my dear aunt——"

"No, no, my dear, you mistake me: it shall be my party at your house, or rather I should say, it shall be your party, for you shall give the supper, but I will issue the invitations; I am very glad indeed that I thought of the arrangement, for I think that it will answer admirably. Your name shall be on the card, of course, dear." And then Lady Glaskill got up and kissed her niece cautiously, and said virtuously that it would be a comfort to her to know that she had done this thing, for what a stepping-stone it would be to society for little Kate.

"Thank you, aunt, you're very good; then I am to pay for the supper, and your friends will be good enough to eat it in my house? That's the plain English of it, isn't it?"

Lady Glaskill nodded and laughed.

"There would be no one to eat it at all, my love, if my friends didn't come," she replied.

"True; on the other hand, it wouldn't be here to be eaten if they were not coming; well, aunt Glaskill, it's a bargain. You supply the people and I will the supper; and both are to be of the best obtainable, remember."

So the compact was made, and dear prudent old Lady Glaskill resolved that the arrangement should be repeated with variations throughout the season. By which means she would put money in her purse, and the better enable herself to gratify certain harmless tastes as to winter residence, costume, &c., which were occasionally rudely crushed.

Kate Galton was a model of absent wifely duty. She never suffered a day to pass without writing to her husband. They were charming letters, those of hers, very charming letters indeed. On several occasions he had read portions of them

to a maiden sister of his, who had girded fiercely at them in her maiden heart, and pursed up her maiden lips at them disparagingly. But then she did not like Kate. On the contrary, she disliked her for divers reasons, all more or less reasonable under the circumstances. The first count in Miss Galton's indictment against her brother's wife, was that her brother had married. "Who knows but that if he had not met that girl he might have been living there as comfortably as possible by himself still?" she would remark to her confidential servant, who would forthwith reply with the sigh of resignation,—"Ah! who'd a thought that Master John would ha' been that foolish, as one might say?" Then again, Miss Galton could not think well of any woman who wore white cambric muslin peignoirs, trimmed with pink or blue ribbons in the morning: "Sits in her dressing-room on purpose to wear them, as I'm an honest woman," she would tell the sympathetic with tears in her eyes. When it is understood that Miss Galton had never in the whole course of her existence been known to even momentarily adorn herself with anything that could be reckoned becoming by any but the most distorted taste, this intolerance to pink and blue will be appreciated.

Then again Kate was the mother of little Katie, and Miss Galton loved the child after an acid fashion, and disliked any woman having a nearer claim to it than herself. Could the child have been her brother's alone, Miss Galton would have adored it. As that in the nature of things was impossible, she would have liked it to be the offspring of a retiring, unassuming woman who would have renounced her first share in it, and meekly sat in subservience at the feet of her own child. But Kate was not at all the sort of woman to do this for an instant; on the contrary, she had been known, on the best authority, Miss Galton declared, to say,—"John, I won't have Katie go very often to your sister's: she'll teach her own frump notions to the child." Frump notions! angels and ministers of grace defend us! Miss Galton was a frump, but she never forgave her blithe sister-in-law for calling her one.

These were the great generals of her army of sins and offences. There were regiments of little ones that Miss Galton would frequently review for the benefit of those "old family friends" with whom the young wife had ever been unpopular. On hot Sundays Kate would put her feet up on the opposite seat and go to sleep. "I am human myself," Miss Galton would say, "and I have been overtaken by sleep in church, but I always sleep uncomfortably and get a pain in my side; John's wife must have her corner, and I call it impious."

Again, Mrs. Galton was not at all domesticated, her sister-in-law averred. "When she goes to the kitching" (Miss Galton, under the influence of emotion, was apt to give a fuller, richer sound to words ending in "n" than belonged to them)— "when she goes to the kitching it is to sit on the table and play with John's pointers. The half of every day did my dear mother spend in her kitching, and John's wife only says, when I tell her of it, 'how she must have muddled and bothered the servants.'"

These accusations and many others had been brought against Kate Galton at a very early stage of her wedded career, and she had borne them with a good-humoured unconcern that was infinitely aggravating to their maker. A tolerable show of friendliness had been been kept up all along between Mrs. John and Miss Galton. But still every one knew that Mrs. John despised her husband's sister, and that Miss Galton disliked and distrusted her brother's wife.

But the decent show had been of a quality to make John Galton believe that beneath the surface bickerings there dwelt a kindly feeling towards one another. He thought that his sister was over anxious though well-meaning, instead of being simply a meddlesome old maid. He also thought that Kate "appreciated Sarah's intentions," which Kate did not.

When Harold Ffrench, the handsome cousin with the atmosphere of mystery and sorrow and romance about him, came down to stay at Haversham, Miss Galton had been—there is but one word for it—portentous. He was of the same family, the same blood, and class, and order as her sister-in-law, and Miss Galton held that no good thing could come out of Egypt. She strove earnestly to make her brother unhappy, and, failing that, she withdrew her countenance altogether from the Grange, as if she felt confident that darksome things were going to happen there upon which the light of her face should not shine.

Huffy rectitude is a hard thing to treat. It may be right in the main, if it may have more than the shadow of a cause, but you cannot go with it entirely, and you cannot make its stony though imperfect vision see any of the softening shades that are so very apparent to you. John Galton knew, when he returned home alone, leaving his wife in London, that he was not doing a wise thing, or Kate a kind thing; yet for all that he felt that his sister was utterly wrong when she implied that it was unmitigated folly on his part and cruelty on Kate's.

Perhaps, however, the worst folly of which he was guilty was showing this litigious old lady Harold Ffrench's letter.

"There," he said, rather triumphantly, "you have pretended to doubt Ffrench's being such a good fellow as I know him to be; read that: no brother could have written differently, and Kate ought to attend to him."

He handed her the letter, and Miss Galton sat down to peruse it calmly, and then did that very annoying thing—pushed her spectacles down and read it over them. There is something judicial and at the same time asinine in the proceeding which drives the beholder to the verge of madness. No wonder John Galton felt angry with his sister when, after reading it in this manner, she put it down with the simple exclamation—

"Humph!"

Not that those letters at all represent the sound that did emanate from Miss Galton's mouth, but I know of no better combination than the time-honoured one which will stand its ground till acoustics achieve the mightiest triumph possible by correctly reproducing an old woman's grunt of disbelief and dissatisfaction.

"I say Kate ought to attend to him," John Galton repeated. Then he went a little beyond what he had ever before said to his sister. "Of course leaving her in town with Harold was very like leaving her with a brother."

"Kate is very obstinate," Miss Galton said, with a shake of her head.

"No, that she is not at all, Sarah; never met with a woman who had so little obstinacy in her."

"I was going to say when you interrupted me, John," Miss Galton went on with severity, "that since your wife has quarrelled with her cousin it would be well for you to discover what it is about. Such very great intimacies broken off so abruptly never look well."

Miss Galton was more portentous than ever, and John Galton waxed savage.

"Oh, bother! I shouldn't have come to you with Ffrench's letter if I had known that you were going to insult me with these senseless suspicions. By Jove! it's something strange if my wife can't have a difference of opinion with a man without a pack being down upon her at once to know the reason why."

Miss Galton grew as angry as her brother.

"Oh, wouldn't you, John? well, since you did come to ask my advice, I shall give it, whether you hurl it back upon me with obloquy—yes, obloquy—or not: I should just bring Mrs. John home, if I were you, before she has a chance of cementing a stronger intimacy with her new friend."

"I shall just do nothing of the kind, for you to raise the common cry that I doubt my wife," John Galton cried indignantly. Then he went away angry and resentfully sore with his sister, and ashamed of the weakness which had induced him to attempt to exonerate Harold from any sort of suspicion. He almost felt as if he had given room for Harold to be accused by excusing him. He quite felt that he had not guarded Kate from the lightest shadow of blame as it behoved him to have done. He was a simple-hearted, single-minded, loyal man; suspicion was so foreign to his own nature that it seemed to him to soil whatever it fell upon. Now through him, he told himself, it had been flung at two who were very dear to him. It was in a very tender frame of mind that he sat down to write to Kate, and when the letter had left, his mood grew softer still, and he felt that he must see her before he slept. So he took the two o'clock up-train from Haversham station, and was in Piccadilly by half-past seven.

CHAPTER XII

OFF GUARD.

KING TURMOIL reigned triumphant in the summer of 1851. A merry madness was monarch of all. Progress mounted like wine into the brains of the majority; under the influence of the intoxicating idea all went as fast as was feasible to some goal, whether good or the reverse was just a matter of chance with the many. There was much public frenzy and private mental aberration. The wildest schemes and most fragile of follies obtained and had a temporary success that was due to the disjointedness of the times. There was such splendour in the metropolis, that naturally there was no inconsiderable amount of havoc in the land. All were gorgeously bedight that year, and, like the lilies of the field, they took no apparent heed of what the morrow might bring forth.

Mrs. John Galton was by nature addicted to the diffusing around her, for beautifying and comforting purposes, of all the dross she could command. Some people call this extravagance; others, lavish generosity. Whatever name you like to bestow upon the quality, the fact remains that Kate possessed it, and the house in which her husband had planted her bore convincing marks of the same. She was going with the tide: and the tide set strongly in favour of following out the advice given, to take no heed of what the morrow might bring forth.

When John Galton reached the door of his wife's temporary residence, in Piccadilly, at half-past seven that night, agreeable odours were wafted up from the kitchen and down from the balcony, as if to welcome him. The perfumes from below were of delicate cates and rich sauces; the scents from above were of roses, and mignonette, and other unpractical things.

"I'm glad Kate has not dined, for I'm hungry," he thought to himself, as he rushed past one of his own footmen, without pausing to notice the irrepressible grin which succeeded that worthy man's first expression of blank amaze on beholding him. Then the sound of many voices smote upon his ear; and as he paused irresolutely on the staircase, there came serpentining towards him a cavalcade from the drawing-room. It was only by an agile bound down into the hall again that he escaped actual collision with the leader of the van—an old lady, who looked as if she were imperfectly riveted together with paint and artificial flowers.

From a dark doorway at the foot of the stairs he watched the descent of his wife's guests. He felt dirty and travel-soiled, and at a terrible disadvantage, as he stood there. They who passed him unconsciously were all so trim and bright. He felt at a terrible disadvantage; but not at all angry with Kate—only rather sorry that she had "not told him about it,"—that was all.

For a minute, a moment, rather, he thought that he would go back again as he had come, unknown, unnoticed. Then he remembered that in such going back without seeing her there would be a mute accusation, at least his sister would so read it, and would force her reading upon Kate some day perhaps. He could not censure her even by implication; he could not shame or distress her by showing resentment at such a very venial offence. So the kind-hearted fellow reasoned as the guests filed down, he unobserved by all of them—unobserved even by Kate, who came last, leaning on the arm of an ugly brilliant-eyed man. So he reasoned, shrinking into an uncomfortably small compass, in order to keep well in the shade, so that she might not see him suddenly, and start and show surprise.

When they were well inside the dining-room door he called the footman who had grinned on admitting him, and bade him unpack a portmanteau containing a dress coat and other articles that were essential to his proper appearance, a portmanteau which had been left in town, fortunately. "And now," he said, when he was ready, "just take this note to your mistress, and lay a cover for me." The man took the note to his mistress, and his mistress read it with the slightest start in the world.

"My husband could not promise me and him

self the pleasure of being here to-night; but he has succeeded in coming nevertheless," she said, handing the note with an untrembling hand to Theo Leigh, as if Theo were to feel special pleasure in the advent of a man she did not yet know. Then Mr. John Galton, judging from those words that his wife was perfectly self-possessed and ready to receive him, walked in, and was received with an air of quiet surprise by the majority of his guests, that made him wish himself back at Haversham.

But for all his own discomfiture he did not let one of them perceive that he had not come up to town fully expecting to meet them. Theo remarked that he scarcely tasted anything, and Mr. David Linley that he "had a habit of silence that was uncommonly pleasant in a bucolic." This was all the notice that David Linley accorded to the husband of the lady whose chains he was reputed (by herself and immediate friends) to be wearing.

Later in the evening, before John Galton could gain quiet speech of his wife that should not appear to be marked, Harold Ffrench came in.

"Has he, that man I wrote to you about, been hanging about her all the evening?" Mr. Ffrench asked of his cousin's husband as soon as they had shaken each other by the hand.

"He hasn't been near her once," John Galton replied. He was thinking of his wife, she being the one woman in the world to him. It did not occur to his single mind to suppose that Harold's question, Harold's anxiety, related solely to Theo Leigh.

"I have not spoken to Kate yet about what you have said, Ffrench; I shall tell her, though, to-night, that you don't think Linley a desirable acquaintance, and there will be an end of it."

"There won't be an end of it, I fear."

"You don't mean that you think Kate will disregard my wishes when I express them, Ffrench? Hang it, man, no one else should hint such a doubt of her affection to me!"

"Kate? oh! to be sure, Kate will be all right about it. It was not Kate I meant at the moment, Galton. I was thinking of that young girl; between us we have got her away from the home where at any rate she was safe and happy, only to throw her in the way of one of the greatest scoundrels unhung."

"Do you mean Miss Leigh and Mr. Linley?"

"Yes. I do mean Miss Leigh and Linley: he is attracted by her, as who would not be, indeed? And I know only too well the sure fate of the woman who attracts Linley. I can't tell you what I feel when I see Kate persisting in exposing that young girl to such a horrible risk."

"What is the risk? He doesn't strike me as being so remarkably attractive," John Galton said in a low tone, looking curiously across the room at his abused guest the while.

"A snake is not remarkably attractive, still it contrives to approach near enough to sting; and a precipice is not pleasant in itself, still it seduces a good many to gaze over its brink until they grow giddy. He's playing his usual double game, the rascal!" Harold Ffrench continued, in a tone of such deep rage and pain that John Galton became involuntarily impressed with the importance of the case, disposed as he was to see only the side shown, and to think well of the world at large.

"What is his usual game?" he asked.

"To apparently devote himself to one woman; to show a surface devotion that may blind beholders. He affects now to feel an interest in Kate, and to find her society charming. His real reason for coming here is to win that poor unguarded girl."

"How do you——. Look here, Ffrench, don't be offended at the question; but *how* do you come to know so much about this man? and knowing it at all, why don't you say it out straightforwardly and have done with it, whatever it may be?"

John Galton looked very anxiously into Harold's face as he thus questioned. The honest, brave, straightforward fellow could not bear to think that the man whom his own dear wife held "dear as a brother" should he guilty of saying that about a man which he either could not or dared not prove.

Harold Ffrench sat down and leant forward, covering his eyes with one hand.

"I have been a fool in my day, Galton; but, on my soul, I have never been a scoundrel or a sneak. I am not offended with you; but your question looks strangely as if you thought me one, or both."

"My good fellow, it's only that I am apt to give out what my own heart holds; I meant no reflection upon you. I don't doubt, or I won't again at all events, that your reasons for distrusting this man, whom that old aunt of my wife's has brought upon us, are good enough. Let me say one thing to you, though—why don't you guard that pretty girl you're so anxious about?"

"I should be a villain to suffer her to see how deeply I am interested in her, Galton; and that fellow knows it, or he would not dare to strive to interest her himself before me. I wish to God I had never gone to Houghton, or brought about an intimacy between Kate and Theo Leigh."

"Theo Leigh couldn't well have a better friend than my wife, I should think."

"Under ordinary circumstances perhaps not. Well, it's useless saying more, since I can't explain everything; but get your wife away from this vortex before mischief is done."

With that Harold Ffrench rose and walked away to a corner of the room where Theo sat talking to Mr. Linley. The latter had remained near her for a long time this evening, speaking to her occasionally with a softness in his eyes and voice that other women had found pleasant and then painful full many a time before. Despite Harold Ffrench's caution, to "beware of this man as·if he were the plague," Theo had given him a full confidence in return for his well simulated one. "I forgot the manner of your introduction to Mrs. Galton. You were mentioning the other day that it came about in a semi-accidental way, much in the same way as Ffrench's introduction to you in fact," he had said, to which Theo replied,

"No, not a semi-accidental introduction· to Mrs. Galton. My introduction to her was rightly and properly compassed. It was Mr. Ffrench's introduction to us that came about by chance. He was wandering about on the marshes, near our house in the country, trying to find his way over a fordless creek. He asked me to direc him, and I told him that he must have a boat— papa's boat—since there was no other; and when I mentioned my father's name,—no, I didn' mention his name, but it came round some way or other that Mr. Ffrench had known him by repute years ago in——Greece."

She had paused before uttering the last word for, as she approached the climax of her ex planation, the face of the man she addressed altered visibly. The soft tenderness, that while it lived almost entirely redeemed his ugliness vanished from his eyes, and in its place there came two light laughing devils of malice and contempt.

"Mr. Ffrench managed matters most ingeniously," he whispered; "he has shown far more tact than I ever knew him to employ before."

"You know him, then, although you never speak——." She stopped herself abruptly.

"Theo, I never speak what?"

"Well of him, or to him. How *can* you dislike Mr. Ffrench, and seem to think things against him?" she continued warmly.

"Shall I tell you?" he asked, in a low voice. The devils had vanished now. The soft tenderness reigned again more powerfully than before, if possible, for Harold Ffrench was advancing toward them to be pained by an exhibition of it. "Shall I tell you why I dislike him?" he repeated. "Because you love him, Theo, and I love you."

CHAPTER XIII.

MRS. JOHN GALTON OFFERS A PERFECTLY SATISFACTORY EXPLANATION.

THEO was but a girl—but a young impression able girl. What need after telling you that to add the fact that all must feel, that she was touched by those last words of Mr. Linley's. Touched not into tenderness, but into that compassionate emotional · frame of mind which after a period may give birth to tenderness. He was much older than herself; his name sounded well mentally, but ill morally; she had heard him much abused, yet nothing definite had ever been brought against him—above all, he loved her! This last was the weight that brought the balance down in his favour. He loved her, and she could not requite his love. Therefore she indulged in a plentiful supply and show of compassionate emotion toward him.

She did not tell him that she was sorry, or honoured, or any other thing that it only comes to one to affect to feel and utter after one-and-twenty. She was not one-and-twenty yet, so, though she was both sorry and honoured, very unfeignedly sorry, and very considerably honoured, she said nothing about either, but just suffered a series of sensations—semi-detached they were, not one of them had fair play—in silence.

The man had tasted the joy to the full in his youth of causing a woman to thrill through all her body and soul to his false words, doubly false in· their apparently enforced frankness. But this silent shiver that possessed Theo when he had spoken was a new thing to him. It was not a shiver of aversion: that he perceived at once. He was no self-deluder, though, and therefore he was also prompt to perceive that it was no light trembling ripple of reciprocation. They had clashed in their earlier years; the memory of their having done so was rarely absent from his mind. Still he did not realise for a few minutes that it was Harold Ffrench's approach which had caused a considerable portion of the trembling that he (Linley) had not understood.

When he did realise it, it stung him far more than if the girl had been antipathetic to him uninfluenced. The sting did not move him outwardly, however, for he reminded him of days gone by, when he, the Satyr, had won what had been vowed to Harold the Hyperion.

"What have you been doing with yourself for the last day or two, Theo?" Mr. Ffrench asked, seating himself by her side.

"Nothing, to-day; you were here yesterday, you know," she answered, inclining her head ever so slightly towards him as she spoke. There was never that leaning action, that barely expressed yearning towards himself, Linley felt, as he watched her from the short distance to which he had retired.

"Was I here yesterday? upon my word I hardly know how the days go." He did not look at her as he said this, but gazed away vaguely into vacancy in a way that caused her to gaze at him with painful earnestness.

"How you look at one, Theo," he exclaimed presently, turning towards her. "Your eyes were going through me then in a way that would make me fancy, if I didn't know you so well, that you were trying to fathom something; what were you reading?"

"Nothing—it's a sealed book to me."

"What is a sealed book to you? my character?"

"Yes."

"I ought to say, thank God that it is, for the reading would not profit you; perhaps I had better break the seals, though; shall I?"

"Do, do; ah! you will trust me."

She spoke in a quick, low tone; every note reached his ear and his heart, but not a sound of the words she used floated across to the eagerly strained ears of the man who was listening for her accents. Love is the best master of acoustics, after all.

"Trust you! yes, but not myself," he muttered in reply; then he rose from her side, saying that Kate was beckoning him. So once again the goblet of explanation, or whatever it might have been, was dashed from Theo's lips.

Mrs. John Galton was a little pinker as to the cheeks, and brighter as to the eyes, when Harold Ffrench obeyed her sign by going over to her side.

"What is this, Harold?" she commenced, as soon as he had seated himself on the small bit of couch which she indicated was at his service. "What is this, Harold? What have you been writing to my husband about?"

She was all the aggrieved matron, nothing more. Harold was aware of her talent for rapid transformations, therefore he was spared surprise at this last one that had come over her.

"About Mr. Linley," he replied quietly.

"Ridiculous! what has the man done to you that you should attack him in the dark?"

John Galton had told his wife that Harold's anxiety related solely and wholly to Theo Leigh.

"He says it would be all right enough for you, of course, dear: you're above suspicion; but he fancies that Linley is fascinated by Miss Leigh, and I—well, I suppose the long and the short of it is that he is jealous."

Jealous! Harold Ffrench jealous of Mr. Linley about Theo Leigh, while she (Kate) was extant! Small wonder that her cheeks grew pinker and her eyes brighter. She would have sacrificed the dawning friendship with Linley to Harold's jealousy of her. But she would not sacrifice it to his fears for Theo.

"Dear John," she had said to him with that air of thorough conviction that may not be questioned, "you know how I always endeavour to palliate Harold's follies, and screen his faults, because he has been as a brother to me since I was an infant; he really tries me a little too far sometimes though; he wants arrogantly to banish Mr. Linley from your house because Mr. Linley is evidently acquainted with some of Harold's juvenile delinquencies. I have no patience with such revengeful narrow-mindedness. Have you?"

"Well, I hardly——"

"Oh, now, John, don't defend him for the sake of sparing my feelings. Of course it's painful, most painful to me, to see Harold give way to such pettiness of disposition, but I can't blind myself to the fact that he does so give way. Mr. Linley is so different, he never says anything about Harold—never alludes to the cause of the aversion that evidently exists between them. I love Harold as a brother," the matron proceeded with creditable emotion, "but I cannot help thinking that he must have been very much in the wrong—it is so hard to forgive any one whom we may have injured."

"Perhaps the less we say about it then the better," John Galton said uneasily. It always seemed to him that the less that was said about anything unpleasant that might not be boldly rectified the better.

"Perhaps so. I will tell Harold that I have given an explanation to you of what he deemed reprehensible, and that you are quite satisfied; shall I?"

"Certainly. Satisfied? I don't like that word, Kate; it sounds as if I had not always been satisfied with you."

"Ah, dear! no one knows better than Harold what reason you have for being so," the fair wife replied. In this speech there was much truth; no one knew better than Harold "what reason" John Galton had for such satisfaction!

So now when Harold Ffrench came to her at her signal, Kate let him feel that he had been unwise in interfering. "Because you do not like him, is that any reason why you should attack him in the dark, and cast unfounded suspicions upon me?" she asked.

"Now you are ridiculous, Kate," he replied quickly. "I was attacked in the dark years ago by that man; but let that pass; what I want now is to do away with the opportunity you give him of exercising his cursed wiles on that——"

"Girl over whom you have already exercised yours," she interrupted. "Pooh! Harold, you ought to be wiser in your maturity than to fear such a kitten face will win all sorts of love and evil for its possessor. I am tired of the girl and her silent non-committal adoration for you and Linley."

"She has no adoration for Linley as yet, thank God," he struck in eagerly.

"Has she not? well, all that I can say is that she tries to blush him into the belief that she has. However, she is going home in a few days; will that set your mind at rest?"

"About her—yes."

"And about whom 'no?'—yourself?" she asked, softening her voice abruptly and placing her hand on his arm with the same quick warm pressure he remembered she had employed once, years ago, when she wanted to learn the story of the forging of the chains that bound him.

"I shall be as much at rest as I have been for more than twenty years," he answered sadly.

"Confide in me, Harold; now, though it's late; confide in me, and I would even befriend you with *her*."

She glanced towards Theo as she spoke, and he replied—

"Befriend her by sending her away home from both of us, Kate."

"I will," she said huskily; "indeed I will; how you love her, Harold! She shall go soon, very soon."

CHAPTER XIV.

MR. HAROLD FFRENCH OFFERS AN EXPLANATION WHICH IS NOT SO PERFECTLY SATISFACTORY.

MRS. JOHN GALTON had promised her cousin that Theo should go back to Houghton and safety "soon, very soon." She thoroughly meant to keep her word. The sight of Theo was painful to the prettier woman whom Theo had eclipsed. This was one reason for the ardent nature of the suddenly developed desire of the prettier woman to banish Theo. But added to this was another and better reason: she did not wish Theo's heart to be wrung or name to be sullied by even so much as the shadow of a suspicion while under her auspices.

Kate had the special grace of doing two or three things excellently well at the same time and without apparent effort. She could be an excellent hostess to the mass contemporaneously with the discharge of her full battery on the one. Moreover, while thus generally agreeable and specially fascinating, she could plan, arrange, and decide upon some important course of action.

This evening, while causing the majority of her guests to hope that these *réunions* would be of frequent recurrence, and weaving a conversational web from which he could not escape around Mr. Linley, she had to settle the form of words in which Theo's sentence of dismissal should be pronounced, together with the manner of its delivery. Kate abhorred the notion of going back to the old Grange, but she felt capable of calmly sacrificing herself even to that degree rather than of remaining a quiescent spectator of Theo Leigh's success in that field where the greatest glories of the day had always been gained by her alone. It was the one thing in life which Kate could not do gracefully—retire amiably into the background,

namely, and from thence watch with kind eyes the fleshing of others' maiden swords.

Mrs. Galton had no very poignant pangs about getting rid of Theo abruptly after almost forcing her to remain. Mrs. John Galton in fact never had any poignant pangs about any one but herself, and she would suffer nothing in the parting. So she resolved to say words to Theo on the morrow that should prove to the latter that it would be well for her not to stand upon the order of her going, but to go at once.

It happened, however, that Kate was not called upon to accelerate Theo's departure after all. The morrow's post brought a letter from Mrs. Leigh, telling her daughter that a long-looked-for appointment under Government had fallen vacant, and been bestowed upon her father. Further, that this would involve the necessity of Theo's returning at once, "if Mrs. Galton could kindly spare her," in order that she might bear her part in the leave-takings and packing-up which were consequent on the change.

"Perhaps you had better start by the two o'clock train to-day," Mrs. Galton suggested, when her young guest made her acquainted with the contents of the letter; "you'll have to see so many people before you leave, and you leave so soon, that I think you had better start by the two o'clock train."

"Ought I to see—I mean, how can I see people if I start so early?" Theo asked.

"I meant that you would have so many people down there to take leave of, not up here at all. I am sure I am delighted to learn that you have such intimate friends up here, I was not aware of it."

"I will start by the two o'clock train, certainly, or by an earlier one, if there is an earlier one," Theo replied hurriedly. Then she added more slowly, but quite steadily and distinctly,—"The only friend I have in London is Mr. Ffrench; I should like to have seen him before I go, but I suppose I shall not."

"No, dear, I don't suppose you will," Kate rejoined affably. It always made Kate affable to see another person baffled in this way. She herself would have obviated the difficulties attendant on seeing Harold Ffrench with a deft readiness by comparison with which Theo's discomfiture seemed a very ludicrous thing. But Theo had no such deft readiness at command, or at any rate would never have brought it to bear on such a matter.

Mrs. Galton's reply to Theo's supposition, that she should not see Harold Ffrench before she left, was therefore given in the most affable tone and spirit.

"No, dear, I don't suppose you will see him; he is sure though to call in by-and-by, and then I will tell him that you are gone."

"That's very kind of you; now I think I had better go and pack-up, Mrs. Galton."

"Why, you seem annoyed! don't you wish me to tell him that you're gone? You funny child! why, I really believe, Theo," she cried, starting up, taking Theo's cold hands in her own and laughing as though the idea were too eminently absurd to be discussed seriously, "I really believe, Theo, that you imagine yourself in love with my cousin Harold!"

She bent her head to a level with Theo's, and

looked with laughing earnestness into her eyes till Theo angrily averted them.

"I don't imagine myself anything, anything of the——no, I *won't* tell a story: I know that I love him! Imagine, indeed!"

She was panting, crimson, trembling, but she did not look one bit ashamed of herself as she made her avowal.

"Poor child!" Kate said half pityingly, half mockingly. "Harold will never marry, you take my word for it; I would prophesy good things concerning your first romance if I didn't know him so well."

Then Kate threw herself down on the sofa again, and affected to look at a book and make notes on the same, and Theo went away broken and abashed now, to pack.

How she loathed her task and herself, and indeed everybody but him. She remembered how she had felt when the trunks were first unpacked in that room, and the dresses first unfolded. Now she wrapped up a hope in every article she folded, and she thought, as she put them away, that they would never be taken out again. Her first romance Kate had called it! It was soon over—how entirely over!

She wearied over the task, as who would not under the happiest circumstances? Packing-up is never nice unless some one is doing it for you, and you are sitting by and are consulted about the position of the things for which you care, and left unharassed about the things for which you do not care. Then the packing-up of the goods and chattels that are to accompany you upon a pleasant tour is an agreeable occupation to witness, though packing-up one's own things is invariably depressing.

Poor Theo wearily put the bonnet that had been on her head to the Academy with him into the well of her box with a sigh, and sickened at the sight of some roses he had given her.

> Ah, those roses something held
> Other roses seemed to lack——

as Mr. Francesco Berger has told us in melodious strains. They were no prize flowers, with big broad deep leaves and the perfume of Paradise. They were just simple "roses red and roses white," but they held something for the girl that every other flower in life would lack.

So at least she felt as she put them carefully away, their poor old dwindled stalks wrapped in silver paper, and some of the faded leaves encased for their more complete security in one corner of an embroidered pocket handkerchief. So she felt then, but people get over things, "love and unlove and forget" in this wicked, weak, changeful world.

It would soon be time to go; happily she would not be compelled to see much more of Kate, whose manner had changed to her so completely and unkindly. She was telling herself this when Kate herself came to the door with a pale face and a constrained mien.

"Harold Ffrench wants to speak to you alone, Theo," she said; "he is down in the little drawing-room; I have agreed to it, go."

She needed no further bidding; she was down by his side almost before the echo of Kate's words had died upon her ear. She was down by his side, and she was happy.

"Theo," he began hurriedly, "I heard what Linley said to you last night; do you believe that it was a horrible agony to me to hear it, and not to be able to save you from a repetition of it?"

She had not deemed it so before, but she believed it now as she watched his face.

"It *was* horrible, horrible, but I was powerless then." He paused and stood further from her, she watching him intently the while; then he went on,—"To-day I learn that a chain that bound me to a silence so painful and ignominious is snapped, broken suddenly, awfully, but thoroughly: I am called away at once, but I must speak to you, though not to the world, before I go. Theo, will you be my wife when I come back, as I shall soon, free?"

She gave a low cry, and held her hands out towards him. He did not take them at first, but repeated—

"Will you trust me? Will you be my wife when I come back, my darling, to whom I dare not even yet show all the love I feel?"

"O Harold, tell me," she began, but he stopped her by saying:

"What this chain was? No, not yet. Forgive me; I dared not risk leaving you with this untold, though all may not be told yet." Then he took her hand and just pressed his lips to it—whispered, "I have your heart's promise, my darling," and was gone.

There was no need to tell Kate what had transpired; she fathomed it all the instant she saw Theo.

"He did not stay long. What is this fresh mystery?" Kate asked, and Theo answered—:

"I don't know; he told me not to ask till he came back and made me his wife." Then the feminine desire for a confidant obtained possession, and she added,—"He seemed afraid to be with me, and kissed my hand as if I had been a duchess instead of what I am to be to him, you know.'

CHAPTER XV.

THE SHADOW DEEPENS.

THE time has passed so quickly—for much had happened in it—that Theo only felt astonishment and no particular uneasiness when the truth dawned upon her one morning that it was just six weeks since Harold Ffrench had appeared before her and asked her to let him carry away with him the conviction that she would become his wife on his return. Just six weeks since that day, and during the whole of that time, he had made no sign, had written no word!

Still she only felt astonishment, no uneasiness mingled with the sensation as yet. She had had plenty to think about and plenty to do during these six weeks. She had had to bear her share in the family rejoicing consequent on this long-looked-for appointment, and in the packing-up and unpacking that it involved. Bodily activity does away with the possibility of much mental bemoaning. Theo had been very busy, too busy to nurse idle fears and doubts that time alone could realize or dispel.

The place was pleasant to her, for it was in summer weather that Theo came to her new abode, and the quarters that had been assigned to Mr. Leigh had an out-look over the river. It was all new and strange, and eminently satisfactory to her father. Therefore was the place pleasant to Theo, and she did not know the people yet.

But when they had been resident about a month, and were considered to have shaken down and to have adapted themselves to their niches, their existence began to be socially recognized in due form. People called upon them with rigorous solemnity, and made them welcome after the decorous fashion of the place.

They were merely names to her as yet, she had had no idea as to their relative importance, or of what station they took in the rigid scale of the place. Indeed she did not know that the place had a scale at this time. She learnt that in company with much else that was pleasant and beneficial by-and-by.

About a fortnight after the calling commenced Theo came into the big drawing-room, whose proportions had been kept intact when the building was apportioned into quarters, and found her mamma entertaining an elderly lady and her daughter, to whom Theo was forthwith introduced. They were Mrs. and Miss Scott, and the elderly lady had no peculiarly distinguishing traits about her, but the girl, her daughter, had.

She was sitting on a couch far away from her mother and hostess when Theo entered; looking not exactly out of temper or contemptuous,—her face was naturally too brightly frank and good-humored for that,—but wearily fatigued at the repetition of that which she had heard so many times before. For her mamma was giving the new-comer Mrs. Leigh a history in outline of the faults and follies of the denizens of the establishment, and Sydney Scott was sick of the subject.

She was a pretty girl, with great deep-grey eyes, a broad brow, and a very fair delicate complexion,—a short, plump girl, with tiny white hands, and a well-cut, laughing mouth. But her greatest charm lay in that aforesaid expression of frankness and in her apparently effortless *bonhomie*.

She had walked to the window and seated herself upon an ottoman which was there, after rising to meet Theo. As Theo followed her and took a place by her side, she commenced the conversation abruptly by saying—

"Are you glad you're here, Miss Leigh?"

"I hardly feel as if I were here yet," Theo replied.

"I asked, because it's the regulation speech, only I don't put it in the proper words. I'm glad you were not impostor enough to say you *were* glad, and that it was delightful. New-comers and outsiders are always told that it's a little heaven, and they pretend to believe it; after a time they rush to the other extreme, and think it a little something else."

"I suppose it's very much like other places," Theo answered, with as much interest as she could throw into her tone. She was feeling that in a short time probably it would matter little to her individually whether this place were paradisiacal as a residence or not.

"No," Miss Sydney Scott replied, shaking her head resolutely, as if such a supposition were not to be admitted for an instant, "that's just exactly what I complain of; it is not like other places, it's unlike anything the imagination of

those blest enough not to live in it can conceive. Let me see, your father is a lieutenant, isn't he?"

Theo nodded.

"Ugh!" the girl exclaimed, shrugging her shoulders. "Well, you know—but are you up in the grades already?"

"I have heard very little 'service' talked; it doesn't make much difference to a man when he's on shore whether he's an admiral or a lieutenant (except so far as the pay is concerned) so long as he's a gentleman."

"Oh, does it not! well, I hope you will retain your illusions. If you do, you will be more fortunate than I have been. It makes this difference here, in the one case you are admitted to the blessings of intimacy, in the other, the sun of patronage occasionally irradiates your path."

"And who is big enough to patronize? Granted that I am very small indeed, still, the patronage isn't a necessity. I can keep out of the way of it."

"Then you'll be cleverer than I have been, and I ain't at all addicted to the virtue of humility. I abominate people who give balls, and ask me to them in a sort of merciful manner, as if I were not quite up to the mark, but should be granted the inestimable privilege of curvetting and capriolling about their rooms. I can't help their asking me, you know, or their manner of doing so either, worse luck."

"But you could help going, could'nt you?" Miss Sydney Scott and her outspoken sentiments were beginning to interest Theo.

Sydney made a grimace.

"Ah! there it is; I am but human, and I like dancing. Now don't look as if you thought me weak, it's one of the effects of the place; you're not a snob now, but you'll be one if you stay here long. If you get the conviction into your mind that in every other house in the place the girls are reorganizing their wreaths and dresses for some particular ball you will want to go to that ball, and you won't think about the manner of the invitation till after it's over."

"Oh! won't I! if the manner's unpleasant that's just the first thing I should think about. But you haven't told me yet who are your big people and who are your little people."

"'Where ignorance is bliss,' &c.," Miss Sydney quoted. "It's hard to say, such a mere accident sends them up. There was a sweet little woman here once, I forget whose wife she was, but few of them knew anything about her, or where she went, or who were her friends, for she never talked large; she was regarded as very insignificant, for she didn't visit the magnates here. But one day the Duchess of ——'s carriage was seen at her door, and then she went up like a rocket. She told me the story herself."

"Unfortunately a duchess's carriage is never likely to be seen at our door; if that is the price of admission into the regions of the select I can never pay it; but do you know" (and she laughed), "I think I can survive my inability."

Miss Sydney Scott looked at her curiously.

"Do you go in for common sense?" she asked dubiously.

Theo shook her head, by way not so much of negative as of evading the question.

"Ah! I'm glad you don't, because if you did

4

I should fight shy of you ; and as it is I have rather taken a liking to you, because you're not a bit of a humbug, at least,"—Sydney hastily corrected herself,—" you don't *seem* a humbug ; but then I've been awfully deceived in women," the frank-faced cynic continued, " and latterly I have been surrounded by such precious queer specimens."

" I suppose we're all humbugs, more or less," Theo answered. She was thinking of Kate's charm and Kate's easily-shifted friendship. Her new acquaintance combated the notion.

" No, no, we are not ; I am not, for instance. I always say what I think, and do as I like."

" Except when you smile and suffer and go to balls where you fancy you are asked on sufferance," Theo interrupted.

" Ah ! that's exceptional ; besides, that isn't all humbug even. I go for a reason ; I go well-dressed, and all the men like me, and that puts my entertainers and their daughters out wonderfully."

Some very real, true, and not unnatural vanity flashed up into the fair frank face as she spoke. Theo could readily enough believe that this girl was "liked," ay, even more than that, by many.

" Come and walk with me to-morrow," Miss Sydney said, rising, as she saw her mamma getting under weigh for departure, " and I'll show you all our purgatorial places of promenade. Oh, yes, and the South Road ; it's a great institution, the South Road."

" I shall be very happy to come. Why is it a great institution ? "

" We all see each other there, and pass each other with little surprised bows, and—oh ! well, you will soon discover for yourself why the South Road is affected beyond all other outlets from this refuge for the destitute. Do you ride ? "

" Yes."

" Will you ride with me ? "

" Yes, if I can hire a horse."

" That's right," heartily ; " don't mind what I have said. If you'll ride with me I shall drop into my old habits again, and not brood over my grievances here. I have only got into the way of growling because I have been cut off from my old occupations. Come to-morrow and we'll arrange." With that Miss Sydney Scott departed, after having administered the most cordial and impressive shake to it that Theo's hand had ever received.

The fair face had wrought its usual charm. Theo was very much taken with it and its off-hand possessor, although she felt that the frankness was partly affectation, and the rebellion against the order of things considerably exaggerated. Still the frankness was pleasing, and the exaggeration was in no wise offensive. Added to this Sydney had seemed to like her (Theo) very much ; and there is a subtle flattery in such seeming, though we may feel all the while that it will soon break down.

They went out for the proposed walk the next day, Miss Sydney armed with a big key, by means of which she procured for herself and companion the inestimable boon of ingress to a park through a door that was closed to the public. To be sure they had to go slightly out of their way in order to avail themselves of this privilege.

But then it *was* a privilege, and as such to be enjoyed. The big key was heavy also, and Sydney soon palpably tired of carrying it. As a badge of office, so to say, it was a pleasure, in itself simply a burden and a mistake. However, Sydney had volunteered to do the honours to the new arrival, and she was resolved to do them with all the attendant glories.

I am afraid that Theo was chiefly familiar with this place to which she had come through the medium of novels. She had visions of the Virgin Queen coquetting over her ruff with Leicester on the terrace, and riding a-hawking through the sylvan shades of the park with ever so many more. It was disappointing to come suddenly on to a flat outside the schools connected with the establishment and find kiss-in-the-ring going on, and a general atmosphere of orange-peel pervading everything.

" So this is the park ? " she asked.

" Yes ; haven't you been here yet ? odious cockney place ? and I don't know whether the common is not worse. Isn't it dummy ? " Sydney asked, suddenly seating herself on a bench and motioning for Theo to sit beside her.

" There is a view that makes up for the 'dumminess' in a measure," Theo said, pointing as she spoke away through a vista that admitted a view of the river.

" Does it make up for it indeed ? I wish it did, that's all ; oh ! it *is* stagnation and nothing else in this place, Theo ; the very worst of its kind, too, pretentious stagnation ; we all make believe to be rather garrison-towny than otherwise, and we get up such surprising animation about such uncommonly small excitements,"

" Why do you make believe about it ? "

" It would be duller than it is if we didn't, and I do it because the rest do ; you'll be the same before long."

" It won't seem dull to me," Theo said, leaning back and looking away over the river. " I have lived nearly all my life in a little country village away on the east coast ; and you know a life in a country village isn't one of dissipation precisely."

" You'll go to the *soirée* next week ? " Sydney asked, without vouchsafing any notice to Theo's last speech.

" I have heard nothing about it. I have had no invitation."

" It is not a case of having an invitation ; your father will subscribe, and so you'll go there with a fraction of a share in the honour of the entertainment : you have the privilege of taking friends with you too, which is something if you have a grudge against anybody," Miss Sydney said, with a laugh of the most affable nature. " The wretched friends get it both ways," she continued merrily, " they have to be grateful to you for giving them some hours of unhappiness ; it's great fun ! "

" I'll keep my friends away, then, till I have found from experience that you are painting the lily."

" My remark applies only to lady friends. We admit of no rivalry on our own peculiar ground ; this is our special territory, you know ; and as we're quite enough to hold it, our name being legion, I think that it's only fair to depress and so drive away interlopers. I only tell you this, in order that you may give any lady against whom you've a mild spite, a ticket for the next. Now I have been candid; don't peach upon me; if you do I will never tell you anything again. Everyone would indignantly repudiate the idea of there being any truth in what I have said, may be (I'll be charitable) they would delude themselves into the belief that there *is* no truth in it. But you take some girl there attractive enough to rival the daughters of the land, and make all the best men visibly eager to inscribe their names on her card, and see if you like what will be said about her afterwards."

" I don't think I should mind what was said, if there was really nothing to say," Theo replied. Then the two girls got up and walked away through the park and over the common, and into a grove, with detached villas on either side, called Rockheath Park.

As they walked along they fell to discussing, with the usual absence of relevancy and reason in such cases, appearances and slander, and their own immaculate conduct and other people's ill-nature. At least it was Sydney who discoursed upon these two latter things—Sydney who looked so bright and cloudless, but who, according to her own account, had been the butt at which countless shafts of envy, hatred, malice, and all uncharitableness had been let fly. It was not until she had listened to energetic and repeated disavowals of being either, that Theo came to the conclusion that her new friend wished to be considered fast and a flirt.

" I am called a *fac simile* of 'Kate Coventry,' just as if I were anything of the kind; isn't it absurd ? "

" Very absurd, unless you're like her, which you say you're not," Theo answered carelessly.

" Ah, but one can hardly judge of one's-self; I don't think it's any bad compliment to be told so, is it ? " Hargrave, of the ——th, said it first, and since then I've heard it till I'm sick of it."

" I don't think it is either a bad or a good compliment; but if I were sick of it I would tell people so, especially Hargrave, of the ——th, who, as he set the ball rolling, can probably stop it."

" You're laughing at me, and I hate to be laughed at," Miss Sydney said, ingenuously.

" Not at all; I was but agreeing with you."

Sydney paused for a minute; but she evidently liked her subject, for she presently resumed :

" That's not so bad, is it, though, as being called a flirt ? Now, could you stand that ? "

" Oh, it's but one of the many things that are *said ;* it's meaningless, because it's said by some one of every one. I heard a frisky old thing of fifty once called a 'a sad flirting naughty thing' by a dreadful toady who knew she would like it; it is not nice, of course."

" No, it's not nice," Sydney said, dubiously; she had rather liked the reputation on the whole, therefore there was not much heartiness in her assent. Suddenly she brightened up again, and spoke with her usual force:

" Mind you do go to the next *soirée*, whether you follow my advice about taking a friend or not. I'll introduce you to a great friend of mine, Hargrave; I wouldn't introduce him to any one else, but I will to you."

" That's very good of you; is he so precious ? "

" I don't know about his being so precious, only he's my great friend, and I don't choose that he should diffuse himself too freely; he's very handsome, in thorough good style; don't you fall in love with him, for I wouldn't stand that."

" I won't try you so far," Theo replied quickly; she felt momentarily indignant at being supposed to be capable of such a weakness, even by one who was ignorant of Harold Ffrench's existence, as well as of that mighty man's claims upon her heart.

" Are you engaged already, then ? " Sydney asked, opening her eyes a little wider, and when Theo had replied " Yes," Miss Sydney went on to ask—" To whom ? what's his name ? " with most engaging, frank curiosity. But before Theo could answer this, a voice came over the hedge of one of the villa gardens to the right which struck her dumb.

" Good-bye till to-morrow, then, to-morrow at five." Then the words grew indistinct, and Theo had time to realise that it was Mr. Linley's voice that she had heard, and to hope that she would not meet him before she caught any more. Then she heard him say something about " Mr. Ffrench," with a laugh, and the next instant he was coming out through the gate and advancing towards her.

" Ah ! Miss Leigh, this is a pleasure ! " Theo had to look as if she thought it one, too, and to hold out her hand.

" You have walked over from Bretford, I suppose ? I heard from Mrs. Galton of your father's appointment ; I congratulate you upon it." Then he lowered his voice and added,—" And about something else more immediately interesting to you, I suppose I ought to offer my congratulations, but I cannot."

She looked up, subduing her blushes as well as she could, and shaking off her discomfiture.

" You are very kind about papa," she said. Then she held out her hand to wish him good-bye, and make him understand that she wanted to go on.

" I am unkind, then, you think, about that other thing ; ah, well ! "—thus far he had almost whispered, at least he had spoken in that low, soft tone which is far more likely to salute the ear *alone* for which it is intended than a mere whisper. He now added aloud:

" You will permit me to walk back across the common with you; I am going to Bretford."

" If Miss Scott—that is, I mean,—allow me to introduce you : Mr. Linley, Miss Scott," Theo said, hurriedly. She was put out at his attaching himself to her in this way; she did not in the least know how to shake him off, and she was well aware that Harold Ffrench would be annoyed when he came to hear of it.

Sydney, merry, loquacious, amiable Sydney, would not assist her in this strait. Miss Scott had given one comprehensive glance at Mr. Linley when he had first appeared, and she thought him old and ugly, uncommonly ugly. His name just struck her as being the same as stood on the back of a novel that she had been reading lately. But she did not think of associating this man with the author, and even had she done so she would have felt no greater interest in him. He was elderly and ugly, and he was arrayed in this bright summer weather in dark and dingy clothes. Sydney only thought well at first sight of those who wore flowers in their button-holes, and the palest mauve gloves, and waistcoats of tender tints. An elderly ill-dressed man was an abomination to her; therefore she walked along now with her pretty nose in the air, and would not assist Theo in bearing this incubus by so much as a word.

It was a terrible incubus to Theo, although she had not a particle of personal dislike to him. Indeed, had her taste been unfettered, she would have been as prompt as the majority of her sex in acknowledging his influence. His ugliness was no drawback at all to the man in her eyes, but he had had the misfortune to win Harold Ffrench's ill opinion, and therefore Theo could not suffer herself to think well of him, though he had told her he loved her. The burden of her mental song as she walked over the common and down to the barrier that was raised around her new home with this man by her side, was, "How annoyed Harold will be when he hears of it! I wouldn't have had it happen for the world." This was the pertinacious *refrain*, and still through it, as it were, came the other thought, that he was "very pleasant and kind."

At the gates they parted. "I am going to dine with two or three men at the 'hotel,'" he told her. He went on to mention the names of the men at once, and Sydney looked at him with greater attention, for they were well-sounding names. There was a drag, too, outside the hotel door; maybe his friends had come down in it, she thought. So at parting the pretty blonde broke the silence she had observed, by saying:

"If you dine in that room, then you'll see the whole force of the place out after nine. It's such a lovely evening, Theo, you must walk on the terrace with me."

───────

CHAPTER XVI.

OUT ON THE TERRACE AFTER NINE.

AT about five minutes before nine that evening Miss Sydney Scott appeared before Theo in raiment so fresh, brilliant and voluminous, that she resembled a substantial, not to say stout, butterfly. The little lady was arrayed in a white muslin, in a great expanse of it, and this was adorned with blue bows, blue ends, and blue runnings of glossy ribbon in a way that was very beautiful to behold. Over this she wore a blue china crape shawl, put on carelessly, so carelessly that it fell back and betrayed the fact of her braceleted arms and pretty white hands being bare.

"You see," she exclaimed, when Theo had declared her "to be got up tremendously," "it's like one's own grounds after nine; we all come out then just as we have been dressed for dinner; you *must* have seen that everybody comes out as much got up as I am."

"I have not seen, for I have not thought of looking. I have not known who the promenaders were, so I haven't been interested, you see. What are we supposed to do now?"

"Put on your hat and come out and walk up and down."

"That sounds cheerful, on those pebbles; can't we go up under the colonnades?"

"Oh, *no*," Sydney cried decisively; "no one

goes there, all the fun is on the terrace; besides, to-night——"

"Well, what of to-night?"

"Why, perhaps if he sees us, that friend of yours might like to come in; now don't be affected, and pretend that you would rather your grandfather did not join you from motives of propriety. Mrs. Leigh, you will come out too, won't you? Mamma's there, and will be delighted to get you to talk to again."

"But who's Theo's friend?" Mrs. Leigh asked. "I must hear that first."

"Oh, mamma, no friend; of course I should have mentioned meeting a 'friend,' but Mr. Linley, a mere acquaintance like Mr. Linley, I didn't think it worth while telling you that I met. I used to see him at Mrs. Galton's, and I met him this afternoon, that is all."

"Linley!" her father ejaculated; "that's a name I ought to know very well." When he said that, Theo knew that she was in for it—in for continued intercourse with that man to whom Harold Ffrench was so antipathetic.

"Come along," she said quickly to Sydney, who was beating the floor with her foot in impatience to be off; "you'll come out and join us then, mamma?" Then, without waiting for a word more, the two girls went out of the house.

"Let us go up to the other end," Theo said; "it's more open up there."

"No," Sydney replied resolutely, "let us keep down here, we shall see the drags go off." Miss Sydney walked along towards the "hotel," with her white robes and blue drapery floating around her bravely.

There were four men out on the balcony of that room in the hotel which faces the west. Without looking up, Theo felt that one of the four was Mr. Linley, and that he would come down presently. Without looking up also, or at any rate without appearing to look up, Sydney knew that three of the men were young, and that they rejoiced in tenderly-tinted waistcoats and flowers in their button-holes.

Presently the four came in and gained the terrace just as the ringing-out bell commenced pealing. Theo's father and mother had come out by this time. And when an inexorable policeman was insisting upon the immediate withdrawal of the quartette, Mr. Linley came up to the Leighs, hat in hand, and said:—

"Will you plead privilege for myself and my friends, Miss Leigh, or will you see us turned out?"

It had come! there was no help for her. Theo felt that she must introduce him to her father.

She shook off the feeling of being a naughty mouse whose guardian cat was absent after a time, when the three younger men had been introduced to them and had succeeded in engaging Sydney and herself in conversation apart from the elders.

"Harold *can't* mind papa talking to him, surely," she thought; "it's only me he wants to keep from being friendly with Mr. Linley, and I have no desire to be it." With the thought her spirits rose, and altogether she was very happy, though the path was pebbly, and though the honours of the occasion were clearly with the pretty creature in blue and white who was being frank and engagingly out-spoken in a wonderful manner.

It was very pleasant, and she wished that

Harold Ffrench could have been there with her when the daylight quite died out of the sky and the moon shone forth in all her glory, silvering everything that she touched with her beams. The old place is fair enough to be set as the scene of any romance : it is all palace at such times. By day the aged seaman is apt to interfere with one's sense of the beautiful.

Some such sentiment as this last one I have penned was being discussed. The two girls had placed themselves on a bench, and the men were standing before them looking down at them, and while evidently seeing nothing save the two pretty faces, were declaring that they " had never believed in the beauty of the place before."

"There's nothing to mar it to-night," Theo said quietly; while Sydney laughed, and said it " was rank heresy to doubt the beauties of the place ; she would introduce them to their notice more fully."

"I like the idea of the aged seaman in the abstract, but he is not pleasant in the flesh, especially en masse. My experience of him is that he is a drunken, discontented old bear, who thinks that the casual visitor ought to bestow perpetual reward upon him for disfiguring what would otherwise be as pleasant an after-dinner lounge as any along the river."

The youngest and best looking of the three men was the speaker. He was the Honourable Algernon Buckhurst, familiarly "Algy Buck," and he meant to be a Lord of the Admiralty one day, and to make the abuses of all things appertaining to the navy his special care.

"I don't object to him at all; he might growl and beg, and be a hundred times more discontented than he does and is already," Sydney said, putting her hand out to see how "strange" it looked in the moonlight; " what I complain of is that my friends will swarm about me and pretend to take an interest in how he's fed and lodged, and so drag me through the halls and wards; that's awful; for when you have been through one there is nothing fresh to be said about anything, and you feel idiotic and stifled at the same time."

"I should like to see you bear-leading," Algy murmured languidly. "Linley and I will come and get Miss Leigh and you to take mercy on us. I ought to go through the thing as a duty, and it would be making a duty pleasant for once."

"Theo," Mr. Leigh called out from a short distance. Theo rose and ran to him, ran up slightly, swiftly, and unrestrainedly as a child might have done, or rather, as the girl she was still.

Her father was standing with his arms folded across his chest and with his head up, but there was a look in his face as if he had received a bad blow, and Theo trembled.

"When did you hear from Ffrench, my girl? you have heard since he left?" he asked as she came up. Then Theo ceased to tremble and answered promptly and coldly, for she resented this inquisition before a stranger, and that stranger Linley, his foe.

"No, papa, I have not heard. Oh! dear papa, what is it?" she cried, as he dropped his arms and put out his hand to her.

"My poor child!" he said in a fervent tone. She asked him again impetuously, "What is

it, papa? what is it?" but he only answered that " my poor child."

"Will you suffer me to tell her?" Linley asked softly. "Miss Leigh, will you kindly trust yourself to hear from me what your father——"

"No, I won't," Theo interrupted, turning on him fiercely. "No, sir," as she saw him about to speak. "Stop, as you are a gentleman: whatever it be—good or bad, true or false—I will not hear it from you."

She had stood alone as she spoke thus : such a little thing she looked to be so defiant: there was not one sign of flinching about her as she stood erect and alone, hurling out her refusal to listen to him. But when she had answered Linley she turned to her father again and clung to his arm.

"Don't let him feel that you can't say and ; can't hear any words that should be said, papa ; whatever it be, whatever it be, say it out, dear, and see how I'll stand it."

It seemed to her to be a point of honour not to quail before this man who hated Harold and whom Harold hated. She felt that that which she was to hear would concern Harold and would be evil. But now as she urged her father to speak she turned her face to the moon and pulled off her hat in order that the light might stream full and clear upon it. Nor did she wince or falter when her father obeyed her by saying in such a broken, humbled tone—

"Poor child! you had better come in to your mother before I tell you what you must hear."

"No, papa, but now, now!"

"The man has deceived you;" then he shouted, " and by God he shall answer for it—he has a wife living!"

"You say it on that man's authority?" she asked, indicating Linley with her hand but not looking towards him. Though she called him " that man," and expressed contempt and hatred for him in every accent, Linley had never been so near loving a woman truly as he was at that moment.

Her father took her hand, but she could not stand caresses yet. She withdrew it determinately and repeated her question, and when her father had replied in the affirmative she cried—

"Harold Ffrench shall thank you for this interest in his affairs at some future time. By way of showing my gratitude for your interference with mine, I will beg you to understand that henceforth we are such absolute strangers that common courtesy will forbid your daring to discuss them with me."

Then she bowed to him—bowed very low indeed—and put her hand on her father's arm to lead him away in a manner that made Mr. Leigh feel that she was not quite so much of a child as he had been wont to deem her. She was something besides his daughter to him from that moment. He began to understand that there were other things in heaven and earth than those of which he in his parental philosophy had heretofore dreamt.

"Are you going in, Theo?" Sydney Scott cried running up to her.

"Yes," Theo replied, "there's your mamma you won't be alone." She shook hands with Sydney, and bowed coolly to Mr. Linley's friends and walked in with what her father thought to be most wonderful sang froid. When she was in her own room, to which she went immediately, "to take off her hat," she said, this *sang froid* deserted her, and she went down on her knees and buried her head in the bed-clothes and sobbed with a bitter agony over the form of assault that had been made upon her absent love.

Meanwhile the man who had assaulted him was watching the horses being put-to, for he was going back to town with his friends.

"That's a poisoned dart that will wound him when he's perfectly cured of the other. Old Leigh will never forgive the insult if Harold Ffrench comes back free to-morrow." Then he thought admiringly of Theo. "She took it grandly, grandly," he muttered. "Harold Ffrench has lost the best thing he ever had yet. I should have gone on a different tack with such a girl as that; until I met her to-day I half fancied she might know the truth."

Mr. Linley told his friends that Old Leigh had been boring him cruelly, and that that was the reason why he had said good night and broken up the party abruptly, as it seemed to them he had. "It was all very well for you fellows who had two pretty girls to talk to, but I am past caring for such things, and haven't acquired a taste yet for old naval men's reminiscences. Fellow never heard of my book either," he continued in a disgusted tone; "what can you have in common with a man who's so utterly out of your orbit as that?"

"There's something about the daughter that I like though, do you know," Algy remarked. "She's not quite so pretty as the little thing in blue, but there was something about her that I liked."

"Next time I see her I will make her happy by communicating your approval of the 'something' to Miss Leigh."

Mr. Linley began to think that it would be rather a refined torture to apply to Harold Ffrench to make some younger man his rival,—some younger man of whom, like the Honourable Algy, it might well be said that Theo had "declined to a lower nature and a narrower heart," could she be led into substituting him for Harold. "But she's obstinate, I see that," he thought; "precious obstinate, and plucky as the devil; *how* she turned on me!"

Curiously enough her turning on him as she had done was the thing that he could not forget, and this not in anger but in admiration. She was the first woman who had ever turned upon him; and she had done it so readily and so fearlessly. He had to thank her for the most novel sensations; he bore her no malice for her candour.

He had called Theo "obstinate and plucky," and it is a fact that she was both these things. Yet it has been seen that she was all a woman in her utter abandonment to grief and despair, when there were none others by to be supported by an outward show of courage on her part. I have shown her to you, kneeling by the bed with her face buried in the clothes, sobbing in a strong agony that such an assault should have been made upon him. But her voice never faltered, nor did her resolution, when she bore her part in the discussion that took place that night. She avowed her intention to be staunch to the man till he told her himself that he was "false and unworthy," and she meant it.

For all that, she went through a terrible ordeal of dread and fear and horrible doubt when she came to be alone again in the night.

CHAPTER XVII.

THEO AND MR. LINLEY BOTH HEAR THE TRUTH.

SYDNEY SCOTT did not mean it unkindly, she meant it the reverse of unkindly, in fact. She wished to prove that her new friend's merits had already received the recognition that seemed the grandest to her. She wished to show that she was already on terms of confidential intimacy with Theo. Above all, she desired to strike a sharp blade into the hearts of several of her acquaintances who were not engaged and who wished to be engaged. These various reasons combined to make her more than ordinarily loquacious, and so, just when the hearing it spoken about was exquisitely painful to Theo, her engagement was made the chief topic amongst all those with whom she was thrown in contact.

"She is engaged to a—I forget his name—but it's a capital match, and she won't be in your way here long," Sydney Scott had contented herself with saying to one or two of her favorite aversions at first. But after a short time this statement appeared tame to her, and she touched it up slightly.

"Do you really think Miss Leigh is too small and dark, and that she looks like a mere fresh country girl? Well, I don't agree with you; however, she won't be a vexed question amongst us long, for she's going to be married; *such* a match, too!"

So rumours arose that were wounding to both Theo and her parents under existing circumstances. How they arose was not quite clear, for Theo had entirely forgotten that she had suffered the hint on which Sydney had built up the full statement to escape her.

"Don't contradict it yet, papa, since it has got abroad unfortunately," she pleaded. "Harold Ffrench will tell me the truth some day; don't denounce him on that man's authority."

It was a horrible grief to her that her father should at this time permit Mr. Linley's visits and give the hand of friendship to him. "He is false and treacherous, of that I am sure, though I don't know how," she would say. So she kept out of the way when he came, as he did frequently, and would neither see him nor listen to a repetition of what he had said.

"Poor child!" Mr. Linley said to her father one night, "she hates me now very naturally for telling you the truth about Ffrench; she'll forget that vacillating fool in time, and when she does she'll cease to think me a devil, and will believe that the 'refined, accomplished man,' was the true embodiment of the Satan she deems me."

But still though Linley would speak freely enough of both Harold Ffrench and Theo, he declined to tell the father of the girl how the fact of Ffrench having a wife alive had come to his knowledge.

"There was something underhand and constrained about his manner to your daughter, and I took an interest in her: some day or other, when this wound is healed, I will tell you why. That being the case, I set myself to work to find out why he was constrained and undecided, and as few things baffle me for long, I soon discovered what I have told you. His pretty fool of a cousin imagined that it was her fascination that drew me to her house so continually: my dear fellow, it was the interest I took in your daughter,—on your account at first, after a time I confess solely on her own. It was hard to stab her, but Theo will forgive me in time."

"Theo is very obstinate," her father replied, mournfully; "she still believes in that smooth-tongued scoundrel."

"Her faith must be pretty well strained by this time," Linley said eagerly; "it must give way before long."

"And she will give way with it, I fear. Strained! the strain is killing her, sir! but she has never let us see a tear or hear a word of repining. I would have given my heart's blood to save my child from this sorrow that she won't acknowledge to be one," the old man said in a broken voice. He admired Theo for not making her moan aloud, but his love made his pity for her a poignant pain to himself.

At last, about a fortnight after Mr. Linley had struck the first blow, the second fell. A letter came from Harold Ffrench, not to Theo, but to her father; but Theo was the one to read it first, for her hand was steadier than her father's, and her vision was clearer.

"Two months ago," he wrote, "I was told, and God knows that I believed, that a chain which had bound me for years was snapped for ever. The curse of impatience was upon me, and the first use I made of my freedom was to ask your daughter to be my wife. My horror and remorse when a few hours later I learnt that I had been told a lie, broke me down more utterly than I had ever thought to be broken down and live. Had my brain been clear I should before this have written the truth which will bring down your curse upon me. To her whom I have so cruelly wronged I dare utter no plea for forgiveness. To you I will only say that before God I thought myself a free man in that fatal hour of parting with your daughter. I left her to find a woman who has been my wife in name for years still alive. I left her to find that I had been tricked into deceiving her—tricked into a more complete destruction than overtook me years ago at the hands of the man you are now admitting to terms of intimacy. Beware of him! he is the cause of the evil that has come upon us all—of the dishonour that you will always associate with the name of

"HAROLD FFRENCH."

She had read it through almost to the last line without flinching; but when she came to those last words a tremor seized her, and she put the letter down and leant her head against her father's shoulder.

"I can't read it to you, papa dear, but I can tell you that it is all black, all black and miserable; we'll never say another word about him after you have read the letter and told me that you *don't* associate 'dishonour' with the name

of the only man I ever can love. Tell me that, and then it shall be done with."

But her father could not tell her that. This man had come and crushed his flower, for though Theo would not be broken she was most sorely bruised; and now he had nothing better to say for himself than that he had been the victim of an idle tale, and that the curse of impatience had been upon him. Mr. Leigh could not forgive him, and could not associate his name with aught but dishonour. Theo had the additional agony of reading in her father's face unrelenting antagonism to the man "who was the only man she could ever love."

But he spared his daughter all allusion to it, as she had desired. "It is all black, let it be done with," she had said. To this appeal she mutely agreed. Theo felt, when she saw her father throw the letter into the fire, that he desired to burn away as much as he could of that episode in their lives which had commenced on that bright spring morning, and was ending now when the leaves were falling fast. "He wishes to burn it away; it shall never be recalled by me," she thought. So from that day Harold Ffrench's name was never mentioned between the father and daughter.

There was no answer sent to the letter which struck the final blow. Mr. Leigh could not write and Theo would not, partly because they tacitly relied upon her honour not to do so, and partly because the great pity that filled her heart for herself and for him, was too near akin to love to be safely expressed to the man whose wife still lived. But through all her silence she hoped that he would do her the justice of believing that, as she had never distrusted or doubted, so she did not now despise or dislike him.

It was a hard thing for the girl to live on and act as usual at this epoch. To get up, and go through the day as the day had ever been gone through in their quiet household, and then to go to her room at night without a hope that this routine would alter for the better. It was a hard thing to do this with external fortitude—more than that, with apparent content. But she did it, never forgetting that she was not alone in the world; bearing in mind constantly that in her face alone the sunshine of her home was found; remembering ever that it is so easy to give up the game entirely.

She had other things to endure soon besides her own heart's gnawing agony, and other efforts to make in addition to the one she succeeded in, of making that agony no household word. Quick upon the heels of the announcement, the injudicious, well-meaning, girlishly premature announcement that Sydney Scott had made of her marriage—came the rumour of the dissolution of it. And Theo had to hear many biting comments through her frank-faced friend, who was a fierce, albeit an injudicious partizan. Nor were comments all: she had to run the gauntlet of an incomprehensible hostility that originated, Heaven only knew in what—an hostility that veiled itself under the semblance sometimes of friendly reproof, sometimes of unwilling disapproval, sometimes of a guarding patronage that was only one degree more absurd than loathsome to her. But however veiled, it was co-existent with her residence there; and she knew it. Altogether it was a hard time to live through from causes pure and simple. In addition, as is general and so perhaps just, her own sex rendered it harder, sometimes by censure and sometimes by commiseration, until Theo came to the conclusion that misfortune must be the worst guilt of all, it is so sorely punished.

"I wish you would tell me all about it, I should know better what to say then when they are going on about you," Sydney remarked mediatively to Theo one day when together they were standing in the square listening to a choice selection of airs that were being performed by a band.

"Who are 'they,' and what do they say?" Theo asked wearily.

"Oh, everybody! and they say—well, all sorts of things; it's very unpleasant for me, being your friend; but what can I say? you have no confidence in me."

"I have no confidence in any one," Theo replied quickly. She simply meant that she confided this bitter sorrow of hers to no one. But Sydney attached a different meaning to the words.

"You must have been most dreadfully ill-used to say that, Theo. I won't believe that you have been to blame, though—though——"

She stammered and stopped, with a blush on her bright face, and confusion in her clear eloquent eyes.

"Though what?" Theo asked, turning her head slightly towards her companion.

"Though they do shy away from you as though you were infected," Sydney said quickly.

"So I am infected—infected with a disease that renders my companionship unpleasant and unimproving," Theo answered carelessly. "I am infected with more than a touch of reserve about my own affairs, and carelessness as to what they or you or anybody else may think about them. Excuse me, but if you have nothing more agreeable to give vent to than your surmises as to their surmises about me, I had rather not hear them; and I think I will go in."

So she went in, away from the candid young friend who told her all that was said and thought and hinted to her disparagement, away from those who treated her, according to that friend's version of the case, "as though she were infected." As soon as she was alone she sat down and prayed unconsciously, gazing awhile over the muddy river, alive with crowded steamers, for a brief escape from the terror of this shame till strength should be hers to bear it better.

"What is thought of me, and what is said?" she asked herself. She shook with rage and scorn at that form of interest which was being displayed towards her, and thought of a hundred plans of escape, and rejected each one of them in rapid succession. Finally, she hoped that frank-faced Sydney Scott had not thought her very petulant.

That Miss Sydney had so thought her she speedily learnt, for Sydney was one who when she had a grievance cried it aloud in the marketplace and from the housetops. This was a favourite form of grievance with her too, which added to the pleasure to be conversationally extracted from it. It has been said that according to her own account Sydney had been the butt at which countless shafts of envy, hatred, malice, and all uncharitableness had been let fly. And these, be it borne in mind, had all been feminine shafts. Perfidy from her own sex, the young philosopher averred, she was well accustomed to meet with. But this was a peculiarly black case of perfidy, "to be turned upon and insulted by a girl she had stood by, as she had stood by Theo Leigh, was ingratitude that could not be easily matched in deepness of dye." It was a lesson to her never to trust a woman again, until such time as she felt constrained to tell how she was called fast and a flirt and a regular "Kate Coventry."

The little lady's wrath was loud, but, as is usual when such is the case, it was not lasting. Sydney could not nurse it to keep it warm; she expended it in airy puffs, and having done so, proposed a fresh alliance offensive and defensive with Miss Leigh in the following terms:—

"I *say* that, after all, if you choose to keep your own counsel you're quite justified in doing it, and I made the Miss Boltons mad last night at their abominable dull musical party by telling them that I would offer them five to one against your being Miss Leigh at the end of the year; they took me,—in gloves, you know; so look out that you don't let me lose."

"You're very good to talk about me and to bet about my marrying," Theo answered, "but if you would be kind enough not to tell me of it, I should be still more obliged to you."

"Now, Theo—however, I'm determined I won't quarrel; I won't expect much from you, but I won't quarrel. Hargrave said, when I told him about you first, that I should find you out in time to be just like every other girl."

"Mr. Hargrave betrays immense discernment and knowledge of character."

"You needn't laugh at Hargrave; he is not stupid, though he's not old and ugly like your hideous talented friend who wrote the book and stumbled upon you in Rockheath Park," Sydney cried indignantly. The young soldier had sung with her, and her alone, the previous night, and he had been the sole military light amidst a lot of rather sombre civilians. The glow of these things was still upon him, so Sydney spoke indignantly in his defence when she deemed that Theo aspersed his intellect.

"The man who wrote the novel, and who stumbled upon us in Rockheath Park, is no friend of mine, God knows!" Even now, though the truth had been made known to her by Harold himself, Theo could not forget that Mr. Linley had been the first to whisper it, and in her own mind she could not hold him guiltless of the evil.

"Why, he is down at your house constantly!" Sydney cried.

"He is a friend of papa's; I have never seen him since that day we met him first."

"Never seen him? How is that?"

"Because I hate him!" Miss Leigh cried hotly. "There, don't look at me in that way. I wouldn't have said it if you had not suggested the possibility of my mentally comparing any other man with him. I hate him!"

"To whom are you so animatedly declaring hatred?" a voice asked behind her. And looking round Theo saw Mr. Linley standing smiling, with his hat raised in such a way that it concealed the expression of his lips. The two girls were seated on a couch midway up the length of the drawing-room, with their backs to the door by which he had entered unobserved.

"Neither papa nor mamma are at home," Theo commenced hurriedly; she would not give him her hand. And he marked her resolve not to do so in time to avoid offering his own. But he stood close over her, smiling down upon her in a benignant manner, and Theo quailed in her soul at that benign false smile.

"Neither papa nor mamma will be at home till night," she repeated. Then impatience conquered, and she threw down her cards.

"How long have you been in the room? did you hear what we were saying?"

"I heard you say you hated somebody, but whom you did not mention," he replied softly. Theo, looking straight into his eyes, read that he was telling her a falsehood, and feared him.

"You will permit me to await your papa's return?" he asked, presently.

"Certainly, if you wish it; but you will excuse my leaving you!"

"You have a previous engagement? Ah! I am unfortunate!"

She would not tell the story that should render her withdrawal from his presence consistent with civility. She simply repeated that he "must excuse her leaving him." She went away from the room, taking Sydney with her, and feeling that David Linley had heard more than her vague declaration of hatred, and that it was ill for her that he had done so.

CHAPTER XVIII.

A GREAT MISTAKE.

SYDNEY had retired with her friend to the little room that was sacred to the latter, leaving Mr. Linley to the solitary enjoyment of the drawing-room, which was as uncomfortable as all newly-furnished and unfrequently occupied apartments are. This spacious lofty room had been felt from the first to be a white elephant. It was incumbent upon them, since it was bestowed upon them, to furnish it. But they had suffered in spirit while doing so, knowing it to be like the bog of Allen, in that it would swallow up sums that had been long held in reserve for other things.

It was a room, everybody told them, that demanded handsome furniture; they abjectly listened to its demands. Its walls "deserved and required" pictures, being really, as one lady remarked, of "palatial proportions!" Accordingly Mr. Leigh purchased pictures, a set of them at a time. Few people, I imagine, require to be told how thoroughly satisfactory works of art procured in this way are to their possessors.

The pervading tint of the room was green. The carpet was green, and the couches and chairs, and even the curtains. Had Theo been in better heart she would have proposed rose-coloured silk blinds inside those verdant hangings. But she had not been in a state of mind to care about her complexion, or indeed about anything save keeping a brave face before her father and mother.

As to the pictures, too, had things been different within, perhaps she would not have left the selection of them so unreservedly to her papa, who

had taken his orders as to what he should buy and what he should leave meekly from the mouth of a picture-dealer.

"The walls are well covered," David Linley had said to him when he had carried that gentleman to look upon them. And so they were, uncommonly well-covered with frame, quite as much as with paint. You noticed the breadth and the rich gilding of the former before you thought of observing the gentleman in black velvet and melancholy after Velasquez, and blowsy beauties after Titian, the "unmistakable Gainsborough," or the "Lady with a 'awk, confidently attributed to Sir Joshua by the most competent critics." But as this is usual in the case of pictures that are purchased in sets, there is nothing derogatory to Mr. Leigh's taste in it.

As may be gathered, however, the room in which these pictures had the first place was not one in which a man such as David Linley could spend an hour or two of waiting pleasantly. In truth, he spent those hours most impatiently and unpleasantly; sneering to himself at the vulgar art and the prevailing hue, and the rigid propriety that marked the disposition of the furniture. Still he waited on and on—why he hardly knew; feeling resentful against poor miserable Theo for leaving him thus, yet half hoping that she would be forced into his presence again on her father's return. It has been said that he was left alone through the withdrawal of the two girls into the small room that was held sacred to Theo. Sydney had followed her friend with aught but willingness. She had felt that it would be more enlivening to stay and hold polite conversation with the man whose name had called forth such a volume of verbal detestation from Theo. True, he was elderly and ugly, but then he was clever, other people told her; and she heard that his voice could soften seductively, and he had friends who were young and handsome, and honourables, and who wore tenderly-tinted gloves and waistcoats, and drove drags, and were otherwise all that was satisfactory.

Miss Scott remembered that he was all these things clearly and distinctly, but she bore the remembrance passively for a time. At last, however, dullness overcame her, for Theo had subsided into a sad silence—a silence she would not have indulged herself in had her father and mother been by to be distressed by the sight of their darling less bright than of old. Silence being ever a thing that Sydney abhorred, she finally broke it.

"I must have left my gloves in the drawing-room, they're not in these pockets," she exclaimed, suddenly starting up and inserting her hands into both pockets of her jacket, but abstaining from searching the pocket of her dress. "I will go in and look for them. No, don't trouble yourself to send the servant, she wouldn't see them if they were not under her nose; it is time for me now to go home to dinner."

David Linley was leaning against the window, looking out at the river with absorbed attention apparently, for he did not turn his head when the door opened, or give any sign of a consciousness of being no longer alone, until Sydney spoke.

"I have come back to look for my gloves. Oh, here they are."

He turned directly she addressed him, and

smiled sweetly, as those rugged-featured men with deep dark eyes can smile occasionally.

"I am sorry that your gloves were on the surface, for you will be off again at once and leave me to solitude."

He walked towards her as he said it, and stood close to her while she smiled and blushed and accurately fitted on her gloves, buttoning them with deliberation, and wondering if the man who described ladies' hands so frequently and well, marked the size and symmetry of hers.

"You must have found it dull here. Theo is not well—that is, I believe she has a head-ache, and a head-ache makes one an insufferably dull companion, you know; but Mr. Leigh will be home shortly." She looked up into his face quite confidingly as she spoke, and she was very fair.

He took out his watch and looked at it.

"Just two hours I have wasted in waiting," he said. "Well! I certainly have no one to blame for it but myself, for Miss Leigh told me her father would not be home till night. I could have walked to Rockheath Park and back in the time, couldn't I?"

"Couldn't you? Of course you could. Why that day we met you we were not half an hour coming back to the gate."

"The time seemed very short then, but your companionship may have been the cause of its seeming only half an hour. I should have been without that companionship to-day. Besides, I really want to see Leigh, and had I gone over, Mrs. Harold Ffrench would not have let me come away again."

He glanced keenly at the girl as he said the name, but he saw that it told her nothing. "For all that, though," he thought, "the chances are in favor of her going back to Miss Theo, and giving a verbose account of all that I have said, together with much that she thinks I ought to have said, and have no doubt meant. In the course of her communication Mrs. Harold Ffrench's name will turn up, and many speculations as to who she is will be dropped." Then he again uttered a regret aloud that he had not gone over to Rockheath Park.

"The man is bored out of his mind nearly; you might just as well have been in there all this time, Theo," Sydney exclaimed on re-entering the room in which she had left Theo.

"Is he? Have you found your gloves?"

"Yes, here they are; Jouvin's best and quite new, I didn't care to lose them. I was obliged to tell him that you had a head-ache."

"To tell Jouvin?"

"No, but Mr. Linley; he's savage, and no wonder, at being left to his own devices; he says he would have gone over to Rockheath Park to call on Mrs. Harold Ffrench if he hadn't thought your father would have been back before."

Theo had known for some time now that the man whose wife she had thought she herself was to be, had a wife living. But she had never before heard another woman called "Mrs. Harold Ffrench." The sound stabbed her like a knife, but in the midst of her pain she could feel rage at the ingenuity with which Linley had made another use the dagger.

"Did he say that?"

"Yes, and no wonder after your rudeness in leaving him in this way."

"Did he say where Mrs. Harold Ffrench lived?"

"Rockheath Park. Oh! he won't go now, it's too late. Do you know her? Is she a friend of yours?"

"No."

"They are pretty houses over there, and such lovely gardens—oh, lovely! It would be nice to know some one living there. Perhaps Mr. Linley would introduce us to her—introduce you, I mean."

"Perhaps he would do even that," Theo contrived to say firmly. But it was well for her that Sydney took her departure just then, for the thought of Mrs. Harold Ffrench's close vicinity was almost subversive of all self-restraint.

Theo told her father a few days after this that Bretford did not agree with her, and asked him might she go away for a time? It was hard for him to part with the pet, especially since her trouble; still he had longed himself to propose a change of scene and society for her. He had only been withheld from doing so by the consideration that her sensitive spirit would perhaps feel that her own father deemed her under a cloud. However, now that she had proposed going away herself, he acceded to her proposition with pleasure.

"It will do you all the good in the world, and you will be back in time for all the Christmas gaieties; but the question is where will you go, Theo?"

"I have thought of that, papa. Norfolk would be delightful, but I know it so well and I want something new. I will put up a humble petition to Aunt Libby to take me for a while; she's often asked me, you know."

"Your Aunt Libby will be all that is kind, if you can stand her."

"Oh! I can stand her, papa; I can stand anything better than—do you know my reason for wanting to get away?"

She looked at him with her honest grey eyes full of tears, but she was less agitated than he was as he answered:

"Yes, yes, my dear; I understand, I understand. You're a good girl," he continued rapidly, holding her off from him and looking at the workings of the young face that still would not be bowed down. "You're a good girl, and a brave girl, by God! and I—I am a poor old fellow who can't bear it for you as you bear it for yourself, my poor child!"

"Ah! papa, don't, don't; this is the worst of all. One sorrow doesn't crush, dear, any more than one sin precludes all chance of salvation; if once you can feel that I am not all wretched, and that he is not all bad, you will be happier."

But Mr. Leigh would not promise not to think the man whose name he could not bring himself to mention "all bad." For all Theo's pride and spirit, her father knew that she had been most horribly wounded, and he could not bring himself to forgive the one who had wounded her.

The old officer could not believe that there was anything good about the man who could offer them this crowning insult, of suffering his wife to dwell in their vicinity. He never stayed to inquire whether Mrs. Harold Ffrench had been resident in her present abode before they came to Bretford, or whether Harold Ffrench had any influence on his wife's whereabouts or not. All he knew about it he knew from Linley, who had told him that "the poor woman who had married Ffrench—to her cost, he believed—was living in Rockheath Park; bad taste of Ffrench to put her there, considering all things." This was all Mr. Leigh had heard, but it had been enough to make him hate Harold Ffrench with an intensity his hate had been wanting in before.

The Aunt Libby to whom Theo wrote, offering herself as a guest for an indefinite period, was the wife of a clergyman in a midland county. The Reverend Thomas Vaughan, thirty years ago, when fresh from college, had married Elizabeth Leigh, and together they had at once gone to the midland county village in which we shall make their acquaintance.

Previous to her marriage Aunt Libby had resided with her brother (Theo's father), who had remained on half pay for a year or two on purpose that his sister might have the advantage to be derived from a brother's protection. This piece of self-sacrifice on his part she had never forgotten, her "brother was one in a thousand," she always said; "she was indebted to him for everything she enjoyed;"—amongst others for the Rev. Thomas Vaughan. These things considered, it may readily be believed that Aunt Libby's answer to Theo's request was not wanting in the spirit of welcome.

Mrs. Vaughan was glad that her niece was coming to her, very glad for many reasons. She liked acknowledging kindnesses, and she liked patronizing any one who would submit to patronage from her. The kindnesses that she had received from her brother were many, and her hopes of Theo's receiving patronage were high. Altogether she was well pleased at the idea of receiving her young niece as her guest, and the whole village soon knew that she was so.

"She writes very kindly; letter reads as if she meant well; but I should judge that it's rather a risky thing to go and put yourself at the mercy of the writer of it," Sydney Scott remarked to ⬤p, on handing the letter back after a swift perusal. Theo had communicated her intention of going away for a time to her friend, but, as may be supposed, she had withheld her reasons for forming ⬤ intention from Miss Scott.

"What do you mean by that rather disparaging allusion to my aunt, Sydney?"

"Well, I mean just this. She writes in sen—⬤—'everybody does,' you'll say—but everybody doesn't; at least the best sort don't. There's something out and dried, that savours of having been copied many times, about her letter. I'm sure she looked up her thing-um-bob Lindley Murray, Lempriere, and all those old fogies, before she wrote it."

"And if she did?"

"Well, if you can sit and see that sort of thing going on, and keep sane, well and good; but it's always a trial to me to see a common-place letter written with circumspection. I shouldn't say that there was much impulsiveness about that old lady."

"That old lady, as you call her, is a very kind old lady, I'm sure, though I haven't seen her since I was a small child," Theo answered. "Impulsiveness in an old lady generally degenerates into fussiness, and I could better endure over

precision than that. You can't set me against going, Sydney."

"Can't I? Well I'm sorry, for I shall miss you terribly. The fact is I have extolled you so frightfully that I have rendered myself obnoxious to most ⬤ the other girls, and I shall be unfriended, solitary, and slow, while you're away. It's not often I venture upon a quotation," she continued abruptly, "and I don't know what that is from, but it just expresses my position here when you're gone."

"I am glad that you will miss me."

"You selfish thing!"

"But I will write to you."

"No, don't, please," Sydney cried fervently. "If you do I shall have to answer your letters, and if you only knew how I hated writing, you wouldn't try me so far. But I really shall miss you, especially as Hargrave is ordered off next week; troubles never come singly."

"The greater trouble will absorb the lesser: you will forget my loss in Hargrave's."

"Perhaps I shall, and won't it be natural? I'm not a stickler for 'woman's friendship,' or any twaddle of that kind, only you suit me, and I can't help feeling a little sorry to lose you. But of course I am more sorry to lose Hargrave, for he can dance with me, and give me tickets for the quarterly balls at Woolwich, and pay me a great many attentions that you can't. It doesn't do to talk about it. I begin to feel low. Good-by, dear, enjoy your aunt to the utmost, and come back as soon as you can. After all, I almost wish I could go with you."

But Theo could not re-echo that wish just then. Her one desire was to get away from all of the old for a time, in order that she might gather herself together the more staunchly to stand any shocks that were to come. Had Harold Ffrench never spoken those words which he had spoken to her, she would have killed her love. Her pride and her modesty would have forbidden her to suffer it to so obtain in her soul without "sufficient cause." But he had spoken words that made the cause sufficient even in the judgment of those who were unblinded by love for him. She had nourished the feeling tenderly for weeks, checking all doubt of him in her own heart, and all symptoms of suspicion on the part of others. And then love and faith and hope were all torn from the heart in which they had been all too firmly rooted, and the wounds thus made were cruel.

"I hope Theo will come back with a little more colour in her cheeks; I suppose the air is good at Hensley," Mrs. Leigh said, when they were sitting round the uncomfortable early breakfast-table on the morning of Theo's departure. Mrs. Leigh was one of those prudent women who, if travellers were about to leave by an eight-o'clock train, would take care to rouse them up at five in the grey dawn, in order that they might not be hurried. Theo's pallor under the circumstances was not surprising, but she dared not ascribe it to the true cause.

"And mind that you get fat while you're away, Theo," her father chimed in. "And—there it's time to go. I wish you were coming back, my child, instead of going."

"I shall come back in a very different case, papa,—as fat and red as you can desire." Then she went away feeling very sick at heart, and doubtful of the wisdom of the move she was making, with a miserable foreboding that flight from an inward enemy was a futile thing.

The early hours of the journey strengthened this conviction, for she was too weary to make acute observations on the beauty of the country to be reproduced conversationally at some future time. Where are the wonderful ones to be found who do mark the land through which they tear behind an express engine, indeed? Others besides love-sick young ladies are oblivious of the beauties of nature under such conditions, and only anxious to reach their goal.

But about two o'clock she did begin to bestir herself mentally and bodily, to readjust her bonnet strings by aid of a small glass deftly inserted in a fan; to wonder who would meet her at the Hensley Station, and how far the Hensley Station was from the Hensley Vicarage; to collect about her her scattered thoughts and her books and shawls, and to otherwise prepare herself for debarkation. By the time she had done this and disarranged everthing again, and began to wonder if she would reach Hensley by day-light, the train rushed up to a platform that suddenly appeared between the hedges, and the guard shouted out a name that an obliging fellow-passenger immediately translated to her as Hensley.

The air felt bracing, and was bright and clear, and so inspiriting as she stepped out on the platform, and everything around, even the porters, looked clean and fresh. But it was depressing to see nothing but cleanliness and freshness—nothing that could by any stretch of imagination on her part be supposed to be specially expectant of her in this strange place. The station was the reverse of an oasis in the desert: it was a barren little ugly spot in a smiling land—a land of rippling streams and glowing plantations, and orchards in which ruddy pears and yellow bloomy plums hung thickly. But there were no houses near, as far as she could see, therefore the glories of nature were rather overlooked by her as she stood casting anxious glances around, in hopes of discovering a road that looked as if it led to the vicarage.

Before despair could become her portion, a grave-looking groom came round the corner of the station-house, and Theo, infinitely relieved, almost bounded forward to meet him, feeling that help had come in his person.

"You're the young lady for hus?" he interrogated suggestively, and Theo replying at once in the affirmative he signed for a porter "bring along the trunk," and led the way to the back of the station, where a good-looking trap, with a fine bay horse in it, was waiting under the auspices of a small boy. Theo's thought, as she mounted up on the front seat, was,—"How imagination leads one astray; I should never have supposed Uncle Vaughan would have been guilty of such a fast trap, and such a splendid horse. What drives I'll have!"

The grave-looking groom took the reins in his hand and his place by her side, and the small boy released the bay's head, a civility which the bay immediately returned by striking at him with his near fore-leg in a playful manner. Then they went out of the station-yard, past a small

pony carriage, and along a glorious country road, at a pace that made Theo feel there was much in life still.

"I should like to drive that horse; I wonder if I might?" she said at last. The groom vouchsafing no answer to this appeal, she resolved to try command, and teach the aged servitor his proper place.

"Give me the reins. I wish to drive the rest of the way. I will explain to your master that I insisted upon it," she began, holding out her hand for the reins in a way that proved she meant to take them.

"M' lord's very particular about Bay Surrey, Miss." The groom was grave and surly still, but he was civil, only why did he bestow a title upon her uncle. "I suppose he's an abject old servant," she thought; then she asked aloud, "how long she was to keep on straight," and dismissed the subject of the reverential mention of her relative from her mind.

"You must take the first turn to the left, then right up through the park to the 'ouse, Miss," was the answer she received to her inquiry. The vicarage must be a finer place, she thought, than she had imagined, since it stood in a park, and she began to feel impatient to reach it, and so gently indicated the same to Bay Surrey, who met her views magnificently.

The first turning to the left was soon gained. Theo took it cleverly, and drove through handsome lodge gates, along a grand old avenue, up to the entrance door of a house that dispelled all her preconceived notions respecting Aunt Libby, and caused her to exclaim:

"Is *this* the vicarage?"

"Bless yer 'art, no, this is Maddington; didn't you know you was coming here, Miss?"

"Good gracious, there's some mistake!" Theo exclaimed confusedly. Then, to her blank amaze, a lady came along the terrace, which was cut in two by the carriage-drive, and said, pointing to a child who accompanied her:

"My little sister pleaded to come out and welcome you at once, mademoiselle." Then she held out her hand to Theo, who had descend from the trap in a state of bewilderment, added:

"And I hope we shall be able to make you feel at home at Maddington."

"You are very kind, but I am afraid I have been very stupid. I left the Hensley Station under the impression that I was going to my aunt, Mrs. Vaughan."

"Oh, dear! Mrs. Vaughan! This is a joke," the young lady cried. "Then you are the Miss Leigh of whom we have heard, and John has taken you for a French governess we are expecting, who must have gone on—missed the station, and gone on goodness knows where! Poor thing!" she continued, with sudden gravity. "Well, Miss Leigh," she added heartily, "we shall know you a little sooner through this mistake, that is all; I must introduce myself: I am Ethel Burgoyne, Lord Lesborough's second daughter, and this is Maddington, a dear old place, of which I trust you will see a great deal while you're staying at Hensley. Now come in, and let me make you and the mistake known to the rest before Mrs. Vaughan comes to claim you, which she will do only too soon."

"You're very kind," Theo replied promptly;

"do you know, you're so kind that I can't regret the mistake?"

Then she followed the young lady along the terrace, and John did something uncalled for to the bay's bit, and declared that,

"He'd thought, that he had, that if *she* was a furriner, then never tell him nothing about their silly ways again: but this passed him, that it did!"

CHAPTER XIX.

AUNT LIBBY.

MISS ETHEL BURGOYNE led the way into a room whose proportions and polished floor made Theo feel very small and rather awkward on her immediate entrance. Space and a slippery boarding are apt to give one these sensations, when come upon suddenly through an error of judgment such as Theo felt conscious of having committed. She recovered herself immediately, however, and comprehended the apartment and its occupants before they had time to mark either fleeting feeling. The inanimate things shall be described first.

The room into which they had passed through a glass door from the terrace was lofty-arched and groined as to the roof, oak-panelled, and well hung with unmistakeable family portraits as to the walls—spacious and imposing altogether. In the centre of the floor there was a richly-coloured Turkey carpet, but the margin that was left uncovered, of polished oak, would have cut up into a good many moderately sized apartments.

One entire end of the room was occupied by a huge bay window; the broad, deep, solid, carved sill, or seat, as it had been formerly, was now made to serve as a flower-stand. There was such a wealth of flowers upon it! They gave to the room what it would otherwise have lacked—a glow of colour, a fullness of tone, that time-darkened carved oak and time-honoured portraits would have been powerless to effect.

For carved oak was the predominant feature in this room, into which Miss Leigh was led. Carved oak writing-tables and cabinets, carved oak chairs, mantel-piece, and screen. The sole piece of furniture, indeed, that was not of carved oak, was a small modern piano in an unadorned modern oak case.

It was not a dining-room, undoubtedly; nor was it a drawing-room; books were not abundant enough for it to be a library; and the most ignorant in such matters could hardly have fallen into the error of imagining it a boudoir. It had been in truth the chief resort of the family when this old oak was new, and it was the chief resort of the family still, the home-room, the heart of the house. They assembled themselves together in it more constantly and comfortably than in any of the modernised rooms, in the fitting-up of which Jackson and Graham had had a hand.

There was a regular orthodox picture-gallery at Maddington—a picture-gallery that was as badly lighted, as long, as dull, as rigorously correct in all particulars, as the picture-gallery of an old family mansion ought to be. But the best pictures, the most important, interesting, and agreeable-to-look-upon pictures were hung here in the oak-parlour.

For by that simple name they called this big room in which Theo Leigh felt herself to be so very small a thing at first. The wife and daughters of the Sir Hugh Burgoyne who had built the mansion back away in those good old days—those dark ages when the Lancastrian Queen was striving to regain the rights her weakly lord had lost—the wife and daughters of the man who was then causing their name to sound in the land had sat in this room weaving silken standards, and had called it the oak-parlour on account of its panelled walls. At a later date, when the knight's descendants had been Lord Viscounts for some goodly period of years, at a date when Addison wrote, and Steele drank, and Marlborough fought for the queen, and the queen quarrelled with Marlborough's wife—at a date when oak-carvings disputed public favour with pug-dogs, the room was furnished anew after the grand substantial fashion of the day, and became more emphatically the oak-parlour than before.

Prominent among the great array of pictures that were on the wall facing the three windows which opened on to the terrace, there hung one that was at once Lord Leaborough's glory and grief. It was that portrait of Charles the First coming out of a wood on a white charger of which Vandyck painted three duplicates. Lord Leaborough's glory was that this was one of the great master's works.. His grief was that friends and enemies alike were unanimous in declaring it to be but a copy, "though a very good one," they inhumanly added, of the exquisite original. The picture was dear to his heart, but, like many well-beloved objects, it was a great trial to his temper. Friendship is ever apt to point out to us with more pertinacity than pleasantness that what we prize as real is but a base counterfeit.

By the side of the mounted melancholy monarch there hung a full-length of his pet courtier, Villiers, in black velvet, and majesty such as even Charles himself did not possess. As a pendant to this there was a portrait of a long dead and gone Burgoyne, a tall, handsome, blonde-haired, bright-visaged young cavalier, whose presentment on canvas arrested Theo's attention, and then enchained it, much as he himself had been wont to arrest and enchain the eyes of all women who looked upon him when he was in the flesh. From the moment her looks fell upon him, Theo glanced no further afield over the well-adorned oak-panelled walls. She could only gaze at the prototype, and feel a faint pity that so fair a thing as this blue-eyed cavalier should have mouldered into dust generations before she was born.

Miss Ethel Burgoyne had taken Theo Leigh into the room, introduced her to Lord Leaborough, "my father," and Miss Burgoyne, "my sister," and planted her on a couch opposite to these three pictures with a quiet celerity that set Theo completely at her ease, through proving to her that Miss Ethel Burgoyne at any rate saw nothing awkward or out of the way in the mistake that she (Theo) had made.

"John made a mistake at the station, and brought away the wrong young lady," Miss Ethel said, when she had mentioned Theo's name to her father and sister. "Poor Mrs. Vaughan will be in despair; I think we ought to send down to the vicarage and relieve her anxiety."

"I think I ought to go to my aunt and explain to her how I came to be so stupid," Theo suggested. Then she mentioned having passed a pony-carriage by the station as she came along in the dog-cart, and the two Miss Burgoynes exclaimed that "it was Mrs. Vaughan's probably."

"Do you know—ah! but I know that you are nearly a stranger to your aunt, Miss Leigh," Miss Burgoyne said, when Theo again proposed going with her explanation in person.

"She is a stranger to me; I was a child when I saw her last," Theo replied.

"Now we know her very well, very intimately indeed," the elder Miss Burgoyne went on earnestly. "Ethel, shall we take Miss Leigh over to the vicarage, and explain the reason of her not being there before to Mrs. Vaughan?"

"I don't see the necessity of our hurrying Miss Leigh away in that manner, Grace," Theo's first acquaintance rejoined, and a faint blush overspread her face as she spoke. "Mrs. Vaughan is sure to drive over here from the station; if she finds that we have already draughted Miss Leigh on to the vicarage she will think the very thing you want to prevent her thinking."

Miss Burgoyne seated herself again in the chair from which she had risen on Theo's entrance. She was a tall, fair, placid-faced woman of thirty-four or five, composed and matronly in her bearing; so composed and matronly, indeed, that she might well have passed for the mother of the younger lady who had gone out on the terrace to welcome Theo. Miss Burgoyne smiled very softly and sweetly on Theo as she reseated herself, and held out her hand to the interloper in a way that bound her to the house of Burgoyne forever.

"Then you must be kind enough to feel quite happy and comfortable with us till such time as your aunt comes to claim you, dear Miss Leigh; my sister is right, I think after all: Mrs. Vaughan is apt to be a little nervous."

"Do you mean a little fidgetty?" Theo asked; she liked these Burgoynes, and was in no particular hurry for her aunt's arrival.

"You must try not to think her so, for she is a dear good woman," Miss Burgoyne replied.

"But she has her foibles, dear old lady," Ethel whispered. Then Lord Lesborough, a fine old gentleman with a great expanse of buff waistcoat and bald head, said he thought he heard the pony-carriage coming up the drive. So forthwith they went out in a body to meet Mrs. Vaughan, and explain to her the reason of her having had her journey to the railway station for nothing—or worse.

It was the pony-carriage that they had heard, and in it was Mrs. Vaughan, the "Aunt Libby," whose name was so familiar and whose *personnel* was so strange to Theo. Directly Theo saw her aunt she appreciated the Burgoynes' motive for desiring to assist at the explanatory meeting between herself and her relative.

"Aunt Libby is a pretty old lady," was Theo Leigh's first thought; "Mrs. Vaughan is fussy," was her second, and when she thought this she

involuntarily threw off a little of the deprecating manner she had been preparing, and stood rather more on the defensive than she had been purposing to do a minute before.

Mrs. Vaughan got out of the pony-carriage and came towards them rapidly, speaking words that were evidently words of reprobation and excuse. The reprobation was to Theo, and Theo (she had ever been a petted child, remember) felt sorely inclined to resent it.

Mrs. Vaughan was warm and excited, therefore, pretty old lady as she undoubtedly was, she looked and felt somewhat at a disadvantage as she came up to the cool composed group who were awaiting her. She was a fair, florid, hazel-eyed and haired old lady, possessed even now at sixty-eight of a neat trim plump figure, and a "well-defined waist." Her glance was quick and keen, her bonnet was gaily trimmed and badly tied, her shawl was expensive, but ungracefully adjusted. Now, none of these things are pleasant to contemplate in the stranger with whom we are bound to sojourn for a period. But none of these sights would have caused Theo a moment's regret had she not observed that Mrs. Vaughan smiled vividly with her thin cleanly-cut lips, the while her eyes were darting unmistakeable sparks of anger.

"My dear Miss Burgoyne," she began, "it's a thing that I wouldn't have had happen for the world." Then she shook hands warmly with the two Miss Burgoynes, and gave the tips of some badly gloved fingers to Theo the offender.

"But we are very glad that it has happened," Miss Burgoyne replied; "your niece has been kind enough to overlook poor John's stupidity; you must do so also, Mrs. Vaughan."

"Ah, my dear, it's not John's stupidity," Mrs. Vaughan replied, with vicious emphasis. Then she clutched her shawl more firmly around her, settled her bonnet afresh vengefully on her head, and endeavoured to smile refulgently upon the Burgoynes and glare wrathfully at Theo at one and the same moment.

"I shall very soon go back to Bretford," Theo thought. The wrathful glare aggravated her; she was quite ready and willing to render unto Cæsar the things that were Cæsar's, in so far as giving honour where honour was due went. Still, she could not feel abjectly remorseful on the subject of the unintentional raid upon the Burgoynes, or her Aunt Libby's vain drive to the railway station.

"We will come over, or at all events I will come over to-morrow to see how you are getting on," Miss Ethel whispered to Theo, as the latter in obedience to rather peremptory orders, strove to adjust herself in Mrs. Vaughan's pony-carriage, when Mrs. Vaughan proposed departing.

"I don't think I shall get on too well," Theo replied: "I have been made to feel such a pitiful offender already, though she has scarcely spoken to me, that I never shall like being with her."

"Try not to mind her weaknesses," Miss Ethel said, with the bravery that is so easy and so customary when the weaknesses in question do not immediately affect the speaker. "She's a dear good woman, as I told you just now, and I should like you to stay at Hensley for some time."

Lord Lesborough's second daughter shook hands very warmly with Theo as she said this, and looked strangely like that blonde-haired, bright-visaged, blue-eyed, young cavalier who had enchained Theo's attention when she first entered the oak-parlour. It was a glorious beauty, truly, and Theo felt it to be so. "Ah, how handsome a living man would be like it," she thought; "it's too bold and bright for a woman that something she has in common with the picture." Then she had to bring her thoughts back to the passing scene ● Lord Lesborough and his eldest daughter came up to say "Good-by" to her, and hope they should see her again.

Mrs. Vaughan maintained an austere silence towards her niece until they were clear of the Maddington grounds and the Burgoyne influence, and she then gave her feelings voice.

"What must they have thought of you for being so awkward, Theo? I am very sorry that the first member of my family that they have seen should have impressed his lordship and the young ladies so unfavorably."

It was a way of mentioning them that caused Theo's blood to run cold, a style of designation that bordered upon the servile, she thought, and that might more fittingly fall from the lips of her maid than her aunt.

"The Miss Burgoynes didn't seem to be unfavourably impressed with me, aunt; don't meet troubles half way."

Theo leant back in the little pony-carriage as she spoke, and strove to render herself comfortable by drawing the wrap-shawl, which they had spread over their knees, around her more closely. Mrs. Vaughan marked the movement and resented the motive. She objected to the one with whom she was ill-pleased striving to attain bodily ease.

"I must say," she observed, viciously whipping up her fat pony as she spoke, "that you take things very coolly, and with considerably more unconcern than is becoming, my dear."

"What things, aunt?"

"Things that vitally concern our interests," Mrs. Vaughan snapped out suddenly.

"Good gracious, aunt! what?" Theo cried, starting erect in an instant; "what have I done? what do you mean? Endangered your interests! how!"

"Lord Lesborough and the Honourable Miss Burgoynes—the *Misses* Burgoyne I should say—are not likely to think the more highly of your uncle, the Reverend Thomas Vaughan, and myself, from seeing how utterly unaccustomed a member of my family is to the usages of good society."

"Oh!" Theo said wearily; "is that all, then?"

"That all indeed! quite enough, I'm sure. To think," Mrs. Vaughan continued, lapsing into a lachrymose tone, "that you should have marred by your own stupidity and ignorance the fine prospect I had opened for you. Ah! it's too vexatious!"

"But after all, aunt, it was a venial offence that I committed. I was very tired; oh! I *am* so tired; and I was glad to meet anyone who seemed to be there to meet me. The Miss Burgoynes were so kind, they quite understood how it happened."

"The mistake was not so bad as the way you acted after it was made, child; you should with 'umble dignity have refused to intrude yourself upon them. 'You do me too much honour, Miss Burgoyne,' you should have said, 'but I think that I had better instantly return to my aunt, Mrs. Vaughan, who is doubtless awaiting me at the railway station. I will not intrude myself upon you,' that's what you should have said. 'Intrude myself upon you,' that would have looked pretty and modest, and have shown them that you knew your own place and theirs. As it is—why, mercy on us, child, what's the matter?"

Theo had been engaged in a sharp mental battle for many weeks; she had been wounded in it, though not worsted in one sense. Still, though not worsted, she was terribly weakened. Added to this she had been further enfeebled by a long, tedious, trying journey, and the sense of having made a mistake that was awkward, though nothing more. These things combined to render her less self-possessed than usual. In combating an inclination to laugh during Aunt Libby's delivery of the speech that she could have wished her niece to have made to the Miss Burgoynes, Theo went to the other extreme and began to cry.

"I'm very tired, and I haven't been well for weeks, Aunt Libby; that's all, indeed that's all" (she strove to explain things as agreeably as possible). I don't mind a word that you have said. Really not a word. I daresay," she continued, trying to clear up, "that I shall be all right when I have had some dinner."

"You require a little camphor on sugar, more than dinner, I'm thinking, child," Mrs. Vaughan replied meditatively, as she turned into the vicarage garden, "or a little red lavender would be better still, perhaps. We shall have dinner at five o'clock, I wouldn't advise your having anything before it; not that I grudge it, of course, but I should like to spare you indigestion the first day you're here."

"Five o'clock will be quite soon enough, Aunt Libby. Shall I see Mr. Vaughan before dinner?"

"My dear—I must tell you, excuse me, since you don't seem to know—it's not the custom for young persons to tell their entertainers that the dinner-hour is 'quite soon enough,' or anything else; you don't know, so I will tell you, and you mustn't be hurt, for I tell you for your own good. As to when you'll see Mr. Vaughan, I can't say; it's prettier for young people to hold themselves in readiness to wait upon their elders and superiors, than to try to make off-handed appointments with them."

CHAPTER XX.

MRS. VAUGHAN ON ETIQUETTE.

THE plump pony was pulled up at the door of the vicarage as Mrs. Vaughan brought her homily to a close. Theo tried to step out of the little carriage and into the house with the light unembarrassed air which is popularly supposed to indicate a bright unembarrassed heart and spirit. But she was weary in body as well as in mind, therefore she failed in conveying to be-holders the desired impression.

The brief lecture to which Mrs. Vaughan had treated her had been depressing in its influence. Youth is ever apt to regard with jealous eyes any proposed amendment of its manners at the hands of one whose own manners do not strike youth as being of a particularly high order. Theo had already discovered a lack of self-possession and calm about Mrs. Vaughan. She distrusted the instructive capabilities of that breeding which broke down on so small an emergency as that of this morning.

She was ushered up-stairs to her own room by a bland middle-aged woman with a soft mellow voice and a soothing manner. The sort of voice and manner, in fact, that must be invaluable in attendants on lunatics, but that is rather aggravating when brought to bear upon the sane.

"Now, missy dear, whenever you feel to want anything, ask me for it, and don't go troubling our missus," she said, when she had drawn up the blind and relieved Theo of her bonnet.

"Whenever I want anything I will ask for it, thank you," Theo replied, in the bravery of ignorance. "Would you be good enough to open the window a little?"

"To be sure, missy; young people like a little fresh air, as I said to missus when I was getting the room ready this morning. My name is Ann, miss, and I have lived here, girl and woman, nigh upon twenty years. Girl *and* woman!"

Ann's voice was very mellow when she said this, and her manner was very soothing; but Theo felt tired and sick at heart; she could not cultivate the qualities Ann was palpably ready to develop just now.

"Oh! indeed; twenty years: that's a long time; a very long time," she added, with sudden emphasis, as she remembered that just so many years had she herself lived in the world.

"Yes, missy, for twenty years, and much I have seen in that time of missus's little ways, as we may call them; she's very kind at heart, but she don't seem so always, and when she don't seem so in some little matters that I can alter, you just tell me, and I will alter them."

The woman went out of the room when she had said that, and Theo thought, "Aunt Libby can neither beat me nor starve me, and in any other case Ann will be unavailing, I should imagine." Then she dressed herself for the five-o'clock dinner in a plain high silk, and wandered forth in search of the drawing-room.

She found it down on the left-hand side of the hall door; a pretty room, with a French window at the end, which opened on to a garden, which imperceptibly merged into the churchyard. "I should like it better if the graves were not so visible," she thought, as she walked to the window and looked out; "but I shall get used to the ghoulish view in time, I suppose; I have got used to worse things than that." Her thoughts always went back to her trouble; she compared every possible grief or annoyance with the mighty one that overshadowed this portion of her life. It really was terribly depressing to find herself fixed for a time in a place and amongst people that promised to be so utterly unsympathetic. But the other day such a different, such a brilliant prospect had loomed before her! But the "other day!"

Soon her uncle—the Reverend Thomas himself—came into the room, and made her welcome with a certain austerity of manner that was strangely at variance with his rotund little person and rosy little face. Then, before she had well had time to realise that the austerity was a mere futile effort after dignity, Mrs. Vaughan joined them, and speedily again Theo wished herself back at Bretford.

"My dear," Mrs. Vaughan began, "I think it only right to tell you that it is not the custom for young people to run at large over a house directly they arrive at it. You don't know any better, therefore I must tell you; you should have waited in your bed-room till I could send Ann to tell you that dinner was ready."

Theo blushed scarlet: few girls of twenty are strong-minded enough to retain possession of their faculties when accused of a breach of etiquette. For a few moments she almost believed she had grossly blundered, and though unprepared to go to the extreme length of declaring "a blunder to be worse than a crime," the dread that she had committed the former was overwhelming. At the end of a few moments reason resumed its sway, and Miss Leigh felt that it was her aunt who had blundered, and not herself.

"I am very sorry, Aunt Libby, that I should have trangressed your rules so soon."

"They are not my rules, my dear: they're the rules of society; I should be sorry for you to betray any ignorance of the sort if Miss Burgoyne should be kind enough after what has happened to invite you to Maddington."

"I will try not to behave like a savage, aunt," Theo replied, with a small laugh. Then Mr. Vaughan had an access of curiosity, and inquired "what had happened?" And Theo had the satisfaction of listening to a slightly distorted version of the affair before a melancholy man in drab came to tell them that dinner was served.

Mr. Vaughan reserved judgment until he was safely ensconced in his proper place at the dinner-table; he then gave it forth, tremulously it must be owned, but it was given nevertheless.

"If his lordship and the Honourable Miss Burgoynes can overlook your niece's little—little error, my dear, I think we, you I mean, may do so also. Pray allow me to send you some soup?"

The offer of soup was made to Theo, whose little error had not at all impaired her appetite. She was young, and hungry, and the soup gave forth savoury odours, and looked of a peculiarly appetising clear brown as it streamed from the ladle. But before she could reply to the offer of it Mrs. Vaughan intervened.

"After such a long journey and no luncheon Theo ought to begin upon something substantial; that soup would be sure to give her indigestion. No, my dear, I won't have you take any; it's my duty to see that you don't ruin your constitution while you're staying here. You shall have some nice plain beef, roast beef, not too much done, and nothing else, not a thing else. I should say by your looks that you're let eat anything unwholesome you please at home."

"Well, Aunt Libby, certainly I am not dieted," Theo replied.

"No, I believe it; your poor dear mother was a very weak girl, so I never expected to hear that she had turned into a strong-minded woman."

"My mother's mind and heart are strong enough to have won me to love her too well to sit and listen to a word in disparagement of her," Theo said, colouring brightly.

"My dear, such a display of temper is very ill-bred," Mrs. Vaughan replied gravely; "or perhaps you're a little nervous and upset after your journey. Well, you shall have a glass of wine, or half a glass of wine; the merest drop, Mr. Vaughan? Do you hear? the merest drop?"

So Theo had the merest drop, with some very under-done beef and a scanty supply of vegetables, "they being bad for her complexion," Aunt Libby affirmed. Mrs. Vaughan then proceeded to remark that she couldn't imagine where Theo had got her complexion. "It's worse than any member of my family ever had before, my dear. Not that it's your fault, I don't say that it is; but it's a great misfortune for you, a very great misfortune indeed; but no wonder, if at your age you're accustomed to eat when and how and what you like. Mr. Vaughan can tell you that when I married him I was like a rose, a blush rose."

"Precisely like a blush rose," Mr. Vaughan struck in promptly.

"Well, Aunt Libby, I feel properly penitent about my complexion, but it's an evil of long standing, you see: I have been brown all my life. May I have a glass of ale, please? I don't care for wine. You're not shocked, I hope?"

"Not shocked, but disgusted," Mrs. Vaughan replied. "No, Theo; ale is not a beverage" (Mrs. Vaughan called it "beveridge" in her emotion) "for young ladies; no! no pudding for Miss Leigh, Thomas, bring it to me. I am sure," she continued, in a semi-apologetic tone to Theo, "that you wouldn't go eating any nasty sweets after your long fast, my dear."

"No nasty sweets, but that appears to be a very nice sweet, Aunt Libby."

"Too rich—far too rich——"

"For the stomach of youth," Mr. Vaughan put in blithely. Then on his wife looking round to give some directions to Thomas, Mr. Vaughan nodded and winked at Theo, and made signs expressive of "something," but what she could not imagine. On Mrs. Vaughan's facing the table again he lapsed into rosy absorption in his own pudding, leaving Theo with the impression that he was a little mad and very cunning.

When the dinner, of which Theo's share had been such a frugal one, was over, Mrs. Vaughan sent Thomas to lock the drawing-room door, and told Theo that she might amuse herself with a book of engravings which she would find in the sideboard drawer.

"We don't sit in the drawing-room when we are alone, my dear," she explained; "it would be wearing out the furniture for nothing. Your uncle will go to his study till tea is ready, and we'll sit here."

"I don't care much for shadowy views of places, Aunt Libby. May I go and get a book from the study?" Theo asked. The prospect was dull that Mrs. Vaughan had held out to her, of sitting there with a book of engravings before her till tea was ready.

"A book! what for, child?"

"To read."

Mrs. Vaughan had been reclining in rather an inert manner in a stout easy-chair before this; she now sprang into animation and an erect posture.

"To read! really, child, it was time for you to come here and be taught the rudiments of manners. Your poor dear father, what can he have been about to suffer you to acquire such ill-bred habits? My dear, it's not the custom for young people to take up books and read when they are staying away from home on a visit; it's considered much prettier of them to sit and talk to their hostess, if she feels inclined to talk; it looks selfish and thoughtless to take up a book and read; you will have many hours to yourself while I am otherwise engaged, then you can retire to your bed-room and read. But when I am here to be talked to, it is your place to talk to me."

"Aunt Libby has her idiosyncrasies, and no mistake," Theo thought, but she was resolved to bear them amiably as long as might be.

"I will just go and get some work, Aunt Libby, and then I shall be able to talk as long and as much as you like."

"Work! like a milliner girl running away for your work directly after dinner," Mrs. Vaughan replied testily, resettling herself in her chair. "I do hope you will learn to be calm before you leave me, Theo, for this restless desire to be doing something betrays that you are accustomed to very inferior society, very inferior indeed. I don't know what the Miss Burgoynes will think of you."

Shortly after this Mrs. Vaughan went to sleep, and Theo sat in the dimly-lighted room with the volume of shadowy engravings before her in a state of semi-despair. "This evening can't last for ever," she kept on thinking, "and to-morrow must be better. I am beginning to hate those eternal Burgoynes."

The late autumn, or rather the early winter, wind went whistling shrilly round the house, and not a sound within the walls interrupted the sorrowful tale the wind told to Theo of coldness, blankness, and nothing better to come. She sat near the window looking out into the garden and graveyard beyond, wondering whether anything bright had ever been seen from that window, whether anyone bright had ever looked forth from it, whether it was always chilly, nipping, early winter socially at Hensley; whether it was imagination which showed her two figures coming along through the tombs towards the house, or whether her vision was to be relied upon.

They came on out of range of her sight, and presently a sharp decided ring at the hall bell proved to her that they had been realities, and that a break was about to occur in this monotony, which was becoming unbearable. Then before she had quite collected her wandering tired faculties, they came in; and "they" were Miss Ethel Burgoyne and the blond-haired, bright-visaged, blue-eyed, young cavalier whose portrait had arrested her in the morning.

5

Had the portrait come out of its frame and changed its garb for the express purpose of mystifying her? or was he a real being, only like unto the pictured one, whose mouldering into dust before her advent she had so poignantly regretted? The dullness of mind and the dimness of light which had been her portion for the last two hours caused her thus to question for a few moments. At the end of them she realised that he was no galvanized Vandyck, but a young English gentleman of the present day, the modern school, and very pleasant to behold.

"Frank has come——" Miss Ethel Burgoyne began.

"To lighten your darkness, my dear Mrs. Vaughan; you're the first person I always look up when I come to Maddington," he interrupted, passing along hastily from the side of the lady he had been escorting to that of the partially awakened and totally bewildered Mrs. Vaughan.

"You always were a most attentive, dear boy," the old lady replied heartily, grasping both the hands he extended to her, in amiable obliviousness of its being the first time he ever had displayed the engaging promptitude he professed. "What a pleasure to see you: that's my niece, quite a child she is, oh, *quite* a child; tell you about her directly," she continued, nodding at him, and blinking at Theo, who disregarded the blinks in consequence of the rapt regard the young, fair, bright, bold beauty of this man won from her.

He had half turned round to look at Theo when her aunt offered him the hazy introduction, and as he stood, one hand still held by Mrs. Vaughan, the other planted on his hip, he made a finer picture than the one that had held Theo's gaze in the morning. He was rather a tall man, and so he had bent his head slightly when he had turned to look on Theo's face—bent his head to an altitude that made his glance at her a level one, that caused it to appear far far more earnest than if he had simply turned and looked as any other man would have done, she thought.

"Frank is my nephew, Miss Leigh; don't you think we're like?" Ethel Burgoyne asked aloud of Theo; and when the young aunt asked this, the younger nephew threw his head up and laughed, and looked strikingly like her at once.

"He is now, he was not a minute ago," Theo replied.

"The seriousness of a minute ago was an unprecedented thing; it's Frank's normal condition to be volatile, as you will find when you know him better."

"When I know him better," Theo repeated vaguely.

"Yes, as you will, of course; you're half asleep, poor child, after your journey; come out in the garden for a turn or two; I know every bit of rock-work and every flower-bed, so you need not fear that we'll be detrimental to your plants, Mrs. Vaughan, in the darkness. Come, Miss Leigh, we will leave Frank with his old friend, and I will take you for a freshening walk, and instruct you as to the importance of the personage who has had the power to bring me over from Maddington at this hour of the night."

Miss Ethel laid her hand on Theo's arm as she spoke, and Theo followed her to the door, and then cast a glance back towards the man they were leaving.

"He's not like you again now," she whispered hurriedly. He had lowered his head again, and was looking straight at her with the level earnest gaze that betokens intense interest and a determination to read all that may be read of the soul of the scanned.

"I am thinking that you two young ladies ought not to be suffered to go out in that goblin garden alone," he said, with a rapid change of expression.

"Come to us presently then, Frank; keep him for ten minutes, Mrs. Vaughan, and then send him in search of us. He does not want to come with us in reality, his great anxiety was to come over here to you," Ethel Burgoyne replied; and then she went with Theo from the room, leaving him with Mrs. Vaughan.

How it had been done, whether his eyes had questioned it, or his lips, Theo could not tell, but she was conscious of this, that when Miss Ethel had asserted that his great anxiety had been to see Mrs. Vaughan, Mr. Frank had telegraphed to her (Theo) an inquiry as to her belief in the truth of this statement, and she, against her will, had transmitted a doubt of it back to him. There was an understanding between them from that moment, she felt—one that might be neither honourable, pleasureable, nor advantageous to her, but that was an understanding nevertheless.

"My nephew is Frank by name and by nature too," Miss Ethel Burgoyne said, when they were outside the hall-door. "Isn't it pleasant out here? Chilly, but nice? Papa and Grace thought me mad when I agreed to come over from Maddington with Frank after dark; he arrived quite unexpectedly, dear boy, and insisted on coming over before he slept to see his 'old friend,' as he called her."

"Frank by nature, is he?—I mean is he an old friend? Is he fond of Aunt Libby?"

"I didn't know that he was till to-night, but it seems that he is, very."

"He is your nephew, did you say?"

"Yes, my only brother's only son; my poor brother died when Frank and I were children, and we've all done our best to spoil him ever since. He's such a darling fellow."

They had sauntered out of the garden away into the graveyard, and now, when she said this, they ceased their sauntering and sat down on a flat tomb-stone, and the early winter wind went by them shrilly.

"How much he is like that portrait that hangs on the left of the white horse," Theo observed in a low tone; then she sank her voice to a still fainter whisper and went on, "Do you know when you came into the room to-night I thought he was something unnatural, I did indeed; don't mind my saying so; I felt that I had seen him before and yet hadn't seen him before, and known him without having known him."

"It was seeing the portrait," Ethel Burgoyne answered aloud and cheerily. "We don't like papa keeping it in that room at all, because it's useless to deny that it *is* unhappily like Frank."

"Why unhappily like him?"

"Because he was such a bad fellow, so utterly unlike Frank in character, as unlike him morally in fact as he is like him personally. He was called 'the bad Burgoyne,' and he was hung in the darkest end of the gallery till Frank grew up like him, then papa had him brought down in order that Frank might not have a chance of forgetting that his great personal attractions couldn't save him from being utterly despicable."

"Does Frank need such a reminder?"

"Well, papa thinks that he does, which amounts to nearly the same thing. Papa distrusts him partly on account of the resemblance to that Hugo Burgoyne, and partly because he never liked Frank's mother. Papa has made what we think the mistake of always trying to keep Frank straight by threats, for though the title must be Frank's eventually, and a good portion of the property, still the major portion of it is not entailed, and if Frank offended papa he would leave it to his immaculate pet, Harold Ffrench, on conditions."

So she heard his name again!—heard his name and a doubt cast upon his being "immaculate," as she would have had her lover supposed at one and the same time.

Theo did not answer when her new acquaintance brought her speech to a close. The girl could not have spoken without betraying more anxiety than might be compatible with those "conditions," which must be fulfilled in order to ensure Harold's succession to that which Frank Burgoyne might possible forfeit. She could not have spoken with the coolness that might be essential to the well-being of the career of the man who had wronged her. Wronged her unintentionally and to his own lasting sorrow, she firmly believed, but wronged her nevertheless. Therefore, though she longed to question and to hear, she held her peace, and trusted that the friendly darkness concealed her emotion from Ethel Burgoyne.

"We—Grace and I—are always in a state of anxiety while Frank is here, dearly fond of him as we are," Ethel went on, after a short pause. "I ought not to mention such things to a stranger, I suppose, and yet after all I don't know why I shouldn't, for they are unimportant."

"What are unimportant?—your anxieties?" Theo asked.

"Yes; our anxieties and their causes are unimportant in reality; we have no reason to fear that Frank will ever go wrong with papa; still, such a little thing would put him wrong, that we do fear it. I always hate Harold Ffrench when I think of it."

"Who speaks of the bogie of my boyhood?" a voice from behind cried brightly, and the next instant Frank himself, the subject of their conversation, stood by Theo's side, and made as though he would have seated himself there had Theo given a movement of encouragement.

"I was speaking of Harold Ffrench," Ethel replied, rather sharply. She was annoyed with her pet for having stolen up to them thus quietly, while she was on the subject of his grievances.

"What were you saying about him Ethel? Do you know anything of him, Miss Leigh?"

He seated himself by her side as he asked it, seated himself there, though never a bit of the encouragement for the lack of which he had at first hesitated was given him; his eyes questioning her, she could see this by the moonlight, even more closely than they had done in the room.

"Yes, and you know I do," she answered suddenly; she felt convinced of this, and she could not resist giving voice to the conviction, injudicious as she felt herself to be.

"Oh! I didn't know that he was a friend of yours," Ethel said, rising as she spoke, "or perhaps I would have held my tongue about him; and yet I don't know either that I should have been so discreet. Come, let us stroll on, I'm cold."

Ethel's speech had saved Frank the necessity of replying to Theo's assertion of his knowledge of her knowing Harold Ffrench. He waited, listening attentively to what Ethel was saying, until she had concluded, then he glided into the conversation again.

"Has Ethel been telling you that he, your friend Mr. Ffrench, has been used 'to keep the beast in awe,' I being the beast in question."

"I have been telling Miss Leigh that Harold Ffrench is a great pet of papa's, who absurdly enough believes him to be immaculate," Ethel rejoined hurriedly. She had no desire for Frank to become acquainted with the full extent of the confidence she had placed in Theo; "darling fellow" as Frank was in her estimation, she knew that he was apt to cloud over at the free mention of family matters when he had not the sole mentioning of them.

"Oh, indeed; was that all?" he said. He was far too well-bred to probe an unpleasant subject when he had nothing to gain by it, and in this case, nothing could be gained, save the pleasure of putting his usually self-possessed Aunt Ethel to confusion. He reflected that "Ethel always stood by him, and most likely always would do so," therefore he spared her.

"Oh! indeed; was that all? Well, Miss Leigh, you know more of him than we do probably; is he all that my respected grandpapa believes him to be? or can we prove him a defaulter in honour, and so leave Lord Lesborough nothing to love and lean upon, and leave his all to, but my worthy self?"

"No one could prove him a defaulter in honour, however intimately he was known," Theo said quickly. But though she spoke promptly and firmly in her defence of the loved and lost, she felt that she was wincing under the interrogatory gaze of the man who had forced her to speak.

"If you say that, Miss Leigh, I shall feel bound to believe in him for the future; ladies generally have good grounds for what they say about such a handsome man as Harold Ffrench," Ethel said, with a laugh.

"I dare say Miss Leigh has good grounds, Ethel; you must not imagine every one as frivolous and easily blinded by appearances as you are yourself," Frank replied, with a mock gravity that was amusing to Ethel and irritating to Theo. "I have not the slightest doubt that Miss Leigh speaks with understanding."

He looked very tenderly down at Theo as he said it, and there was a most sympathetic inflection in his voice. But then Theo remembered that men are tender and sympathetic occasionally without sufficient cause; and so she strove to stifle the conviction that he knew her story. "He *can't* know about Harold and me," she kept on saying to herself; "who could know it, excepting a few people at Bretford? It is only his way to say things as if he meant something more than is said."

"I speak with the usual amount of understanding, I suppose," she said, trying to speak carelessly. "Mr. Ffrench would always have my suffrages, because he looks as if he deserved them. I believe in the jewel having a fair casket; I should have lost Portia, and chosen the wrong box, I am persuaded, if I had been Bassanio."

"So should I, I think," he replied, laughing; "but I should have chosen the gold, hoping to avoid her. I should have felt convinced that such a strong-minded woman as Portia would eschew baubles, and encase her counterfeit in lead; and as I have no fancy for being special-pleaded out of my mind, I should have avoided her."

"And lost the fortune! No, I don't think you would have done that, Mr. Burgoyne," Theo said, as they paused at the hall-door. "Won't you come in again? do."

"You don't give me credit for magnanimously throwing away a chance; well, Miss Leigh, I am not guilty of such weakness often, I assure you. No, Ethel, we won't go in to-night—it's too late; I will come and make my apologies to Mrs. Vaughan for not saying adieu to-morrow morning."

Then he took Theo's hand and pressed it gently, and told her that he looked forward to meeting her on the morrow, as perhaps they "might find out that they had some more mutual friends."

When Ethel Burgoyne and her handsome young nephew turned and departed, Theo went in slowly and unwillingly, for she wanted to think about many things, and thought and Mrs. Vaughan's presence were not wont to agree. She found her aunt sitting erect, brightly expectant, and wide awake, and her uncle looking rosily resigned to the animated state of affairs at this late hour, just opposite to her.

"Why! where are they?" Mrs. Vaughan asked hurriedly.

"Gone home: they thought it too late to come in," Theo replied: then she thought of a sop for Cerberus, and added, "but Mr. Burgoyne is coming to see you to-morrow morning, Aunt Libby."

"Now look here," Mrs. Vaughan said solemnly. "I have had the candles lighted in the silver candlesticks instead of burning the lamp for your sake, Theo, for *your* sake, my child—it's such a much more becoming light. We'll put them out now, and go to bed, so that you may have some beauty-sleep, and get up looking fresh in the morning. Control your inclination to be pert, and keep very quiet; dashing men like Mr. Burgoyne like that, and who knows what may happen. Lord Lesborough doesn't want his grandson and heir to marry money. Good night, my dear."

"Good night, aunt," Theo replied, just touching her own cheek against the one Mrs. Vaughan presented to her for a kiss. Then she went swiftly up-stairs to her own room, angrily repeat-

ing "dashing men," "who knows what may happen." "What horrible phrases! To use them to *me* too, to *me!*"

"Frank, dear," Ethel Burgoyne said fondly to her nephew, as they walked briskly along through the park, "I wish you would make up your mind to marry, we should be so much happier about you, and papa would be so much better satisfied about you?"

"I don't think he wants to be well satisfied about me, Ethel."

"Ah! you wrong him there, you do indeed. I am on your side, you know; still, now you are unjust to papa."

"Besides, I haven't seen the woman yet who can take and hold me, Ethel: I find them out too soon, and then they become uninteresting."

CHAPTER XXI.

POOR FRANK.

"THE best plan will be to keep Frank out of papa's way as much as possible," Ethel thought the next morning, as she stood fastening her cuffs at her dressing-room window, preparatory to going down to breakfast. She had passed an anxious night about this "boy," as she termed him, who was more like a brother to her than a nephew. Hitherto Frank had appeared to be brightly oblivious of the fact of his grandfather having no overweening affection for him. But now evidently the fact had dawned upon him, and from what he had said to her the previous night, when she had suggested that he should marry, he was rather more disposed to resent it as an injustice than to strive to alter it.

"Papa feeds his wrath by looking at that wretched picture. Sir Hugo, you were a bad Burgoyne, for your fatal influence is at work even now, making papa believe that Frank's little follies will develop into big crimes. There he goes," she continued, throwing up the window and leaning out to look after Frank, who was cantering across the lawn towards some hurdles. "Don't be late for breakfast, Frank. Good gracious, you have papa's horse," she added hurriedly; but Frank did not hear, and so cantered on, waving his hat to her as he rode. "A fool John must have been to let him take the Baron," she said aloud, in a vexed tone, as she watched the old brown hunter with the short dock going over the lawn with Frank on his back. "The first morning of his visit too, and he knows what papa is about that old horse; how could John let him make such a mistake!"

She turned from the window and went downstairs into the oak-parlour, their breakfast-room when they were alone. There she found her sister, but not her father, as she had hoped. For the oak-parlour windows did not command that lawn over which Frank had been cantering, and she had hoped that his error of judgment might still pass unknown and unnoticed.

"Where's papa, Grace? Do you know that silly boy is riding the Baron? What is to be done?"

"I don't know, Ethel; I must answer that to all three of your questions. Oh, here's papa."

They went forward to kiss him as she spoke, and read in his face that their troublesome pet was safe still. Lord Lesborough's brow was serene.

"The old man is the first afield," he said, seating himself and opening the paper. "Master Frank not down yet, I conclude."

This not being a direct appeal, Miss Burgoyne busied herself with the coffee, and Ethel with the Times advertisement sheet, and neither answered it.

"While I," Lord Lesborough continued, "have already been down to the home farm walking."

"Walking! what was that for, papa?"

"The old pony caught his leg over the halter and threw himself down and lamed himself in the night, and so, as I shall want the Baron after breakfast, I thought I would walk."

Both daughters trembled a little guiltily as the father spoke. The Baron had been spared by him at his own personal inconvenience, to what end!

"I ought to have thought of reminding Frank last night that the old brown horse is still held sacred," Ethel thought, with a twinge of self-reproach. "How could the poor boy be expected to remember such a trifle?"

The breakfast proceeded slowly, and still Frank did not come in.

"Had you not better send up to Mr. Burgoyne's room, my dear?" Lord Lesborough asked, as he sent up his cup for a second supply of coffee; "your late walk last night, Ethel, has knocked up a young gentleman, who doubtless keeps much earlier hours when he is away from us."

When he said this his two daughters felt still more uneasy, for Lord Lesborough was invariably waxing angry when he attempted to be ironical, and called Frank, "Mr. Burgoyne."

"Oh, papa, now he wouldn't pretend that it was the walk—but he had a long journey yesterday, you know," Ethel remarked deprecatingly.

"I suppose his mother carries his tea up, when he condescends to live with her, whenever he's lazy." Lord Lesborough rarely failed in lashing himself up into a rage with his grandson, when he began to speak of that grandson's mother.

"I dare say his mother is quite wise enough not to question his right to please himself in such matters," Ethel exclaimed. It seemed to her that there would have been disloyalty to the dead brother in suffering a disparaging remark on the living sister-in-law to pass unrebuked.

"Here he comes—such a cup of coffee for you, Frank," Miss Burgoyne exclaimed, smiling brightly at him as he entered; but the offender did not recognise either the offer of the coffee, or the smile that accompanied it. He went directly up to his grandfather; he still held his hat in his hand, and he looked pale and agitated.

"Good morning, sir," he began. "You will be very much annoyed with me, I fear, when I tell you what I have been unfortunate enough to do this morning?"

Ethel's heart sank, and her prophetic soul told her that her fears when she first saw him on the Baron had not been groundless.

"Good morning, sir. What have you done?" his grandfather replied, quietly, putting down the paper, and pushing his spectacles up on his forehead as he spoke. There was little of either cordiality or conciliation in Lord Lesborough's manner, and his grandson keenly marked the want of these things.

"I took the Baron out this morning, and I have been unfortunate enough to let him down and cut his knees in landing him over a hurdle and ditch at the end of the west lawn. I am very sorry, both for the horse and your displeasure."

He said nothing of his own dislocated elbow, and Lord Lesborough saw nothing of it. The old man was moved to a deeper anger than his soul had known since his only son had married this present offender's mother.

"Had you regarded my displeasure—had you given one thought to my wishes—you would never have touched the horse," was all he said. Then Frank turned away from him, and Ethel rose, crying out, "Don't you see he is hurt himself, papa—don't mind the horse; he is hurt. Where is it, Frank?"

"My arm is broken, I believe," he replied, going and throwing himself on one of the couches. "Had it been my neck, Lord Lesborough would have forgiven me for marking the Baron's knees; as it is——"

"I will send for a doctor," Lord Lesborough interrupted, rising and walking towards the door; "he will be more beneficial to you just now than my forgiveness."

"Things look well for Harold Ffrench, don't they, Ethel?" Frank Burgoyne asked with a faint attempt at a smile, as Ethel knelt down by his side, and shuddered over the disabled limb. "He will remember this against me, I'm certain."

"Dear Frank, how could you be so reckless?"

"Don't ask questions, dear Ethel. Aunt Grace, you'll stay with me till the doctor comes, won't you? And Ethel, you go and write a note to a man called Linley, telling him of my accident, and that before it happened I had time to go and see that the shooting-box at Lownds will just suit him. He may take it with the greatest safety, tell him; and add, that the sooner he comes, the better I shall like it; will you, Ethel?"

"I will, Frank. But Linley, he's just one of the very men papa does not like you being so very intimate with; is he coming?"

"Not here—catch him at Maddington! But I suppose Lord Lesborough will suffer him to come into the neighbourhood and shoot the harmless partridge, and by-and-by hunt the depredating fox without questioning his right to do either. Yes, write, and don't worry me, Ethel, for by Jove this arm of mine——"

He paused, and did not say what that arm of his was precisely, but Ethel guessed that it was too painful to permit of polite conversation even with her just at present. So she went and wrote the letter, and then brought and perused it for his approbation.

"Will it do?" she asked.

"Yes, it will do. You have said just the right things, and not too many of them. 'Pon my word, Ethel, our understandings match so admirably, that I have often thought it a pity that a man may not marry his father's sister; don't forget to send it off by to-day's post. Ah, here comes the apothecary."

The gentleman he thus irreverently designated being the Hensley surgeon, who had come up to do his best for the injured limb, the two ladies left Frank with his doctor, and his own man, who had entered at the same time.

"His arm is worse than broken. I believe his elbow is dislocated," Miss Burgoyne said in a melancholy tone—"poor Frank!"

"Papa is too hard, too hard," Ethel replied, warmly. "It's cruel and wicked to be so prejudiced against your own flesh and blood, as he is against Frank; and Frank has always taken it so beautifully, hasn't he, Grace? Never seemed to see it till to-day."

"Perhaps papa would have been better inclined towards him, if he had seemed to see it and feel it a little more; and yet one doesn't know; nothing, I fear, would ever have made him heartily fond of Frank."

"When Mr. Burch is gone, we will hear how Frank is, and then have the car, and go down and call on Miss Leigh, shall we, Grace? and we'll get Mr. and Mrs. Vaughan and her to come up to dinner; it will be better to have some one, than for Frank to be alone with only papa and us in the evening; shall we?"

"Yes, we will, dear. Not that I see how it would be possible for Frank to get wrong with papa, when he is obliged to keep quiet on the sofa; we always are in a terrible turmoil while that boy is here," the placid lady continued, calmly. Then they went their respective ways till such time as the doctor departed, and they might learn how great Frank's injuries really were.

Mrs. Vaughan was in such a satisfied frame of mind, that she seemed to be another woman on the morning after her niece's arrival. She had gone to bed big with hope, and had straightway fallen into dream-fraught slumbers, that were far more refreshing than dream-fraught slumbers usually are. She had supped on the reflection that Lord Lesborough did not desire his heir to wed for money, and the supposition that Mr. Burgoyne was or was going to be attracted by Theo. She had supped on these, and the supper did not disagree with her.

"I shall take you round the garden and over the village this morning, Theo, my dear," she said, briskly, when Theo came into the room, and seated herself at the breakfast table; "that is, if you'll like to go, I will take you; later in the day we may expect Mr. and the Misses Burgoyne."

"He said the morning, Aunt Libby."

"It will be 'morning' whenever they come, Theo; remember that. Theo, on no account call it 'afternoon;' even if they should come at five, it's morning to them, and they must suppose that it's morning to you also. Can't you eat anything, my dear?"

"Nothing, thank you," Theo replied. She hated the prospect of going over the garden and round the village in Mrs. Vaughan's wake—it destroyed her appetite, and made her wish herself back at Bretford again. Something of this must have been visible in her face, for presently her aunt said:

"You must stay with me till you get your appetite and your roses up, my dear; you must stay with me a long time, Theo; I shall have you stay a long time."

Theo tried hard to think of something nice and proper to say; the effort resulted in a simple "Thank you, aunt," after all.

"I wish you to stay. I'm very anxious indeed that you should stay a long time," Mrs. Vaughan went on with a slightly flushed face, "and you ought; and so ought your parents—if they knew what was good for you, which they don't—to wish it as well, instead of looking as if you thought you'd be dull."

"I do, aunt. I do wish it; dull, I don't mind being dull, I assure you."

"Well, my dear," the old lady rejoined with a perceptible softening of manner and spirit, "so much the better, and you have more good sense than I gave you credit for; I shall keep you with me for a long time, and, if you have any young friend you would like to have with you to make a change, you may ask her to come and stay with you: there, what do you say to that?"

"That I am much obliged—you are very kind, I mean," Theo replied absently. She was wondering whether she should or should not avail herself of this offer, and invite Sydney Scott down to share with her the desperate dulness of Hensley, and the dubious delights of Maddington. "I needn't decide yet," she thought, "but if it's any one, it shall be Sydney."

She however decided that Sydney should come long before that morning walk came to a conclusion. Mrs. Vaughan was disheartening in the garden, and distressing in the village. She would, while in the former, indulge in a prolonged weeding of a bed of variegated geraniums; and she would not suffer Theo to assist her in the task, or accede either amicably or at all to Theo's suggestion that she "might as well just walk round by herself, and come back to her aunt when her aunt had done the bed." Mrs. Vaughan ordained that Theo should remain within conversational range, and Mrs. Vaughan's ordinations admitted of no appeal. Theo resigned herself to the situation—strove to appear interested in the account of the Maddington *ménage*, with which her aunt diversified the running commentary she was pleased to deliver on "Theo's chances in that quarter"—and resolved that when the subject should be mooted again of the "young friend coming to make a change," she would mention Sydney Scott as one peculiarly adapted for the honour.

"At all events we shall be able to take long walks together, and escape from Aunt Libby with less appearance of design than I see I shall ever be able to effect alone," she thought. Then her meditations were cut short by Mrs. Vaughan requesting her to fill a watering-pot out of the garden tank, which Theo did to the detriment of her well-starched morning dress, and the consequent downfall of her aunt's amiability.

"So careless of you, child; however your father can afford to clothe you at all, if you ruin your things in this way, I can't think. Don't tell me that 'it's nothing,' and 'that it will wash;' I know it will wash, and I know that it's not nothing, for washing costs a great deal of money, and a great deal of money is what your father can't or oughtn't to spend about you. Our income wouldn't stand it, I know that."

"I don't carry watering-pots about and spill their contents daily, Aunt Libby; this is an out of course proceeding, remember." Theo was ceasing to be seriously affected, in other words "cut up," by her aunt's habit of reproaching stormily. She found it tedious simply, terrible no longer.

"A lady should be able to do all such things neatly, Theo; I have no patience with that ridiculous air of fine ladyism you affect. Not accustomed to carry water-pots, indeed; absurd in your position to be above such things: you would be thought far more of if you could do any little thing of the sort in a neat, graceful way, instead of being as awkward and untidy as an untrained country-girl."

Mrs. Vaughan rose from the crouching position she had taken up over the bed of variegated geraniums with the abruptness of unmitigated but doubtless most righteous anger. She was checked midway in her effort to regain the upright by a terrible jerk, which made a wide rent in the white China crape shawl she had unwisely arrayed herself in prematurely for the walk through the village. On Theo's going to her assistance, it was discovered that Mrs. Vaughan, in the heat of her argument in favour of graceful carefulness and neatness, had fastened the end of her shawl securely to the rich, heavy soil with the trowel.

"It's ruined! ruined!" she exclaimed almost tearfully. "It's one that your father brought home the first voyage he made after my marriage; I wouldn't have had it happen to my brother's gift for the world."

The allusion to her father touched Theo, and saved Mrs. Vaughan receiving from her observant niece the information that she had stuck the trowel into the ground with heart, and heat, and force to the words, "I have no patience with you," in reference to Theo's far slighter accident.

"I won't do any more gardening this morning; change your dress, Theo, and we will go into the village. I won't have you dress yourself finely, though; I *will not* have you deck yourself out just to walk through a little country village where the people will not think one bit the better of you for being dressed like a peacock."

"It would never have entered into my head to change my dress just to go in the village, Aunt Libby, if you hadn't told me to do it; even now —see I'm nearly dry—I don't see the necessity for it."

"Do break yourself of that habit of setting your own judgment in opposition to the judgment of your elders at every turn, Theo; and pray be careful how you utter disparaging remarks about the places people live in. I do see the necessity for your making a nice appearance in the village, however much you may despise it. Not that I mind it. I attribute it to your ignorance of the world. But be careful before other people."

Theo stifled a laugh. "I'll promise to be very careful, especially before the Misses Burgoyne," she said demurely. "But I assure you I am so far from being silly enough to despise it, that I felt quite anxious to get a friend of mine down here to enjoy this pretty place with me."

"To see Sydney with Aunt Libby will be rare fun, and I shall enjoy it," she added to herself as Mrs. Vaughan, now recovered from the torn shawl, gave a gracious assent to the proposition she herself had first made.

It was a pretty village, a very pretty village, with a brawling stream running through the centre of it, and white rose-covered cottages climbing up the hills on either side. An unpretentious village too, that made no attempt to elevate itself into the dignity of a town, but that was content to be a simple village still, with a walking post and a shop that contained an olla podrida of eggs and bacon, calico, tallow-candles, hair-pins, peppermint lozenges in very dusky bottles, and all the other articles that are ordinarily found in aught but sweet profusion in a country store.

Mr. Burch represented the professional element in Hensley, and on Mrs. Burch the first call was made by the vicar's wife and Miss Leigh. From her they heard the story of "Young Burgoyne's accident." Mrs. Burch always called him "Young Burgoyne," when neither he nor any of his immediate friends were by, in order to impress her hearers with a notion that she was on terms of careless intimacy at Maddington. Under the influence of the presence of his immediate friends, she fell into the equal error of speaking of Lord Lesborough's heir as the "Honourable Burgoyne."

Mrs. Vaughan looked annoyed in a bright-eyed way when they came out of Mrs. Burch's house and wended their steps towards one of the white rose-covered cottages. This accident would keep Mr. Burgoyne in the house for some time, and the impression that she flattered herself her niece had already made, might wear off before he saw her again. She began to have her doubts also as to whether she had been wise in her generation in authorizing Theo to invite another young girl down to Hensley. What if this young girl were prettier than Theo? She was not wont to brook uncertainty, therefore she asked:

"Is your friend, Miss Scott, better-looking than you are, my dear?"

"I don't think she is," Theo answered frankly. It was one of those things about which Theo could not get up confusion and mock-modesty. Very candidly would she have confessed her own inferiority of appearance had the inferiority been patent to her. But it was not patent to her in this case, therefore she replied with such an air of thorough and frank conviction that it carried conviction, and consequently comfort, to the heart of her aunt.

The white rose-covered cottages that climbed up the hills which rose in gentle swell on either side of the sparkling, brawling stream known as "Hensley Water," were nearly all of them occupied by maiden and widow ladies in a state of decay. Not bodily or mental decay by any means, but commercial decay that rendered them meek and quiet in spirit, and remarkably amenable to the chronic advances of the vicar's wife.

A species of lull came over Theo as she followed her aunt into one of the prettiest of these houses, to which they were admitted by a small domestic of tender years and irreproachable neatness. Deborah was her name, and subdued was Deborah beyond her years, and thoughtful beyond conception—when in the house. What Deborah was when she had her outings and join-

ed the youth of both sexes in a brief tour of festivity to some neighboring town, may not be
told here. But a rumour of the transformation
that came over her at such seasons had reached
Mrs. Vaughan, and Mrs. Vaughan had now come
fraught with the design of shocking the souls of
Deborah's too confiding mistresses with a repetition of this rumour.

These mistresses were the two daughters of a
gentleman long deceased, who had written a
classical dictionary, and immortalized his name
in the annals of learnedom. His two daughters
had retained that name, and were not likely to
change it now, for one was seventy and the
other sixty-five. But whether they had retained it of their own free will, or because of no
man having been forthcoming sufficiently daring
to propose an alteration in it, this deponent say-
eth not.

Miss Dampier and Miss Margaret Dampier—
never in her earliest youth had any one been
rash enough to call her Madge or Maggie, or ab-
breviate her name in any way—were busily employed at their usual morning avocation, namely,
discussing the village politics and knitting little
socks and parti-coloured shawls to be disposed
of at bazaars. The windows were closed and
the crevices hermetically sealed, for they belonged to that unwholesome class who "dread a
draught," and apparently feed and flourish on
the foul air in which they delight.

"This is my niece. Theo, my dear, pick up
Miss Dampier's ball of wool," Mrs. Vaughan
said, introducing Theo to her friends.

"Ah, very like you; very like you, indeed,
isn't she, sister?" Miss Margaret Dampier replied, with the palpably assumed air of benignant blandness that old ladies frequently adopt
towards contumacious cats and refractory small
relatives who are brought to see them. "Deborah said, as you came up the hill, that it must
be Mrs. Vaughan's niece by the likeness; she
had just brought me my twelve o'clock arrow-
root—never forgets it, never—the comfort she
is I can't tell you; and we never can be grateful enough to Miss Ethel Burgoyne for recom-
mending her from the school."

"If I had been consulted, Deborah wouldn't
have been the girl I should have recommended
for such a place as yours," Mrs. Vaughan replied, bridling up in a moment. Then Theo sank
into obscurity while Mrs. Vaughan made known,
and the two Miss Dampiers groaned over, Deborah's supposed enormities. So passed two weary
hours.

CHAPTER XXII.

MRS. GALTON FEELS THAT JUSTICE IS NOT DONE
'HER.

KATE GALTON was back at Haversham with
her husband and her child, attending to all her
wifely and maternal duties in her usually exemplary manner. She had made no sign, had uttered no word of dissatisfaction when her husband had carried her back to the Grange. She
never did make a sign or utter a word of dissatisfaction, when the d ing so would not further
her own ends. Mrs. Galton would have been a
first-rate political economist, she never wasted
her material.

She made no exception to her ordinary rule
in this instance. There had been a surface show of
willingness to go home as soon as ever she found
that the going home was inevitable. A surface
show was always quite enough for John Galton.
It was not in him to suspect that there was
aught that was not perfect, pure, and fair beneath that perfect, pure, and fair exterior, which
was so dear to his heart—so golden to his eyes.
So he believed his wife, and never deemed that
this prompt acquiescence in his wishes about returning to Haversham was due to the fact of
town emptying itself fast. Confidingly had he
accepted the acquiescence, and conspicuously
had he flaunted it before his sister. "I shall be
glad of the peace and quiet, and so happy to be
alone with you at the dear old Grange again,
John," Kate had said to him on the morning of
their leaving town; "and as it's always as well
to please people in this world if possible, we
won't ask Harold down for the shooting. Sarah
does dislike his being there, and I should like to
please her in something as she's your sister."

"Oh, nonsense, let him come. Why shouldn't
he come?" John Galton had replied. But
though he had thus replied, he had deemed it a
very sweet concession that his wife had offered
to make. It never occurred to his honest,
manly mind to suppose that the concession to
his sister's idle prejudices was made solely because his charming Kate could not help herself
in the matter. Harold had refused to go to
Haversham for the shooting, therefore Mrs. Galton utilised the occasion, took the honours that
were to be had, and declared that she would not
have him. Mr. Ffrench was what Kate termed
"buffed," that is to say, he was too unhappy at
this juncture to endure either to flirt with, or be
flirted at by his bright cousin. He had shown
himself the reverse of amenable to the little advances she had made towards a better understanding springing up between herself and him
from the ashes of the Theo Leigh complication.
He had responded as gruffly as was compatible
with such a melodious voice as he possessed to
her suggestion of an invitation to the Grange.
So Kate paused on the brink of the invitation,
and consoled herself with the reflection, that
John could be taught to appreciate the sacrifice
she had been compelled to make.

They arrived at Haversham one bright Saturday afternoon, in October, and even Mrs. Galton
—fractions of whose heart were in divers places
—was fain to confess that the Grange was not a
bad place at that season of the year. Scarlet
geraniums and October peaches blushed them a
joyous welcome, and the steward came to John
Galton's office door presently with tidings of
much game being about. There was a wealth
of fruit in the garden too, and the best of qui-
nine in the air. Altogether Kate felt that things
might have been worse—at the same time she
set herself the task of determining how they could
be bettered. "I'll redeem the time by being
agreeable to Sarah—till some one else comes in
my way," she said to herself, while graciously
preparing to accede to John Galton's request
that they "should take a stroll through the
grounds and village" after dinner on the evening of their arrival.

She found it dull work strolling through the
semi-darkness in the soft autumnal evening air

with the man she had married because Beelzebub had won. Now and again she found herself seeking about for something to say to him, and not finding it. Ah! there had never been this strain on thought when Harold Ffrench was by her side! Words had come glibly enough then, and not words alone, but something that words were well employed in clothing. Nor had speech and good cause for the same been lacking whenever Linley had been near.

She never once told herself that this mental oppression was due to some defect in her own nature—some flaw in her own heart. She walked along by him struggling with the silence she always desired to indulge in when her husband was by her side, and declared to herself with emphasis that he was dull. "Why didn't he marry a woman who could care for the things he cares for, and enjoy the eternal talk about them," she asked herself; and her conscience never once told her, that it was because she had willed that he should marry her.

She had no interest in his pleasures, she had no joy in his interests. His pointers jumped about her boisterously, and she only thought of how her dress would suffer, and permitted the dogs to feel that they were troublesome—a discovery which it is grievous for a sensitive dog to make. In fact, the horrible curse was upon her more strongly than ever, of being bored by that from which there was no escape.

"It is too late to go into the stables and look at the horses, I suppose, John?" she asked after a long silence, during which she had been declaring to herself that they had not an idea in common—more than that, that he had none but the commonest ideas.

"We'll look at the horses before church to-morrow," he replied; "you said you would go on and see Sarah, to-night."

"Then if we are going there, I will go in and get Bijou," Kate answered, hurriedly. Stagnation seized her soul at the thought of going down alone with her husband to the dulness of her sister-in-law's house. Bijou would be a mutual friend, on whom their uncongeniality might meet, and expend itself less markedly.

Miss Galton had been seething within herself for hours. She had heard from a biped retriever—one who was warranted to fetch and carry more abjectly than any dog—that the squire and his lady had come by the 4.40 train. Informant had been unable to say whether or not any one had accompanied them, having only caught sight of the heads of the aforesaid, as the carriage passed her on its way to the Grange. This doubt as to whether they were alone or not, was the primary cause of Miss Galton's seething; but as the hours went on a fit of feeling neglected set in with aggravated symptoms, and she raged furiously in her soul, for that "John never thought of coming near his sister, no, not he."

She was in this mood when they came in with their child, John laughing and talking to his small daughter with the unforced vivacity of perfect satisfaction with all things; Kate making the air ring with her bell-like voice, because it suited her to make Sarah believe her to be in brightly overflowing spirits, though she had been torn from London and Harold Ffrench.

"We only waited to have dinner before we came to see you, Sarah," John Galton said, extending his hand to his sister.

"Yes—we were starving. Immediate cause of your dear Norfolk air was to compel us to appear impolite, and stay to eat before we came to see you, Sarah," Kate added, holding her face down to grim Miss Galton to be kissed.

"As you waited so long—not that I expected you before—it would have been more prudent to have waited till to-morrow morning," Miss Galton replied, gruffly. "Coming out at this hour, at this time of year, with nothing over your shoulders, and a thing on your head that doesn't half cover it, seems to me the height of folly."

"Oh! I never take cold," Kate replied carelessly, but her blue eyes dilated curiously as she spoke. She was superbly indifferent to Miss Galton's opinion at most times, but on this occasion she had sought (with no very noble motive) to win a good one from that acrid lady; therefore she felt resentment kindling.

"But the child may—poor little dear," Miss Galton said, snappishly. "Come here, Katherine—ah! as I thought, not half wrapped up," she continued as she wound the cloak little Katie wore closely round her till the child resembled a mummy.

"I don't care to treat her like a sick chicken, thank you," Mrs. Galton said, quietly; "loosen your cloak, Bijou, you're not cold, you little hypocrite."

"No, I'm not cold," Katie cried, laughing; "I don't want the old thing."

Bijou touched her cloak as she spoke, but she looked at her aunt at the same time, and Miss Galton felt that she was the "old thing" to whom allusion was made. Her brother's child was very dear to her, but now, strengthened by the presence of her disliked sister-in-law, she resolved that justice should take its course.

"John, you ought to punish that child for her impertinence," she began with severity; and at this Katie laughed a young laugh of derision. The idea of being punished by her papa struck her as being humorous, and she read partisanship and the promise of support in her mother's bright speaking face.

"My papa won't scold me for saying 'old thing'—and you mustn't, may she, mamma?" Katie was a fair, ethereal-looking child, winning, and pretty to an extraordinary degree, but it is astonishing how intensely disagreeable such a child can be to any one on whom it feels it safe to empty its small vials of contempt.

"I think, as poor little Katie has offended you, Aunt Sarah, that we had better go home," Kate said, rising gracefully; "we came to spend the evening—didn't we, John? However, it can't be helped."

"Oh, nonsense: sit down," John Galton said, rather nervously. He hated feminine sparring matches. They always, he observed, commenced about and ended in nothing, and he liked tangibilities. So now he told Kate to sit down, and called Katie to "come and tell him what she had been doing while he had been away." This last was unwise, for by so doing he left the belligerents to their own devices.

"That child is ruined by being left so much to servants," Miss Galton commenced. "You won't send her to school, and you go away and leave her, as my poor dear mother never thought of leaving us—never thought of it."

"The result of your mother's practice is enough to make me follow it, certainly," Kate said, coolly: the propriety of conciliating Miss Galton, if possible, now at this dull season when there was nothing else to do, was ceasing to be so vividly before her.

"At all events the conduct of my mother's children never brought a blush to any one's cheek," Miss Galton replied fiercely. She was quite ready to take the daggers, ay, and use them too, for she had expected Kate to be contumacious about this coming back to the Grange, and Kate, instead of being contumacious, had been surprisingly quiescent. Altogether, Miss Galton felt disappointed in her sister-in-law, and she was not one who brooked disappointment, or one who could take an unlooked-for turn in events nicely.

"What uninteresting courses you must all have run then," Kate said, languidly. "Fancy having been so discreet all your lives as never to have made even 'goodyness' blush and tremble for you and for itself in your society."

"It's more than *every one* can say,—more's the pity." Miss Galton almost snorted as she said this.

"As you say," Mrs. Galton said, affably, fastidiously fitting on her glove as she spoke, and buttoning it with precision. "'Tis true—'tis pity—pity 'tis, 'tis true.' Every one can't say it. I can't, for instance. I never had such a vaulting ambition as to attempt to pass through this world unblushed for. I have only been careful never to blush for myself. Now Bijou, look sharp, dear; don't stand gaping, but put your hat on and come home."

"I thought you said you had come to spend the evening with me, Mrs. John?"

"So we did."

"Do you call this spending the evening?"

"No, I don't."

"Well, why don't you stay a little longer then —unless you have left company up at the Grange, when *of course*——"

Miss Galton, who had drifted into softness for a moment, relapsed into severity again at the bare mention of the company—the creature of her own brain.

"No, we have no one with us; but you haven't made it too pleasant to-night, Sarah, I must say," John Galton said, deprecatingly.

"Never mind, dear. Pray don't say anything, John," Kate murmured soothingly. Meekness under unmerited rebuke was a strong card— therefore Kate played it. "We ought not to have come and taken your sister by storm to-night, but I hadn't seen her for so long, that I thought she'd excuse it being late."

"I never thought—— But there, you will twist and turn my meaning," Miss Galton replied bitterly. "Late! I never care for John coming late; but I'd better not speak, I'm always wrong."

When a woman declares that she had better not speak, and that she is always wrong, the wisest thing to do is to flee her presence immediately, before she has had time to say a great deal in the endeavour to prove herself right. These self-accusations are signals for departure that it is worse than folly to disregard.

John Galton would have stayed to combat these low opinions which his sister had formed respecting herself. But Kate was wise as well as wary, therefore she developed inflexibility of purpose, and went away, taking John and Katie with her, and leaving Miss Galton a prey to unuttered spitefulness.

John Galton did not speak as they walked along the village street, but when they had passed into their own grounds, and the gate was closed behind them, he began:

"I wish to heaven, Kate, that Sarah and you could hit it off better? I don't say that it's your fault, dear."

"Still you think that it is, John. Now don't be unjust, but acknowledge that Sarah is too litigious for an angel even to agree with her long. I very rarely do take any notice of what she says, but to-night I was tired, I suppose, and I had gone down meaning to be amiable, and rather hoping that she would see that I meant to be amiable. That being the case, her manner was enough to put any one out; now wasn't it?"

"Yes, it was."

"You see she's the same whatever I do, John, —whether I try to please, or whether I do not try to please her, I am always wrong in her estimation. What hurts me most," Kate continued, with virtuous emotion, "is that sometimes I feel she impregnates *you* with her unjust views about me: on more than one occasion she has succeeded in sowing seeds of discord in your breast, John."

"Never, Kate, never! Jove, though, Katie ought not to hear such things." He said this in a low tone, but presently he forgot his precautions, for he burst out heartily with: "Succeeded in making me distrust you!—no; she never has, and she never will! Distrust you, Kate, darling! Do you know that would be death to me?"

He did not say it in the tones a young, impassioned, chivalrous boy would use to the object of his first love dream. The declaration that death must ensue when distrust sets in is common enough under such circumstances, and is to be taken for exactly what it is worth. John Galton meant all he said, and Kate, whose hand he had taken and placed securely within his arm, felt that he meant it.

She tried to get a peep at his face without his seeing her, and she succeeded, for his eyes were bent steadily on the ground before him. She succeeded: she saw his face and marked that it looked graver than usual, but frank and kind as ever. Then, for all the frankness and kindness —for all the love he had but just expressed for her—for all the thousand bonds of sympathy a nine years' union ought to have caused to spring up between them—Kate Galton felt that she was weary of life at the Grange, and of the man who had brought her there to be its mistress.

"The night air is chilly," she said, with a little shudder; "I shall go to bed at once, I think, for the journey has tired me—and I shall not speak again till the morning."

Then when his wife said that, John Galton crushed back the desire that was in his heart to have some quiet conversation with her, in the course of which he could tell her how he had always loved and trusted her, and how nothing that mortal could say or do could cause him to love and trust her one atom less. It would have been pleasant to him to tell her this, not in romantic phrase—he was not a romantic man,—but in some plain, strong sentences that would have gone straight to her heart. However, she was sleepy, and the journey had tired her, therefore he never said the words, and Kate rejoiced in his reticence.

"The dream of being nice to Sarah is over," Kate said to herself when she reached her dressing-room; "but I have made him see how wrong she was to-night, and that's a good work, for it will pave the way to his often finding her very wrong. Oh, dear! to-morrow and all on for ever so long will be like this evening. Poor old stupid! he will sit and look as if I ought to speak to him, and I have nothing to say."

Then she gazed in the glass and took pleasure in her beauty, and congratulated herself on her management of it, and wished that Beelzebub had run second for the Two Thousand, and that Mr. Linley lived near enough for her to cultivate an intellectual friendship with him—for "he thoroughly understood and appreciated her," she told herself; and perhaps she was right.

John Galton sat alone for two hours after his wife had retired that night. He sat alone, plunged in thought, not in anxious or unhappy thought by any means, but still in vexed thought for all that. He was not a man to cherish idle dreams of universal harmony, but he keenly desired that peace and good will should reign amongst those who were of his own household, and his own kith and kin. It had only come to him lately to see clearly how antagonistic his wife and his sister were to each other. For years his vision had been indistinct in the matter, he had seen dimly that they "didn't hit it off," as he called it, but it had never occurred to him to seek for a reason why they did not do so. Now, to-night they had forced him to see more than one reason—his sister had implied that she did not deem his wife too prudent, and his wife had suffered him to see that she had long been aware of this adverse opinion, and that she regarded it as less than nothing, in fact that she despised it. "And well she might—being what she was," he told himself, proudly and honestly. Yet, though his honest pride in Kate was unshaken, he could not forget that the opinion she scorned, the judgment she held in such obvious contempt, had emanated from his sister.

He sat alone, neither unhappy nor anxious, but just a little sore and vexed that "some people couldn't be satisfied unless the rest of the world was cut after their own pattern. Sarah would like every one to go to heaven in her carriage," he finally decided. "It comes of her having lived by herself at Haversham all her life. Kate's too bright for her; some people would tell me that she is too bright for me too, but I know her so well."

He meant that he loved her so well—too well for her to be anything but perfectly congenial and admirably adapted to him. In his case perfect love had cast out fear—and Mrs. Galton knew it.

A week passed away, during which Mrs. John Galton and her husband's sister abstained from each other entirely, and John Galton shot and rode and broke in a new setter, and was happy.

There was plenty of game that year, and as he never tired of shooting it, so he deemed it possible that Kate would never tire of seeing it shot; therefore he would issue cordial invitations to her every morning over the breakfast table to drive into some field which he would mention, and bring him some luncheon about one. In former days, when three or more guns would be out, Kate had joined thus far in her husband's sports and pastimes with a charming vivacity, that had made him feel her to be specially designed for a country gentleman's wife. But now the case was altered; it was a weariness and woe to her to go. Still she went daily as he asked her, remembering that other days might dawn.

On the Friday after their return, they received a note from Mr. Linley. I say "they" received it—but the note was to Kate. "I have taken a shooting-box at Lownds, and I want Galton to bring his dogs and have a few days amongst the turnips with me. Do you think you could make up your mind to come with him, and put up with the rough accommodation of a bachelor's establishment? If you will do so, I shall be eternally grateful to you; as you will, with your customary amiability, take the office of tea-maker upon yourself, I feel sure."

"He has evidently only asked me because he thinks you wouldn't go without me, John," Mrs. Galton said, handing the letter to her husband, and arranging a pout for his edification when he should look up after perusing it.

"Oh! I don't know; I daresay he will be better pleased to see you than me. Your style of talk suits him better, you see, Kate," John Galton replied, honestly.

"I don't believe that—but I'll go, dear. I know you can't bear being without me," Kate said, virtuously. Then she sighed, and added, "but it is hard to leave the Grange so soon again."

CHAPTER XXIII.

WAVERING!

FRANK BURGOYNE had done himself no ill-service by that piece of reprehensible carelessness of his which had terminated so badly for the Baron. That is to say he had done himself no ill-service with those powerful partisans, the women. His aunts, for instance, idolized him and his injured limb with a wealth of idolatry no amount of perfect health would ever have been able to call forth. They made him and his patient endurance of sufferings, that they slightly over-estimated, the theme of a hymn of praise, in which Theo Leigh eventually joined. For—be tolerant, reader—Theo was young and impressionable, and it is not in the nature of women to hear eternally that a man is a hero without going into a state of worship for him. She had given her heart, she had been ready to give herself, without doubt or fear, to Harold Ffrench—she had suffered a horrible agony of baffled love and hope on his account; she had defied censure for his sake, and set up her belief respecting him in opposition to her father's. But now—now, though the time was young since all this had been—this young blue-eyed man, who to his cost resembled the bad Burgoyne, had a large share of her thoughts; to say nothing of the power he possessed of making the old smile that Harold had banished irradiate the face of Theo Leigh.

She was not false, she was not fickle, she was not weak in affection even, or ~ votary of that luxurious creed which holds it lawful to make love to the lips that are near when the lips that are loved are not by. But she listened too long to the before-mentioned hymn of praise respecting Frank for absolute indifference to continue its reign in her heart about every other man than Harold Ffrench.

A good deal of the bloom of her beauty had been brushed off; her glow was gone, and her eyes were brighter and less soft than of yore. The bound was gone from her step, too, and the highest notes of her voice were rarely, indeed never called into requisition now. Every one knows the difference these changes make in a girl, surely. We have all marked it in ourselves, or others, and felt sorrowfully that the first great experience has been learnt, that the brook and river have met, and that another fellow-creature is freed from the most glorious of all illusions—the belief in the enduring nature of love's young dream.

But though the best of her beauty—its brightness, bloom, and freshness—was gone, enough remained for her to seem a very fair thing in any man's eyes. A tenderness had come in the place of the lost buoyancy, that was soothing; and as Frank Burgoyne had not known her in her buoyant days, he was well pleased with that which had come, and incapable of lamenting its inferiority to that which had vanished.

She got to think more about him than she otherwise would have done, and to like him better out of the very generosity of her nature and the depth of her love for Harold Ffrench. She heard this young man, in whose society she was thrown through no design on her part, spoken of as one whom Harold might be made to injure in a measure. They were rivals in the race for a prejudiced old man's favour, and right she could but feel was with the man who was before her, suffering,—the man who never pushed that right or sought to disparage that rival, or took the shadow of an advantage: all he seemed to desire, all he sought to win, was a higher opinion of his character from his grandfather, not the suffrages of Lord Lesborough. She felt him to be very noble and very disinterested, and this question began to torture her, "Would there not be foul meanness and cowardly falseness in Harold taking from this gallant young gentleman what would never be given to Harold did Lord Lesborough know of him that which to her cost she knew?" She could not breathe the story that had been reft from Harold in an agony that she felt, though she had not seen it! She could not breathe it: but if he knew of Lord Lesborough's intentions and still suffered that story to remain untold! the only thing that remained to her now—her faith in his honour—would be gone.

Through all these changes of feeling she could not refrain from identifying herself with Harold, though she knew him worse than dead to her. Whenever she identified herself with Harold she was doubly kind and attentive, and softly, gently devoted to the man whom Harold might possibly injure; and he marked her manner and responded to it, and made her read poetry to him, and painted little word-pictures of vanished dreams that he had had, of longings and aspirations after "a career," which had assailed him at divers periods. So a friendship sprang up between these two, a friendship that would have been love but for the memory of the man who had brought his maturity to bear upon her mind, down under the sun on that marsh-bank that had witnessed her transformation.

What were the poems we read in '51? I ask, because to them was due the temporary lapse from that perfect fidelity which poor mistaken Theo believed that it behoved her to keep unimpaired. She read mellifluous verses to him—to Frank with the blue eyes and the bandaged arm—and he looked as if he felt all the rhymes expressed, and altogether it was very dangerous.

Dangerous, but uncommonly agreeable, for they were eminently sympathetic, these young people; they both had an ear for unforced easy rhyme, and an aversion to a false quantity. They both liked suggestive poetry, too, and as Alfred Austin and Owen Meredith had not illumined literature in those days, they were compelled to fall back on those fountain-heads of suggestive sweetness, Byron and Moore.

So she read with a deeper pathos in her tone than she quite intended, because she was thinking a good deal of the one who had vitalized Byron to her; and he, the interesting sufferer, listened with a deeper pathos even than here in his looks, because it was the habit of his eyes to look pathetic things on very small provocation. Then before the reading or the listening had palled upon either, Theo put her aunt's offer into execution and sent a cordial invitation to join her to her Bretford ally, pretty Sydney Scott.

"I shall not be able to come up to-morrow morning," Theo said to Ethel Burgoyne one day, after sitting for an hour or two with the young aunt and nephew, who were so singularly alike at times, so oddly dissimilar at others. "I shall not be able to come up to-morrow morning: a friend of mine is coming to the vicarage."

"Bring him up with you," Frank suggested languidly. He was out in the garden for the first time since his accident, and the two girls, Ethel and Theo, were following him about in a state of admiring awe, for that he was able to walk and stand the full light of day.

"My friend is a Miss Sydney Scott," Theo replied quickly, but without anything that could be construed into a blush; "she's such a pretty girl, too."

"All the more reason for bringing her up, Miss Leigh. I'll do no end of politeness in the calling line as soon as ever I can ride over; but just at present you must be lenient and teach your friend to be lenient, too. She must call on me, as you have done—will she?"

"I have no doubt she will," Theo said.

"That's right, that's well; not one call only, but many, for you must not let her keep you away: I couldn't do without you, Theo." Then he passed round close to her side, and whispered as Ethel paused to gather a flower. "You do me more good than you can imagine. If I had but known you two or three years ago I should have been a different fellow."

There is something extraordinarily touching

in this statement always. A woman may not care to see a man different in anywise; he may appear in her eyes incapable of improvement; yet his assertion that had he known her before he would have been a different man, is a tribute to her power that she can but feel. It sets her wondering what her influence might have been, and what would have called it forth, and in what way he would have altered under it. It makes her think about him in connection with herself, throws open a wide field of conjecture, and gives her the idea of there being that something sympathetic between herself and him —that something which is so sweet while it lasts, so sad when it is over, even though love does not spring up through its agency.

So when Frank Burgoyne told Theo Leigh in a low tone of voice (that low tone of voice does a power of mischief in itself) that he "would have been a different fellow had he known her two or three years ago," it set her thinking of him with a degree of gentle turbulence that, if well managed, will assuredly develop into something more exquisite still.

The average young lady of this world and age says, when such a speech is made to her, "Oh! now what nonsense," or "How can you say so when you know you don't mean it?—ridiculous!" But Theo was just a little different to the majority; neither better nor worse perhaps in reality, but a little different decidedly. She neither blushed nor called that statement of his "ridiculous," but she began wondering curiously whether indeed she might have influenced this man for his good whom Harold, her love, might injure. But of that wonder came a thought which clothed itself in these words:

"I would have taught you to be careful; I would have taught you to remember about the Baron!"

"You would have taught me something else," he said.

"Ah! but that first, because it means pleasing your grandfather; and you ought to please him, you ought to be careful."

"For who's sake, Theo?—I am alone in the world,—that is to say, I have only a mother. No one will be injured or much benefited whether I stand or fall with Lord Lesborough. Who would care? Would you?"

"Yes, I would—I would!" She flamed her answer out upon him, in a way that made him think the little girl was further gone than he had intended her to be in the time. "She's got over that fellow quickly, and no mistake," he thought, for he adjudged that this prompt interest which she betrayed was a heart-felt one for him.

"So! you would care to see me keep straight with my mighty relative?"

"Yes; how like a German that 'so' was."

"What do you know of Germans?"

"Just nothing."

"Then how did you know that there was aught Germanic in my way of expressing gentle surprise and acquiescence?"

"Well! I've heard some one I know very well say 'so' in that way so often,—oh! so often;—and he told me that without being an imitative animal he had picked up that most non-committal of expressions during his residence in Germany."

"And who is your friend?" he asked; "who is the happy man whose rather weak reasons for a rather weak result are worth remembering?"

Theo felt older than Frank Burgoyne on the spot. None but a very young man ever indulges himself in these verbal impertinencies.

"I never questioned either reason or result, therefore they never seemed weak to me," she replied. "You have given them importance, so you ought to be the last to find fault with their having it."

"You haven't told me who your friend was."

"He was Mr. Harold Ffrench," she answered. Then, at the sound of her own voice mentioning his name, all her love for him, all her fears for him, all her longings that he might come out scatheless after all, welled up, and she went on, "Oh! I wish I had known you sooner, Frank Burgoyne, or that I had never known you at all."

What wonder that Frank Burgoyne dressed his mental plumes more carefully from this moment, and deemed that Theo was in love with him.

Ethel had gathered her flower and adjusted it in her belt by this time. "Pretty, isn't it?" that young lady asked abruptly, coming up, and taking Frank by the sound arm, and pointing to the result of her horticultural labours. "Scarlet geranium goes well with anything; this blue dress might have been made for it, and so might every other I remember that I have worn with it."

"I should think it would look pretty in your dark hair at night, Miss Leigh," Frank suggested.

"It does look well in my hair at night," Theo answered, rather absently.

"The next time you come here to dine I'll have a bouquet of it ready for you, shall I?"

"If you will."

"No, but if you will I shall do so."

"I shall be much obliged; I always like flowers."

"I won't prepare them carefully only to have them accepted in such an indifferent spirit; if you won't accept my simple flowers I shall be indeed unblessed; but even that would be better for me than the seeing them taken and worn negligently."

"They shall be worn with such care and consideration that they shall last the whole night, Mr. Burgoyne; what more can I say?"

"And what more can I or any other man expect? 'Last the whole night!' why it's a colossal triumph to hear that an offering, a sacrifice, shall have a lady's attention for a whole evening. So you'll really wear them till they wither."

"They look equally well in fair hair, Frank, let me tell you," Ethel struck in. "I'm rather fond of adorning my yellow locks with crimson and scarlet; I know some people think they are too pronounced for a blonde to wear, but then some people are wrong."

"It's very little consequence what blondes wear, in my opinion," Frank said languidly; "you're an exception, Ethel, but as a rule I can't say I admire fair women sufficiently to regard with attention anything in which they may please to array themselves. I like depth and intensity," he continued, turning to Theo, "and that you don't get, you know, in ninety-nine fair faces in a hundred. I like intensity, colour, and warmth, such as you have," he added in a whisper.

"Aunt Libby will be developing colour, and warmth, and intensity of anger if I don't go home soon," Theo replied, laughing. She would not treat his speech with tender silence, but it made her thrill. She was very loyal to the lost love; she was almost resentful against herself for being an atom touched by this man's approbation and manner of showing it. Yet she was conscious the while that she was touched, and that there was nothing very reprehensible in reality in her being so. One always feels a little nervous when drifting, drifting away!

"Don't make her angry enough to put any obstacle in the way of your resolve to bring your friend, and come again to-morrow," he said aloud.

Then Theo replied "certainly not," and gave him her hand in farewell with eyes averted from his gaze. It was the first time those honest grey eyes of hers had ever fallen before him, and there was something of triumph to him in the thought that they had been done so at last.

She drove herself home in her aunt's little pony-carriage, and then, after reporting herself "returned," and "Mr. Burgoyne much better," she asked for and gained permission to go on to the station and meet Sydney.

"You may go if you like, my dear," Mrs. Vaughan told her, for Mrs. Vaughan thought that things looked well for the Burgoyne alliance, and was therefore tolerant to all the "whims," as in her heart of hearts she called them, of the one who might compass it. Then she weighted her consent with a veiled reprimand.

"Not that I should have supposed it possible that you couldn't wait till to-morrow morning to make those confidences to your friend which I am not to hear; however, go, by all means, and meet her at the station."

"Thank you, aunt; with the pony, I suppose? I have no 'confidences' to make, I assure you, but I should think it kinder, were our positions reversed, for Sydney to meet me than if she sent a servant; so I'll go."

"Oh, my dear, I'm neither jealous nor suspicious, I assure you, Aunt Libby rejoined quickly; "and I know that young people like to talk their idle folly unhampered by the presence of their elders. Well, if you're going it is time to go, for the train must be nearly due."

So Theo, who did not care to combat the insinuation, went to meet and make welcome her friend.

She saw Sydney's face at the window as the train stopped—saw Sydney before Sydney caught sight of her, and marked that the usually beaming blonde looked less bright than of yore. But a minute after she caught sight of Theo, and sprang out on the platform, exclaiming—

"How jolly of you to have come yourself, Theo! well, dear, I'm so glad to be with you; but what a hole of a place it seems."

"Just the station; the village is pretty, and there are some nice—well, I can't tell you now, but I don't think you will be dull," Theo replied, thinking as she spoke of the antidotes to dulness that were to be found at Maddington. "I have

brought the pony-car up for you: I suppose it will hold all your luggage?"

They had turned the corner of the station house by this time, and come in view of the pony car, which Sydney surveyed with a critical eye.

"What a little beast of a trap for that handsome little pony to be put in, Theo; what a mistake to spoil his look in that way, for he's as handsome as a harness-pony need be. Hold my luggage, my dear! I respect my dresses, and always travel with them laid out straight in a box that will take the length of their skirts; box won't go into that car, I know."

"You must please to send it up, then," Theo said, turning to the station-master.

"Any time this evening do, miss?" the man asked.

"Oh! yes; I suppose so, at least?" Theo rejoined, looking interrogatively at Miss Sydney, who forthwith drew a small watch from her belt, and inquired—

"What time do you dine?"

"Directly we get home; you won't be expected to dress."

"But I expect myself to dress, thank you; the porters must bring my big box up at once. You had visitors the first night you came, and who knows that I may not have visitors too? I'm not vain a bit: I know that I can't stand inspection after a long journey till I have got myself up afresh."

Then she stepped into the car, and asked Theo "might she drive?" and on Theo willingly acceding, she plied the whip so freely on the handsome lazy pony that Theo trembled lest the sound of that flagellation should by any chance reach the ears of her aunt.

"What is going on at Bretford? How did you know that I had visitors on the night of my arrival?" Theo asked, when they were fairly on their road, and had told each other three times that "they were very glad to meet again."

"Oh, the usual amount of envy, hatred, and all uncharitableness. I don't care for it, though; I know that I am tremendously unpopular with the ladies."

"But I don't think that you are unpopular," Theo urged; "I never heard any one speak anything but well of you there yet, do believe me, Sydney. It must be horrid to fancy oneself disliked in the way you do."

"Oh! it is horrid of course," Sydney rejoined, with a bright smile; "but I know that I am unpopular. However 'I care for nobody, no not I, and nobody cares for me,' as the old song says: besides, as Hargrave says, after all it's easy to know why I am unpopular. I'm not vain, but I can't help knowing the reason. No, it wasn't Hargrave said that, it was Mr. Linley."

"Mr. Linley! what! have you seen him again?"

"I should think so!—rather! He has taken a shooting-box down near here, at Lownds, and he has asked my permission to call on me at your aunt's, which I needn't say that I have graciously. They always taught me to be provident when I was a child, so I take care now to provide against dulness whenever I can. I hope I shall have time to dress before dinner."

Miss Scott had ample time to dress before dinner, for the porters had been rather impressed by a certain something that savoured of liberality, not to say lavishness, in her manner, and her long box followed her quickly. The toilette was made, and successfully made too. Still disappointment enthroned itself upon her brow as the evening wore on, for nobody came. She could but feel that her efforts to appear fresh after a long journey were wasted, since none but the Vaughans and Theo were by to see them.

The following day brought a note from Miss Burgoyne inviting them up to luncheon at Maddington. They went, both in higher spirits than usual, for the communion with a bright unclouded girl of her own age had been good for Theo. They set each other off, and became each other so well that Frank Burgoyne experienced difficulty in deciding to which he would award the palm of beauty. "Theo has more in her, and is therefore the more attractive girl," he said to himself; "the other's pretty, but only pretty, nothing more."

Judging thus, he still devoted himself chiefly to Theo, a course of proceeding which laid him open to Sydney's righteous indignation. She was not accustomed to be put in the background, and the feeling that she was occupying that unpleasant position now caused her spirits to collapse after a time, and made her adopt an air of complete indifference to the young man who had suffered her to lapse into it—an air of such complete indifference that it might have deceived a man who had had no experience of her sex into imagining it real, but that was as a veil of the thinnest gauze over her sentiments to Frank Burgoyne. He saw that she was *thinking about him*, and began to question whether, after all, there was so much more in Theo Leigh.

CHAPTER XXIV.

MISS SCOTT PROMOTED, VICE THEO LEIGH, RESIGNED !

"GIVE my compliments to Mrs. Vaughan, and tell her that I shall be over to see her to-morrow," Mr. Burgoyne said, when the two girls were leaving. At this statement of his intentions Sydney elaborated her former indifference, and got up an expression of utter weariness, and Theo blushed scarlet, for he was shaking hands with her as he spoke, and he bestowed more than a warm clasp upon what she still held sacred to Harold Ffrench.

"With Miss Ethel?" Theo asked.

"No," Ethel replied for him, "he has thrown me over for a younger and lovelier—he won't take me."

"But you oughtn't to ride, Mr. Burgoyne; indeed you ought not to ride yet, and you can't drive yourself?" Theo questioned eagerly.

"And you do give me credit for having sufficient good taste to eschew being boxed up in a carriage, or being driven about by a trustworthy groom like a helpless incurable. Well, you're right, Theo—Miss Theo, I mean. I have a friend in the neighbourhood, and he'll tool me over to Hensley, if we shall not bore you."

"You won't do that," Theo answered candidly, and Sydney shrugged her pretty plump shoulders, and said:

"All things are relative, you know, Mr. Burgoyne; most likely you'll be the great diversion of the day at Hensley; you may safely come without fear of falling flat after other brilliant excitements."

"You're very kind," he said languidly, "but the fact is I'm hardly up to chaff to-day; I have been away from the regions of it for a long time;" then, while Sydney blushed hotly with the consciousness of having blundered in this her first onslaught upon him, he turned to Theo, and murmured:

"And I am not so capable of appreciating chaff you see, Miss Theo, as the young heroes whose wits are sharpened by incessant intercourse with garrison-town belles are; your friend is overpowering, teach her to be merciful."

So far he had spoken in a light, almost scoffing, way, but now he altered his manner suddenly, and whispered:

"Teach her to be as sweet as you are yourself, if that be possible."

Theo could but think of him as she drove back to the Vaughans. Sydney ensconced herself in the corner of the car in silence, and did not even ask for the reins this time, for she was seriously put out, she scarcely knew why. Miss Scott maintained an absolute silence too, therefore Theo had full opportunity to think of him, and think of him she did.

He had called her "sweet," and he liked her, and trusted her, and believed her to be what a woman should be! She felt that he did all this; she felt sure of it, for his eyes told her so, and his words and manner corroborated and bore witness to the truth of what his eyes said. While she!—knew that of his rival, Harold Ffrench, which, if known to Lord Lesborough, would cause Lord Lesborough to cease from thinking Harold Ffrench "immaculate," as Ethel phrased it. She knew that Harold Ffrench had been what the prejudiced old peer would consider a "defaulter in honour," at the same time she knew that the man who would be injured by the retention of that knowledge, believed her to be frank, and sweet, and true.

"Oh, if Harold would only tell all, and lose all, and brave the blame!" she thought, and her heart went low, and her brow blanched as the fear began to dominate that she had given the first fruits of her heart to a coward.

Better that it should be proved that his deserts were small; better that he should be adjudged and denounced as unworthy, than that he should go on evading judgment and denunciation by keeping silence. While she had thought that it was to gain her love alone that Harold had held his tongue, she had never blamed him once. But now she felt that perhaps there might have been another motive for that secrecy which she had held to be only weak, not wicked! A sordid motive—a motive that it nearly broke her heart to think could actuate the man she loved. Ah! she was all a woman in giving birth to this fear. Every crime under heaven will be of small account in a woman's eyes if the man she loves stops short on the commission of them,—of cowardice and meanness.

You see hers had not been a purely feminine training. She had been an only daughter, an only child, and so the principles of honour that her father would otherwise more assiduously have grafted upon sons, had he had them, were made portions of Theo's education. She had been her father's companion and confidante all her life, and she had early had a proud appreciation of his renown for courage and honour. To be fearless and to be truthful were such vital points with him, that Theo never deemed it possible that a "gentleman" could shrink from or evade anything. That Harold Ffrench had maintained reserve, had shrunk from making the great event of his life public, for the sake of some commercial benefit which might accrue to him were privacy kept, was a bitter thought to a girl who had been taught to brave everything that came in her way without blenching. She would have been horribly shamed to show fear for herself for any less cause than love! Think what she was when she felt that the man she loved had shown it! She would not give the thought words even to herself, but as she drove home from Maddington that day she was miserably conscious of feeling that had it not been for those past passages of hers with Harold she could have loved (as a sister of course, nothing more!) the brilliant, brave carelessness of Frank Burgoyne.

Will she be deemed very weak, very greedy of that sweet something which she might not reciprocate when I say that Theo felt a throb of something like pleasure when she remembered that Frank Burgoyne had drawn no unfavourable parallel between herself and Sydney Scott. She wanted no more than a sister's quiet love from him, but to have seen that gentle moonlit affection out-blazoned at the first by the sun of passion or admiration for her fair-faced friend would have been painful, very painful. It is easy enough to resign gracefully after a time, but not at first, not abruptly, not till one gets used to the idea of being compelled to do so.

Sydney Scott said very little about her new acquaintances that day, to Theo's relief. "They're very nice, not a bit snobbish," she remarked when Mrs. Vaughan asked her if she had not "found the Honourable Misses Burgoyne truly agreeable, and Mr. Burgoyne very different to the majority of the young men one met."

"They're very nice, not a bit snobbish. Different? no, I don't think him exceptional at all; all young men who get petted up as his aunts pet him want taking down; but I didn't remark him much."

Mrs. Vaughan would have liked to have told Sydney that she was not called upon to remark Mr. Burgoyne much, or at all even. She would have much liked to have told her niece's young friend thus, much with the point and emphasis, not to say spite, with which she deemed it well elderly ladies should address young ones. But Sydney Scott had the air of one who might not be attacked with impunity, even for her own ultimate good; therefore Mrs. Vaughan bore this light mention of one of her articles of faith in silence.

"Let us be out in the garden, if possible, when those men come from Maddington," Sydney said to Theo the following morning; "a state call from them in your aunt's drawing-room and presence would be too much for me."

"We'll be out in the garden when they come, if you like, but don't flatter yourself that we shall be suffered to remain there while they're here; don't you wish to see Mr. Burgoyne?"

"Oh, yes, if he comes in my way, but not under Mrs. Vaughan's auspices, if I can avoid it. I shouldn't feel myself. I should feel at a disadvantage, for I'm certain she will never think anything I do or say nice."

"She has a way of appearing terribly particular, but it's half appearance; she is very kind in reality."

"I could see that she thought me too fast," Sydney began animatedly; "now didn't she, Theo? say, didn't she?"

"No, I don't think she did; she isn't up in the term, and so she is not on the look-out for the quality."

Sydney's animation flagged. She had been more than ordinarily debonair and out-spoken last night, and Mrs. Vaughan had failed to observe it!

"O Theo, don't you wish you were so dowdy, and quiet, and uninteresting that no one would notice you?" she asked presently.

"Indeed I don't," Theo replied heartily, "and you wouldn't find half the pleasure in lamenting being so, that you do in bewailing being quite the reverse."

Which assertion Sydney gravely negatived and questioned, till Theo grew weary of it, and bitterly regretted having made it, for nothing that in any way concerned herself was lacking in interest, or immaterial to Miss Sydney Scott.

"I won't drag you out, you'll like to be in to see them," Sydney said to Theo, when the hour that Frank had mentioned as the one of his intended call drew near. "I can go out and amuse myself, don't you come."

Sydney had her hat on when she spoke, and a wonderful pair of well-fitting gauntlets, to say nothing of a broad leather belt across one shoulder from which hung suspended a pouch.

"You look as if you had been getting yourself up for a 'specimen collection stroll,' Sydney. Where are you going? Wait, and I'll come too."

"No, don't; no, please don't, for why should you? This means nothing: one always wears certain things in the country whether one wants them or not; I shall just rove about till your aunt's grand guests have been and gone; don't you come, you'll be wanted."

She walked off, hastily waving her hand to Theo, and evidently meaning the latter to take her at her word, and suffer her to go out alone.

"I shouldn't like to miss Mr. Burgoyne, after all," Theo thought. Then she went back into the drawing-room, and sitting down at the window, she suffered her thoughts to play round that "all," after which she felt that she would be sorry to miss Mr. Burgoyne.

Sitting there she perceived that Sydney, after all her elaborate preparations towards avoiding the expected guests, was taking the only path by which it was possible they could reach the vicarage. "Stupid of her!" Miss Leigh thought; "however, she can just bow, and pass on when she meets them. I wonder who'll be with him."

She felt a bright colour rush over her face as she caught herself thinking of "him" thus, and remembered how he had pressed her hand unreproved, and found occasion to tell her that she would have had the power to make him a different fellow had he met her before. Then, while the colour was at its brightest, her aunt came into the room radiant, and told Theo that her complexion was vastly improved, and that she heard a horse's trot coming along the Maddington Road. Which combined information rendered the colour permanent, and caused her explanation of Sydney's absence to be rather rambling and vague.

Mrs. Vaughan had entered the room radiant, for she liked the idea well of the young heir of Maddington paying his devoirs at Hensley at this early stage of his recovery. But minutes passed, and she grew less radiant, and after a time she grew very impatient.

"Just half an hour since I heard a horse coming along that straight bit of road from the Maddington turn; they might have been here over and over again," she exclaimed angrily, looking at Theo as if Theo were answerable for the delay.

"Perhaps it was not them after all."

"Stuff and nonsense, child! who else, can you please to tell me, would be coming along that straight bit of road from the Maddington turn, eh?"

"I don't know, aunt."

"Then don't talk about things you don't understand," Mrs. Vaughan returned loftily. "I wish you would break yourself of that habit you have of setting up your judgment in opposition to everybody else's, Theo."

Theo having nothing to reply to this the pair relapsed into silence again for yet another dismal ten minutes. At the expiration of these minutes Mrs. Vaughan solemnly announced her belief that the horse whose trot she had heard at the Maddington turn had fallen down and done fresh damage to Mr. Burgoyne.

"At all events we will put something on our heads and run down to the gate, and look along the road, Theo," she said, excitedly.

"Very well, I'll get my hat, not that we shall do any good by going."

"Pray permit me to be the judge of that; no, don't stay to get your hat, this will keep the cold from your head," and as she spoke, before Theo could interpose an objection, Mrs. Vaughan had enveloped her niece's head in a small shawl of ill-conditioned texture and unbecoming hue.

"Keep it nice and close under your chin,—stay, I'll put a pin in for you," the energetic old lady continued. So Theo, after the feeblest remonstrance, submitted to an arrangement that was not comfortable enough to reconcile her to its unbecomingness. Theo felt that she looked very plain in that wretched little brown shawl, and that her abnegation of the pomps and vanities of this wicked world was complete indeed as she walked soberly along the drive by the side of her aunt.

The gate was closed, but they opened it, and passed through, Mrs. Vaughan still apparently hopeful of coming across some pieces at least of the Honourable Mr. Burgoyne. About ten yards from the vicarage garden gate there was a hazelnut copse, and immediately against this copse they saw not pieces only, but Mr. Burgoyne intact.

The dog-cart was drawn up to the side of the road, and Miss Sydney Scott stood by the horse's head, patting his nose, and calling him "good boy," and "poor fellow, then," and asking him,

"was he a nice horse?" after the most approved feminine fashion. By her side Mr. Burgoyne stood, breaking the husks away from nuts, which, when thus far prepared, he handed to her; and inside the hedge, assiduously gathering the nuts for the pair outside, was a man, whom Theo with a start and, no, not "a stifled cry,"—stifled cries are not uttered in real life—recognized to be Mr. David Linley. She could but feel the full force of the unbecomingness of the abominable little shawl as she came abruptly upon this road-side picture.

"My friend Mr. Linley—allow me to introduce Mr. Linley, Mrs. Vaughan, Miss Leigh—met an old acquaintance in Miss Scott, and insisted on getting down to gather her some nuts; I was powerless to drive on by myself," Frank said, making an effort to look as though he did not think that Theo would think that he was transferring his half-sworn allegiance from herself to another.

Mixed feelings agitated Theo. It was hard to meet Linley again, hard to mark the feeling Frank had been apparently ready to develop but yesterday for her had veered away to Sydney, hard to have that shawl upon her head! that odious little shawl, so unbecoming in hue, and texture, and arrangement.

She had not encouraged the development of that aforesaid feeling as she might have done in all maidenly dignity. And she had resolved to encourage it even less in the future. Still, for all this resolve, a sense of disappointment came over her as she marked that the resolve would be no more tried. When we have elaborately armed against temptation it is disappointing not to be led into it!

Sydney Scott looked up, beaming and bright; devotion always pleased her, and some show of it had been made this morning by the man who had played at absolute indifference with her yesterday. Her coming out along this road had not been altogether purposeless, and yet she had not aimed at that which she had attained. She had merely desired to show herself to them apparently regardless of their coming: to show herself prettily dressed, bright, fair, and fresh as the morning, and at the same time to show them that this charming combination of dress and good qualities was not mindful of them at all, but was actually conveying itself away from sheer indifference.

This had been her motive in coming out, but the motives of the majority of girls are susceptible of change, and Sydney was no exception to the rule. When she met the dog-cart and found that the friend of whom Frank Burgoyne had made light mention the previous day, was no other than her own acquaintance, Mr. Linley, she came to a halt, and brought her hand to her hat with a graceful gesture of salutation that reminded them of a pretty page, and compelled them to stop.

Miss Scott had looked forward to a meeting with Mr. Linley at Hensley with pleasure, while she had deemed that there would be no one else. But now, since she had seen Frank Burgoyne and found him possessed of that tawny beauty that she specially affected, Linley's age and plainness recurred to her in all its force, and she began to hope that "Theo would take him off, and leave her the other."

She told them that she had come out to explore, because it was impossible for her to keep

6

in the house when there was anything new to be seen, or any nuts in the neighbourhood to be had. After a moment or two she appended frank regret that she should have done so this morning. "As you were coming," she continued, looking at Frank, who responded by jumping down from the trap at once and declaring that he too would earn his nuts by honest toil.

"We had better go on and put up the horse, hadn't we?" Linley asked. He wanted to see Theo, and to see how she acted upon Frank, and how something that he had to tell would act upon her. Pretty Sydney Scott was all very well, but he had not taken the shooting-box at Lownds for the purpose of witnessing Frank Burgoyne and that young lady eat nuts towards a better understanding.

"We'll go on directly—lots of time," Frank rejoined. "Here, be a good fellow and just pop over this fence, and get some of those nuts for Miss Scott."

"For you to help her to eat them,—that will be the amount of your honest toil."

"Never do anything for yourself that you can get another fellow to do for you. Yes, hasn't he a handsome head, Miss Scott? Do you like horses?"

"That I do," she replied. And there was no affectation in the warmth this time, for "that she did," thoroughly. Then she saw Linley safely over the hedge, and went on for the benefit of the heir of Maddington alone.

"They never turn round on you and deceive you."

"That depends upon whether you're up in their little ways or not," he said, laughing; then he altered the expression of his eyes, and went on:

"A horse deceive you—no! none but an ass could do it. So you had the heart to come out this morning? How done I should have been if I had missed you, which I might have done if you had gone into the wood."

"Yes, if I'd gone into the wood before you passed, we might have missed, mightn't we? What nonsense, though, as if you would have cared! Oh! thank you, Mr. Linley, what clusters! there's another bunch—no, farther on still—that I should so wish to have if you wouldn't mind taking the trouble to get it for me; you can't help seeing it if you walk down, but it's a shame to ask you."

"Not at all, don't mention it," Linley replied, grimly. He felt that he was being foiled by this girl of twenty, and he resolved to make her wince for it. He had a trusty ally, before whom this young lady would go down like corn before the reaper.

It was while he was away searching for the cluster that was so difficult to find that Mrs. Vaughan and Theo came up, and Frank made his praiseworthy effort.

It was but for a few minutes that Theo permitted herself the indulgence of feeling sore and wounded for—she knew not what. At the expiration of those minutes she reminded herself that she, who loved another—"God help me and forgive me," she murmured—could not in reason care for the beat of this young man's liking. It is always, however, more agreeable to be the first, always soothing to feel that you are the primary consideration with some one who is present and congenial to you. Of course every true woman

is capable of resigning this position to a friend who may legitimately take it. But again, be it acknowledged, that she is not a true woman if she does not feel to some degree the being compelled to do so. It is easy enough to resign gracefully after a time; but not at first; not with a shawl adjusted so unbecomingly upon your head that it makes your resignation appear simply a matter of course. No, no! under such circumstances one does indeed feel it hard to resign.

CHAPTER XXV.

"IF SHE UNDERVALUE ME, WHAT CARE I HOW FAIR SHE BE?"

THE whole party walked back to the vicarage together, and the task of leading the horse devolved upon Mr. Linley, who disliked doing it, and showed that he disliked doing it.

"I will drive you, Miss Leigh; you will get up, and graciously pilot me, will you not?" he said to Theo, when he had come back over the hedge and joined the group. And Theo had negatived the proposition with more promptitude than politeness. She would have been glad to escape from Frank's society just then, but fresh as her eagerness was, it could not quite conquer her well-established aversion to Mr. Linley.

"It's not worth any one's while to get up in the trap again—distance is nothing; lead the horse, there's a good fellow," Frank interposed, before Linley could press the point again. Then Theo felt a spasm of gratitude towards Mr. Burgoyne, in beautiful unconsciousness of the interposition being the fruit of his fear that Miss Scott might be the one asked next, and that she might go, and leave him to walk home with Theo.

The walk home, short as it was, was a failure, looked at from every point of view. It is always unpleasant to keep step with a fast stepping horse, and civility compelled them to accommodate their pace to Linley's. Sydney Scott was annoyed at her rural court being broken in upon; it was far more in accordance with her ideas of enjoyment to have two gentlemen in waiting upon herself alone, than to share their attentions with any one, even with her dear friend, Theo. Added to which not wholly unnatural feeling, she was mortifyingly conscious that Theo might imagine that there had been design in her (Sydney's) morning's course of conduct. Miss Scott had an intense dislike to being found out in any of those little moves of hers that were made with such winning careless frankness—such utter absence of thought, apparently. She marked now that Theo appeared slightly downcast, and, with feminine keenness of perception, she read the cause with tolerable clearness; therefore, though she triumphed slightly in her soul, she was also mortified, and, consequently, quiet.

"Things had not gone very far with either girl," Frank Burgoyne told himself. How should they have gone far in the time indeed? Still he was aware that he had shown that in his manner to both which he might not with impunity continue to show to both if he desired to make progress with either. There were two points to be settled, he felt, and settled right quickly, too. The first point was, did he desire to "go further" with either one of them? The second, "which of them was it?" It would be hard to decide!

Things had not gone very far with either girl, and they seemed likely to remain where they were during the greater part of that call. Under the influence of the angry glances which Mrs. Vaughan could not refrain from darting at Sydney, that young lady passed from a semi-repentant state into one of defiance. She felt virtuously indignant that her pleasing pastime should be so palpably deemed faulty, and she included Theo in her anger for being the niece of the lady who so harshly regarded it. She pouted and flushed, and looked very bright-eyed and pretty, and talked in a tenderly-mournful undertone to Frank Burgoyne, and altogether aggravated Mrs. Vaughan. She depressed Theo, too, and Theo went down to dismal depths in her own estimation for feeling this depression, and Mr. Linley marked that she did so, and deemed it well to give her a counter-irritant in the hopes of stringing her up to the attractive point again.

"I have some old friends of yours staying with me at Lownds, Miss Leigh. Mr. and Mrs. Galton came last night; they'll be delighted to hear that you're in the neighbourhood."

"The Galtons here?" she asked. She was obliged to reply to his communication; so she made her effort, and said out her little conventional phrase, without emotion, apparently. But it was only "apparently." In reality there was a dull, numbing pain at her heart; they were drawing around, they were closing in upon her again, those who knew the story of her love and sorrow—worse still, of the brightness of her former hopes, and the blackness of the cloud that had overshadowed them! It was horrible! The light pangs that she had been lately feeling at the fading away of the friendship that might have been love, were as nothing now. She sat there, compelled to keep a fair front before them, to hear what they said, and to hold herself in readiness to answer them, with a sense of being utterly crushed, utterly shamed, utterly (this was the bitterest drop in her cup!) unable to help herself—powerless to be anything but a patient, enduring woman. Mr. Linley saw how entirely his tidings had beaten her down, but he did not bestow much sympathy upon her, for he knew the elasticity of her nature, and was aware that the beating down was a mere temporary affair, and that the rebound would come all in good time. He liked the girl for many things,—for her pluck and her pride, and, above all, for her power of holding on to her own opinions. This liking would have merged into something far warmer—it had done so, indeed, but he had repressed it nearly entirely now—had she not betrayed one of those shrinking aversions to him which are not to be surmounted. But, though he liked her, he would not have spared her a single stab that might stir her up to be the bright Theo of old—capable of winning and retaining the taste and heart of this young man, who could thus be made to rival and outshine Harold Ffrench in all things. "Then, when the match is made, I'll let him know that it was I who brought them together," he thought; and the thought was soothing and agreeable to him to an extraordinary degree. Once before he had robbed Harold Ffrench of a

woman's love, and though he could not do it himself in this instance, he could do it vicariously, he hoped. He decided on throwing Frank and Theo together more than ever. "I'll get them both to Lownds," he said to himself; "Theo will come to Ffrench's cousin, I'll be bound—women are so infernally foolish and sentimental about such things; and if Miss Sydney stays here and threatens to mar things, I'll tackle her myself—she's more amenable than Theo." In his heart he firmly believed that Theo was the exceptional woman who could resist him, and his belief ought to have been founded on experience, for he had lived and loved.

Mr. Linley put a stop to those before-mentioned "Undertones" after a time. He appealed to Sydney about a book that she had professed one day at Bretford to have read, and that he felt persuaded she had not read. He put her through a brief catechism concerning it now, held her looks and words securely, though he was powerless to enchain her attention, and by so doing he gave Frank a fair opportunity of addressing Theo, which Frank took sheepishly, for he knew that he had swerved from his manner of yesterday.

"Jolly well those scarlet geraniums look, Miss Leigh," he said, walking to the window that commanded the churchyard; "that bed, I mean, on the near side of that stumpy tomb with a cherub's head sitting on the top of it; the roses are gone though—I'm sorry for that."

"But the dahlias are come, and one can't have everything," Theo replied, going up to his side at the window, and determining to be as she had ever been to him, though his friendship, perhaps, was a fleeting thing.

"That's the worst of it, one can't have everything; this morning, for instance, we hadn't you at our Arcadian repast——"

"But you had nuts, and they are better," she interrupted. "Oh! I wanted to ask you, do you know the Galtons?"

"No," he answered; then he went on, in almost a whisper—"She, Mrs. Galton, is *his* cousin, isn't she?"

Then Theo nodded assent, and looked up almost piteously into his eyes, for the manner of his mention of Harold Ffrench told her plainly that he knew a portion of her story, and she feared that he might even know the whole of it, and, knowing it, deem her all that she deemed herself just now. She remembered the keen gaze he had bestowed upon her that first night of their meeting: she remembered the fear that had assailed her then, the fear that had slept since she had been so much with him, and had come to like him so well. But it returned now, and she felt that its slumbering had been a sort of disloyalty to Harold, for it had been lapped to that slumber by the worst foe tha one she loved could have—the man he might possibly injure.

It was very hard to maintain composure from the moment of the resuscitation of this fear, but she was a practical girl to a certain degree, and so she contrived to calm herself into propriety of manner by the reflection that it could do no good to give way at all. Nevertheless, she was glad when the necessity for the strain was over, and the call came to a conclusion.

But Sydney was not glad, and Sydney could not affect gladness. The catechism relating to the unread book had been replied to by her with a stifled impatience that had been marked by Mrs. Vaughan; and, now that the guests were gone, Mrs. Vaughan reprimanded that impatience, and not the impatience alone, but sundry other acts, and looks, and words of Sydney's in a way that young lady did not like at all.

"I must tell you, my dear," she began, "that I had rather you did not go out to meet gentlemen in the roads about the house; it doesn't look well."

"Go out to meet gentlemen! Mrs. Vaughan, I wouldn't do such a thing; I assure you I know perfectly well——"

"So do I, my dear; I know perfectly well that I am only doing my duty as your hostess in telling you of conduct that every right-minded person would disapprove of. I must beg that you won't go out to meet gentlemen in the roads——"

"But I didn't do anything of the kind," Sydney cried hotly.

"You can't deny that you met them *in* the road, *as* I say," Mrs. Vaughan rejoined stiffly; "and your manner to Mr. Burgoyne was not what was thought pretty in my young days: talking in low tones never looks well. Of course you mean well, my dear, it's only ignorance of the ways of the world that makes you commit these little errors."

"Ignorance!" (choking with wrath and surprise); "you must allow me to correct that statement as to my ignorance of the ways of the world, Mrs. Vaughan. I'm excessively sorry if I have offended you in any way: as I have done it, unfortunately, I had better——"

"There, there, say no more about it," Mrs. Vaughan exclaimed hastily. A row that she could not regulate precisely as she wished was painful to her to the last degree. Miss Scott appeared willing to show fight, therefore Mrs. Vaughan deemed it well to hoist the white flag, and so she said, "say no more about it."

"I'll go home at once, I'll start this day, this hour," Sydney said to Theo, as soon as they were alone, which they were quickly, for Theo promptly suggested an adjournment to her bedroom when her aunt had finished speaking. "It's only the thought of her being an old woman that kept me quiet, I can tell you, Theo."

"I can only say I'm sorry—I'm very sorry."

"Yes, but there's no balm in that after having been downright insulted by a—a—well I must call her it—an old bully. What *did* I do so very bad? did you see anything wrong in anything I did, or didn't, or said, or looked?"

"No, nothing wrong, of course not," Theo replied, flushing up, and speaking with extra warmth on account of her lively remembrance of the depression she had felt.

"I couldn't help Mr. Burgoyne being very attentive—now, could I, Theo?"

"No, you couldn't."

"How should I have known that they would want to get out, and get me nuts? I didn't know there were any nuts even; I wonder your aunt doesn't accuse me of getting up that copse for the furtherance of my evil designs upon—which of them is it?

"Don't think anything more about it. Aunt Libby will have forgotten all about it when we go down, and you'll forget it when you see Mr. Burgoyne the next time."

"Perhaps I shan't see him again—I can't if I go to-day."

"But you won't go to-day, dear," Theo said quickly and earnestly. "You won't make a mountain of a mole-hill; I'm sure you won't."

"Mr. Burgoyne says he thinks he has seen me before. I told him that mine was not by any means an uncommon face, so perhaps it was only some one like me he had seen."

"Ah! very likely," Theo replied; she knew that Sydney would remain and suffer wrath to go by for this time if discreetly suffered to report dialogue.

"*He* said he didn't call it a common face—quite laughed at the notion."

"I don't wonder at that—I mean at his laughing—no, I mean at his saying——"

"He says (and Hargrave has often said it too, so I suppose it's true) that my eyes are just the colour of Mary Stuart's." Sydney cared very little what Theo meant, she interrupted Miss Leigh's attempted elucidation rather ruthlessly.

"I dare say they are; so many people's eyes seem to be like Mary Stuart's," Theo said wearily.

"Oh! I don't take any sort of stand upon it; they do very well for every-day life. When are we going to Lownds?"

"I don't think there was any day fixed."

"Mr. Burgoyne will be there too; I hope your aunt won't go, for if she does, and he devotes himself to me, I shall have a pleasant time of it. Does Mrs. Galton get herself up well? If we go there to luncheon I shall wear a costume that I had for a luncheon at the —— barracks the other day. Stop, I'll show it to you, it's violet silk, and a lace mantle lined with the same, and a violet bonnet, and parasol, and gloves. I *wish* I had had a double row of flat bows on the skirt,—it was an awful error not to have them, wasn't it?"

"Yes," Theo said, "awful;" and wondered silently whether she would ever again feel earnestly interested about flat bows. To be capable of experiencing poignant regret about them was a state of beatitude to which she might never more hope to rise, she told herself, but would she ever be interested about them at all, just ever so little?

There had been no day fixed for this going to Lownds, to which Sydney looked forward with hopes that were high. No, happily for Theo, there had been no day fixed as yet, and something might occur to avert the necessity for going at all. If it came to pass that she must go down to the gates of the foe, and expose her head uncovered to the arrows that would surely be flying, then she would go down without a word and only flinch inside. Still she hoped that she might not be made to go down. No good thing, nothing more than the tamest maintenance of her present position, could be gained by the pain she must feel and bear quietly did she adventure into the midst of Harold's friends and foes when they all met together. So she hoped that Lownds might lapse from the minds of her aunt and Sydney Scott, and that they might lapse from the minds of those at Lownds.

She had an unconscious ally in Mrs. Galton.

who was now the presiding genius at Lownds. The shooting-box arrangements were very much to her taste, for Mr. Linley had not transported himself thither to be uncomfortable. He was not keen enough sportsman to regard all things as of little worth in a sporting establishment save the game that might be around it, and the dogs that were to point and set at the same. All things were done decently and in order at Lownds. Kate found herself lodged luxuriously. It suited Mrs. John Galton to reign, and reign alone, and always give the law; therefore it was that she unconsciously aided and abetted Theo's fervent hopes; she desired not the presence of any other of her own sex who might come and share this empire which was all her own now.

Now Mr. Linley, who marked the majority of things with tolerable clearness, marked very soon this disaffection of Kate's to the proposed introduction of Theo and Sydney to his bachelor quarters. He did not run counter to it openly, for he wished Mrs. Galton to remain; and in that she might be useful to him, he ardently wished her to remain good tempered. But all the same he resolved that Theo and Sydney should come, and that Kate should invite them affably.

He carried his point on the Sunday morning following Mrs. Galton's arrival at Lownds, one bright sunny autumnal morning that they had agreed would be far better spent out in the garden than in the Hensley church.

"I will go in the afternoon if you like," Kate had said when her husband asked her if she meant to accompany him. "I will go in the afternoon, because probably it will be dull then, and one may as well be in church as not; but I won't go with this sun shining. I shall get more good by sitting out there and thinking."

"Out there" was on a low garden-chair under a walnut-tree whose boughs reached nearly to the earth on all but one side. There they kept them short and open for the sake of the view that stretched away to Maddington, and there the sunbeams fell profusely now in that golden warmth of theirs that they do occasionally displa▩red October.

"▀e have left you all the week for the partridges; it would be a shame for us both to leave you this morning for the good of our souls," Linley said, in answer to this statement of her intention. "Shall we all sit out there thinking, Galton?"

"I like to go to church once in the day, and after dinner always seems to me——" John Galton began, but Mr. Linley interrupted him by saying:

"Indiscreet after one arrives at years of indigestion; yes, you're right; well, then, we will manage it in this way, you go to church this morning, because you like to go once in the day, and I will stay at home and try to make Mrs. Galton think better of us than she must have been thinking all the week."

So John Galton walked across the fields to the little church at Hensley, and believed in all that he heard, though he did not heed it much on this occasion, for he was just a little sorry that Kate was not there. You see he had grown up with this notion, that there was something after all in these forms and ceremonies, and he wished in all honest sincerity that those

who were dear to him should attend to them. It in no way altered his own opinion of her, still he did wish that Kate could "think" on sunny Sunday mornings in church as well as under walnut-trees.

Mrs. Galton took a shawl, and a rug, and a book, and a dog, and went and ensconced herself under the tree with the sunbeams at her feet. The book was speedily dropped, for Mr. Linley soon followed her and went down upon the rug where the sunbeams were never shrinking from the light they threw upon that ugliness on which men said he presumed.

"What a good fellow Galton is," he began; "he has all the qualities and all the qualifications that both men and women like."

"He can ride straight to hounds, and hit a bird if he aims at it," she replied laughing.

"Women—and men too—like a fellow who can ride and tell the truth without swerving," he answered.

"There is an impression abroad that we weak-minded women 'go in,' as you call it in your slang, for the athletic," she rejoined.

"And don't we honour you by giving credence to such an impression? Isn't it better to be able to ride straight at any hedge, moral or physical, than to tell in glowing language how another fellow does it?"

"No, I don't think that it is better," (she remembered how well he did these things in print himself, how game he was in the hunting-field, and how prompt to resent everything, or nothing, in post octavo)—"no, I don't think it better, Mr. Linley." Then she recalled to her mind how Beelzebub had won and how that winning had been brought about, and she felt that she would have flown at higher game had higher things been shown her. "Better!" she went on, rather sadly, "no, the one who simply tells about them in type cannot talk of them eternally as those can who really do them;—were you under the impression that I was quite contented with ranking with, but after, the horse and dog and gun?"

"I was under the impression that you were a very clever woman, and I am under it still," he replied, picking a walnut as he spoke, and endeavouring to get it away from its husk without staining his fingers, "you are, with much tact and talent, to say nothing of kindness, trying to make me feel that you don't look upon me as quite an inferior creature to your husband, the man who rode into your affections one day in a not long past memorable Newmarket year. Of course you feel a certain degree of pride in him, you must, whenever you compare him with your cousin Ffrench, for instance. God! it's enough to make any man blush for the possession of brains when he reflects on the use Ffrench has made of his; with such opportunities as he has had too—such marvellous opportunities!"

"Harold is full of transcendental nonsense that makes one rejoice in not being bound to stand or fall with him," she replied; "but as to the pride I feel in my husband's achievements in the field—well, the less said about it the better."

Mr. Linley had always thought her a very pretty woman before this morning, very pretty and rather affected. The affectation he had condoned, for it had been displayed for the purpose of pleasing him, and as is usually the case under such circumstances it had pleased him though he had seen through it. But this morning she looked less pretty than she was wont to look, and there was a certain fractiousness in her manner that he liked less than the normal affectation. She had not stayed away from church for the purpose of hearing her husband's praises intoned, nor, though she regarded Linley favourably enough now, did she quite like her idol of the old days disparaged. He may have fallen from his pedestal, that aforesaid idol, but to hear aught detrimental to him is disgusting to the last degree to the woman who placed him there, unless she can charge the utterance of these detrimental speeches to jealousy, when she can bear it better.

But vain as Kate was, she could not charge them to jealousy in this instance, at any rate, not to jealousy about herself. She felt that there was a certain element of truth in what Linley had said of Harold Ffrench, and that it was his thorough and conscientious opinion that Ffrench had made a poor use of such good things as nature and education had given him. So fully was she impressed with this belief that she resolved to abstain from giving Linley to understand that Harold had been her slave in the past. As Linley did not believe in him her triumph would be small, therefore she was compelled to fall back upon vague statements of the "influence she had had through no efforts of her own over a mighty mind—an influence that had been so thrillingly acknowledged that it had rather spoiled her for the sober happiness and the calm appreciation of her merits which she had afterwards gained by her marriage with Mr. Galton."

It was very hard to come down to this tame theme. Here was all a cousin's love for Harold Ffrench now—nothing more, nothing warmer; but as she had liked him well, as she had gloried in the halo his supposed gigantic intellect had thrown over their attachment, it was not agreeable to wake to the cold truth, and hear that there had been nothing particular to glory in, in the dispassionate tones of the man who now had the power to sway her mentally.

After the bells of all the neighbouring churches had ceased tolling, and that strange lull had come over the air which can only be found in perfection in a country locality where dissent does not obtain, where Salem and Ebenezer chapels are not, they heard footsteps crossing the lawn that intervened between the house and themselves, and Kate gave a quick gesture of annoyance and cried, "It's John." A moment more showed them her mistake, for through the opening where the boughs were short, over the sunbeams that lay down (like Linley) at her feet, came Frank Burgoyne.

"I made sure I should find you at home, Linley," he began, raising his hat to the lady, and in his eyes she read that he had made sure also that he should find Linley alone. "He's too young for me to care to make amends to him for his disappointment," she thought, as she looked lazily up at him, and told him how such a morning as this was a poem, and how Mr. Linley and herself had decided on reading it in preference to going to church at Hensley. Frank Burgoyne almost felt as though he had

interrupted the reading; strange sensations of being unwanted, unwelcomed, set in. His annoyance at finding the lady there when he had come to talk privately to Linley faded away before his annoyance at finding the lady was far from well pleased to see him.

"Cannot the poem go on?" he asked. "I trust my advent has not spoiled the rhythm; the fact is, Linley, I wanted to ask you," he went on hurriedly, "if any day was fixed after all for the Hensley people to come here? I promised to come with my aunt, Miss Ethel, when they came, and she wouldn't like me to make any other arrangements that would interfere with that appointment."

"There was no day fixed; I left that to Mrs. Galton, who I believe is going to be kind enough to call and give the invitation in person to-morrow," Linley replied, looking at Mrs. Galton as if he had not known such had not been her intention a minute ago.

"Of course I will do your bidding, as you compel me to act as hostess while I am here; but a family party?—All the people out of a country rectory, to be asked, does sound very awful; do you mean that they're to be asked to dinner?"

"That by-and-by," her host rejoined, "we'll invite them to luncheon first, a sort of preliminary canter before we run that race of intimacy which people are compelled to run in the country if they would avoid dying of themselves."

"Then to-morrow I am to commence my pilgrimage along that interminable vista of entertainment that I see looming before me? I'm to ask them to luncheon, to say something to that very demure young lady, Miss Theo, about her being good enough to come and relieve my solitude? I shall never die of myself, Linley, believe me, I don't get bored alone; but with a family party on my hands for hours perhaps ——" She paused and shrugged her shoulders, but did not specify what might be expected to happen.

"You heard Mr. Burgoyne say that he was coming with Miss Ethel?"

"Ah! forgive me, so he did say it; it won't be quite a family party, then, if Miss Burgoyne can stand it?"

"I count for nothing, I perceive," Frank said, and he tried to say it as if the counting for nothing was a great joke, which he relished very much, but he did not quite succeed.

"You! why, you will be out with my husband and Mr. Linley," she said glancing carelessly at him.

"I can't carry a gun yet," he replied.

"To say nothing of Linley not having the slightest intention of leaving you to bear the burden and heat of the day alone, Mrs. Galton; we shall have had plenty of sport before one; and we will lunch at two—at two on Tuesday, Burgoyne,—will that meet your views?"

"Yes, perfectly," Frank answered. He wished that Mrs. Galton would look up and betray a little interest in whether it met his views or not, he was not accustomed to be utterly disregarded by women in this way, for Kate's was a genuine disregard, very different from the one Sydney had got up at first. But Mrs. Galton did not look up and betray interest in him, or his coming or his staying away. Mrs. Galton evidently looked upon him as very young indeed, far too young to disturb herself about. This was a manner of looking upon him that was eminently distasteful to him, for he had no tenderness for his youth, he never cared to see it brought to the fore.

"She's a lovely woman, lovely," he thought, as he walked slowly back to Maddington; "that sort of nonchalance which she assumes is disgustingly out of place, though. By Jove! the devil's in it if I am to be taught that my existence is very immaterial by a woman of that rank." He reminded himself more than once of how far superior a cast of character both Theo and Sydney were, how much better bred they were, and how much more they thought of him.

------◆------

CHAPTER XXVI.

THE LUNCHEON AT LOWNDS.

THERE was a sweeter, softer cadence in the poem after Frank Burgoyne took his leave of them that morning. It rose and fell with more pathos than before, for Linley felt that the pretty woman who was reading it with him liked him better than the interruption, though the interruption had come in a guise fair enough to have won its forgiveness from ninety-nine women out of every hundred. There was a dulcet flattery in this; Kate had been very judicious for once without design, the fact being that very young men did not interest her, she having the sense never to forget that she was thirty, and to leave rather than be left.

"I suppose it's time to go in and look for your husband and luncheon; it's nearly one o'clock," Mr. Linley remarked, looking at his watch.

"I suppose it is: it always is time to go and do something else when one would rather not, I observe, in this abominable world."

"The world's as good as any we shall ever know anything about, I expect."

"Probably; nevertheless I should like it to be all sitting in sunbeams that have no scorch in them, and being made to feel that that is enough. I have not thought once of what is to follow while I have been sitting here, and now I am recalled by hearing that I must rise up and go in." Then she rose up, gathering her shawl around her as if she indeed felt that she was going out of the sunbeams into chill life again, and adding, "Pious exercises always make my husband very hungry, I observe; don't let us keep him waiting." She went in, and the poem was at an end.

The call came off, and the invitation to luncheon at Lownds on the Tuesday was given and accepted. There was not the shadow of embarrassment on Mrs. Galton's part at this her first meeting with Theo since Theo had been so honoured, as she deemed it, by Harold's choice of her—so disgraced by his defalcation. Theo had nerved herself to bear a sympathetic word or look, for she judged it impossible that such a thing as had befallen her could be passed over as though it had never been, by one who had known of its occurrence. But the event proved that she had armed herself against nothing, for neither the sympathetic word nor look was given. Mrs. Galton rather desired to sink the subject of Theo's wrongs, out of no special love or consideration for Theo, but because a recognition of Theo's wrongs would have been an acknowledgment of Harold Ffrench having been more serious in the matter than she even now liked to believe he had been.

"You're not looking half as well as when you were staying in London with me, Theo."

"She looks better than she did when she came down." Mrs. Vaughan regarded the remark resentfully as a slur on her hospitality. "She came looking squalid."

"It is the Bretford air that disagrees with you, I conclude."

"The Bretford air is good enough; it's not the air that disagrees with us at Bretford, is it, Theo?" Sydney struck in. Sydney had not played a prominent part in the conversation yet, and it occurred to her that unless she were prompt she might miss an opportunity of telling a stranger how sorely she was tried, and what general injustice was done her at Bretford.

"I'm very well; it's my way not to look in such rude health in the autumn as I do at other times," Theo answered, unconsciously spoiling Sydney's golden opportunity, and averting the song of Miss Scott's injuries and independent resentment of them.

"When I was young I had sense enough myself not to go about looking moody and melancholy, and if I had not had the sense myself, my parents would have drilled it into me; but now-a-days——" Mrs. Vaughan stopped and shook her head nervously, and Mrs. Galton asked—

"Yes—what?"

"Why, now-a-days girls are so inconsiderate; selfishly inconsiderate, I will and must call it; as to ruin all chance of establishing themselves, by going about with a downcast moody air, as if they had known all the woes of the world. There's Theo, now, I speak to you as a friend, Mrs. Galton" (Mrs. Vaughan frequently spoke as a friend to utter strangers, to the dismay of those who dwelt in the tents with her)—"Who would think Theo a mere child both in years and experience to see her? Never known a care, never known a sorrow, in her life: my dear brother has sheltered her like an exotic, and this is how she rewards him. Oh! I have no patience with it! no patience with it!"

Mrs. Vaughan had had small patience with all things since Frank Burgoyne had cracked nuts for Sydney; none at all with Theo's pallor and occasional depression.

"I am very sorry that I don't look as I ought to look, Aunt Libby," Theo replied: the reprehensible pallor had given way to a scarlet flush at Mrs. Vaughan's declaration to Kate, to Kate who knew better, to Kate who knew all about it, that she (Theo) had never known a care or sorrow in her life, and that she had been tended like an exotic.

"I must say good-bye now," Kate said, rising: "I can only hope that the bloom requisite for Theo's establishment will come back when the autumn is over. We shall see you to-morrow at two, then? There will be a cavalier for you, Theo: an interesting one, with his arm in a sling, and melancholy in his eyes."

"Oh! Frank Burgoyne, do you mean?" Syd ney asked, with animation.

"Yes, I mean Mr. Burgoyne," Mrs. Galton replied sweetly, but through all the sweetness she contrived to make a tone of amused surprise run at Miss Scott calling him "Frank" Burgoyne. Sydney detected that tone instantly, and felt keenly that it would impart a rich flavour to the story when Mrs. Galton should tell it to the man now spoken about. Need I say that after this Miss Scott lavished no great amount of good feeling on the pretty woman who was always in such full possession of her senses, that she never lapsed into Christian-naming men, however intimately she might think of them?

In addition to the car to which the lazy pony belonged, the Vaughans kept a hooded box upon four wheels, known in the village as "our carriage." Theo had viewed it surreptitiously through the half-open doors of the chaise-house on two or three occasions, but she had never ventured upon a close inspection of it, on account of a lively remembrance she had of her aunt having made a statement of intoleration to all stable tastes on the part of young ladies.

This day, however, on which they were to go to luncheon at Lownds, Theo made its nearer acquaintance, and she was fain to confess after a five miles' drive in it, that creeping over in the car would have been preferable to this state transit, upon which Mrs. Vaughan had insisted. Mrs. Vaughan was a staunch advocate for etiquette, too, therefore she had desired that Theo should occupy the seat of the lowly with her back to the horses, while Miss Scott, the stranger, had the place of honour by her (Mrs. Vaughan's) side.

Being seated with her back to the horses would, under ordinary circumstances, have been a light evil to Theo. But the circumstances were extraordinary, so to say, for it was a gala-day, and on gala-days Mrs. Vaughan belonged to what she called her "very best cap."

Throughout their wedded career Mr. Vaughan had heard at what appeared to him as hideously short intervals, of his wife's "best cap," and he hated it with a hatred that was demoniacal in its intensity for so good a man. It had been a thorn in his flesh and a saddle on his loins during the earlier and less prosperous portion of his career, for he had frequently been compelled to carry it in a box that resembled an ark for weary miles when they were going to those convivial gatherings yclept tea-parties. Such days were over for the Reverend Thomas now, and he no longer trudged out to tea with Mrs. Vaughan's prodigious best cap in his hand. But he keenly remembered those sufferings which he had borne with such exemplary fortitude, and the sight of the ark-like box was odious to him.

It was specially odious on this occasion, for Mrs. Vaughan had declared that "it would ride comfortably between Mr. Vaughan and Theo, if they would only sit as close to their respective sides of the carriage as they could." Which they did accordingly, and then had the box wedged in tightly between them, where it rode comfortably at the cost of considerable personal inconvenience to them both, but that was nothing to "the annoyance of not having a cap to put on your head when you go to a place," as Mrs. Vaughan observed.

They found their host, together with the Galtons and Frank and Ethel Burgoyne, in a room in the fitting up of which they saw at once the fitness of things had been studied. It was the perfection of propriety as the chief room in a shooting-box, and for all that, women looked thoroughly in their places in it.

It was a long, low, lattice-windowed room, with a broad rafter crossing the length of the ceiling, in which he received them. To have removed that rafter, whose normal condition it was to look heavy and burthensome, would have been impossible. To utilise and make it conduce to the beautifying of the room had been Mr. Linley's task as soon as he came to Lownds. It was very ornamental now, that formerly obnoxious rafter, for it was of oak, and he had had it polished, and its grain brought out, and a substantial line of gold beading placed along it on either side. Above all, nailed to its centre were two pairs of antlers, and from these antlers trailed long, creeping plants that hung down low, and then turned up again abruptly in a most extraordinary way, and that took their rise in tiny pots that lurked between the horns.

The fashion of the furniture, too, was extraordinary—as extraordinary as this gamey and floral combination which I have described. The material savoured of the chase, for it was of the skins and horns of animals: the shape savoured of a Sybarite.

The faces of tigers snarled at you, and the claws of bears looked ready to catch and hug, and the fangs of one grand lion grinned at you, from the backs and tops of chairs and couches. When you turned these round you found soft seats of delight, elastic, warm, and cozy, and the wild sports of the field and forest that they had suggested vanished from your mind.

A pleasant room, with an atmosphere that was agreeable to breathe, for there was a fire in the grate—a bright, leaping little fire, that threw out no more heat than could be well endured in October—and the windows were open for the free admission of the rarified autumn air. A wide door at the end was open also, showing them the luncheon they had been invited to eat, laid out on a large round table, sparkling and bright with glass and silver, brilliant with October fruits and flowers.

"Shall we go into the other room? I believe we are all here: there is no one else to wait for, is there?" Mrs. Galton said, after a few minutes had elapsed, during which few minutes Mrs. Vaughan had been suffering agonies of uncertainty and qualms of doubt as to whether her cap-box had been brought in, and whether she was to be invited up-stairs to adjust it properly or not.

"No, we have no one to wait for. No probability of Ffrench coming, I suppose?" Mr. Linley asked, carelessly, turning to Frank Burgoyne.

"None at all—that is, I fancy he is engaged with Lord Lesborough," Frank answered, and Theo saw that he glanced uneasily at her as he spoke.

Mrs. Galton rose, and led the way into the dining-room, and Mrs. Vaughan was fain to follow, with her bonnet on.

"It's rather singular," Mrs. Galton began, in an explanatory tone, when they were seated, "a cousin of mine, Harold Ffrench, has come down to stay at Maddington."

"Oh! indeed!" (Mrs. Vaughan was but indifferently interested in the cousin of a woman who had shown such lack of consideration for her comfort and her cap.) "Oh! indeed! Harold Ffrench."

"Yes; such a nice fellow. I wish he could have come to-day, don't you, John? He would have been quite an acquisition, wouldn't he?" Mrs. Galton addressed Theo this time, and glanced at her from between half-closed lids in a way that Theo found very hard to bear.

"He would," she said. She had been shocked by the abrupt announcement of his being in her vicinity, but she felt that it was intended to be a shock to her, therefore she resolved to make the signs of its being so as few and little visible as possible. In such a case it is surely pardonable to deceive observant friends.

"Ah! to be sure, Theo knows him," Ethel Burgoyne observed, in all innocence. "He's a great friend of yours, isn't he, Theo? I forgot to tell him till this morning that you were here."

"I never heard Theo speak of him," Mrs. Vaughan struck in, with prompt indignation; "why didn't you tell me you knew him, child? I hate——" she was going to add that "she hated such sly ways," but the Burgoyne alliance should never be frustrated by her. Frank might revolt at anything underhand.

"There was no occasion to speak of him, aunt, more than of any other man whom I have known and you have not."

Theo was seated next to her host.

"Let me give you some Chablis with your oysters," he said; then he went on in a lower tone, "Bravely said, Theo; you have known him, and, knowing him, feel that there is 'no occasion to' speak of him again."

"I did not mean that at all, Mr. Linley," she said aloud, and he raised his eyebrows and shrugged his shoulders, as though he would say, "If she would be indiscreet, well!"

"What didn't you mean at all, Theo?" Mrs. Vaughan asked, sharply. There was an element introduced into the conversation that was beyond her comprehension, and the being compelled to eat in her bonnet always "muddled her," as she expressed it. "Sire, I hit where I dare," is a principle that is frequently acted upon. Mrs. Vaughan, under the influence of wrath, felt that it behoved her to be rigorous as to Theo's meaning and manners.

"I didn't at all mean that Mr. Ffrench was not worth speaking about," Theo answered.

"And who (pray, Mr. Vaughan, allow me to say a word to my own niece without trying to put me down with such looks) thought you did mean it?"

"Mr. Linley thought so, and it's not at all what I meant." Theo was nearly choking with wrath now, for Linley was smiling (derisively she thought,) and Kate gazing at her with admirably pourtrayed astonishment.

"I am sure my cousin would be very much obliged to you," Mrs. Galton said, coldly. Then she murmured in a low voice to Frank and Ethel Burgoyne who were seated near to her, "Heaven preserve me from friends who tilt at windmills on my behalf."

"It did seem rather uncalled for—unless there's more in it than I know of," Ethel Burgoyne replied, looking at Theo curiously. Then Mrs. Galton played with her rings, and said:

"Theo Leigh is rather imaginative, you know, and imagination often leads people astray; don't mention this absurd scene to Harold, please: I should be sorry that he should know what a little fool she makes of herself."

"Was it his wife,—that Mr Harold Ffrench's wife,—you were going over to Rockheath Park once to see, Mr. Linley?" Sydney Scott asked. Miss Sydney had been slightly in the background for a short time, and she hated being there; she came to the front again most effectively.

"His wife!" Ethel Burgoyne exclaimed, "his what?"

"Shall I betray him?" Linley shot these words in a low whisper at Theo, and she saw that Frank Burgoyne was watching her.

"Not now," poor Theo answered, and almost before the echo of her own words had died away, she heard Linley saying—

"My dear Miss Scott, I little thought that spoken words of mine so dwelt in your mind. This Mrs. Harold Ffrench is the wife of the man I knew long ago, Mrs. Galton,—the man I thought your cousin might be when I heard his name first this year," he continued, addressing Kate.

"Oh! I see," Kate replied, and from Kate's tone Theo knew that she too was ignorant of what had been the barrier between herself and Harold Ffrench.

Theo was longing ardently that Harold Ffrench might tell the truth concerning himself to his possible benefactor, but she did not desire that anyone else should tell it; she trembled indeed with a sick pain at such a contingency. So now it began to afflict her sorely, this doubt she had as to whether Frank Burgoyne knew all about Harold or not. If he did know it, what motive had he for keeping silence with his grandfather? And if he did not know it, what motive had he for gazing at her curiously, as he had done from the first? She could but think he knew it, she could but fear he knew it; and if so, what must he, so frank, so honest himself, think of Harold Ffrench?

This statement of Harold Ffrench being in the neighbourhood appeared to cast a something that was partly gloom and partly restraint over the little party. The spirits of all flagged at that luncheon-table, though it was a round one, and no one person was isolated from another. Mr. Linley took Theo at her word—he did not betray the secret of Harold Ffrench having a wife to the Burgoynes, but he made her feel that it was a mean thing to have pleaded for that protecting silence, and that Harold Ffrench was a something meaner still to need it. Over and over again as she sat there trying to partake with appetite of those viands for which the oysters and Chablis were intended to give her a zest, did she say to herself with a quailing heart,—"O Harold, why won't you tell all, and lose all, and let the world say the worst?"

That there was gloom and constraint over all things was visible enough to others besides Theo. Kate was annoyed by what had passed relative to

Harold Ffrench. She was annoyed at Harold Ffrench's having elected to stay at Maddington, instead of having come on to Lownds to see her. She was annoyed with Linley for having addressed Theo in tones too low for her (Kate) to have caught the sense of them several times. Above all she was annoyed at the prospect that loomed before her, of having to entertain Mrs. Vaughan for so long a period as that estimable matron might choose to remain there. For Theo was palpably now—for some reason or other that remained a secret to Kate—absorbed with Linley. And Frank Burgoyne would probably devote himself to Sydney, when the ice of reserve that was over all just now should be a little thinner. The gentlemen remaining would be her own husband and excellent Mr. Vaughan alone, and neither excellent Mr. Vaughan nor her husband had been in the list of her panaceas for the woe of this luncheon, when the obligation of presiding over it had been finally thrust upon her.

As for Sydney Scott, she was labouring under a sense of most cruel injustice. That nutting episode and two or three brief chance meetings since it, had made her very intimate with Frank Burgoyne. He had shown himself willing to come round entirely from the side of her friend Theo to her own. He had paid her many compliments, buttoned many refractory gloves in her service, and been generally devotional to her, in a way that had made her remember keenly that he was Lord Lesborough's heir. She knew by experience what these long hours in a shooting-box, with a luncheon as an excuse for them, are almost sure to bring forth. She had gone with high hopes, she had gone prepared for anything save finding Frank Burgoyne distraught to the degree of being more on the alert when Mrs. Galton spoke, than when she, Sydney Scott, uttered notes that but the other day he had seemed to think were dulcet.

Frank Burgoyne was distraught, horribly so, and horribly conscious of being so. Mrs. Galton was no fairer, no sweeter, no softer, or more enthralling than were dozens of women whom he had known, and who had smiled on and been forgotten by him: but she would not smile upon him, or at least she would not smile upon him particularly, nor would she particularly refrain from doing so. She caused him to see clearly that he was no more to her than another, that she considered him rather young—that she scarcely thought of him at all, in fact. So Frank Burgoyne, being unaccustomed to such a light regard from any woman about whom he thought at all, seethed in spirit, and was distraught in manner as he sat at Mrs. Galton's side, and Mrs. Galton's eyes were turned away from him languidly. He felt convinced that "those two girls had little in them," in comparison to this delicate woman with the material husband. He began to wonder why she had married the honest-hearted gentleman, who was obviously unable to reach the heights of regarding her in the dim religious light of semi-romance that he (Frank) was throwing around her. He questioned whether the "bogie of his boyhood," as he had once called Harold Ffrench, had been an active agent in the creation of that air of gentle melancholy that hung about her. He marvelled whether or not she had children, and if she had, were they that "all" to her that the "something dearest"

should be to such a woman? In short, he thought about her more perhaps than he should have thought of his neighbour's wife, and, not being vicious, he was sorry for it.

Sorry for it, and ashamed of it, though there had been no guilt in those thoughts. Still he was ashamed when he looked at John Galton's honest face, and Kate's apparently pure brow. There was all the sanctity of the married woman about her in Frank's eyes; spoilt and petted as he had been by women all his life, he had never learnt to think ill of them, for Ethel he knew to be pure and good, and Ethel was as a sister to him; all the weaknesses that she had, he knew.

So he turned himself resolutely from Kate at last, and found that the pretty girl whose gloves he had buttoned and whose nuts he had shelled, would not suffice to banish all thoughts of Mrs. Galton, even for those few short hours. Then once more he told himself that "there was more in Theo," and subsided into his old friendly relations with Miss Leigh, who responded to him half deprecatingly, as to one who was very generous, or very much deceived.

The shadows of dissatisfaction deepened when they rose from the table at last. For the first time Theo was panting to gain private speech of Linley, and Linley apparently had no design that she should do so. Instead of suffering the party to drift asunder and divide into pleasant knots of twos, or more, he collected it together in the room they were received in first, and installed himself in their midst, in a way that did away with all hopes of anyone's gaining private speech of him. Then, even as her aunt raged in her soul at being compelled to sit in her bonnet with a full knowledge of her best cap being up-stairs, did Theo rage at not being able to speak to him, to have it out with him, about Harold Ffrench and Harold Ffrench's wife.

She longed to tell him that she could bear it all as it was, and to put it to his manliness not to make it unbearable by speaking of it till Harold Ffrench deemed the time ripe to speak of it himself. "Till Harold deemed the time ripe;" she would put no harsher construction on his reticence than that, even to herself. When he deemed the time ripe he would cease to live this lie, and be the candid gentleman she so hardly, so vainly, sometimes strove to think him.

CHAPTER XXVII.

AFTER LUNCHEON AT LOWNDS.

HAD he come there unwittingly? or had he known of her being there, and come, hoping to see her again, without apparent design? She had not questioned thus when the note of his arrival had been first sounded, for all her thoughts had been of him then. But that first flush of excitement was over, and she was standing now at a window in the drawing-room, rather apart from the rest, asking that question keenly—asking it with an anxiety she could not subdue.

The dread that she had about him! There would be danger in meeting him, and danger in evading him, danger and pain. She could not foresee anything but discomfort arising from this combination, and when she thought of how it might strike her father, she felt pitiably helpless and uncertain how to act.

If he had come knowing that she was there, and designing to see her, he had erred, in that he had been guilty of something underhand. She could not bear to think this of him; she put the fear of it away from her resolutely, and told herself that he had come in ignorance, and that he would go to-morrow perhaps, and spare her the pain a meeting here, a meeting now, must cost her. She looked up, disturbed by a slight sound, and she saw that Frank Burgoyne had come over, and was standing by her side.

"Ffrench did not know you were here, Miss Theo, till Ethel told him this morning," he said, and Theo drew a breath of relief that was a half sigh, and replied :

"You say so—you mean it ? "

"I do, indeed. I would have affirmed it before this, and more solemnly, had I known that you attached such importance to it."

"I do attach importance to it, Mr. Burgoyne, and I think you know why," she said quickly. She was longing to test his knowledge to the utmost; she was capable of ruthlessly probing her wound for the sake of finding out whether or not Frank Burgoyne was wholly in Mr. Linley's confidence.

He blushed more than the girl before him as she spoke, he knew well how this must pain her, and he was so sorry for her pain.

"Do forgive me," he murmured earnestly; "I had no right to broach the subject; but I do know enough, Theo, to make me feel sure that the assurance of the truth, the assurance that Mr. Ffrench did not know you were here, would be agreeable to you."

"Then you knew that I——" she stopped, half choked for an instant, and the blood rushed up in a flood to her brow, "Then you know that I—thought myself engaged to him once ? " she went on, in a voice that she strained so hardly to steady that Frank felt more than pity for her.

"I know that he was engaged to you, and that for some cause he has lost you, Theo," he replied, so lovingly that Theo thought how pleasant it would be to have such a brother as this sympathetic Frank Burgoyne.

"That cause, that cause ? " she interrogated eagerly, but Frank did not say whether or not he knew what it had been, and so Theo was still in doubt as to the extent of his knowledge on the subject. He only sat down on the broad seat of the latticed window, and talked to her of other things, of indifferent things, looking past her against his will the while at Kate, who saw him not. He could but watch her and her graceful affectations, and half sneer at them to himself, and watch them still, and finally gird at her in his heart for not playing any of them off upon him. He chafed under her neglect, under the spectacle of so much more being lavished upon Linley than upon himself, the "younger man." He set himself to watch her keenly; he tried to detect the minutest atom of assumption or unreality in Mrs. Galton's manner of regardlessness towards himself. To his ultimate loss he failed in detecting aught that could have put him on his guard; the lady was prepared to meet and baffle all suspicion of this unconcern of hers being other than the undesigned pure and simple offspring of her feelings towards him.

Mrs. Vaughan had thought of ordering her carriage directly after luncheon, for she was warm and weary. The day had been a failure, an utter failure, in her estimation. Frank Burgoyne had been planted as far from her niece as was possible at the table. Theo and her host had spoken in low tones ; her best cap had not been suffered to see the light ; and Mrs. Galton palpably was at no pains to entertain her (Mrs. Vaughan). The sense of these evils was upon her strongly as they came back into the room with the oaken rafter, and it caused her to tell Mr. Vaughan that she should order the carriage, and go home at once ; and why they had come she for one could not tell, for certainly they were not wanted.

"It will scarcely do to go just yet, will it, my dear ? " Mr. Vaughan had replied, and there was a something about his manner of saying it that showed Mrs. Vaughan that the day had not been such a failure to her lord and master as it had been to herself. In truth he had been discussing church-rates and parochial matters generally with John Galton, and was very happy, and in no hurry to be put away on the back seat of the carriage and galled by the cap-box again.

"Whether it will 'do' or whether it won't (and why it shouldn't I should like you to tell me), I shall go at once," Mrs. Vaughan had rejoined. But just then Frank Burgoyne followed Theo to the window, and Mrs. Vaughan resolved to be all the thoughtful relative, and bear her bonnet and Kate Galton's neglect for yet another little while.

For Kate, graceful lady, charming hostess as she was, and could be at times, was negligent of Mrs. Vaughan. She had not wanted Mrs. Vaughan and her party here, and now that they were here, she let it be seen, not that she had "not wanted them," she was too well bred for that, but that she felt that she could not entertain them ; that she lamented this incapability, but still was helpless. "It's a cruel kindness asking people to come so far and having nothing to amuse them when they do come, Mrs. Vaughan," Mrs. Galton said once to Mrs. Vaughan. "I am afraid you find it very dull." Then Mrs. Vaughan had rejoined, "Oh ! pray don't mention it : very nice and pleasant, I am sure," and had thought that were Mrs. Galton properly afflicted with fears as to its being dull she might ask her to "walk round the garden," or, "look into the dairy," or, "see the house," or propose any of the many other things ladies of an inquiring turn of mind and an active habit of body like to do when they find themselves in strange quarters. But there was no dairy to see at Lownds, and Mrs. Galton would not have offered to do the honours of it had there been one ; and as for walking round the garden, she read at a glance that Mrs. Vaughan would have bored her as to the names of flowers and plants. Therefore Kate did not propose any of the pastimes that Mrs. Vaughan had come to consider customary in a country house, and so Mrs. Vaughan felt herself neglected, and cast about for a vessel on which to wreak her wrath.

Theo was employed profitably, her aunt hoped, harmlessly she could but see, with Frank Burgoyne in the window. The legal recipient of her sorrows and angers was deep in the discussion of a large-hearted scheme for the furtherance of decency and order in labourers' cottages. It wounded his wife to see him so rosy and comfortable while she was crimson and uncomfortable :

It hurt her that he should be discoursing in such a friendly spirit with the husband of the woman who was leaving her to her own devices; it aggrieved her horribly that he should permit enjoyment to appear upon his countenance when all was vexation of spirit with her. She was preparing to swoop down upon him with some significant reminder, with something that should at once and thoroughly rouse him to a sense of his baseness in being gay when she was sad—and savage—when her eyes fell on Sydney Scott, and wrath was averted from the head of her spouse.

To no one had the day been a greater failure than to Sydney. She had come prepared to see Frank Burgoyne do very terrible things in Mrs. Vaughan's eyes; she had come joyfully expectant of Frank and herself infuriating her hostess beyond those bounds of fury she had seen Mrs. Vaughan observe hitherto. She had thought herself round into rather a soft state of mind about the handsome young man whose prospects were so good, and had cashiered Hargrave of the —th, who had nothing but his pay, and not too much of that. She had told herself that "Frank understood her," and had bitterly lamented the lacking violet bows. It was hard on her, therefore, to come and find him preoccupied with his own thoughts at luncheon (that refection, which former experience had taught her can be lingered over so long and pleasantly, and at which two can absorb themselves, and separate themselves from the rest so much more easily than at a more formal dinner). It was harder still to find him occupied with Theo in the wide latticed window after luncheon. These things were hard; but harder than all else was the fact of there being no one who could take Frank's place, and assist her in proving her indifference to this unlooked-for desertion. She was compelled to sit and look on, and to know that they knew she was compelled to be thus quiescent, which was worse than all else.

She could not even fall back upon Ethel Burgoyne, for Ethel had picked up a book and was evidently interested in it; besides, conversation with Ethel just then would have been as panada after caviare. His aunt was all very well as one of the family, but it was with the nephew that Sydney had proposed conversing principally to-day. Twice Mr. Linley attempted to draw her into the conversation with Kate and himself, but Kate did not back him, and Sydney did not respond. She had no intention of playing second to Mrs. Galton, so she made her answers to his polite attempts in good-tempered monosyllables, and waited.

Sydney had a marvellous power of looking bright, and unconcerned, and good-tempered, when in reality she was none of these things. She was none of them now, as I have shown, but she seemed them all; even clear-sighted Mr. Linley thought so, when he passed near her to get a screen for Mrs. Galton, and she (Sydney) said to him—

"Very jolly it is, being here."

Her tone challenged an answer quite as much as her words, and after giving Kate the screen he came back to make that answer, standing before her in the way she liked to see men stand—in a way that showed lookers-on they were devoting their words to her alone, and looking down at

her youth (she was redolent of that same wonderful spirit of youth) with the admiration those alone can feel for it who have left it behind.

"I was afraid you were not finding it jolly at all. I am an old bachelor, and I forgot that when I invited a couple of pretty young ladies I ought to have provided against monotony reigning by inviting a corresponding number of cavaliers."

"Well, I wish you had thought of it, Mr. Linley" (she was franker than ever, for she was resolved not to lapse into obscurity again). "Well, I wish you had thought of it, Mr. Linley, for my sake."

"I will be more provident the next time you honour me," he replied, and there was ever so small a tone of chagrin in his voice. He had hardly anticipated the pretty flirt telling him so jauntily that she wished for the society of another man, though he had been neglecting her.

"That is right, do," she answered, and then she lowered her voice, but not her eyes, and went on, "and then perhaps Mrs. Galton will be good enough to monopolise him, and leave me a chance of having a word with you, Mr. Linley, for you're the oldest friend I have here, you know," she went on pathetically, "except Theo, and I only knew her one day before I knew you."

When she said that, Mr. Linley remembered the night on the terrace, and the nutting the other day, and the way she had thrown him over then for Frank, and many other little episodes in this young lady's life that he had marked. He recovered the judgment he had nearly lost when she seemed to be frankly lamenting that there was no young cavalier here this day. He recovered his judgment about her, and declared her to be but a bungling coquette after all. However, he remained there, standing before her, and looking down admiringly on the fair youthful head, until at last he took both her pretty little plump white hands in his, in order that he might read their palms and something of her character, "which was a mystery to him," he said, to her delight. It was at this juncture, just at the commencement of the reading, that Mrs. Vaughan's eyes fell upon her young guest, and wrath was averted from the head of the vicar of Hoosley.

"I think it high time that we were going, if we are to get back to Hensley to-night, Mr. Vaughan," Aunt Libby exclaimed, rising up with a flutter that sounded through the room like the springing of an agitated hen.

"Surely not yet, Mrs. Vaughan; don't go yet," Mr. Linley answered, looking round at her, but not releasing Sydney's hands.

"But indeed I shall." Mrs. Vaughan snapped rather than spoke these words; they went off with a click in Theo's ears, and made her come away from the window, for they betokened anger.

"Will you order the carriage, Mr. Vaughan, or must I? I will you be good enough to say goodbye to Mrs. Galton, and not keep the carriage waiting, Miss Scott?" The old lady was bridling her head at Sydney, and flashing glances of unmistakeable anger at her, but Sydney would not cast her weapons from her and cry for mercy.

"There will be plenty of time to tell with what I am, and what I'll be, Mr. Linley, if you make haste. I won't keep the old horse waiting, Mrs. Vaughan; poor old fellow! I wouldn't be the cause of his getting a cold, and roaring more than he does already, for the world. That means that ' I shall be fortunate in all I undertake,' does it? how nice. And that other one—what's that? I never noticed my hand being so full of ugly marks before. Let me see if you have any of the same lines, Mr. Linley; here's one—no, it's a cut; how ever did you get that *tremendous* scar, Mr. Linley?"

He dropped her hands suddenly.

"It's not tremendous, it's a mere scratch, you little exaggerator," he said quietly. Then Frank Burgoyne, who had come up to hear what they were all talking about, said:

"Ah! I've often remarked that, Linley; it's a sabre cut, isn't it?"

"I am sorry there is no time to tell a story about it before Mrs. Vaughan leaves us to gloom," Linley answered. "You have had one little specimen of my skill in the art of narration, haven't you, Miss Leigh?" he added inquiringly.

"Yes," Theo replied curtly.

"Oh! yes," Mrs. Galton put in; "you told us some amusing nonsense the night we met you at Lady Glaskill's, about a girl being torn through some bars, and being married to the wrong man, and Harold Ffrench would be grand about it, and refuse to have his name given to the fictitious hero."

"You honour me too much by so clearly remembering the pith of my poor story," Mr. Linley said, bowing to Kate. "You remember it better than that, don't you?" he added abruptly to Theo, and Theo answered "yes," again, and asked him piteously with her eyes, "why she did so remember it?"

To which mute question he did not make reply, but perhaps that might have been because the leave-taking became general at the moment, and Ethel Burgoyne was rather loudly demanding to know whether they would not all of them go to Maddington the following day, and see Mr. Harold Ffrench.

"Perhaps we may, my dear, if I feel equal to it," Mrs. Vaughan murmured; "but the charge that girl is to me words can't tell. I wouldn't have had her down if Theo had given me a hint —no, nor half a hint."

"Oh! she's all right, dear Mrs. Vaughan," Ethel said hopefully.

"Well, I hope she may be, but I don't think it," Mrs. Vaughan replied, relapsing into a state of doubt as to Sydney with virtuous celerity. "*Such* ways, and such manners, and such assurance in a girl of that age, makes me tremble! actually tremble!"

And Mrs. Vaughan trembled forthwith to an extraordinary extent, considering that she was neither cold nor hungry. Perishing starvation could not have shaken more vigorously than did Mrs. Vaughan under the influence of feelings that may not be analysed with regard to this young charge of hers, who suffered men to hold her hands and read her character the while.

CHAPTER XXVIII.

HAROLD!

"HE will not come." Over and over again the girl said this to herself, and over and over

again she felt a blinding shame that she hoped she might be telling herself a lie. He would not come, she tried to feel sure of it. He ought not to come, she knew that full well. But it would be so sweet to see him, it was so hard to know that he was so near and yet so far.

That drive home from Lowndes had been dreary, not so much "dreary," Sidney averred, as disgusting. Mrs. Vaughan had striven— striven arduously, and with partial success—to make her voice heard above the grinding of the wheels. Now the roads were dry and stony between Lowndes and Hensley, and the result of this striving on the part of Mrs. Vaughan was that Theo was nearly maddened by, and Sidney simply maddening to, Aunt Libby.

For Miss Scott had an aversion to being screamed at (especially in reprobation) over the stones, therefore she avoided as much of the unpleasantness as she could by putting over her ears the plump white hands which Mr. Linley had been holding. It was this gesture which made Mrs. Vaughan deem herself more of a wronged woman than ever, it was this that made her see Sidney's misdemeanors of a crimson hue.

Mrs. Vaughan had her little idiosyncrasies. There was no doubt about her possessing them, and no doubt about her fatal facility for developing them on the smallest provocation. She elected to give them full play to-day, so she went to bed with a headache immediately on her arrival at home, and sent a message to the cook to the effect that the luncheon at Lowndes had been an early dinner in fact, and that consequently they would not require the dinner she had ordered before leaving in the morning, or indeed anything at all till they had a cup of tea at nine.

The two girls, in ignorance of this private embassage, came down at half-past six dressed as usual, and finding the drawing-room a blank, they fell to wondering why it was so, and to wandering about the dining-room like two stray spirits. Everyone knows the discomfort of a period of this description. Daylight is not dead in the sky, yet it is too dark to see to do anything; nor is it cold, yet a fire would be pleasanter than a grate full of shreds of white tarleton. Again, dinner is what you are in the habit of expecting at this hour, and though you are not hungry you expect it now, and your heart swells with more anger than sorrow at seeing no signs of it. Theo and her friend had both been set wrong in a measure, and this was not the sort of thing to set them right.

"There goes the ghost of our chance of a dinner to-day, Theo," Sydney said, when the servant came into the room about a quarter to eight with the lamp, and asked them if they would like some bread-and-butter cut for tea. They were both lying down on sofas, and one girl was very miserable, and the other very cross.

"Bread-and butter! no, none for me, thank you," Theo said; and then the servant looked at Sidney, who shook her head vehemently.

"No, none for me, either; bring me a bedroom candlestick."

"You're not going to bed at this hour surely, Sidney," Theo said, turning round on her couch, and gazing with amazement on the little blonde who had lifted herself up on the opposite sofa, and was now employed in carefully dishevelling her long fair tresses.

"I should think I am indeed; I'm utterly worn out; these arrangements don't agree with me. I have been made very ill often by an unavoidable delay in the dinner-hour, and this is an avoidable one, therefore it's ten times worse. I feel shivered and ill, and *dull* to a degree you can't comprehend in your abominable placidity, Theo. Mrs. Vaughan might have mentioned that she was in the habit of cutting off one's rations when one annoyed her."

"It would have been a break to have sat down and dined," Theo answered; "not that I am hungry."

Pending the arrival of her candle, Miss Scott stood up and commenced divesting herself of her rings and bracelets. She was very delicately careful over these things: she polished them up with her filmy handkerchief one by one as she took them off.

"What's the matter with you, Theo? Do you take that affair (isn't this a fine opal? there, you can see it when I flash it so!) to heart much, after all? How about the presents? You have never told me whether you returned them or not."

"Oh, don't! I had none to return."

"How mean of him—horribly mean! and yet I doubt whether they're not more bother than anything, it's so awkward to go and give anything back; it looks as if you suspected a man of being low enough to regard the worth of them; besides, I get to like things, don't you?"

"Yes."

"Now, there's that ring, for instance, and a stud-brooch, opals and diamonds to match it. I begin to feel that I ought to give them back, because, you know, when Hargrave gave them to me I think he understood that I—understood what he—I meant what they——"

Miss Scott having rambled slightly during the whole of her explanation, now lost her way entirely, and stopped.

"Meant," Theo suggested.

"Yes, meant, if you like it; for my part, I hate things that are 'meant,' they always put one in the wrong place, and of all earthly things I hate being in the wrong place. Hargrave has been like a brother to me; he's such a dear fellow, you know; we are great friends, and I could love his wife, if he had one, like a sister; but if I have to guard against what he may 'mean,' or defend myself against what he has 'meant,' why, it will be a hideous nuisance."

"Has a necessity for guarding and defending yourself arisen?" Theo asked. She asked it with a fresher interest than she had yet betrayed, for Sydney's speech savoured of a certainty of something—of something concerning Frank perhaps.

"It hasn't—not exactly, at least, but one's always open to its arising; and then if one has to explain, and apologise, and say 'sorry' for a whole heap of things that would have been nothing if a lot of people hadn't talked them up to your misery, it makes it odious. No tea for me; I'll go up to my room, and you can come and say good-night to me when you come up, Theo."

With this permission she withdrew, leaving Theo alone—quite alone in the dull, cool drawing-room, that looked out on the garden which merged almost imperceptibly into the graveyard.

Miss Sidney Scott had no special gift for playing the martyr without sufficient cause, and she deemed the cause insufficient to-night, therefore she rang for Ann when she reached her own room and suggested to that benign woman that a fire after what she had suffered below would be soothing.

"And missus is that queer that she doesn't care for dinner like, when anything have put her out; but, at your age, miss, lor, 'tain't likely but what you're fit to eat whenever it's the right time; now, couldn't you pick a bit of something for supper?"

Miss Scott thought that she could pick a bit of something for supper.

"That's right," the woman went on cheerily; "I know her ways and I pay no regard to them, and I would have had Miss Theo pay no regard to them either. I'll warm up a partridge in a little gravy, and bring up the tray in ten minutes."

"Go and tell Miss Leigh when its ready, Ann; it will be a capital arrangement," Sidney called out, as Ann was closing the door. But by-and-by the tray came up, and no Theo appeared to partake of its contents.

"Miss Leigh isn't in the drawing-room," Ann said, in answer to Sidney's inquiries.

"See if she's in her room, then."

But Theo was not in her room, nor did a carefully-conducted search, which avoided Mrs. Vaughan's room, succeed in finding her. "Perhaps she has gone to sit with her aunt," Sidney said, but even as she said it she doubted the probability of her surmise being correct, and the warmed-up partridge was eaten with a far less zest than would have attended its consumption had she not been marvelling greatly "where Theo could be."

The lone chill room had been too much for Theo; the lamp cast unpleasant shadows—lamps always do if you are in a room by yourself and your heart is low. She did not dare to disturb her aunt; she did not care to disturb her uncle, who was in his study, engaged in a tough tussle with a text which he did not understand, and which he was going to make clear to the church-going Hensley mind on the following Sunday. There were no books in the house that she cared to read, there were no thoughts in her heart that she cared to lie still and analyse. She was in that condition of mind when action is not alone meet and well, but an absolute necessity for the sufferer. So she rose up presently, and went out through the window, which opened like a door, out into that garden-graveyard where she had strolled with Ethel Burgoyne, and sat down on the tombs with Frank the first night of her arrival.

Rapidly along the paths, in and out from one to another with no cessation of speed, and no settled goal, Theo walked for a while. Then the sound of the gravel under her feet grated harshly on her ears, and she went yet farther from the house, away on to the grass, and commenced threading her way amongst the tombs, in and out, in and out, till her progress grew into a quaint pattern, and she became gradually conscious of it.

Of it, and of something else that caused a cord of feeling that was almost fear to tighten round her heart. She was some way from the house now; a spreading cypress, a yew or two, and a weeping elm intervened, and made her isolation seem a perfect thing; and the tombs that marked where the quiet dead were laid were about her, ghastly pale in the moonlight.

For the moon was up; her beams fell through a dense plantation that rose from the side of the garden, fell shattered into a thousand bits of living gold through the leaves down at Theo's feet. And moving along there, sometimes in the shade of that plantation, sometimes obliterating the golden bars, sometimes showing dark against the whiteness of a tomb, she, sheltered from observation herself by the dark cypress branches, fancied she saw a form.

For an instant she was startled, and she fell back involuntarily still further into the shade of the gloomy branches of that solemn cypress tree. Then she shook off the feeling that she feared might be superstitious dread, and went forward again, out from beneath the branches, from the concealing shade, from that dark haven of calm, along the silent turf, across the shimmering moonbeams, on to the form that had moved, that was moving still, which had troubled her for awhile.

There was no presentiment in her mind to prepare her for that to which she was going, to urge her on, or to restrain her. As unconsciously as the great majority in real life she went on in an unprepared state to that which nothing in reason could have prepared her for. At the worst she deemed that lurking form could be but a stray village dog or child; she went on to pat or reprove it, as the case might be—went on with a conscience void of either fear or hope, and found herself face to face with Harold Ffrench.

No Romeo waiting in the garden with the warm pallor of passion and a southern night upon his face, but visibly a middle-aged gentleman who felt the cold, for his coat was closely buttoned, and he seemed to shudder. Only for an instant had she time to observe these things, in the next he was coming close to her with extended hands, and the words "My God! Theo! *you* here," on his lips.

"I am so glad." Freely she rendered up her welcome, honestly she showed him that it was joy to her to see him again. It might have been that five minutes before each had been feeling sore and sorrowful at heart on account of the other. But now, in this first moment of greeting, no sign was made by either of aught but genuine joy at once again having met. Life is very short. God be praised that some natures seize the golden moments without dimming them by retrospective tears! It was nothing that the girl forgot that she had been injured by, and had suffered for this man, but it was grand in him to forget that he had so injured, and caused her to suffer.

He had taken both her hands in his in his first agitation, for though he forgot the sorest part of the affair, he remembered quite enough to be agitated. And now he released them one by one as he remembered more. Then she spoke again rapidly, for she pitied him so keenly for being there, and dared not show that

pity, and knew that he knew she dared not show it, and bled at her heart for them both.

"I suppose you're on your way—you've missed the way to Maddington."

"Yes, I'm on my way to Maddington," he replied. It was disconcerting to him to be found out in this weakness, even by Theo herself. "What brought you out in the cold?"

They were such cool words—they were spoken in so calm a manner—and yet Theo could not quell her pity, or kill the fear she had of the hot thoughts that dwelt in both.

"The night looked so fine, and I—ought I to ask you to come in, Mr. Ffrench, or will you come another day?"

"Another day," he replied affirmatively; then he walked away hastily for two or three yards, and came back to where the girl stood trembling.

"What did you think of me?"

"When?" she answered. She was a coward then, poor child, and strove to fence with the necessity for understanding him at once. It was all rushing upon her now, and she could hardly bear it.

"When! when you learnt that I had been a mad fool, and that you had to suffer for that mad folly! Theo, I had lost my trust in man long before that day, but I lost my trust in God then."

He put his hands up before his face, he bowed it down upon them as a man who had lost his trust in all things, and still felt he could not put himself out as the snuff of a candle would do. She stood shuddering strongly, for his words were very horrible to her, and she dared not essay to comfort him.

"Go in, child," he exclaimed suddenly. "Go in; it would be absurd to tell you to forget that you have seen me here, but remember it only as one of the thousand follies of a man who is old enough to be your father; go in."

She tried to obey him, but she could not go till she had pleaded for himself against himself. She had loved him so well "once," she told herself, adding that she liked him so well now, that she could not bear him to continue this silence which others might construe into shame.

"You are going to Maddington; the Burgoynes often talk of you," she began tremblingly.

"Do they?" he rejoined carelessly. He could not think about the Burgoynes just then. He was occupied in wondering where God's mercy had been when he suffered the calamity of which he had been the means to this girl to come to pass. The alteration in her was patent to him.

"Oh! Mr. Ffrench, if you would only——" she paused half fearfully as the question obtruded itself—what right had she to counsel or direct this man, who was another woman's husband?

"If I would 'only' what, Theo?—explain my curse to you? No, I cannot: don't ask me to do it——"

"No, not that," she interrupted eagerly, "but go and tell Lord Lesborough that—that you are——"

She could not say "married," the word clung to her tongue, and rendered it incapable of articulating.

"Go in, for God's sake," he said hurriedly, as he marked her huskiness and gathering confusion ; "tell me what you have to say another time—another time, Theo," he continued, inwardly swearing the while that this was the last time he would ever risk putting the girl to such pain. Then the wistfulness of her face wrought upon him, so that as she almost sobbed out "good night," he caught her hand again, and pressed his lips upon it with the fervour that is generally put into the last intended caress.

There was a step behind her—behind the girl whose hand was being held to the lips of the man who loved her, and whose wife lived, and Harold Ffrench, raising his head at the sound, started erect, as though he had been stung, and cried out :

"By my soul, this was undesigned."

"By my soul, you are a scoundrel !" was the quick retort, in tones that made Theo cry out with a pain she had never thought to feel at the sound of her father's voice.

- - - - - ◆ - - - - -

CHAPTER XXIX.

AN EXPLANATION.

THEO had been loved like a daughter, and trusted like a son by her father. He had never been deceived by her ; he had never anticipated being deceived by her in any matter, whether small or great, since the hour when she had first looked at him with understanding, and the great love of his heart had gone out to his daughter. It was very horrible to him to come upon her thus, and to have a doubt of her perfect integrity forced upon him for the first time in such a way.

It did not occur to Theo to tell her father at once that this was no assignation, no planned romance under the moon, no trifling with his honour or her own. She did not suppose it possible that he could deem it such ; she gave no thought to the fact of appearances being horribly against her. She only felt stung to her soul to bear such words as those he had given vent to used by her father to Harold Ffrench.

"Don't call him that," she cried, going up, and trying to cling to her father's arm as she was wont to cling to it, and feeling that he would not suffer her to do so,—why she could not tell. "Don't call him that, dear," she repeated. Then the recollection of her desolation came upon her, and she put her head on his shoulder, and said :—

"Kiss me, papa ; oh, my dear father ! I am so glad you have come."

"Don't add hypocrisy to it," he returned sternly : then, while Theo looked up at him with sad, wondering eyes, he went on with a sob in his voice : "By God, I have trusted you so entirely, my girl, it breaks my heart to think how you have deceived me. I didn't deserve this, Theo, I didn't deserve this."

"Papa ! do you think I came out here to see ——" she did not name Harold, but she glanced round at him as he stood there with his hat off, waiting anxiously to speak.

"God help me, I do," her father rejoined.

"She did not," Harold Ffrench exclaimed, "on my honour."

"Your honour ?"

They were only two words, but they were enough for both who heard them. Theo read in them all her father's hatred and contempt for the man she loved, and that man writhed under them. The position was a pitiable one for them all, and she felt the full pitiableness of it. But hurt, cut to the soul as she was to know herself suspected and Harold wronged, she pitied her father the most. She knew how he would suffer when she made him feel the truth. She knew how he suffered now in doubting her.

"Let us go away,—back into the house, I mean,—before I tell you how I came to be here," she said, very quietly. She had no desire to make a scene, or be emotional ; she only wanted now to get in quickly, and right herself in her father's estimation.

"Good night, Mr. Ffrench. I shall tell my father, and then he will be only sorry, not angry, any more, that we came here to-night."

Theo held her hand out to Harold Ffrench as she spoke, and he took, and pressed, and released it, without a word. Then he doffed his hat to the old man, who stood looking on angrily, and turned away to leave them.

"And now we will go in," Theo said, bringing her eyes back from that glance, that was half after Harold and half away into the past, "and you will soon say that I am no sneak, and that he is no scoundrel."

She did not say this in either angry or injured accents. She had a masculine way of looking at many things, and it seemed to her neither opposed to justice nor reason that her father should be aggrieved and wrongfully suspicious of her. The knowledge that he was so had been slow in dawning upon her, but as soon as it did dawn upon her she felt that appearances were against her, and that it would be idle folly to resent his having judged her by them.

They went in, and found Mrs. Vaughan down in the midst of the assembled household, recovered from her headache, and freely offering suggestions as to Theo's whereabouts, and Mr. Leigh's reasons for having come down in this way, and confusion was rampant for awhile. Confusion which Theo cleared up eventually in her own honest straightforward manner.

"We have so much to say to each other, let us go into a room by ourselves and say it, papa," she exclaimed, going away to the door. Then her father followed her, trying to smile in apparent lightness of heart at his sister as he passed, an attempt which did not impose upon Mrs. Vaughan for an instant, or blind her to the fact of there being something wrong.

They went back, that father and daughter, into the room the drear dulness of which had wrought the evil of driving Theo to escape from it into the open night. When they had entered it, and Theo had shut the door, she turned to him, with a world of love in her outstretched hands and flashing earnest eyes, and began :

"I can't tell you quickly enough, that as little as I thought to see you to-night, did I think to see him out there."

"Theo, is this ——" he interrupted.

"Stop, dear" (in a lovingly imperative tone, a tone that made him feel she would not permit him to be unjust to her). "I only heard of his being at Maddington this morning while we were lunching at Mr. Linley's. Now tell me what has brought you here, papa, and let us have done with that other subject."

Her father's arms were round her now, and he was kissing her on the forehead, and calling her by her pet name, in a way that proved to her right clearly that her simple statement had been accepted.

"The reason I came," he said, "(don't be hurt, child) was that I learnt from a friend that there was danger to my daughter in the neighbourhood, and so, despite his offer to do so for me, I came down to guard her from it myself."

"Danger! from whom?" she asked; then a sudden recollection came over her, and she cried:

"Don't say, don't say, for it's untrue, you know, and you'll be so sorry."

"Sorry, by God, no!" he almost shouted, "I can never forgive him for being the cause of my having doubted my child."

She could not weep and moan, she could not lapse into the lachrymose. Those women are happy who can do so, for it gives them something to do, and aids in passing away an awkward time. But Theo could not cry; neither her mind nor her face grew blurred. So now, though her father was more affected than she cared to see him on her account, she only said:

"It's the friend who scented out a danger that didn't exist, that has caused the doubt; but you'll forgive even that some day or other, so I'm sure you will forgive the one who never hurt or wronged us knowingly."

She uttered this steadily enough, without the shadow of an alteration in her usual tones, but she shivered and trembled when he replied:

"Sorry for having been blind enough to distrust my daughter, even for an instant—yes; sorry for having called down God's curses on the man who would have wrecked her honour had he not been found out in time, and who still pursues her when she is away from her father's protection,—never!"

"Oh, my dear, my dear, you were never so hard, you were never so hard; and you think you are right, and I can't make you feel the truth, though I feel it all so entirely myself."

"We'll say no more about it," he said, huskily; "only this, that I'm sure of you again."

Then she asked him to make her feel that he was by staying there a few days, and then letting her go back to Bretford with him. When he had promised this, she, like a true woman, asked for one proof more.

"And you will scorn to turn informer, won't you? you will keep the secret that was told to you to save,—not that—but to cure me?"

"If you are cured, yes."

She drew a long breath.

"I think I am."

"There is but one thing will make me think it," Mr. Leigh replied.

"And that one thing, papa?"

"I shall believe you cured of the folly I was foolish enough to encourage once, when I see you wipe this thing away from your life."

"What will make you believe that I have wiped it away?"

"When you can look forward, child."

"I can do that now; I shall be very happy

with you and my mother, though my best happiness is gone."

"While you say that, while I know you feel it, how can I forgive that man, Theo?"

He thought of her as he asked this—thought of her as she had been on that day when Harold Ffrench first came down to the rough old sea-coast village. He thought of her as she was then, with all her young bloom about her, with her heart and cheek and mind fresh and unsullied as those of a child. As he thought of her thus, he showed in his face that his unrelenting words were not words merely, they were meant.

"What would make you, then?—and yet don't say, don't say" (putting her hand over his mouth); "it will come in time, even that, perhaps, and you will quite forgive, then."

"Yes; if anything can make me quite forgive, my darling," he replied. "Now let us go back to your aunt; I will stay here a few days, and take you back with me, if you like."

"I think it will be better that I should go; yes, much better that I should go and be with you; then no 'friend' need write you false notes of warning about me, papa, wringing your dear old heart for nothing."

Miss Sydney Scott came to Theo's room that night after the latter had retired, and questioned her severely. "Why did you go out? and where did you go, Theo? Why didn't you ask me to go with you? I should have preferred it to coming up to bed, and then if we had been out together there wouldn't have been such a hullabaloo when your father came."

"I only went out in the churchyard."

"And meditated amongst the tombs: how ghoulish your tastes are for a girl of your age: didn't you feel creepy out there by yourself?"

"Rather."

"I should think so. I wonder what would induce me to go out there," she continued, walking to the window which commanded the graveyard, and placing her face against the glass, and her hands closely on either side of her eyes, and peering steadily for a few seconds into the darkness.

Suddenly she started, and said softly:

"Come here, Theo; gracious! come quick."

"What is it?" Theo asked, going up to her side.

Sydney turned a pale face round to look at her friend, her eyes were sparkling brilliantly, and her teeth almost chattering. She was ecstatic and alarmed.

"There's a figure moving about down there, Theo—a man, I'm sure! do look."

"No," Theo said, shrinking back.

"But do, do! he can't see us." Then Sydney pressed her nose against the glass again eagerly.

"I see him now in the shade, I mean just out of the shade of a tree; I see him quite plainly, that is, I can see one shoulder and his hat. Oh! Theo, who can it be? oh! Theo, did you see any one?"

Poor Theo faltered.

"You know I have not looked," she replied.

"Ah! but I mean when you were out, did you see any one when you were out? Who can it be?"

"Don't let whoever it may be see you at the window, Sydney; pray don't, its nothing extra-ordinary any one being in the churchyard at night, after all."

"But I think it is extraordinary at this hour; all the village people would be gone to bed. Theo, I tell you who I think it is,—Frank Burgoyne."

Theo looked sharply up at Sydney, who had again brought her face away from the glass. The face was flushed now, and a smile of gratified triumph irradiated it; Miss Sydney evidently meant what she had said.

"Maybe it is Frank Burgoyne," Theo said, tremulously, feeling very grateful to the vanity that was ever ready to suppose what it wished.

"And if it's Frank Burgoyne, what can have brought him here? *Did* you see him when you were out?"

"Indeed, indeed I did not, Sydney; do believe me, I did not."

"He must come hoping to see one of us; why else should he come, you know?"

"Probably it is to see one of us, but it's not to see me."

"Oh, Theo! what a thing if, after all, I'm Lady Lesborough; what a jolly take down for all those people at Bretford!"

"Why on earth should you care to take them down? and how could it affect them? You do attribute such a lot of motives to people, Sydney. I hope you will be Lady Lesborough, not for the sake of seeing other people savage, but for the sake of seeing you happy. I think Mr. Burgoyne such a nice fellow! now come away from the window," she continued, coaxingly; she was very much afraid that some stray moonbeam might show Sydney presently that the one she watched was not Frank Burgoyne, and, above all things, Theo desired to avoid remarks being made about the nocturnal visitant at to-morrow's breakfast-table. While Sydney imagined it to be Frank Burgoyne she would hold her peace.

After a time Sydney consented to withdraw, and go to her own room, the window of which did not command the garden and graveyard. And then poor Theo set herself seriously to work to decide on what she ought to do, should she ever see Harold Ffrench, or should the contingency at which her father had hinted, and for which he evidently hoped, arise.

In the order of things it would be only natural that in time to come some one else should see in her a portion of that which Harold had seen, and so perchance desire to possess it for his own. She felt this, she acknowledged it to be but in the order of things; perhaps (she was only a woman) she did not feel strongly averse to such a thing occurring. But how would she take it, what ought she to do when it did occur? Would the ashes of the fire that had burnt out her childhood, that had seared her youth, go on smoulder-ing for ever, and scorch the tendrils of any new hopes that might arise?

It seemed a terrible thing even to herself as she did it, to sit there and weigh the merits of such a case, and calculate the chances of what she might be able to do in order to, at any cost, make her father think that the blight he so re-sented had not been eternally blasting in its ef-fects on her. It seemed unwomanly, unworthy of one who had been dear to Harold Ffrench. But then, again, she owed it to a prior love, to the love her father bore her, to banish as many as might be banished of the signs of that early blight.

And all the while she sat there thinking of these and sundry other things, she could not lose the consciousness that was half agony and half bliss, that every flicker of the little candle that lighted her vigil was watched from below by one of whom she scarcely dared to think.

At last she came to a resolution that gave her a strange kind of strength, that imparted a feel-ing of endurance, a sensation of being able to bear things, which she had long lacked, despite that quiet treading of the path of duty which I have portrayed. She resolved that this early dream which her father, whom she loved so well, had denominated a "folly," should never stand in the way of her following any path upon which he placed her, and which he wished her to pursue. Her sorrow had caused him sorrow enough al-ready; he should never, willingly, be given another pang through her.   •

There came a strong party over from Mad-dington the following morning: the two Miss Burgoynes, and Frank, and the Galtons, and Mr. Linley. These last had reinforced the Madding-ton party on the road, so they all came along together, with a view of taking luncheon with Mrs. Vaughan, "if Mrs. Vaughan would have them," Frank said, which Mrs. Vaughan was only happy to do at his instigation.

Kate Galton was on horseback, in a light-blue habit, seamed with black braid, and in immense spirits, and Frank was palpably in a bad case, though no one save Linley, and perhaps Kate herself, guessed the cause of it. It was Kate's speciality to be lighter-hearted in exact propor-tion as others were depressed, particularly if that depression arose from herself. She marked Frank's moody manner, this morning as she had marked it on that day when the first seeds of the disease that was affecting him were sown, and as she had no feeling with regard to him, she re-solved to play the model matron, and discreetly point out to her husband how foolish young Mr. Burgoyne was, when she found a fitting oppor-tunity.

"We couldn't get Harold Ffrench to come with us to-day," Ethel Burgoyne said to Theo: and Theo, calm as she was externally, quivered in her soul as she glanced at her father, and saw him drinking in the words. "He leaves us in a day or two," Miss Burgoyne went on; "but I daresay you will see him before he goes."

"I leave in a day or two also; I am going back with my father," Theo replied.

"And I am going back with her," Sydney Scott whispered to Frank Burgoyne. She re-flected that if he had deemed it worth his while to risk rheumatism in a damp graveyard at night for the sake of watching her shadow on the blind, he might even risk being rebuked by the pro-fane, for being rashly romantic, and bringing things to a climax under fear of so soon losing her.

But all he said when she told him that she was going back with Theo was, "Oh! are you?" and he did not look much more at the moment. But his manner had lost so much of its former buoyancy, that she was not much disheartened at his being so undemonstrative at the first shot. She would fire a few more before they finally parted, and give him another chance.

Before they had left the Lowndes shooting-box that morning Mr. Linley had received a telegram from a man in town who was more than a servant and less than a friend to him:—a man who wrote his letters, and corrected his proofs, and disabused the minds of too despondent duns of dread, when they came and waited in the hall, urged to this repulsive line of conduct by thoughts of the "heavy accounts they all had to make up next Tuesday,"—a man who was his secretary in name, and who was divers other things in fact.

The telegram was very brief; it consisted only of these words,—"Going fast; he does not know it; will shortly." But brief as it was, and relating as it did to such a pleasant thing as the freedom of somebody or something, it plunged Mr. Linley into a state of melancholy that lasted until they had been on the road for some time, and joined the Maddington party. When that event came to pass he recovered a little, and entered into a very lively disquisition with John Galton as to the respective merits of a couple of colts the latter possessed, one of which was shortly to go into training.

It so happened that John Galton directed his whole conversation during the ride to Mr. Linley and Ethel Burgoyne. His wife therefore fell to the share of Frank, and Frank's elder aunt, whose mind was fully occupied with the management of her horse, and who consequently rather neglected Mrs. Galton. It was an opportunity which he dared not hope, which he did not "hope" (for he wanted to do that which was right), might arise again, so Mr. Frank made the most of it according to his lights.

There was a variety of interests and counterinterests, there was a wealth of plotting and scheming, innocent and the reverse, assembled that day inside that quiet rectory-house.

Events did not march far however this morning. Linley was the only one who made a decisive move on this board which I have endeavoured to place before my readers. He made it by saying when the hour of separation was coming on:

"What do you all say to meeting to-morrow at Lowndes, all of you who are here now? I want my old friend (I may call you my old friend, though, in years gone by, we had but a cursory knowledge of each other) Mr. Leigh to come and see me in my country quarters."

They all promised to go to him, all except Mrs. Vaughan, who did not care to take her best cap a perilous journey a second time for nothing. She declined on the score of the parish requiring her supervision the following day. "There was no occasion for her now," she said; "her young ladies could go with Mr. Leigh."

"And in order not to interfere with Galton's sport, and at the same time not deprive him of such delightful society, what do you say to dining in my bachelor-hut at seven, instead of lunching there at two?" Linley asked, in that sort of generous, liberal way that implies "you may find a Barmecide feast or a baronial festival, my dear fellow, but you'll be heartily welcome to either, especially the latter."

They all said that it was a good change, and assented readily to the plan.

"You will be liable to Harold Ffrench, of course you know that, Linley?" Frank said, interrogatively.

"If Mrs. Galton's cousin is with you still, I shall be most happy to see him."

"I believe he will elect to remain with papa again," Ethel put in.

"Papa, would you rather I didn't go?" Theo whispered, drawing her father into the bay-window.

"Certainly not, you are not the one, nor am I the one to let you, shrink from a meeting that's fair and above board," her father replied.

"Then it's settled that we all meet at Lowndes at seven to-morrow," the master of Lowndes said, rising up; "that is right. Now, Burgoyne, had we not better have round the horses?"

They went off, and took the road at a swinging trot. It happened that the two fastest trotters of the lot were Kate Galton's horse and Frank Burgoyne's: this being the case they soon distanced the others, for there was no good cantering ground between the Vaughans' house and Maddington Park gates.

"Never mind, Galton," Linley muttered to John Galton as the pair turned a corner out of sight of those behind; "the young fellow is foolish, that's all."

John Galton turned with a look of honest inquiry on his face towards the man who was speaking to him. Something in that man's eyes struck him apparently, for presently he flushed, and asked:

"What am I not to mind? and how is the young fellow foolish? I think he's one of the nicest young fellows that I ever met with in my life."

Linley laughed. "My dear fellow, all right; I am ready to think so too; on my word, Galton," he continued in a sort of admiring burst of enthusiasm, "you're one of the most sensible fellows I ever met in my life." Then he drew rather nearer to Ethel Burgoyne, and began speaking to her, for John Galton was looking at him with a queer expression in his eyes. Mr. Linley had made another move.

When they reached the Maddington gates there was nothing to be seen of either Frank or Mrs. Galton. "They have kept up a trotting match to Lowndes, probably," Ethel said; "never mind, Mr. Linley, we have our own man with us; we can ride up without Frank. Mr. Galton and you shall not come out of your road for us."

But Mr. Galton and Mr. Linley insisted on doing so, since the Miss Burgoynes' cavalier had deserted them for the lady for whose conduct Mr. Galton, and Mr. Linley too, in a measure, were accountable.

When they were riding back through the park, after seeing their charges safely off their horses, and not so much as catching sight of Harold Ffrench, John Galton commenced:

"What did you mean just now, Linley? I'm not quick at taking things, but I hardly liked your allusion."

"'Not easily jealous, but, being wrought, perplexed in the extreme,' eh!—no offence; I am but making a quotation, you know."

"It would have improved the play, to my mind, if that hound, Iago, had received a score or two blows from a well-loaded hunting-whip before they set about judging him like a man," John Galton said slowly.

Mr. Linley looked askance at him as they rode slowly along.

"Iago's is an ungrateful part; how the devil are *we* to know that he didn't mean well though he was a little over-zealous in the cause of 'finding out' Desdemona? But let me see; what gave rise to all this? oh! I remember; I ventured to hint to you that that foolish, impressionable boy, young Burgoyne, was boring your wife, and you treat the hint as though I had aspersed *her*."

"I fancied you were falling into the mistake into which a lot of fellows have fallen with regard to Kate,—through no fault of hers," he added hastily. "Because she has no end of good-nature, people think she is guilty of levity, very often when it's as far from her thought as—as—anything bad can be," he continued energetically.

"Of course, of course, that is all very apparent to a man who has seen life, and known women as I have," Linley replied hastily; "but Burgoyne is just one of those young asses who would sell their souls to be spoken about with a married woman; to be a diluted Don Juan, that is the best ambition he has at present, I'm afraid; and that sort of fellow, little dangerous as he is in reality, is awfully compromising to a woman. I like Burgoyne very much," Mr. Linley went on frankly, "and I wish with all my heart that you would give him a setting down, or empower me to do it for you, for his grandfather has the memory of that wretched Hugo who did something or other bad ever present in his mind, and he would be down on Frank to Frank's detriment at a word."

"Set him down for his own good as much as you please," John Galton replied, "but I will not have my wife censured even by implication; here they come back to meet us," he added hurriedly, and his face grew violently red as he said it. He wished he had not used the word "they" in speaking of Frank Burgoyne and his wife after what Mr. Linley had said.

"We have had a charming trot; where are the Miss Burgoynes? my horse never broke once, did he?" Kate exclaimed animatedly, appealing to Frank.

"Not once," he replied abstractedly, staring at her.

"You have blown him, poor fellow," John Galton said, leaning over, and patting his wife's horse; "let us walk home quietly now."

"I'll turn back with you, Burgoyne; don't be alarmed, Mrs. Galton, I won't be a moment late for dinner," the master of Lowndes said, politely taking off his hat to his fair guest as he turned back on the road to Maddington with Frank Burgoyne.

"I say, young fellow," he exclaimed, as soon as the Galtons were out of ear-shot, "you've done it, and no mistake; Galton is as jealous as the devil; how do you stand with her?"

"Good God! what do you mean?" Frank asked agitatedly.

What Mr. Linley meant, however, must be reserved for another chapter.

CHAPTER XXX.

SYDNEY'S SURMISES.

Miss Scott was sorely distraught both in manner and mind, for all her normal steadiness and self-possession, and for all her experience of this species of light skirmishing, till she could get Theo alone, and relieve her feelings by speech.

"He never hinted to me that he was there last night," she began; "those old cats of aunts of his watch him so closely."

Theo felt herself to be the meanest of all impostors, knowing so well as she did the one who had been "there" last night. For an instant she felt tempted to make a clean breast of it: the next instant she felt tempted to do nothing of the kind.

"It's useless mincing the matter," Sydney went on (there was this great bliss in conversing with her, she never waited for your answers)—"it's useless mincing the matter; he's immensely fond of me, I can see that; and I have never made a mistake yet," she continued, with a large air of experience, so large an air in fact that it might have been gained from the passionate and apparent attachment of the whole army, nothing less. "If he does not know his own mind before I go, though, I can't be expected to wait till he does, can I?"

This was a downright question; besides, Miss Scott had to pause for more breath; therefore Theo said, "certainly not."

"Certainly not," Sydney repeated after her, with a mocking emphasis; "you're like every other girl in the world, ready to agree to anything that one doesn't want you to agree to; I didn't expect spite from you, Theo."

"You will never get it, either. I am not quite sure what I ought to say to you about Frank Burgoyne; if I only knew what to say, I'm sure I'd say it."

"You're very kind, uncommonly kind; now, Theo, have I ever come in your way? I ask you, have I ever taken away any of your gentlemen?"

Theo laughed. "I never had any in my possession to be taken away."

"Then you *can't* be jealous of me."

"I am not indeed," Theo replied heartily.

"Ah! I'm delighted at that," Sydney said, in a tone in which disappointment would make itself heard. "I'm delighted at that; there is nothing that would be so odious to me as the idea of making any one jealous of me. I couldn't bear it; oh! I wouldn't do it, not on any account, if I could help it. I have done it sometimes unconsciously, for men *will* like me, you know; of course that's pleasant, but the other is horrible, isn't it?"

"Very pleasant—I mean very horrible; oh yes, I quite agree with you."

"I can see Mrs. Galton hates me," Sydney said, letting her hair down before the glass, and trying the effect of a different arrangement. It was always gratifying to Miss Scott to think that Mrs. or Miss anybody else hated her.

"Why should she hate you?" Theo asked.

"That's what I say to myself!—why should she? But she *does*, any one can see with half a glance. I'm not going to be put down by Mrs. Galton, though; she could have slain me to-day when he handed me the butter at luncheon."

"You don't suppose she wanted all the butter, do you?" Theo asked, laughing.

"No, it wasn't that; she didn't like to see Frank paying me so much attention. The butter, indeed! how absurd you are, Theo! You must have seen her look. Ouf! she glared like a pretty-faced cat; I'm sure, though, there ought to be no question of cutting out in the matter; *she* is a married woman, and I have never attempted to cut her out."

Theo tried very hard to interest herself in Sydney's surmises. It seemed ill-natured not to do so. Theo had perfectly recovered the little sore feeling that came over her on that first day when Frank Burgoyne had paused on his path to her to provide nuts for Miss Scott.

"Then you really feel that he likes you, dear, and you are sure you like him?" she said, sympathetically. Sydney, however, was not one to care for the tone sympathetic,—it threw too serious a hue over all things.

"Oh! I don't know about 'really feeling' and 'being sure;' how can one be sure of anything, especially when a man is hedged in between a lot of old aunts?"

"It is ridiculous to speak of the Burgoynes in that way; Ethel is very little older than we are, if she is at all."

"I don't want to say a word against them, only I hate being watched and glared at as if I were the most outrageous flirt in the universe." Sydney fervently prayed at this juncture that Theo might say she "thought she was;" but Theo neither thought nor said it. Her friend's ambition had not been fully fathomed by her yet, and even had it been Theo Leigh was too conscientious to gratify it.

"Did they glare at you too? I thought Mrs. Galton did the glaring? And all this fierceness was thrown away upon me; I wish I had seen it, Sydney."

"I wish you had, because it is great fun to see a lot of women spiteful to choking point, and unable to help themselves; Frank would go on, you know."

"Go on what?—handling you the butter?"

"Paying me attention generally, Theo," Sydney replied loftily. "If you didn't see it for yourself, I am not the one to tell you about it. I detest talking about myself. What shall you wear to-morrow? I shall be pale, and go in pink."

"You *will* be pale?"

"Yes; I turn very pale at night if I am at all thoughtful, and I shall be thoughtful to-morrow," Sydney replied, deciding on her *rôle* for the morrow with the gravity of a judge; "and one white flower in my hair: bother this sudden move of going back to Bretford just as I have got used to all your aunt's vagaries!"

"I am sure my aunt would be glad to keep you longer, if you'll stay. I must go back with my father; he wants me, and I want him. I have been away from him too long already," she continued sadly.

"Then of course you must go; and it won't matter whether you do or not if Frank proposes to me, for then I can go and stay at Maddington," Sydney replied, suffering her selfishness to crop out in the frankest manner; "and if he doesn't why then the sooner I get away the better, for I should be bored out of my life here: isn't mine a charming philosophy?"

"Very charming, indeed,—what there is of it; the philosophical portion of your speech wa microscopic, though."

"Perhaps you will like the philosophy of th one I am about to make better. I always mak the best of things; I shall make the best of m house when I've one of my own, by having yo there as much as possible. That's rather pretty speech from one woman to another now I wouldn't say it to any other girl in the work than you, Theo," Sydney said brightly, in bles oblivion of the scores of school companions and friends of later days to whom, in moments of confidence, the like speeches had been made by her.

"Very pretty indeed, and very nice of you if you could mention at once in what direction your house is likely to be, I could take a yearly ticket on that line, and so be in a position to rui down to you often," Theo said, smiling.

"Rather witty, and more than rather vicious,' Sydney replied cooly. "Well, women are al alike! even you have the taint, Theo; you're a wee bit; I won't say 'annoyed,' but 'astonished' at my being so liked. Shall I wear my hai turned back or over my forehead to-morrow night?"

"You look very well with it either way."

"Do I really now," Sydney exclaimed with the freshest delight; "no one is less conceited than I am; I never thought myself pretty for a minute in my life; I wonder other people do, don't you?"

"Think you pretty?—yes."

"No: wonder at other people thinking me so; they *say* they think me so, at least. I don't believe them. Of course I know that I am not hideous, but then my mouth is wide, you know (don't you hate a button-mouth? *I* do), and my nose isn't quite straight, and, as Hargrave says, I have ever so much more mind in my forehead than any Greek statue that was ever chiselled."

"I agree with Mr. Hargrave; and your nose is nicer than any stupid straight one."

"Oh, you're delicious, Theo! you're not a bit like other girls, making people uncomfortable whenever they can. I think *you* charming, and I don't mind telling you so; but then I very seldom meet with any one like myself and you, who is equally open and above any little paltry jealousy." Sydney pranced about the room as she spoke, with her head aloft and her face flushed with excitement. The sound of her own praises was to her as the smell of powder to the young war-horse.

"Hargrave, you must know, Theo, abominates anything statuesque in real life, and his taste is perfect,—oh! perfect. He always says, 'Fancy waltzing with the Venus of Milo, or having a Juno to pour out your tea.'"

"No, I can't fancy his doing the one with the Venus, or Juno doing the other for him," Theo replied, laughing, as a vision of the crisp carroty locks, and the stiffly-carried head which surmounted the well set-up form of the gallant young officer rose up before her. "It's quite a treat to hear you speak of Hargrave, though, Sydney; he has been absent from your conversation for a long time."

"He has; not only absent from my conversation, but from the country; he is in Dublin now, going to Lords-Lieutenant's balls, and flirting with Irish girls, probably. He *was* very nice, though," she continued, seriously, " so nice that I should not wonder, dear, at your falling in love with him if you saw much of him. When I have a house of my own you shall see a good deal of him ; he will be safe to like a friend of mine."

" Poor Hargrave ! if he could hear you, how gratified he would be : can't you let him manage matters for himself for the future ? "

" Theo, I only meant it kindly towards you," Sydney replied, with severe gravity. " I should not benefit by it at all, further than the benefit it would be to me to see two people of whom I am fond—yes, very fond—happy together.'

Theo looked at her wonderingly. "She really believes herself for the moment," Miss Leigh thought; " she plays so many little harmless parts, and rushes into them all with such spirit that she really believes herself; she is quite exalted now."

Presently Sydney came down from her temporary pedestal, and resumed the manner of every-day life.

" I won't be so selfish as to keep you here talking any longer, dear, for I'm so sleepy that I can hardly keep my eyes open, and if I don't go to bed now they will be heavy to-morrow with too late sleep. Now go, I won't be selfish enough to keep you a minute longer. Good night,—and, Theo dear, if you do see Ann, tell her I'd like some biscuits and a glass of sherry. I'm tired."

That evening, while Theo had been sitting, listening to her friend's frivolous surmises, Harold Ffrench had received a telegram, and had started off at once in what appeared to the Burgoynes a most extraordinary state of excitement as an answer to it. " I have received news from town which will take me away by the next train," he said to Lord Lesborough in a broken, altered voice; and when Lord Lesborough said, " Dear me, no bad news, I hope, my dear Harold ? " he could only say in a bewildered manner that he " did not know yet."

Nor did he, in truth. Once before he had received a somewhat similar telegram, and he had acted upon the supposition of its truth, to his own lasting remorse, and Theo's lasting sorrow, he feared. The former telegram had told him of the death of his wife, this one which he now held in his hand told him that she was dying.

He dared not believe it, he endeavoured not to hope that it was true. And he failed ! From the bottom of his heart there rose up a big prayer that would be prayed—a prayer that, fervent as it was, mingled itself with the gurgling of waters, with the sound of the soft Greek tongue, with the noise of a cry that had burst from his soul through his lips years, years ago, when a veil had been torn down by a mistakenly impassioned hand.

If that prayer were realised ! if that prayer were only realised ! " My God ! " he thought, " what a vista opens before me, for the girl loves me still."

He went off, and took his ticket, and wrapped himself up in a corner in his railway rug, just as though his journey were one of the commonplace things towards a common-place goal which

men take every day. Went off and took his ticket, and started on the journey towards death and liberty about the same time that Theo was hearing that Sydney would wear pink and be pale on the following day, and praying God to give her grace to bring sunshine on her father's heart once more, if it might be that the option of doing so should be offered her.

It was in the dull grey morning that the train by which he was travelling reached the London terminus. The out-look over the house-tops of that east-end district, that he had had as the carriages crept slowly homeward, was a disheartening one. All was murky and cheerless, cold, ugly, raw, and uncomfortable that morning in the world (so much of it as he could see) and in his own heart.

Life was not up and doing in the homesteads of that business locality yet, save in a few instances. Still looking at those houses over which hung that deep air of all being at a standstill within, which marks the exterior of the abode where all are sleeping; looking at these houses, steeped in quiet as they were, gave him no sense of rest, no respite from that soul-fatigue which was bowing him down. He called to mind—the carriages the while lazily creeping home—early hours that he had known in other scenes, when his heart had been hotter than now it was, and sorrow and waiting had been harder things to endure. Hours when the night, the dark gloomy night, had merged into a clear, grey, bright childhood of young morn, that found him standing on some hill, perhaps, at the foot of which a village wrapped in slumbers lay. Hours which had brightened imperceptibly, and brought a certain soft peace to his soul as the greyish tints grew warmer, and a little shade of pink came over the east, and blushed away the mists in a way that made him know that hour to be the maidenhood of day. Hours when life, the sleeping life around him, had wakened up, thrilled into being as it seemed by that blush, when action had resumed its sway, and rest had been rather softly laid aside than broken rudely. Such hours he had known often :—how often !—and he passed many of them in review before him as the train crept slowly home over the summits of sordid-looking houses, which in their grim repose gave him no sense of rest, but only of stagnation.

There was an hour in his past that was given back to him more vividly than the others which he remembered. Memory has an artist's hand very often ; she photographs a " something," and then touches it deftly with gorgeous tints, with tender accuracy, with loving skill. She brought him back such an hour now : she touched it in such a way : she galvanized that golden hour from the past !—between the taking of the tickets and the final stopping of the train.

This was the scene, bereft of the tints by which memory enriched it : this was the hour, devoid of the colour and glow !

He was a boy ! Not that, for the law allowed him just three days ago the honours and dignity of manhood; but a boy in heart and feeling though his years were twenty-one. A great indignant cry, followed up by cantos of melodious strains, had throbbed over from the land of classic story, to the university at which he had been studying. The time for doing this was over now (at the hour I speak of), and he was on his way to "Greece and the struggle for liberty;" that was all, he thought. In reality he was hastening forward to the worst of bondage and slavery.

There was with him one who had been his sworn friend and comrade through numerous school-boy joys and sorrows, through various college difficulties, through so much of the weal and woe of life as either of them had yet known. A sharp, brilliant young fellow, this latter, a year or two older than Harold; a man with a limitless faith in himself, and that which he was destined to achieve; likewise with a limitless faith in the folly or the vice of the rest of the world.

Such the *dramatis personæ*. The scene was the deck of the yacht. Time, that moment when the purple-pink hue broke over the brow of the morning, and blushed away the mists that had prevailed before.

They were on deck together. Harold, then the more active, as he was ever the more impassioned, of the two, was leaning over the bulwark, looking eagerly along towards the east, gazing with his soul in his eyes at the first sign of the sun-burst which should presently flake the sea, flood the scene with living gold. The other man, his friend, was lying down by his side, and both were silent, and the heart of one (of the one who now recalled that hour) was very full of the glory of the world God has made, and of faith in the goodness of the creatures He has placed in it.

Well! that hour and its illusions were long past; nothing was left to him now, save the memory of it.

The train stopped: even that memory was gone.

He stepped out on the platform shiveringly, and looked round for a porter to fetch him a cab, while he endeavoured to get himself a cup of coffee. As he did so, a man rushed past him from a carriage that was farther back than the one he had occupied—a man whose gait and figure he seemed to know. But he did not pause to think more about the man, whose face he had not seen. The atmosphere was cloudy even under shelter on that chill foggy morning, and his mind was troubled about matters so important that they had the power to cast out all thoughts of possible acquaintances.

He had to take a long dreary drive through a wretched part of London, and then another train for a short distance in order to reach the suburb where lived the woman, if still she lived, who was his wife. As fate would have it, the sole cab that could be found for him was a four-wheeled one, drawn by a horse about which there could be no manner of doubt. A horse whose head was so low in the world, and whose knees were so hopelessly broken and swollen, would be safe to miss every train his unhappy "fare" might be desirous to save. However there was no other cab to be taken, so he took this, and went away at an excruciating jog-trot that was worse than a walk, inasmuch as it was no faster and jolted him more severely.

Huge drays lumbered up at every corner to obstruct him, gigantic loads of cabbages perpetually blocked the way, the earliest of all

butcher's-boys locked his wheel in a fast embrace, and then swore at his well-meaning but unquestionably irritating driver for full five minutes. He was taken down a very "short cut," and when at the extreme end he was ignominiously draughted back again, because the "road was up." The horse grew lamer every minute, the driver more considerate to that luckless quadruped. The busy stream of life poured faster and faster through the streets every instant. London had shaken off slumber as far as his eye could penetrate, and every one was going the usual pace but himself.

Delay was awful to endure; he had never known aught so slow as this progress he was making, save a day's old Times or an evening party. Delay was maddening, for she who had injured him so might die deeming him cruel at the last.

He would get out and walk; he would hail the first hansom. This was a good thought, a bright thought: it irradiated two long streets in the which no hansom could be found. They either did not grow in those regions, or at that hour; anyway he could not see one, look out of which window he would.

He gained the station from which he had to take the train for a short distance at last, and then he found that the train he had hoped to catch was gone, but that in half an hour there would be another; so there was more waiting to be done. More waiting, and more writhing under the consciousness that he might stab at the last, the solemn "last," and he misjudged.

That half-hour passed, the brief journey was over soon, and at the station at which he alighted he found a hansom and a horse that was not lame. The day was clear and bright now, well on her way to her first grand junction, the breakfast-hour of the great majority. But his spirits and his brow could not clear and brighten in company with her. He was afraid to think or hope in fact, and he could not help doing both.

A sharp drive through a street or two of houses, which you cannot pass without marvelling who on earth can live in them, they are so devoid of all purpose in point of architecture, so guileless of design in their turrets, which are far too tiny for any one to harbour the thought for an instant that a room lives inside those symmetrically arranged bricks,—up a stupendous hill that rises right away out of these streets in a way that suggests to you that if ever you have a spite against the denizens of these latter you can go up there with a proper apparatus and pour a sufficient quantity of molten lead upon their dwellings with extraordinary effect,—and then across a common, the last thing between himself and those abodes of pretentious suburban bliss, in one of which he was going to meet his wife.

We have seen this man only as a lover, as Theo Leigh's lover, heretofore; we shall now see a little of him as a husband.

The garden gate of the "villa residence" where she who had borne his name, and had the power to keep that name sacred or to dishonour it as the case might be, had lived, stood open when he reached it, and on the gravel path that led up to the door there were the marks of a pair of wheels, double marks,—they had been, and they had returned. He saw them without remarking them, and his own hansom wheels crushed these previous ones out with speed as he dashed up to the door.

The door was opened to him in a second by a pallid boy, whose trembling fingers had refused to adjust his jacket round his young person with that perfect propriety which it is the ambition of a "Buttons" to achieve. Harold Ffrench stepped over the threshold, through the portiere, into a carpeted hall,—out of the fresh, clear winter air into an atmosphere that was made up, God knows of what! There was an unearthly sweetness, a languid fragrance about it that he had never met with before.

He went on, he had not seen her for years; he went on, knowing now that she was dying.

The door of a room was open opposite to the head of the flight of stairs by which he ascended to look his last upon her. He went through it, and then he paused for a minute, and, with his head bowed upon his hands, prayed for strength to bear whatever he might see, whatever he might hear. Then very reverentially he approached the couch shrouded by silken curtains on which lay that the existence of which had clouded Theo Leigh's life; approached at the signal of a man who rose from his knees at her side—a priest of her own faith, of the Greek Church, to which she had returned of late years: and so, after long years, once more he looked on the face of his wife.

CHAPTER XXXI.

AT THE LAST.

DEATH'S seal was upon her: but for all that it was such a common-place face to have caused such a wealth of anguish to such a man.

She was lying with her eyes closed when he first knelt down by her side, and all the casual observer would have seen was a large white face, coarse features, and ill-marked brow, and a mouth that had been voluptuous in youth, but that now was pinched and drawn. He saw more than this: he saw the face of the woman he had vowed all unwittingly to love and cherish years, years ago, while still a boy; the face of the woman whose own conduct had forced him from the hard task; the face of the woman who had been the cause (innocent in that, though) of his seeming a scoundrel to Theo Leigh.

She opened her eyes after a while, and asked, "Is he there still?" in a querulous whining tone; and they told her in response that "her husband was," and so presently she turned her eyes upon him.

"So, you could come for this?" she asked; and there would have been sarcasm in the poor dying voice, had he allowed himself to hear it.

He stooped down: he was very tender to aught that was weak or womanly. She was very weak now, in this parting hour, and very womanly withal in her mild attempt to embitter it.

"Zoë, let us forgive," he said, as softly as though she had anything to pardon in him.

She moved her head wearily on the pillow, this woman with the beautiful soft Greek name, who was dying.

"I can forgive," she muttered; "take my hand," (she drew it from beneath the coverlet) "and tell me you will too,—everything."

He took her hand.

"Everything, everything," he whispered.

"Then raise me up, and with my head upon your shoulder, I will tell you truly what became of her whose head would have been more welcome there than mine has ever been."

"Of Leila," he said mournfully, obeying her.

"Yes: she did not die."

"He lied, then, even though all was so long over." Harold said, more to himself than to her.

Her breath came quicker and shorter. "You must lean me back," she muttered brokenly; "lean me back, and listen! Leila lived for years. Harold, do you remember when I was first false to you?"

He bent his head in bitter assent: had she merely sent for him to stab him?

"I gave myself to him on condition that he should never let you know that Leila, who loved you still, and whom he had forced away and kept till—till——"

"God! She was never his, say?" Harold Ffrench cried; and the answer was a weary closing of the eyes, a weary movement of the lips, a weary, sad, painful fleeing of the soul from the frail body. The Greek woman, the bride won in such a romantic way (for Linley's tale had been Harold's true story, with the substitution of Constantinople for Athens), the wife who had been a curse to him, the sister of the girl who had first waked love in his soul, was dead?

Her last words had been perhaps the bitterest drop in the bitter cup his connection with her had forced him to drink. For years, from the date of that rash chivalrous marriage which had marred him, up to the day of Linley's introduction to Kate Galton and Theo Leigh, Harold Ffrench had never heard of Leila. He had never dared to seek tidings of her while his love for her lived, because of his wife, her sister. And when at last time killed that love, the day for seeking tidings of her was long, long past. So he went on till that night when Linley told him that Leila had "expiated her offence against the heaven-born passion Love in the dark blue waters of the Bosphorus."

He had grieved at the hearing; grieved as a man must grieve when he learns that the lovely thing he loved has come to a cruel end. He had grieved and believed; now on her own death-bed, his wife had deepened the grief by abolishing the belief, and substituting for it a fear that a deeper wrong had been his, a deeper degradation Leila's than he had ever feared.

He moved away presently: away out of the presence of the senseless form that had been a burden to him so long: away down into the drawing-room of the suburban villa where the signs of her, its late mistress, were manifold.

A luxuriously furnished room, heavy with perfume, and reeking, as it were, with ornaments. Not with the ornaments that tend to elevate the taste of those who look upon them, but of an order that told clearly what manner of woman she had been who had selected them.

There were gorgeous vases, vases all red and gold, of queer fantastic shape, standing on the floor, with their bases buried in deep wool mats dyed of a brilliant scarlet. In these vases gaudy flowers bloomed or drooped rather, for the heavy air, the atmosphere of artificial perfume, was killing them.

He looked round at the low soft couches, on which soft furs and oriental rugs were thrown, at the little Maltese dogs, their hair tied up with pink and blue ribbons, that were lying upon them. He marked the colour and the warmth, and the mighty amount of everything that could tend to relax and enervate the body and mind, and the absence of all that could purify, brace, and refine. Then he sat down with a sigh, and thought of how the ignorant strong-natured girl he had married had been true to her fleshly instincts, true to her disregard of more ennobling influences to the last.

There were gilded toys about, movable figures arrayed in the last Paris fashions, that waggled their heads and wriggled their hands when you pulled a wire. There were many volumes of coloured engravings, whose bindings caused you to blink. There was a wearisome waste of all such things as a tasteless woman with plenty of money to spend and an eye for bright colours is sure to collect about her. But there was not a single thing about the room which told that the woman who had occupied it had possessed either heart, soul, or mind.

He had never been in that house before. The little dogs, the only things that had loved and lived with his wife to the last, came round him cringingly, as Maltese terriers will, expecting either a kick or a biscuit, but there was no recognition in their servile eyes, no friendship in the wags of their time-serving tails. He had never been there before, he had never seen his wife since that hour to which she herself had alluded, when he first knew her false to him.

He had never known a moment's love for her; but when he had first recovered from the stunning blow the deception which made her his wife had dealt him, when first he recovered from that, and along through a series of years that appeared interminable, he had striven to "make the best of things" for her and for himself. She was a babyish-minded, ignorant, plain young girl. She had already shown herself an adept at intrigue in a way that had wrecked his life; still he reminded himself that she was his to guard and improve now, let the means by which she had become so be ever so reprehensible. He strove with all his strength and mind to so guard and improve, and her low ignorant cunning baffled him at every point, till he sickened over the task.

Then there came a day when the man who had aided him in carrying her off "under a mistake," as he (Harold) still supposed, appeared upon the scene. She brightened a little, came out of her apathetic languor, seemed to throw off a few of her wearingly childish ways and tedious lazioess, when this friend came, till at last Harold knew that both friend and wife were foully false to him.

The men could fight. Harold had the poor consolation of leaving a scar that never wore out on the hand of the man who had wronged him. But the woman,—the plain soulless woman who had been the cause,—what of her? Her lover—the one who for some cruel spite

had played at being so—would have none of her, that Harold knew. She relapsed into her former apathy, making no defence, caring not what became of herself; so he, reproaching himself a little perhaps for that he had never loved her, suffered her to remain a clog to him, sought no divorce, and separated from her only to her greater comfort.

The friend who had done him this last injury was David Linley.

It seemed such a motiveless wrong, such a causeless injury. It remained a profound enigma to Harold Ffrench why David Linley should have wrecked their friendship for this woman without a charm, till on her death-bed she told him brokenly that Leila had been loved by Linley, and had never loved Linley in return. He saw it all now: there had been a motive, and the motive was jealousy, which sought to sting, no matter how or when.

His "love for Leila was a long-dead thing," as he had once said to Theo Leigh. But he could not help thinking with some of the old passion of the glorious-faced girl whom he had loved and lost in his youth. She had been true and tender, then, after all; she had loved him and her fate had been so hard, so horrible! It was so vague to him even now.

He roused himself from this dream of the past, and the thoughts of the present came to him and caused his heart to bound. Life held much for him still. The past would be swept away like an ugly dream; the future was all his own to give to Theo Leigh.

How he longed to hold her to his heart and tell her all!—his early love, his wrongs and sufferings; to lay bare his life before her, in fact, and hear her say that she would take what was left of it. How he longed to do this, and to bring back the bloom to the fresh young cheek that had blushed its best blush for him, and that the moonlight told him but the night before had grown so very pale.

But he had been over hasty once. He would wait now till none could censure him for being premature. There would be safety in such waiting he felt proudly, for Theo Leigh was true as steel he knew.

By-and-by he summoned the confidential servant who had lived with his wife for years, and she told him, rather more whiningly than was well, how her mistress had cared for him and craved for his presence at the last. He tried to believe it, though; he wished to believe it, wished to think that she had been only weak and erring, not wicked and heartless.

After a time he asked the question which he had summoned her to ask, and which parched his tongue in the asking.

"Mr. Linley never came here?" he said, lifting up one of the little dogs as he spoke.

"Never, sir. That you should think such a thing, with my poor dear mistress——"

"Hush!" he interrupted; "I meant the question as no reflection upon her; I only want to know the full measure of my debt to him," he muttered, putting the little dog down again.

The woman coughed and sighed before she spoke again.

"He never came near this house, and I was always with my poor dear lady when she went out. Would you not like to see her, sir? She looks so peaceful and happy, it might comfort you."

He could not refuse it: it would have looked brutal to do so; besides, a refusal might wring this woman's heart, and she had been faithful, and was true according to her lights, he thought. Still he could not avoid going along to the chamber of death lingeringly and slowly; there was something in going at all from which his soul recoiled.

He went in very softly. "All that was left of her now was pure, womanly." She lay there in raiment that was not whiter than the face, which did look very happy and peaceful. There were flowers on the pillow, and on the coverlet, and between the waxen fingers of the gently-folded hands there was a broken lily. It all looked very pure and stainless, and there was a solemn hush in the room.

He stood there gazing upon that which was left of the woman who had been his wife, and his heart was filled with as solemn a hush as that which pervaded the room. He could not tear himself away. He could only stand and think very softly of her and of the solitary life she had led for years in loveless penitence.

Presently there was a sound of tiny pattering feet, then a rushing, and worrying, and scraping, and the little Maltese terrier came from under a chair that stood by the head of the bed, with something in her mouth. "Here, Julie! Julie!" the maid cried affrightedly. But before she could rescue it, Harold Ffrench had taken from Julie's mouth a scarcely-worn glove, and read on the inside of the wrist the name of "David Linley."

CHAPTER XXXII.

SAVED AND LOST.

"Good God! what do you mean?" Frank Burgoyne asked.

"Mean? Why, that that fellow, who is not the fool you take him to be, has fathomed your feelings for his wife. You have been mad," David Linley replied sternly. His game seemed very clear to him now; he liked Theo himself, and he would have won and worn her if he could have done so. Failing that, however, as he felt that he should fail, strive as he might, he resolved that Harold Ffrench should never have her. It had been Harold's misfortune through life to win love where Linley coveted: Linley had still one arrow in his quiver to let fly into the heart of his former friend.

Frank Burgoyne grew flushed and uneasy.

"You exaggerate in the most horrid way, Linley," he began hotly; "there has been nothing in my manner to Mrs. Galton, for whom I have the deepest respect——"

Linley groaned impatiently.

"Talk that trash to women, they'll believe you perhaps. My dear fellow, there's been that in your manner to Mrs. Galton, and, by Jove! that in Mrs. Galton's manner to you, that if Harold Ffrench gets hold of it you're ruined with your grandfather."

"I will not allow Mrs. Galton's name to be handled in this way, or her conduct to be called in question," Frank replied indignantly.

"Then teach her to be more careful, show her that it is incumbent upon her to be more careful, not alone for her own sake, but for yours. Good Heaven! your grandfather will fancy himself justified in anything—a married woman! his favourite cousin!" Linley said earnestly.

"You are making the most groundless accusations in your anxiety for my welfare, Linley; you are over-shooting the mark altogether," Frank said nervously. He was miserably conscious of the state of his own feelings towards Kate, and miserably uncertain as to how far he had betrayed them. This uncertainty kept him under as it were, and gave David Linley the mastery.

"I can only tell you that Galton is on the alert; he told me to speak to you. I don't wish to asperse Mrs. Galton, but when a married woman sees a man is in love with her, it looks rather fishy if she suffers the thing to go on."

"I have never thought of her for an instant save as an agreeable companion," Frank replied moodily.

"It is most unfortunate, *most* unfortunate, then, that your manner should have implied so much more. Knowing that she is a flirt, and that you are impressionable, I ought never to have thrown you in contact; the fact is, I fancied you were sweet on that charming girl, Theo Leigh."

"So I am," Frank said hurriedly. He was ready to say or do anything to avert the possibility of the shadow of suspicion falling upon Mrs. Galton's admired head. The folly had all been his; he alone would pay what penalty that folly cost.

"I am heartily glad of it. No, I won't come in, thank you; I must get over to Lowndes, and dine as quickly as possible. I have to run up to town to-night to see my lawyer. I shall tell Galton before I go that Theo Leigh is the one, and I'll let *her*, Mrs. Kate, know it too, or she will be compromising you."

"For God's sake don't say too much," Frank said in a bewildered tone.

"If you regard your interests at all, too much cannot be said," Linley replied firmly; "*you* know the trifle that's required to make a very considerable difference in your grandfather's will. By Jove! I shall think that Mrs. Galton has gone a little further than I gave her credit for, since you are ready to risk so much for her favour."

"I have never had her favour in the way you imply: I have never been scoundrel enough to seek it. Say of me what you please, but for God's sake don't saddle her with the consequences of my confounded stupidity." Frank spoke quite warmly; he was ready to do anything to establish that guilelessness of Kate in which he himself so firmly believed.

"I wish I could credit you quite, my boy," Linley said. "Be careful, that's all I can say. Don't rouse John Galton's jealousy, or it will be all up with the woman, as well as yourself. Don't look savage, Frank; I have spoken for your good. If you say 'drop it for the future,' good; I will do so. Come over to dinner to-morrow at seven, I will make a diversion by bringing back a lot of town news, and *be* careful."

"I will," Frank replied eagerly; "you'll see I will."

David Linley shook hands heartily with Frank Burgoyne, and then rode rapidly back to Lowndes.

"You'll excuse my dressing to-night, won't you, Mrs. Galton?" he said, going into the room where Kate and her husband were. "I have to run up to town directly, to see my publisher about that confounded book of mine."

"Nothing wrong, I hope? Certainly, don't dress; you will be back to entertain your guests to-morrow, I presume?" Mrs. Galton said languidly.

"Oh yes," he said, he should be back; and there was nothing very wrong, only some "copy" missing. Then he offered his arm to Mrs. Galton, and they went in, and he made a choice selection of viands, and flavoured the same with the right sort of wines, and had altogether a capital dinner, partaking of it with the keenest appetite, just as though he had not heard that morning that the woman to whom he had been one colossal wrong, from the moment he first palmed her off upon his friend so falsely, lay dying.

When it was time to go off to catch the train he did it as quietly and blithely as possible, making jokes the while with Mrs. Galton about the new-born dandyism he was betraying in gloves. "It's a shame for you who never used to wear them at all to travel in such as these," she said, taking up a pair of pale lavender ones, in which he had written his name delicately and legibly; and he agreed with her "that it was a shame; but I have rushed from one extreme to the other under your auspices." He travelled up in those gloves nevertheless.

It is not essential to follow him upon that journey; the scenes through which he passed are perhaps better left untouched. It need only be told that he was more fortunate than Harold Ffrench, in that when the train crept slowly up to the terminus in that grey morning hour he trusted to his own wit rather than to the porter's, and so procured the solitary hansom waiting there, which wafted him speedily on towards his goal. But he was more unfortunate in one thing: when he reached his goal he lost a glove, while Harold found one as we have seen.

The host was back in admirable time to recover his fatigue, and receive his guests on the following day. He wore an outside mantle of extreme good humour and high spirits, but Kate had a habit of lifting up corners of such mantles and looking beneath. She did so on this occasion.

"Something has gone wrong with you," she whispered, after the Leighs and Sydney had arrived, and while they were awaiting the Burgoynes, and were all trying not to look as if they were anxious for the Burgoynes to come. "Something has gone wrong with you, I am sure. Can't the missing copy be found?"

"No, and it makes me awfully anxious; but cover that anxiety if you can, that's a good creature," he replied; and Kate promised, but did not believe him.

It was easy enough to cover his anxiety, and conceal it from the earliest arrivals, for Mr. Leigh went back into the past at sight of Linley, and enlarged upon the same for John Galton's special behoof. It was a rare treat to Mr. Leigh to meet with some one who felt an interest in that particular epoch which was brought to his mind by the meeting with Linley. John Galton felt and looked genuine interest at once in Mr. Leigh's reminiscences, just as he would have felt and looked about anything that concerned any one whom he liked however remotely.

As for Theo and Sydney Scott, they had not come to that age yet when we mark the mien that is not shown to us.

But when the Burgoynes appeared upon the scene David Linley became what he had never had cause to accuse himself of being before—a fidgety dispenser of hospitalities. "I am awfully afraid of things going wrong even now, though they're well in train," he said, half to himself and half to Kate Galton, with a startled look, when she laid her hand on his arm gently and told him he must take her in to dinner. "How should they? and what matter if they do?" she answered rather scornfully. She was becoming weary of this reigning at his shooting-box, and having to play the hostess to "so many women."

"Ah! you don't know how I have set my heart on it: how should you?" he replied. Then he laughed, and got himself together with a shake, and asked impressively, when they had all seated themselves, and there was the usual silence, "why he had not the pleasure of seeing Harold Ffrench?"

"He had to go up to town last night," Frank Burgoyne replied.

"He received a telegram which carried the day against my father's dismay at his departure," Ethel explained. "Do you know we have all, even Frank, come round to liking Mr. Ffrench very much; he is so nice when you know him, and he has such a story!"

"Has he indeed? Should you have thought he looked like a man 'with a story,' Miss Leigh?" Mr. Linley asked of Theo, who sat shivering, and thinking, "now it will all come out, it will all come out."

"But he has," Ethel persisted; "a story that there can be no harm in telling if we Burgoynes don't mind telling it: the secret of our father's liking for him is to be found in his story."

"Do tell it, if it isn't long," Kate Galton said, uttering the first portion of her sentence aloud for Ethel, and the latter part in a dulcet whisper, that fell upon Mr. Linley's ear alone.

"It might be made a great deal of by aid of your gift," Ethel Burgoyne replied, looking at her host; "as I haven't your gift, however, I will not draw it out to its ruin; it is simply this," Ethel began to blush, and her colour brightened as she proceeded; "my father fell in love, desperately in love, with Harold Ffrench's mother, after he was engaged to our mother; and she, who was afterwards Mrs. Ffrench, was so honorable that, though she loved my father, he believes to this day nothing would ever tempt her to make another woman miserable; that is all the story."

"How unlike a woman," David Linley said, laughing.

"How like her son," Theo Leigh cried quickly.

"How uncommonly lucky for your mamma that she met with such a generous rival, that is all I can say," Mrs. Galton remarked quietly.

And then they went into the question of whether it be nobler to give up everything or to brave everything for love, which topic imparted a piquancy it would otherwise have lacked to Theo Leigh's soup.

Frank Burgoyne, in accordance with the plan he had proposed of misleading everyone as to his sentiments regarding Mrs. Galton, had taken Theo Leigh into dinner. He had devoted himself to her in the marked manner which men will show without an end or aim at times, and Theo, feeling grateful for this lapse he was making into those habits which had been his during the days of his broken arm, had responded sympathetically. The devotion, conventional as it was, and the sympathetic response to it, were both patent to Sydney; therefore, though Miss Scott had adhered to a portion of her original intention by wearing pink, she waived the paleness, and came out with such a brilliant colour through annoyance that she looked remarkably pretty.

Pretty in so brightly blooming, so unmistakeably *young* and fresh a way, that David Linley saw with bitter vexation that she quite put Theo Leigh out. The latter should have had the winning warmth and colour to-night, if Frank Burgoyne's heart were to be caught in the rebound, when warned off the premises by regard for Mrs. Galton's fair fame. However, he hoped that a lot of wine and a few judicious words might place Frank in the right groove. Once there, he would run easily enough. The matter, if it were to be managed at all, must be managed quickly, he told himself, for Harold Ffrench was free now, and unless this thing settled itself speedily, Harold Ffrench would soon know a better happiness than the one he had lost at starting.

"I am not going back to the drawing-room with all those women alone," Kate whispered to her host, when dinner was over; "can't we all move together?"

"Do you want to flirt with Frank Burgoyne?" he asked, directing her gaze at the same time to Frank and Theo.

Mrs. Galton glanced hastily toward the pair, and tried a little laugh.

"Indeed I don't," she said, shaking her head; "were I free to have any offered me, I would have no boy's love."

She said it in a very low tone; but Frank Burgoyne had a habit of hearing her lightest accents. She despised him, then, despised and disregarded him. She had fathomed that he loved her, and resented the impertinence in the orthodox "noble matron" manner. Frank felt very guilty and terribly cast down.

Presently he looked up, across the table, at the husband of the lady on whose account he was enduring sensations of humiliation and remorse. He looked up, and found John Galton's eyes fixed on him with an expression of pitying contempt. The expression was not there in reality; it was only Frank's distorted judgment which read in that interrogatory look such a meaning. But the mistake did him good: strung him up to "have done with this folly at once."

"Before you go to-night I must speak to you, Theo," he whispered, bending his head towards her in such a way that all at the table marked the action. And when Theo looked up at him with frightened eyes, and tried to stammer out an answer that should sound as if she did not know perfectly well what he meant, he felt that he was, as he expressed it to himself, "in for it, and no mistake, now."

David Linley disregarded Mrs. Galton's suggestion as to the simultaneous return of both sexes to the drawing-room. He was nervous and excited himself, and he wanted more wine than he cared to take before women to steady his nerves. It was as much to him as his hopes of heaven that this last best joy should be taken from Harold Ffrench, for he (David Linley) had loved Leila, and Leila had never loved him. He desired that Frank Burgoyne should warm his imagination Theo-wards as much as was possible with wine, and Frank forwarded his desires in this respect freely.

In the drawing-room, meanwhile, things were not going so fast. Stagnation generally seizes the souls, and manners, and tongues of women when they retire for that privileged twenty minutes or so after dinner, unless they happen to have babies, or contumacious cooks, when their conversation is a maddening thing to those other women who have not either.

The Burgoynes were old enough and well-bred enough to conceal the extent to which they were bored. For full five minutes Ethel, gently seconded by her sister, made conversation, and contrived to make her words fall trippingly off her tongue. But there was no response made by the others to these efforts of hers. Charming, vivacious, fascinating as Mrs. Galton could be, and was ordinarily, she could also be quite the reverse of these things on occasions. One of these occasions presented itself now. She had nothing further to hope from the Burgoynes; such social radiance as they could shed upon her would be over soon, for it could not extend into Norfolk. While, as for Theo Leigh and Sidney Scott, they were wearisome to her to the last degree. Therefore Mrs. Galton sat in an easy attitude and complete silence before the fire, and gazed with much satisfaction at the reflection of her own pretty face in the back of a highly-glazed screen.

Nor were Theo and Sydney enlivening as companions on the whole. Theo had had her nerves considerably shaken by those meetings with Harold Ffrench and her father out in the goblin-garden, as Frank called the graveyard the other night, and they had not recovered their usual tone again. More than this; she began to see, it began to dawn upon her, that it was within her ability to do or accept a something that would heal the soreness of the past, if she could honestly obliterate that past from her heart. And this she began to feel she could do.

In fact, the girl was in a flutter—in the throes of the dread that it did not lie in her to act honourably and well towards everybody, herself included.

Life is very hard!

As for Sidney Scott, she was simply "huffed," as the phrase goes, and huffiness, thank heaven, is a thing to be got over. There was not a particle of malice in the girl's composition, and on an emergency arising she would have been capable of doing and daring anything for anyone who would ask her so to do and dare. But in the meantime, while quiet reigned, and humdrum was prime-minister, Sydney could but feel just a little splenetic and rosily indignant with Theo for having come between her and all the admiration that was going.

The pretty blonde was so pretty that she might have been more generous even in her own heart. But it was the thick spot in that otherwise transparent porcelain, it was the flaw in what would else have been a perfect copy of a glorious little Venus,—this strong desire that she had to take and enfold, to have and to hold, all that was sweetest in the looks, and words, and manners of all the men who might be within her range. She could not help it. She meant no harm, and she paid whatever penalty might be due, in the bitter, sick soreness which seized and cramped her when she did not get all she desired.

At the same time, though this might all be guileless enough, it must be acknowledged that there was a touch of something quite the reverse of noble in her suffering wrath to obtain in her soul against Theo, simply because poor Theo had been the recipient of some of the looks, and words, and manners that evening for which she (Sydney) hungered.

"You are soon going to leave us, Miss Scott, I find," Ethel Burgoyne remarked to her at last.

"Yes, in a day or two. I'm going to travel up with the Leighs."

"Miss Leigh and you live very near to one another, do you not?"

"Ye—es," Sydney replied, as if the admission compromised her rather.

"That is very pleasant for you," Ethel Burgoyne went on, feebly it must be confessed, but really because she had nothing better to say.

"Yes; it is pleasanter to have one's acquaintances near to one than at the other end of the world, I suppose," Sydney replied, again in the same dubious tone, and with a certain monotonous drawl that was aggravating to listen to.

"But you are very intimate, are you not?" Ethel persisted.

"Oh! we see each other often. I don't know about being very intimate; I haven't known her—I mean she hasn't known me very long."

"Isn't that the same as your not having known her, that you corrected yourself? I fancied that you were great friends from your coming down here to stay with her."

Sydney almost shuffled on her chair, and felt hot and flushed. Miss Ethel Burgoyne was most innocently (or was she doing it out of malice?) putting her in an awkward position. On one side was a strong inclination to ignore all special intimacy with or kindly feeling for the traitor Theo, who had dared to let some loose laurels that were flying about light upon her own brow instead of bowing her head to the dust, and suffering them to waft along to their proper destination on Sydney's. And on the other side was the reflection that her position at Hensley altogether was incompatible with a declaration of utter indifference to and cold regard for the cause of her being there at all.

"I came down here because she was so dull and wanted me," she said, almost snappishly, and very loud; "but I hate the country: so

much is made of every trifle, and you hear of a thing till you hate it. It's all very well for Theo," she went on in a lower key; "she likes flirting, I suppose, and while there's any one to flirt with she's amused, or seems to be; but I never *do* flirt, and——"

"You don't care to see any one else indulge in such idle folly, do you?" Ethel Burgoyne said, in a laughing tone; then she took Sydney's morsels of white hands in her own, and went on, looking into the now sparkling blue eyes, "My dear, talk in that strain when you're ten or fifteen years older, but not now—no! don't even do it then, or people may say that you are a spiteful, soured woman, which you never will be in reality; but the habit of saying whatever may first come upon the tongue grows upon one, dear."

She was too young and too good not to take a small semi-flattering lecture from a still young and pretty woman well and gracefully. So she threw off a few smiles on the spot, and shook off the appearance of chagrin at once, just in time in fact to be her own best self when the men came into the room.

There being only four gentlemen, a rubber seemed inevitable; but David Linley knew better, even while suggesting it, than to suffer it to come to pass. He knew well that from a sober respectable game of long whist such as Mr. Leigh would play, Frank would not arise prepared to go to extreme lengths about Mr. Leigh's daughter. The rattle of a dice-box on the desperate uncertainty as to red or black would have urged him on to commit any madness; but not whist, not debates to where were the honours, and who perchance would gain the odd trick.

The inevitable, or rather the apparently inevitable, rubber was evaded therefore deftly.

"We'll have a rubber; you'll like a rubber, Leigh?" the host asked, in a genial tone.

"Yes, certainly; I shall like it of all things. Won't some of these ladies——" Mr. Leigh was beginning, when Linley interrupted him.

"By Jove! I punched a lot of wads out of some cards in the gun-room before dinner! I hope we have another pack; I will ring and ask."

He rang and asked accordingly, and great search was made throughout the lodge, and, of course, not another pack found. Whereat Mr. Linley expressed much concern; so much, indeed, that Kate, who fathomed him just at this special place, almost determined to make him feel what he expressed for a few minutes by declaring that she had a pack in her dressing-case. She relented from her purpose, however, on the birth of the reflection that it was not well to rile Linley for nothing.

"It being impossible to accomplish a rubber without cards, we will put up with music; you shall play to us," Mr. Linley said to Sydney.

"I hate playing."

He sat down by her.

"When *I* ask you?"

"When you say you'll put up with it I should think so."

He made in reply one of the silly speeches shot with satire which his experience taught him to believe would tell upon a woman.

"I would 'put up' with strains from Pandemonium, provided you were the singer of them, or from Paradise, supposing I were in Pandemonium, on the same conditions. Do you believe me?"

She did not believe him, but she was charmed with him,—charmed, odd as it may seem, by that very ugliness from which she had at first revolted, —charmed with the flattery that she felt to be false,—charmed into obliviousness respecting Frank and Theo.

Mr. Burgoyne had seated himself near to the father and daughter. He had refrained from the only spot in the world on which his foot would willingly have rested just then, that spot, namely, that was nearest to Kate Galton, and had put himself close to the girl with whom (to avert suspicion from that other one) he had declared himself to be in love. Then Theo's heart sank a little, with—was it hope or fear?—and her father's rose.

Her heart would have sank still lower could she but have looked into Frank Burgoyne's. He was compelled to brace himself, to string himself to the point by constantly reminding himself that he "stood committed after what he had said to her at dinner." She deluded herself with the notion that the embarrassment he was evincing came from love for her, and a knowledge that she had loved Harold Ffrench.

It was a "very nice evening, and *thank* you so much for it, Mr. Linley," all the ladies said to him when they were going away. Before it was over Frank Burgoyne had redeemed the verbal pledge he had given Theo, and she was bound to bury all thoughts of the man who had come to her under the slanting sunbeams on that bright spring morning down on the rush-covered bank. In making the announcement of what "he had done" to Linley, Frank Burgoyne felt that he was saving what by his idle attentions he had risked of Kate's fair fame; and in hearing it, Linley felt that once more "though his wife was dead Harold Ffrench had lost."

◆

CHAPTER XXXIII.

"MY NIECE'S ENGAGEMENT."

IT was a very tender subject to touch upon with her father. Theo knew that he would be glad to the point of being blind to what she might be feeling, if the art were hers to conceal feeling at all. But still it was so tender a subject that she dreaded touching upon it.

All the way home from Lowndes that night she, sitting silently in the corner of the carriage, wandered about the English language, seeking for words that should best tell the tale of Frank Burgoyne's offer, and her acceptance of it. She wished that she possessed Frank's graphic gift, for, on thinking it over, really she could not remember that he said more than a word or two. Yet he had made himself intelligible—sufficiently intelligible, that is to say.

Mrs. Vaughan was sitting up awaiting them on their return; and Mrs. Vaughan was much depressed, as was only natural on the part of the solitary waiter for the gay and reckless who were out enjoying themselves. Mrs. Vaughan had all the materials for utterly subduing and rendering them miserable and downcast immediately they entered ready at her hand. Over her injured head (she felt injured at being left at home, though she had distinctly refused to go) she wore a pallid little shawl, that looked as if it had seen some suffering, to represent chilly weariness. On her lap she held a large book of a religious nature to show how she had been enabled to endure said chilly weariness. These means accomplished her end. They all felt profoundly sorry—for themselves—the instant they came into her presence.

"Ugh! I'm cold; I'll go to bed," Sydney said quickly.

"It will be but a short night," Mrs. Vaughan remarked, in sepulchral tones.

"I am afraid you have been dull by yourself, my dear Elizabeth," Mr. Leigh suggested, cheerily, sitting down and stirring the fire. He could not help feeling cheery; he saw in Theo's face that she had something to say to him; and an undefined feeling of satisfaction with all men and women and things sprang into being in his soul at the sight.

"I am never dull with this near me," Mrs. Vaughan replied, patting the book rather fiercely: and then the Reverend Thomas essayed to cough down a sigh that arose at the thought of the pleasant night that was in store for him and choked himself.

"And what sort of an evening has my little girl had?" Mr. Leigh asked, in that tone of affected liveliness which is so ghastly, and so hard to bear at unseemly times. Theo felt this present time to be unseemly for the display of such facetiousness, and therefore did not know how to respond to it.

"The evening was well enough; why shouldn't it have been? Of course it was nice there; but then the drive home is long and cold, you know," she answered, putting her arms across her father's shoulder, and her head down upon her arms with a weariness that made her uncertain as to whether she was very happy or not.

"*You* seemed to find it pleasant, anyway," Sydney exclaimed abruptly. "Now to me there is nothing particularly pleasant in going out to see people all bored with one another, as all those people seemed to-night; Mr. Linley is the only one who ever has anything to say for himself, and he was knocked up with that journey he had taken about his rubbishing book, which isn't worth it, I dare say."

"If she thinks Mr. Linley the only one who ever has anything to say, she won't mind when I tell her what Frank has said to me to-night," Theo thought.

But here Theo reckoned without her host, or rather without due reflection on the various intricacies of Miss Sydney's nature. When rest and apparent peace were over that clerical mansion that night; when Theo had told her father the tidings that were so hard for her to tell in the precise manner in which she desired to tell them to him, so hard for her to tell partly because they were so joyous for him to hear; when Mrs. Vaughan had made incidental mention for the forty-eighth time, because he'd counted, within the hour, to her own special fraction of the Church, of "my niece's engagement,"—when all these things were, and many others besides that may not be catalogued here, Theo went in, like a restless spirit in plaited hair and cambric, to communicate as much as she should have the rash daring to communicate to the sleepy Sydney.

Miss Scott was in the debatable land between slumber and waking when Theo entered her room, that is to say, she had just gone over a precipice with velocity, and her heart was thumping, partly with the bound she had given in her bed, and partly with honest indignation at the idea of anything so puerile as a precipice which didn't exist coming between herself and the sleep she coveted. The entrance of her friend at this moment with a candle that looked like sitting up was not calculated to restore her equanimity. She asked somewhat snappishly, "What do you want? Is the house on fire?"

"Nothing so bad as that," Theo replied; "only I—I want to talk to you a little."

"Talk away, my dear; you won't mind my going to sleep, I hope, if your talk's to be long."

"It won't be long, Sydney; do just turn your head and look at me. You know what you said to me yesterday about going to Lowndes to-day." Theo was getting nervous: she feared that the event would lead Sydney to accuse her (Theo) of something like dishonesty in having listened, as she had listened, to those sayings of "yesterday;" she was getting nervous, albeit she was innocent of this great offence, therefore she stammered.

"What I said to you yesterday about going to Lowndes to-day?" Sydney repeated after Theo. Sydney felt intuitively that something antagonistic to her statements of yesterday was forthcoming, consequently she was non-committal now, and prepared to act upon the defensive.

Theo found herself on a wrong course; she therefore "tacked across," and made a slight progress on her way to elucidation.

"Sydney, dear, I thought to-night that Mr. Burgoyne was very much attracted—I mean, was very fond of you. Of course he is 'attracted' by you, every one must be that." Theo spoke very hurriedly, and there was almost an apologetic cadence in her voice, hardly as she strove to eradicate it, for she knew that such would be precisely the cadence which would be most offensive to Miss Sydney.

Sydney looked fearlessly right out of her eyes, as it were; she saw very clearly what was coming now, but she was determined to make no sign of having been punished in this race which she had run with Theo. After all, this was but a rehearsal,—practice is always good.

Thinking thus, Miss Sydney looked fearlessly, as I said before, right out of her eyes, and said: "And to-night, I suppose, you have found that Mr. Burgoyne rather prefers your noble *self?* You don't think that I didn't see that too, do you, Theo? Well, dear, all I can do is to congratulate you both on his offer, if he's made you one, and on your having had the sense to bury your dead, and give up going about and doing the victim to man's perfidy business any longer."

Theo looked guilty, miserable, in a moment; it was an unkind thrust from her little friend; but her little friend was capable of doing a good deal in that way.

"Good night, Sydney; I thought I would tell you at once, because——"

"It's rather nice to receive an offer from the future Lord Lesborough: oh, yes, dear, I quite understand. Good night. You must say, Theo," she continued virtuously, "that I have been a regular brick. I have been discretion itself, for your Master Frank isn't averse to flirting."

This being kind and unanswerable, Theo did not attempt to answer it.

"You didn't see my joke last night when I was talking to you, Theo," Sydney went on with the most joyous frankness; she *did* rebound very soon; "you didn't see that it was I who would have to come and stay with you when you're married, and be got off. How dense you were!"

"I suppose I was: the truth is, I was not listening to what you said, Sydney."

"That was civil, but I'll forgive you. Now I'll give you a bit of advice, for I am not blinded by being spoony on Mr. Frank, which you are," (how heartily glad Theo felt that she was!)—"don't give him too much rope, for he'll take it, and if I know anything at all of men, which I rather flatter myself I do, he's one who will always make love to the lips that are near: and don't be jealous, for that is a bore to yourself; and good night, Theo, I am so glad you have been so lucky."

Perhaps it was not the nicest or most soothing parting-speech that could have been uttered: doubtless the bright little blonde meant it to be both these things; still she felt a trifle disappointed when she marked how very faint was the impression that it made on Theo Leigh.

There was such a universal air of elation over the whole house the following morning that Theo almost expected to see her esteemed relatives, together with the tables and chairs, burst into Terpsichorean demonstrations. It was almost mortifying to discover what a mere nothing she had been before in the eyes of her uncle and aunt by the light of this sudden refulgence with which they beamed upon her. Viands were lavished upon her, fears as to her complexion no longer assailed Mrs. Vaughan, she heard her manners described to her father as being so "innately well bred that Mrs. Vaughan felt, after seeing them in a niece of hers, that she had nothing further to wish for in life." Mr. Leigh, in his satisfaction at what had transpired, accepted these tributes to his daughter radiantly, believing, after the manner of honest people, that they were honestly paid to Theo, and would have been paid to her in any case. In fact, Theo was nauseated by her young success before it was one, indeed; for though Mr. Burgoyne had spoken the conclusive words to her, there was still Lord Lesborough, Mr. Burgoyne's grandfather, to be consulted. What would *he* say to this contemplated marriage of his heir? Theo was the only one who could answer that question without flinching; though she felt that, if he said "No," not all that wild brawling Hensley water would suffice to put out the flame of Aunt Libby's wrath.

"I suppose you won't go out this morning in case?" Mrs. Vaughan said to her brother with a transparent air of mystery, and an abrupt halt on the word "case," which said more plainly than aught else that she meant in "case Frank came."

"No-o, I shall look at the paper," Mr. Leigh said. "You young ladies will be ready to go back to-morrow?" he continued, addressing Sydney Scott and his daughter.

"I shall, papa."

"And *I* shall, Mr. Leigh," Sydney replied promptly; then, recovering her politeness, she added, "although I'm sure we have had a most delightful visit, Mrs. Vaughan."

Mrs. Vaughan was too well pleased to be down, as she otherwise would have been, upon the first portion of the speech. She accepted the latter part with smiles that were so broad, so free and flowing, so rich in colour, and gorgeous altogether, that they really resembled flags of triumph. When she had waved these over the heads of her own household for a while, she went out to make the village happy.

"I hope to goodness Aunt Libby won't say anything in the village, papa! did you caution her?"

"Bless my soul, no!" Mr. Leigh replied; "but of course she——"

"Will," Theo interrupted; "yes, she will, I'm sure,—she always does."

"Dear old lady! Yes, she always does say what she oughtn't to say," Sydney said, in a low tone; "shall I put on my hat and run after her, Theo, and stop her from talking? I know I can stop her, frighten her into complete prudence, and yet only tell the truth."

Sydney's eyes sparkled with fun as she spoke. Theo was much melted by the sight of this earnest interest on behalf of her affairs.

"Yes, do, Sydney; I wouldn't have a word said till—till——"

"Oh! all right, I understand," Sydney replied, rushing off blithely.

In the meantime the momentous subject had been broached at Maddington, and, as was only just and natural, Lord Lesborough was violently opposed to that for which he had been verbally anxious for years. "It was true that he had desired to see Frank married," he acknowledged; "marriage was the only safeguard against that destruction towards which he was distressed to see Frank drifting." Here he left off being tender, and burst into wrath. "But such a marriage as this! It would be but a repetition of the d——d affair that ruined—yes, ruined—his father."

"Having made her an offer, and she having accepted me, I'm not going to be hounded off it," Frank said doggedly. "I shall stand to it, sir, which will save you the trouble of looking out for a cause for quarrelling with me any longer."

In his heart Lord Lesborough loved his grandson, but being obstinate unto death himself, he had always elected to believe that obstinacy had been the rock upon which Frank's father had split, and that in the natural course of things obstinacy would be the rock upon which Frank himself would split. Still, he loved his grandson, and he was horribly angry with those words, which appeared to cast a doubt upon that love.

"You know you like her yourself, papa," Ethel said to him, reproachfully, when Frank had gone out of the room.

"I do: nevertheless it is not the match for Frank to make."

"I think he's very fond of her," Ethel pursued, not that she was in reality very firmly convinced of anything of the sort, but it is a nice womanly thing to say on such an occasion, so Ethel said it.

"He'll get over that," Lord Lesborough replied stiffly.

"Not if he's the true Burgoyne I take him to be," Ethel went on, warming to her theme and feeling, as was natural, ten times more interested in Frank's love now that she was put in the position of counsel for the defence than she had been before,—"not if he is the true Burgoyne I take him to be. Why, papa, you of all men would disown him for it if he could 'get over' a genuine thing soon. What did you tell us the other day? —that, well as you had loved our mother, you never loved her with the deep wild love you had for Harold Ffrench's mother? You never got over it,—why should Frank?"

"I wish Harold were here," was all Lord Lesborough's answer.

"So do I, with all my heart," Ethel replied; "he would plead for Frank, he—do promise one thing, that if he thinks well of it you will too; he knows Theo, you know."

Accordingly Lord Lesborough promised, and Ethel went into suspense for at least ten minutes after the incoming of every train, and eagerly awaited the advent of Harold Ffrench, who had promised to come back to Maddington as soon as he could. He was, in truth, on his way to them now, for after Julie had transformed herself from an innocent bundle of floss silk into a ruthless detective, he had no heart to stay in the house where was lying the dead body of her who had been his wife. He was on his way back to his friends and Maddington—Maddington that was so near to the spot made sacred to him by love. He was on his way back, he was free, he was happy with a feverish happiness; he was on his way back to—what?

Mrs. Vaughan had a very pleasant progress through part of the village before Sydney ran her to ground and unearthed her. The mere mention of "my niece's engagement to Mr. Burgoyne" took away the breath of the majority of her auditors, and as the majority of her auditors would have burst their kindly hearts rather than have suffered her to perceive how staggered they were, the delight was doubled. Mrs. Vaughan had, it must be confessed, no bad notion of what constitutes success and imparts the extra sheen to it. She painted quite an effective picture of Theo's having come, and seen, and conquered in an incredibly short space of time. She mentioned, in a light and airy manner, the youth, the extreme youth, the childhood almost, of said conqueror, who was put back by her excellent aunt to "between sixteen and seventeen," in a casual kind of way that of course made an immense impression on old ladies between sixty and seventy. Mr. Burch's three daughters, who were all pronounced at the county and assize balls to be "remarkably effective, handsome girls," and who all made a point of grouping in the window according to their lights whenever Mr. Burgoyne rode past it down the village street, and who had individually and collectively hoped a great deal from the way in which he had raised his hat to them at divers times, said, "Ah! how very nice! Soon be married, of course; there being nothing to wait for if Lord Lesborough were agreeable." At which poor Mrs. Vaughan, not having the faintest notion yet whether or not Lord Lesborough would be agreeable on this occasion, went into the smiles of uncertainty, and the Burch trio were partially avenged.

But the Miss Dampins were as water in the desert to a panting heart; they were sympathetic, rejoiced, intensely curious. They plied Mrs. Vaughan with questions in a way that made her love them, and resolve to buy a lot of their unpleasant comforters and cuffs, and other results of their incessant knitting. They went into the matter in an able-bodied way you would not have expected from such gentle old ladies. Their joy at the hearing was a genuine thing, and they wound up by sending such abject messages of congratulation to Theo in the warmth of their hearts, that Mrs. Vaughan was ashamed to deliver them.

Mrs. Vaughan had always been a little what her more envious neighbours about Maddington termed bumptious; but this day Maddington, as it were, oozed out at every pore. She even hurled it at the heads of the harmless peasantry, promising those who were out of it, work, and those who were in want of it, soup, all from Maddington. "I will speak to my niece, Miss Leigh, and she will let Mr. Burgoyne know; you may have heard" (this in a condescending way, as if the benighted wretches should be forgiven even if still oblivious) "that Miss Theo and Mr. Burgoyne are," &c., &c.

She had gone half through the village dispensing her news and her smiles, making some miserable and herself happy, and still she had a fair field, the other half, before her. She had left, wary old sportswoman that she was, the best bit of land for the last. In the portion still to be beaten there lived her husband's predecessor's widow and four maiden daughters. And these had never taken kindly to Mrs. Vaughan, and Mrs. Vaughan had never taken kindly to them. They disliked one another simply in the unreasonable, motiveless way some women do dislike those of their own sex who have gone before or followed after them. The dislike had never grown into a feud, but always remained what it had been at first,—a bitterly civil, cantankerous, and hopeless aversion.

Before, however, Mrs. Vaughan could enter and make their home too hot for them to dwell in it calmly, she met Sydney Scott, who had been sauntering about looking for her for some time, and who was hot and tired, and consequently just a little cross.

"Well, Mrs. Vaughan," she began, "have you done your rounds? Why didn't you bring me with you to carry your basket?" Miss Scott's tone was cordial to a degree, but as she made no attempt to withdraw her hands from her jacket pockets as she spoke, the suggestion as to the basket was idle.

"I have not been to my paupers to-day," Mrs. Vaughan replied; and Sydney, being merely a frivolous worldling, felt her blood run cold at hearing such mention made of some of her fellow-creatures. "I have been making a few calls."

"Oh! you've made some of your calls already; they hadn't heard the big news yet, had they?"

"No, they had not heard—when I went in," Mrs. Vaughan said, with a little cough.

"Did they hear while you were there? How quickly things must fly," Sydney asked innocently.

"I shall leave you here, my dear, for I must go in and give the Blands a look," Mrs. Vaughan answered testily; she was very unwilling to be baulked of this crowning joy.

"Very well, good-by, I'll go home then," Sydney said, turning away. Then, as she saw that the Blands saw from their window that Mrs. Vaughan was designing them the dubious

honour of a call, and that the old lady was therefore fairly committed, and could not follow and question her (Sydney) at once, she added, "Poor Theo's first affair! To think that it should all have gone utterly to smash, as it has gone! There, don't wait: they're looking: go in."

"Lord bless my heart!" Mrs. Vaughan panted, as she walked up the Blands' garden. "The monster!—the wicked, unfeeling, little monster, —to deal me such a blow here in the gate of the enemy! Oh, my poor heart! that I should have lived to boast too soon to any of the Hensley people: but, thank God! it wasn't the Blands."

In the nature of things, no call could be a comforting thing after this. Mrs. Vaughan went in weak and came out worsted. The Blands had numberless easy triumphs over her that day. She was dubious in statements, deprecating in style, dolefully depressed in soul. She had been brave, she had not feared her fate too much, or held her own deserts and the deserts of her niece as small. She had answered a victory to the world before it had been officially declared to herself, and now she learnt from a well-informed ally that it was defeat, and that she had been over-anxious in the well-doing of making her acquaintances throb with envy.

It may seem a small thing to some people, this blow that had been given her. But when her position in the parish is considered, in conjunction with the earnest desire common to all women to better the same, the full force of the blow will be understood. Henceforth she would be known as one who had striven, and had a fall. Henceforth she would be open to ribald mention as one who had overrated the amount of toleration felt for her at Maddington; as one who had intrigued to ensure the heir of Maddington for her own niece, and been promptly put into her proper place at the very moment when success appeared to be about to crown her unworthy efforts.

Such thoughts as these rushed through her mind as she constrained herself to sit and talk to the Blands, in the sketchy manner that was the natural result of the morbid dread she had every time the garden gate swung open that either the butcher or baker were coming in, and would "tell all" to the Blands' servants. She pictured the scoffs that would be uttered in that case immediately she removed herself from the house, and the glances of mingled pity and contempt that would fall from the Blands' eyes upon her discomfited back as she went down the garden. As she pictured this scene she pitied herself so profoundly that she could scarcely constrain herself to talk at all.

No thought of any possible pain that Theo might feel in what Sydney had termed the smashing of her first affair arose to soften her. Not that she was an unkind or a cold-hearted woman; but her own position in the parish, her social status as the clergyman's wife, and the own familiar friend of the Burgoynes, was very dear to her, so dear that when peril threatened it, no matter how remotely, she could not entertain the idea of another's sufferings. During the whole period of her sojourn at Hensley she had been eminently respectable. She had never made a mistake, she had never seemed to aim

at much, and she had never fallen short of that
at which she had aimed. Scoffers had essayed
on more than one occasion to throw derision on
that best bloom of her life—the Burgoyne connection; but they had failed, for no man or
woman could say that in that quarter she strove
for more than was willingly ceded to her. But
now!—her heart quailed as she thought of how
now, in steering clear of the Charybdis of the
Burgoyne distrust, she would infallibly fall foul
of the Scylla of general discriminating contempt.
These thoughts were very hard to bear; so hard
that they would not admit of one gentle, pitying,
sympathetic one being given to Theo. Her
niece's engagement, instead of being the crowning glory she had anticipated its being in the
morning, would be the one spot on the hitherto
undimmed radiance of her Hensley career.

CHAPTER XXXIV.

"WHAT MATTER A LITTLE MORE WAITING TO
ONE WHO HAS WAITED FOR YEARS?"

To have stayed in that house where the life
had fled and the glove had been found, and
David Linley had to the last, to the very last,
been falsely friendly with that false wife, was
more than Harold Ffrench could do. Had Julie
suffered things to remain as the more discreet
and deceitful human beings in the house would
have desired, Mr. Ffrench would have done one
whom he deemed faithful (the servant who had
stayed with his wife for so many years) the
grace of remaining to see that wife buried. By
way of justifying what he had mistaken for
affection,—by way of rewarding that woman's
fidelity with a show of supposition on his part
that such fidelity and affection was not unmerited,—he would have stayed, and have shown
that he believed the best of her who was gone.
But not now, not now.

Not now, with that woman laughing in her
sleeve at his having been hoodwinked so long
and so well. Not now, with the echo of the lie
she had uttered to him but just now still ringing
in his ears. It would be unworthy of him now
to stay and seem to sorrow and to sympathise
in ever so small a degree. Let her be buried
decently and in order, for the sake of humanity;
but he was exempt now from all claim on his
special interest in the sorrow of the surviving
maid, and the dignity of the dead mistress.

For she, that mistress, had degraded him.
Not once in hot youth alone, not in agony and
shame, not with a sudden fury repented of and
atoned for afterwards through long, weary years
of well-doing and remorse. She had degraded
and deceived, and been coldly, systematically
false to him since the day when they were both
young, to the last, to the very last.

So he could not stay there in the house with
the mocking falsely humble and respectful
glance of the one who had aided and abetted,
ever ready to fall upon him. He could not take
up his London life again at once, that cold solitary life which he had led in stagnation of soul
for years. The life which brought him in contact with nothing warmer through the live-long
day than some well-known page from some well-
loved book read in youth, and cherished now as

one of the very few things that were still the
same as then. The life which left him long
solitary hours to be disposed of God knows how
at those periods of the day when other men of
his age and standing went from the cold of business into the warmth of home. The life athwart
which the shadow of a friend so seldom fell that
when it did that life seemed strangely darkened
and saddened through the rarity of the thing.
The life which, if he had known was to be his
for so long when first it was thrust upon him,
would have been cut short by the horror of it
and the utter inability to face it. The life that
should be ended soon and swept away from his
memory by the charmed notes of promise which
should be uttered, the clouds which should be
melted away before the light of love which lived
for him in the eyes of Theo Leigh.

Even with the prospect of this joy before him
he could not take up that life again, though but
for a brief space. He would go back to Maddington. He wanted reassuring, he desired to
feel the sense of security the sight of Theo
would give him. He needed to be with people
who thought well of even if they did not like
him, and for whom that sorrowful story of his
was not written upon his brow legibly in type
that those who ran might read. All this he
needed, and all this he would have down at
Maddington.

Together with something brighter still: the
sight of Theo's face when she should hear the
truth from him, and turn to him with such balm
for what he had suffered in it, and such a joyous
pledge of recompense in the future. How she
would forgive him for that fond folly of his,
divided by such a tiny line from guilty selfishness, which had caused him to linger by her
side down on those bleak marshes alone on the
rush-covered bank. How she would forgive
him and love him. The train sped slowly after
that thought arose.

It was scarcely absent from his mind during
the whole journey. It was present there and
vivid the whole time, and it was very comforting.

The only thing, the solitary shadow that fell
across and marred the brightness of it (and that
very seldom) was the thought that would arise
once or twice of how many more years had passed
over his head than over hers. So many years as
he had known beyond her must he strike off from
the roll of those which he might hope to know
with her. He found himself regretting his age,
and fervently praying that the blood of youth
could bound through his veins once more. For
youth would be her portion for many years to
come, and the richest bloom of womanhood,
especially with such a physique, would be hers
when he was grey-haired and maybe decrepid.

The train seemed very slow to him. It was
useless his asking himself "what matter a little
more waiting for one who has waited for years?"
The "little more waiting" that was rendered a
necessity by space intervening, by space alone,
thank God! he said almost aloud, was more bitterly hard to bear than aught had been for years.
He so longed to lift the sorrow from the young
heart, and the cloud from the young eyes that
had been the one so light and the other so bright
when first they turned towards him.

His greatest, his only ambition now, was, to

have a home where Theo would be also, and to be at rest with her. Had this incubus, which was but just removed from him, been lifted away from him years ago while youth and the desire to do something, to make a stir in the world, had still been his, he might have striven and failed, and been more embittered than he was as things were. So he looked leniently back upon that long series of desultory attempts to do so little that when those attempts failed he scarcely marked the failure of them. Failure on a larger field might have driven him down into depths from whence there would have been no arising—into depths from which he told himself now no man could have arisen to Theo Leigh. Therefore he felt leniently towards that long inactive career which sometimes he had regretted while still leading it, and thought that as that inactivity had led him into comparatively little evil, so now after it he was fairly entitled to nurse the sole ambition left to him—to cherish, and dwell upon, and yearn to realise the vision of the peaceful, quiet, loving life which should be his with Theo.

"What matters a little more waiting to one who has waited for years?" How had he borne that enforced quiescence? he asked himself. How had he suffered this clog to chain him away from all that was most prized by his man's heart! How had he been enabled to keep love from being the lord of all during those last few months especially? From what portion of his passionate weakness had come the strength which had enabled him to refrain from testing whether love were indeed powerful enough in that girl's heart to make her consider the world well lost for it?

He had been sorely tempted, horribly tried! Tempted and tried by that very unguardedness and perfect trust of hers which after all had been her tower of strength. He shuddered, now that she would so soon be his own in all honour, to think of how often he had cursed the social bonds that bound them both, and been on the point of bursting them, when he had reflected on how brief a thing after all life was, and how benighted were those who laid down laws for themselves, only, as it seemed, to make that life miserable. But there was nothing between them any longer, nothing; neither shadow nor substance. Nothing save the green fields and hedge-rows which lay between the train and Hensley.

Harold Ffrench walked fast when he got out of the train at Hensley, walked fast as a man is apt to walk when he has something pleasant to do and is in haste to do it. He was in mourning, in such mourning as a man can go into at once in these sombrely clothed days without making any material change in his dress. But there was no mourning in his face, and none in his heart. He was a brighter, happier man than he had been for long years, and he was a better man too, as is often the case when one is happier.

He was in broad charity with all men except David Linley, whose heart even then, in that happy, gentling hour, he could have torn from his breast and flung to perdition without compunction. But for the rest of the world he had such glowing kindly feelings, such a wealth of toleration, such a mighty sympathy.

All things were fair, fair as the future that had opened to him, fair as the face of the love of his boyhood, or of her who had wakened this later love in his soul. Nature smiled so softly that

her child, the winter season, grew rosy and warm in her rays. There was a promise in the sunshine, and on the light wind that was up there was a hope, as he walked on towards the fate that was in store for him.

"God! what days we'll have together!" he said aloud to himself, as he got into the Maddington grounds and walked along even faster than before, impatient to announce himself and then go on to Theo. "Dear little thing! she who was satisfied with the prospect over those bleak, hard marches, while I talked to her of better things and more luscious scenes; to take her where I have been myself, and see her whole soul leaping towards me while I tell her what I was suffering then. It is worth having lived for, this; it will be no bad reward for the hell I have known."

Faster and even faster along the avenue, with many of the hopes that were his in his long-left youth coming back to him, and crowding tumultuously through his brain. Resuming all unconsciously the very gait that had been his in youth, carrying his head more buoyantly, his hands in his pockets more carelessly, his heart in his breast more blithely than ever he had done since that day when he had stood on the deck of the English frigate and lifted the Greek girl's veil.

He made as many plans as a girl with her first pocket-money for giving pleasure to others—to those to whom heretofore he had unhappily given little else save pain. He bethought himself of where it would be well for Theo and himself to take up their headquarters when they were in England, in order that they might be within an accessible distance of her father. He even laid down a plan very susceptible of improvement of cultivating that mind of hers which in its uncultivation was still so inexpressibly dear to him. He never thought for an instant, as he strode along like the man he felt himself to be once more, but that he should have her for his own, to do with her as it seemed good to him so long as he should live.

So on to the house where he seemed to be expected, and wished, and waited for, in a manner that was very pleasant to behold, especially by Ethel, who had never been wont to be demonstrative towards him. But now she came forward through the whole length of the oak parlour when he entered it and found her there alone, and gladly made him welcome, telling him how happy she was to see him, and how much they all had been and were wanting him, in tones that had the genuine ring of the metal.

"That's very good of you," he replied; "I'll hear what you want me for when I come back. I'm just going over to Hensley."

"Oh! do wait a little," Ethel began earnestly.

He shook his head, he was in no mood for more waiting; he had been waiting for years for much, for months for this very thing which now he was about to make his own.

"I shall be back before long," he answered, thinking the while that it would be extremely probable that he should be nothing of the kind; "but I have something to do and I must go and do it at once."

He was about to leave the room as he spoke, but Ethel checked him.

"Mr. Ffrench, do stop."

He stopped and went back to her, and she held

out her hand, and when he gave his she held it fast.

"What is it?" he asked.

"Oh! it's about Frank; do sit down and I will tell you, but you mustn't be impatient, will you?"

"I will try not to be impatient, if you will try to tell me quickly."

"So I will; as if your Hensley business, which is probably about a gun, or a dog, or a saddle couldn't wait! I always find when men have particular business down at Hensley that it's at the farrier's or the vet's."

"Mine is neither; however, go on."

"Well, then; you know what a dear boy Frank is, and that papa is often just a little perverse with him?"

Harold Ffrench nodded and asked,

"Has he smashed the Baron again?"

"Oh, no! nothing bad, he has only fallen in love."

"Ay, and with whom?" he had no suspicion, not the faintest shadow, as to what her answer would be, and Ethel had none either as to how it would touch him.

"He has fallen desperately in love, poor boy, and proposed and been accepted, a thing papa has always been wishing him to do if the girl was nice; and here now when they are both tremendously in love, and no girl can be nicer than Theo Leigh, papa——What's the matter?"

He had not started, or smote his chest or his forehead, or fainted, or gone ghastly white, or given any other melodramatic sign of emotion. He had merely flushed; a strong man's flush of disappointed passion and cruel jealousy is no pleasant sight to witness.

"What's the matter?" Ethel repeated wonderingly.

"Nothing; an old wound that I am apt to feel after exertion; go on."

"Well, Frank—but I didn't know you had ever been wounded."

"Long ago, and it was to death I thought at the time; go on." It was to death now—the death of all good within him, but he would hear to the end.

"Well, Frank can't get papa's consent to their engagement—it's cruel to him and to her too, poor girl, but if you——"

"Are they so devotedly attached to each other?" Harold Ffrench interrupted bitterly.

"I believe they are, and you can't wonder at it; any girl would be sure to be won by Frank if he tried to win her; he has every quality to attract and endear him to a woman; do speak to papa, Mr. Ffrench," she went on earnestly, "he promises to be influenced by you; and even if you don't care for Frank, you like Miss Leigh, so just think of what she must have been suffering all these days—with her temperament to be subjected to such a mortifying uncertainty."

"She shall know no further suffering if I can avert it; I will go to your father at once."

"That's good of you; before you go to Hensley?" she added inquiringly.

"Yes, before I go to Hensley; in fact, my Hensley business was very unimportant."

He was sitting now with his elbows on his knees, his hands clasped together, and his head bent down low, as though he were gazing earnestly on the pattern on the carpet. Miss Ethel, looking at him, marked the deadening influence that seemed to have come over him suddenly, and also for the first time observed the black clothes.

"I have been so selfishly interested in dear Frank's affairs that I didn't see—" she began hesitatingly, then she added more rapidly, "I fear you have lost some friend since we saw you."

He saw her eyes travelling down from the black tie and jet studs to the band that was round the hat which was lying on a chair by his side.

"I have lost the only being in the world who was dear to me," he said savagely, "don't speak to me about it any more; lost! I have been losing all my life."

He rose up as he spoke, and Ethel, feeling very sorry for him as she did, still hoped that he was going to put the memory of his losses away from him for the nonce, and proceed on his mission on behalf of Frank the favorite without delay.

"Are you going to papa now?" she asked.

"I hardly know; I think, if you'll allow me, I will take a stroll first; the young people," he smiled grimly as he said it, "can exist for an hour or two longer in uncertainty—cheered and supported as they are by their mutual passion."

"I don't expect you to have much sympathy with that sort of thing," Ethel replied, smiling; then she looked at him, and wondered why she had not expected him to have much sympathy with "that sort of thing;" there was no incongruity between himself and the subject. "But I know you will do Frank a good turn if you can," she went on earnestly, "and you see, if he is banished in this thing, the very thing we have all been urging upon him as a sure means of pleasing papa, why, there's no saying how it may affect him; is there?"

Harold Ffrench did not answer for a minute or two. He was asking himself during that pause why he should interest himself in the matter?—why he should obey the behest of Miss Ethel, and strive to smooth the path of his rival?—why he should interfere between Frank and the possible perdition a disappointment might drive Frank into? But when he had asked himself why he should do this thing, which would be putting his hand to the fatal wheel of fortune which was crushing him he remembered Theo. Remembered Theo, and resolved that never another pang, another doubt, should be hers, while he could save her from it.

"No, there's no saying how it may affect him," he replied in an indifferent tone; "well, my voice shall be raised for the happy pair; where is your father?"

"He keeps in his own study, and declares he feels the gout coming on."

"And where is Fra——, your nephew?"

"Gone down to see Theo, I believe," Ethel replied laughing; "I never thought to see Frank so completely upset; he was as pale and agitated as a girl this morning, and so touchy."

"Is he?" Harold Ffrench replied sarcastically. "Miss Leigh will, without doubt, repay him for his anguish."

Then he went off to speak with Lord Lesborough; but had he known the true cause of Frank's pallor and touchiness, he would have, even at the risk of seeming to play Frank false, carried out his original intention and gone over to Theo at once.

Lord Lesborough was sitting by the fire in his study, with a table covered with bills by his side, and a portentous frown of calculation on his forehead. The bills were all duly docketed, and they were all paid; therefore at first sight the frown appeared to be a work of supererogation on the part of his noble brows. But they had a mission, those bills, and they were fulfilling it. They had been incurred by Frank at divers periods of his career, and they had been assiduously looked up this morning by Lord Lesborough in order to feed the flame of his wrath against his grandson. One of Lord Lesborough's legs was extended straight out before him, too, after the manner of one who is suffering from the gout.

"How are you, Harold? glad to see you back again," he exclaimed, shuffling his papers about with a great air of business, as Harold Ffrench came in.

"I'm here only for an hour or two," Harold replied, shaking hands with his host.

Lord Lesborough picked his leg off the chair in most unseemly haste.

"You don't mean to say you're going off again to-day?" he asked, "I wanted to talk to you about that boy; he's got himself into a d—d mess."

Harold Ffrench felt the blood rising to his face and throbbing in his veins. It was hideous to the man who loved her better than he had ever loved any thing in his life, to hear Theo Leigh alluded to in this way. He could not answer the allusion immediately, so he said—

"I'm sorry to hear that you have signs of the gout about you."

"Yes, I'm afraid it's coming on," Lord Lesborough replied, promptly acting on the reminder, and replacing his leg on the rest, with much circumspection and many facial expressions of anguish.

"Been taking too much port wine?" Harold suggested. In reality, he neither cared for nor believed in Lord Lesborough's gout or its cause at this juncture. He only wanted to gain a little time before the subject of the death-blow of his hopes was mooted.

"It is not that," Lord Lesborough replied quickly. Port that had been ten years in bottle and three in wood, was much affected by him, and he had an exceeding great dislike to hearing that its effects were not invariably all that was desirable. So now he replied somewhat testily, that "It was not that," and then went on to add—

"It's chiefly mental with me; if a thing weighs on my mind, it's almost sure to fly to—to——" he hesitated, and rubbed his leg; he had not quite made up his mind whether he would say to his "knee" or his "foot."

Then Harold Ffrench determined that he would no longer strive to evade the subject which he had come to discuss.

"What is weighing upon your mind now?" he asked, rising up and leaning his back against the chimney-board.

"That boy's folly—you have not heard yet?"

"Yes, I have heard from your daughter that he has engaged himself to Miss Leigh. On my life I can't consider it a folly on his part." .

Once more Lord Lesborough forgot the effect of his mental excitement; he took his leg down from the rest and planted both feet firmly on the ground.

"You're about right, perhaps," he said; "the girl is more foolish still to have imagined for an instant that I should permit the thing to go on."

Harold Ffrench stood silently looking down on his old friend with a glowing face and steady eyes for a few seconds. At last he said, holding his hand out to Lord Lesborough as he spoke—

"You have treated me as your son for years, and I am very grateful for the love you have shown me for my mother's sake; Heaven knows your unswerving friendship has been the only light in a preciously black career; but, if wrong or insult is offered to Theo Leigh at your instigation, or from a member of your family, I shall banish that solitary light, and say good-by to you and Maddington for ever."

"Are you mad, Harold?" Lord Lesborough asked, wonderingly.

"God knows I have enough to make me mad. No; I think I'm sane enough now. Come, Lesborough," he continued abruptly, "grant me this favour—let your grandson be happy with that girl, who is far too noble for him, or for any other man that I know."

"It's not the match he should make," Lord Lesborough replied, shaking his head and rubbing his leg.

"Not the match he should make; I agree with you in the letter, but not in the spirit. What do you want him to marry? Not money, I know. She has no rank certainly, but she is a gentlewoman born and bred, and she has a heart of gold; if it is set upon your grandson now" (he gave a gulp over the words), "don't try it, for God's sake."

"You speak very warmly of the young lady," Lord Lesborough said. "One would think——"

"Stop! I don't 'think' about it," Harold interrupted. "I will tell you why I speak so warmly of the young lady, and when you have heard it you will put no obstacles in the way your grandson is going if you're the man I take you to be."

Then Mr. Ffrench sat down, and in a low voice, for his heart was heavy, he told the man who had loved his mother the story of that first meeting down on the bleak marshes, the love that grew out of that meeting, the constraint, the suffering, the blight that ensued; and, lastly, the cause of that constraint and suffering, and its recent removal.

"If this was broken off you might have her still," Lord Lesborough said, somewhat huskily.

"Have her still, after she has found out her first mistake, and loved another man according to her years! God bless her, no. It is natural that this should have come about. Let her be happy at last."

"If she can be happy with that boy after you," Lord Lesborough said somewhat scornfully. "However, I won't interfere; and you will come to Maddington as usual while I live, won't you?"

Soon after this, Harold Ffrench went away; and late that evening Theo Leigh received a note from Ethel containing warm congratulations from the whole family, and a promise of coming to call on her (Theo) the following day. Frank was with her when she received the note, but instead of handing it to him, she kept a nervous hold on it long after she had read its contents.

"What more does Ethel say?" Frank asked.

"Not much," Theo replied.

"Let me see," he said; then she handed it to him, and he read:—"'Harold Ffrench came down for a short time to-day, and won a most complete consent from papa; it seems he has a great admiration for you, Miss Theo, and he has quite succeeded in making papa share the feeling.'"

"Curse him for interfering," Frank thought, as he gave the letter back.

———◆———

CHAPTER XXXV.

CONGRATULATORY.

THE engagement and the agreeable consent to it from Maddington was not allowed to interfere with the original arrangement. Theo and Sydney Scott were to return to Bretford with Mr. Leigh, and Hensley was to be left to its normal quiet.

Lowndes was to be left to itself too. The Galtons were going almost immediately, and David Linley declared he would not remain there in solitude. Lowndes had answered his purpose entirely, he had no reluctance to quit it now. It had been the centre of that sociality which had resulted in Harold Ffrench's stumble on the very threshold of happiness.

Mr. Linley heard of Harold Ffrench's brief visit, and its pleasing results, from Ethel; Mr. Linley was "intensely interested in the young people," he said. He also averred that he had quite a fellow-feeling with Ffrench in the matter; and on the strength of this fellow-feeling took occasion to expatiate largely on Harold's good-natured share in the affair to Theo.

At first Theo listened in silence to his speeches on the subject, but at last she told him that he need not say any more about it. "I quite appreciate the kindness, and good-nature, and 'right-feeling,' as you call it, Mr. Linley, that Mr. Ffrench has displayed; you needn't din it into my ears constantly. I don't see that he could have done anything else, for my own part."

"I won't; but I must say Ffrench has acted unselfishly at last," he replied; "generally he lets other people manage their own affairs without let or hindrance from him; but he really took the trouble to put the thing properly before that old dunderhead Lesborough."

"Do you call Lord Lesborough a 'dunderhead' to Frank?"

"Possibly I do; why do you ask?"

"He oughtn't to let you, then; at any rate, I won't let you speak of Lord Lesborough in that way to me."

"You're mounting guard over the family dignity rather early; have you anything else to say?" Mr. Linley asked suavely.

"Yes, that I don't need to be told now that Mr. Ffrench is unselfish; I know it, I've known it all along."

"I don't think you're aware of the full extent of his unselfishness in this instance, though," he said impressively; "and you ought to know it: really, such an act of self-abnegation as his ought

to be made known to the one for whom he has made it."

"What do you mean?" she asked quickly; "why do you—how dare you talk to me in that way about Mr. Ffrench? He has been kind, but he would be the last to desire what he has done to be looked upon in the light of a sacrifice; the last to desire it," she repeated scornfully; "he would think such a supposition an insult to me."

"Then you are what I half fancied you might be—ignorant of the death of his wife. He was free to renew his vows, you see, but he has ceded you to the better man and the brighter fate," Linley said quietly, watching her sharply the while.

He had no wish to pain her in the matter. That is to say, he had no desire from the beginning to pain her much. He only wanted to wound her in such ways through Harold and about Harold as should prevent her ever being able to give Harold a taste of that joy in the autumn of his life of which Linley had defrauded him in the spring.

David Linley had no wish to pain Theo in the matter, but he was watching her keenly to see "how she would take" the intelligence; and she, marking the keenness of that glance, answered with the most unaffected coolness—

"His wife dead?—poor thing."

"Poor thing truly!" he said, with something like emotion, as old recollections crowded upon him.

"I know nothing of their story, but whatever it is, her's must have been a very hard life. Did she love him much?"

"I believe she did, at first; hardly in a way you would understand, though. Poor Zoe! he represented liberty to her when she played off her little ruse; when she got the actual thing, she ceased to care much for its representative."

"I know nothing of their story, and I don't want to know anything of it," Theo said quietly; "but I should like to hear that all the fault was not on his side."

"All what fault?"

"The fault that caused those long, long dreary desperate years of separation, and all the harm that came from it. I can't think that it was all his fault; but I should like to hear."

"Oh, she was harmless enough, poor little soul, when I knew her," Linley replied, with some embarrassment. "You see, that habit of amusing himself with every girl he comes across, is never a pleasant sight for a man's wife to witness."

To which Theo replied, "No, it couldn't be," very decidedly; and then paused for a few seconds, and then shook her head and said, "no, it wasn't," more decidedly still.

This conversation took place in the evening of the day before their return to Bretford. The Lowndes party and Frank Burgoyne were at the vicarage, and they were all as restless and ill at ease as people who are assembled to be happy together on a last evening almost invariably are. Mrs. Vaughan had invited them in a burst of enthusiasm, which faded out the moment she discovered that their acceptance of her invitation would cause a great disturbance in her household. Not only had the enthusiasm faded, but truth to tell, a certain something that strongly resembled ill-humor reigned in its stead. "I suppose I needn't give those people supper, Theo," she said to her niece the day before, in a tone that made Theo feel herself to be a miserable sinner on the spot, and the cause of all things unpleasant. "I *suppose* I need not give those those people supper, Theo."

"Don't give it to them on my account, Aunt Libby," Theo replied, indifferently. Truth to tell, she was very indifferent as to whether her friends fed heartily in her presence or not. It never occurred to her to think her friends hungry when they came to see her.

"Instead of scoffing at my well-meant endeavours to make things pleasant under existing circumstances, I *wish* you would give me the benefit of your advice," Mrs. Vaughan exclaimed, tearfully.

"My dear aunt!—Well!—let me think. No; give them tea and coffee when they come. They all dine late, and don't want anything more."

"Don't want anything more," Mrs. Vaughan repeated, sarcastically. "My dear child, one would imagine you had been accustomed to entertain paupers, hungry paupers, to hear you talk of people 'wanting' anything more; you *must* learn to be more careful in your conversation, with your present prospects." And Mrs. Vaughan threw up her head, and flattened her little back, and thrust forward her little chest like an enterprising pouter pigeon, or a mistress of deportment for the upper classes, as she spoke.

"Oh, give them the supper. Let us have the supper by all means, Mrs. Vaughan," Sydney Scott cried. The supper appeared to her the sole element out of which pleasure might possibly be extracted which was left in Hensley. "If we don't have supper, how on earth are we to get over the evening?" Miss Scott asked of Theo later in the day. "It may be all very well for you, Miss Theo; but for people who are not just engaged to each other, let me tell you, a country congregation of this sort is tedious to the last degree."

Finally, the supper was decided upon; and when once the fiat for it had gone forth, Mrs. Vaughan went into the clotted cream, blancmange, and whipped syllabub questions in a way that relieved her guests most completely and entirely of the onus of entertaining her.

If the truth and the whole truth be stated, though, it must be told that when the evening came, it was not the "people who were just engaged" who found it the least tedious. It may have been, that excess of happiness made Frank remarkably quiet, not to say subdued: at any rate, something had that effect upon him. As for Theo, after that conversation which has been recorded with Mr. Linley on the Harold Ffrench subject, a conversation which took place before tea, she grew remarkably quiet, too, but quiet in a gentle, tender way that offered a marked contrast to Frank's unmistakeable sullenness. She was not regretting anything; circumstances had killed anything like love for Mr. Ffrench. David Linley, too, was very thoughtful. He could not help thinking a little of the dead woman who had been his toy, his tool, his slave, but never his love. He could not help thinking of her now as he sat looking at the one he had intended to be the third victim of his hate to Harold Ffrench.

For the rest: Mr. Leigh was happy in an unfeigned sober way that neither sought to hide nor to make itself manifest. He was exceedingly

gratified at the climax to which things had come. He had arrived at Hensley anticipating all manner of unpleasantness, in consequence of that warning he had received as to Harold Ffrench's proximity to Theo. The turn things had taken was delightful to him, and he showed that he thought it delightful, but he showed it so quietly that none who knew him less well than Theo could have discerned it all.

Mrs. Vaughan was happy, too, but in a qualified way. She had her doubts about many things, amongst others whether Theo felt properly impressed by the honour that had been done her, and also whether Theo felt duly grateful to her excellent aunt for that aunt's share in bringing the honour about. Mrs. Vaughan also had her doubts as to the lobster-salad, the construction of which she had in an evil hour of blind confidence entrusted to Sydney Scott, turning out well. "She's *sure* to have put in too much of something, the giddy-pated thing," the old lady said to herself, constantly glaring at the unconscious Sydney, who disregarded the glances, and suffered them to pass without verbal retorts in an unprecedented manner.

Sydney, in fact, was finding the evening far from tedious, though her friend Theo was the nominal heroine of the occasion. Miss Scott was agreeably occupied in watching Mrs. Galton—Mrs. Galton's silken skin was so visibly rubbed the wrong way by this latest achievement of Theo's.

This was the second head of big game that had fallen to Theo's gun before the eyes of Kate, the far more skilled sportswoman. Mrs. Galton was not precisely envious or jealous, but still she did not like it. She had thought but little of Theo, honestly thought but little of her, for Theo's was not the type of grace to touch Mrs. Galton. It was hard, therefore, to feel that Theo was on the highroad to all that for which she (Kate) had ever pined,—rank and position.

Mrs. Galton began to think more of Frank Burgoyne from the moment his engagement was made known to her. The shock his proposal to Theo caused throughout their circle, the talk and speculation, the surmises and excitement it created made her feel him to be the important man he was, in a flash. In the order of things it was out of the question that he could have married her, but for all that she did feel sore at his selection of Theo Leigh.

She had offered Theo congratulations in due form; however. Theo had on Mrs. Galton's arrival that evening unwarily accompanied that lady up-stairs, for the purpose apparently of seeing her take off her bonnet; and as soon as they were alone Mrs. Galton said what it is proper to say under such circumstances. She took both Theo's hands in her own, kissed Miss Leigh on the brow in the approved beneficent feminine fashion, and said:

"I find I have to congratulate you, Theo; really, you lucky girl, I'm very glad."

"Thank you," Theo replied.

"Thank you. Is that all you're going to say to me?"

"What more is there to be said?" Theo asked. "Have some eau-de-Cologne?"

"No; I won't have anything but a free confession from you that you are very thankful now for not being linked to my cousin Harold in any way that would have caused you to miss the chance."

"I don't know that we need talk about that now," Theo replied.

Kate looked out through the veil of nut-brown air she was re-arranging.

"There's no harm in talking about it if you have quite got over all feeling for Harold, Theo; of course, if you have not, I will keep silence on the subject. Shall I?"

"Just as you please," Theo replied, quietly.

"No, dear, it shall be as *you* please. The recovery has been rapid, marvellously rapid, I own; still I hope, that is, I *hoped*, that it was a recovery; if it is not, as I said before, I'll keep silence on the subject. Shall I?"

"If I say 'yes,' she'll take that as a declaration of the recovery not being perfected yet," Theo thought; "and if I say 'no,' she'll go on talking over till I'm frantic: anything is better than talking of it; and, after all, what does it matter what she thinks?"

"If it is not, as I said before, I'll keep silence on the subject. Shall I?" Mrs. Galton asked once more. To which Theo replied,—

"Yes." And so the matter dropped.

Dropped, that is, as far as conversation on the subject of it with Theo was concerned. But there was still Frank to be congratulated.

Now Mrs. Galton did not set about doing this in the manner that is especially odious to men—publicly, that is, in the face of the whole congregation. Had she done this she would have had the pleasing knowledge that Frank was feeling exquisitely uncomfortable and ashamed of himself, as publicly congratulated men are apt to feel; but she would also have had the fear of his being annoyed with and suspicious of her. She could not risk this, for at last Frank Burgoyne had become interesting to her.

So she, knowing that to the one who can wait all things will come, waited for a quiet opportunity to say her little speech to him. That opportunity came at last, and she seized it promptly like the active quick-witted woman she was. Seized and utilised it at once unobserved, as she imagined, by all then present. In this, however, she was mistaken: Sydney Scott saw and marked her.

The occasion taken by the fair strategist was the move in, or rather the confusion arising from the anticipation of the move in, to supper. Mrs. Vaughan was one of those excellent women who, through the very intensity of their desire to see all things done decently and in order, create, entirely by themselves, confusion, disorder, and consequently rank anarchy and despair.

The first sign of the approaching supper was given about an hour and a half before it was to be eaten, by Mrs. Vaughan's partially subdued but palpably uneasy desire to get out of the room. She had a presentiment that grew and strengthened in a frightful manner each moment that she was delayed, that somebody was doing something that ought not to be done to the table, or the viands, or the silver, or the glass. "I could'nt tell what it was," she explained, after the guests were gone. "I could'nt tell what it was, my dear, but I felt it in my throat; and, sure enough, when I *did* get out at *last* there was cook rubbing up my second-size silver salver with a glass cloth, and the grey-cat licking his paws, and looking at the trifle; and I wish," Mrs. Vaughan continued, with a rapid linking

together of cause and effect,—"and I wish, my dear Miss Scott, that you wouldn't put your chair right in the doorway when you see a person wishes to get out of the room quietly and without any fuss."

"I did'nt know what you wanted, Mrs. Vaughan," Sydney replied. "I saw you were very uncomfortable, but I didn't know what about. Of course if I had known you wanted to go out and look at the grey-cat licking his paws, I'd have let you pass; but I didn't, so I sat still."

Sydney had sat still, and Mrs. Vaughan had thus been compelled (as she fancied) to confine her flutterings to the room, the doorway of which was partially blocked by Miss Scott. But Mrs. Vaughan had not done this calmly. She had disturbed the deep repose, not to call it the dull quietude, which had been hovering over this small celebration-gathering of hers previously. She had broken up the deep repose, and caused people to wonder whether they were expected to make moves towards a departure yet, or whether there was anything more coming.

"Don't you think I had better order the carriage?" Mrs. Galton whispered to Theo.

"Oh! dear no," Theo replied.

"I'll just ask the Burgoynes what they think. I know she doesn't like late hours—she told me so herself," Mrs. Galton said, rising, and moving a little apart from the group of which she had previously been one, a move which brought her closer to Frank Burgoyne in the most undesigned way.

"Mr. Burgoyne, you'll hear for me what your aunt thinks about the propriety of making a move, won't you?"

"Yes, if you like," he replied aloud. Then he crossed over and spoke to Ethel, and then returned with her message, "No, certainly not; don't think of going yet," to Mrs. Galton.

He was near to her at last, and no one was within earshot. Her opportunity had come.

"You have not thought me remiss or indifferent because I have refrained from doing aloud what everyone else has done — congratulating you?" she asked, in her lowest voice.

"I have not."

"I suppose I ought to do it now. I suppose it is a settled thing?" she went on softly, and (he thought) anxiously.

"Thank you; it is a settled thing, I suppose," he replied, somewhat confusedly. This was a very newly-born thing, this interest which Mrs. Galton was displaying towards him, and like the majority of newly-born things, it was perplexing to a man, he did not know how—to handle it.

"Then now I may venture to express a portion of the deep interest I take in you; you will be so happy, for you have won her, and you must have loved her dearly to have sought her so soon."

It did not occur to Frank to question why Kate should be more now to express interest in him than she had been hitherto. He was but a man, and it was pleasant to have this admirable creature feel and express interest for him at all—doubly pleasant, since he had doubted her feeling the slightest interest in him previously. He thought more about the former portion of her sentence, but it was the latter part of it that he answered. "I ought to be happy, for she's a dear good girl."

"That she is," Mrs. Galton replied, glancing at

Theo; "and you may imagine how peculiarly
sed I am, and what my feelings are now that
e such a fair prospect before her."

rank made no answer; he knew that Mrs.
.on was making allusion now to Theo's first
-dream. He did not care about it, but he
not quite sure that he liked to hear it spoken
at.

It is an inexpressible relief to me," Mrs. Gal-
went on; "before this I have really felt
med to look Theo in the face; not that I was
onsible for my cousin's idle folly, but still he
my cousin, and I always remembered that
n I looked at poor Theo."

That's all gone and past," Frank said gloom-

Of course it is: utterly and entirely gone
past, and no one can rejoice more heartily at
being so than I. I little thought, Mr. Bur-
ne, that morning when you came to us under
walnut-tree, and just broke our monotony
r to let us relapse into it deeper still by your
edy departure—I little thought that morning,
; I should be offering you *such* congratulations
ore we parted."

I don't believe you thought about me at all
; morning," he said; and then he felt pro-
adly ashamed of himself and his imprudence
hus betraying chagrin.

'his was the small scene which had been re-
ied attentively by Sydney Scott, and found
lciently recompensing by her for the burden
heat of the evening. Sydney told herself
; it was righteous indignation on Theo's ac-
nt which made her look with an unfavourable
upon the free display of fascination Mrs. Gal-
was making to Theo Leigh's lover; in this
deceived herself, as is by no means uncom-
n even with those who judge themselves more
rously than did Miss Sydney Scott.

t came to be understood before the Leighs
, that the marriage should be in the following
gust. In the commencement of that month
nk would come into possession of certain prop-
es that had been bequeathed to him by an-
er relative; and though Lord Lesborough
given his consent to the latest arrangement
heir had made, and was on the whole well and
erously disposed towards him, it still seemed
e only judicious that Frank should not em-
k upon the sea of matrimony in entire depen-
ce on his grandfather.

'heo was taken in possession by the Bur-
nes to Maddington, before her departure to
e an interview with the head of the house.
d Lesborough kept his leg on the rest during
whole of it, in order to be able to lapse into
liminary twinges of the gout did the meeting
short in the smallest particular of any one of
requirements. But the meeting did not so
. Theo Leigh had great tact, and she was
y fond, in a grateful, clinging way, of the man
ore whose mighty relative she was now being
ted out.

[er father was with her naturally on the occa-
. He had gone with her to the important
mony of her solemn recognition as Frank's
rothed, fraught with the determination to
w Lord Lesborough that he got as good as he
gave. In other words, that Theo Leigh was not
held to be overpoweringly honoured by any man's
choice of her. This determination was rather

thrown away, however, for when they reached
the audience chamber it was made patent to them
(despite that lurking gout-symptom) that Lord
Lesborough did not deem Theo to be overpoweringly honoured himself.

Of the journey back to Bretford little need be
said. So much of my story remains still unwritten, that I need not essay to draw it out by
throwing a great air of importance around, and
spreading the description over several pages of a
transit by train. So I will only say that my party
of three, Mr. Leigh, his daughter, and Sydney
Scott, travelled from Hensley to Bretford in perfect safety, since it would not suit my purpose to
kill or maim them just yet.

Average reader, sojourner in the every-day
paths of life, you do not require to be told what
the majority of Theo Leigh's acquaintances said
on her return to Bretford as soon as the report
of this new engagement of hers made itself heard
amongst them. They spoke of Mr. Burgoyne as
"that poor young man," without having the
faintest idea in their innermost hearts why they
pitied him. "He can't know how she has been
jilted once," some of the matrons said, in a tone
that made some of their young military heroes
wince, and resolve solemnly to be extra careful
as to the quality of the soft nothings they were
wont to whisper to said matrons' daughters.

CHAPTER XXXVI.

"AS WE FORGIVE THEM THAT TRESPASS AGAINST
US."

HER lines were cast in pleasant places, or, at
least, they bid fair to be cast in pleasant places
in a very short time. They all said at Bretford
that it was a marvellous match for her, and that
she was a wonderfully lucky girl to be going to
make it. She told herself the same things constantly, for she loved Frank with a true healthy
love, and her father walked more erectly than he
had done for months; indeed his daughter's engagement had removed nearly all of that gall and
bitterness which had embittered his existence of
late from his heart, and left it free to beat health-
ily again. The cloud that had covered Theo's
head had been removed, he told himself, by a
higher hand than had placed it there. Theo
would be guarded safe and sure now from everything from which a man could desire his daughter
to be guarded. She would be a viscountess; better than this, she would be the wife of a man
whose past career was unsullied by secrecy or
subterfuge—whose future was bright as such a
past deserved.

Mr. Leigh was very happy in these prospects
of Theo's. He was happy to see that Theo's was
a far soberer, truer joy than she had had in that
first unauspicious engagement of hers, which had
been far less brilliant outwardly, and so far less
calculated to touch the majority of girls than this
one. This love of hers for the younger man,
though by no means so young a love as that
which had blazed up little more than a year ago,
and burnt itself out, was still a better love. It
was calmer, less exacting, less fearful. It was
likewise far deeper, and more likely to last.

She clung very much to her companionship
with her father in these days, talking to him fre-

quently of the old days down at Houghton, the days before Harold Ffrench had come there. They never spoke of aught that had transpired after that bright April morning when I brought them before you first. They dropped their lives at that epoch, as it were, and took them up again in these days, passing over all that had gone between.

All that had gone between. All the sweetness, and the sorrow, and the sympathy that had made that period the richest portion of her life. Rich in such thoughts as could never be hers again. It was hard sometimes to pass it over in silence, but she knew that Mr. Ffrench's forgiveness was not perfected in her father's heart as yet, and until it was so, she could not bear him named. For though her love for him was a dead thing now, she thought kindly of him still.

They spoke more of her approaching marriage than most fathers and daughters do : such a topic is the mother's more especially; but in this case it was with her father, that she made little plans for the future—plans in which he always had a share. Was this because of some doubt she felt that in his heart he was not well-assured of her perfect satisfaction with that future, and that until he was so assured he would remember the happiness she had felt in a widely different one, and remember the one who had changed that happiness into misery for a time.

Lord Lesborough was suffering from a tedious wasting illness, and Lord Lesborough's heir—because his aunts willed it so lovingly—spent much of his time at Maddington. But even when he was in London he was not extortionate in his demands on Theo's time and attention. He never sought to withdraw her from her father's society; and though always pleased to be with her, and to speak with her about his future life, and his public hopes, he would stroll about for hours alone when he went to spend long quiet days with them.

From time to time pompous messages were wafted up from the sick-room at Maddington to Theo *vid* Ethel. "You are first favourite with papa," that young lady wrote; "he discourses on your merits by the hour together to Harold Ffrench, who comes here sometimes, or rather by the five minutes together, for that's the extreme length of time which Mr. Ffrench stays in his room. When papa is better, and you're Mrs. Frank, Hugo Burgoyne will retire into the obscure corner of the gallery again."

These things were very pleasant to Theo, and they made her feel more tenderly still towards Frank. It was not in her, she feared, to "forward" in any other way this man who was to be her husband. But in his own family, or rather with the mightiest member of his family, she had done him good service already. Occasionally a fear crossed her mind that Frank, though he liked her to be well liked by all his family, did not care very much for the larger meed of toleration that was now awarded to himself, and that he only accepted the situation because it was not worth while to dispute it. But she strove to put that fear behind her. She desired to believe him to be all that was good and dutiful.

These messages from Maddington were balm and oil to her father and mother. Mr. Leigh would have regarded with unfavourable eyes any alliance, however brilliant, for his daughter, to which the family of the one who might desire to make it with her did not incline. From the Burgoynes there had been no demur; more than that, from the Burgoynes there had been every evidence of a satisfaction as complete as his own; therefore was Mr. Leigh happy with a fulness of content that made Theo feel that some things could not be too dearly purchased.

On the whole, it will be seen, that this was a happy time enough, for there was much to make life very bright to the girl who had known much sorrow, to the girl one of whose most poignant sorrows had been the knowledge that through her had been dealt the blow which had bowed a head never before bowed by aught approaching to shame—her father's. It was a happy time; for unless two lives could have been entirely unlived, there was no possibility of her life to come being brighter and safer than it promised to be.

If Time could have been arrested there, if he would only have stood still and suffered those who sorrowed so much to be at rest, at peace! There was a dead lull, such a lull as we see and feel sometimes after a mid-summer tempest, when Nature seems too tired to do any more, and so lies down, showing us how grandly calm she can be in fatigue. But if you have lived on the brink of the ocean, as I have done for years, watching all its changes, and marking all its moods, you will know that Nature's power is but taking a brief respite, and that she will rise up soon in such a storm as must wreck many.

She wakes from her lethargy, from that fear-disarming torpor, by such gentle degrees at times that you disregard the signs, and fall as prone before her fury as though no such indications of waking had been given. A feeling of something has been over you, perchance—of something that is not fear, and that "resembles sorrow only as the mist resembles the rain"—which, after all, is resemblance close enough to make the majority melancholy.

This lull had lasted then for a space that was all too brief to look back upon, but that had not been so very brief in reality. Summer was over everything once more—summer as warm and soft, but a trifle less bright, perhaps, to some than that past one of '51.

The lull was very perfect, very soft, and full, and deep, one gentle June evening at Bretford. Out on the terrace in front of Mr. Leigh's house they stood enjoying it. "They" were the father and his daughter, and that daughter's future husband.

The marriage that was to be in August, towards the latter end of August, had been spoken about freely between them that evening.

"We shall come here first, Frank, when we come back from the Continent—here, before we go anywhere else, shan't we ? "

"Certainly we shall," Frank replied. He was rather indifferent, to tell the truth, as to where they should go first when they returned from the Continent. He would have said "certainly we shall," had Theo suggested the Bights of Biafra.

"I don't ask that; you'll have other places that you must go to first, but by-and-by. What days we shall have together again, Theo ! " her father said to her.

"Ah! what days we *shall* have, dear; there

will be hardly any break, papa, not so much of a break as when I went to Hensley, in fact."

She left her lover's side as she spoke, and went round to her father's, looking up into his eyes with some of the old sweet gladness in her own that he had missed so long, so sorely! He was very happy then.

"Theo will have to rely principally on you next season," Frank Burgoyne said. "You see, if things stand as they are (he meant if Lord Lesborough still lived), I'm to come forward for West——shire, and I must make a show of attending to my electioneering interests, and I shan't care to know that Theo is out alone."

"Theo won't be out alone much," Theo replied. "I can promise that much, can't I, papa? I suppose you won't be much interested in reality, Frank?—I'm very ignorant about politics."

"Remain so; that is all I ask," he rejoined, laughing.

"I don't think Theo would have been the ideal wife for a man who had had to work out his own career," Mr. Leigh remarked. "Yours was made for you."

"Which accounts for my indifference concerning it, and for hers too, for that matter. I wish I had been compelled to work for a career; by heaven, it's the only thing to make a man of a fellow."

"It's a very fine thing, and answers occasionally," Mr. Leigh said quietly.

"Papa, don't pretend to think that it has not answered in your case," Theo began earnestly. "Why, mere success would have been nothing to what you gained so early, and have kept so long; to have made a name for such gallantry so young, and to have held it untarnished all these years! I had rather have that knowledge of my father than any other that could be given me."

"You see, the child can be enthusiastic," the father said, turning half away and scanning the offing, because he would not let them see that he was touched by her loving proud mention of that which he never talked about himself. Then the trio walked on in silence for a few moments, in complete silence till—there! when the blue, crimson, and gold, the tricolour of departing day, was flaming over the west, when the broad bosom of the water that rolled on at their feet was studded with a myriad diamond stars that were again momentarily shattered into yet a myriad more, when the voices of the seamen weighing anchor in the river were raised aloft in that evening strain that is less sweet than solemn, when the pall of silence was over all else around, and the grey mantle of the grand still night was descending rapidly, when the day was done, when the hour of deepest calm had come—then it was that Theo heard the first breath of the coming storm.

They had walked along in silence for a few minutes—in a silence that not one of them felt impatient to break. Suddenly Theo heard an exclamation that was partly a groan, and she looked and saw that her father had crossed his arms firmly, as he had done that night when the tale of Harold's shame, of Harold's wife, was told them.

He had stopped, clasping himself over the chest with that firm clasp which he had often been wont to give himself when standing in the bows of his boat he would be leading on a cutting-out expedition. The attitude was the same, but there was a touch less of "something" over all that wrung her heart to tears, for that clasp lasted but for an instant, then it relaxed, and his arms fell prone.

There were no tears in her eyes though, and no falter in her voice, as she moved closer to him quietly, and asked him had he spoken to her, had he said—anything.

While she questioned him thus quietly, Frank Burgoyne stood near to her, looking more startled and anxious than the girl whose heart was shedding tears, and for a few moments there was no answer.

Only for a few moments, but, "my God," Theo thought, whenever in after years she recalled them, "the agony of them, the agony of them!" Those moments were of dread and horror so condensed that they might have been spread over a whole lifetime, and have made that life bitter.

Theo could not have said what had come over her father, no word-painting can describe that change, none could have said precisely in what way he was not as he had been a minute before. There had come a tinge of pallor over that bronzed old face that might have been the work of months of sickness, and there had come a weaker compression of the lip, and a trembling where before there had been power in the frame.

The anguish of it! of that standing there, and being as powerless as the stones at her feet to avert, or assist, or understand, indeed, this fell visitant, whatever it might be. The anguish of standing in that melting summer air, knowing nothing, save that the only rock she had never split upon—the love that existed between her father and herself—was being shattered then.

He spoke at last, and even his voice was changed. Is it worth being born into the world to see such things come to pass? So they led him in helpless as an infant between them, and the doctors came, and told sorrowfully how the strong man was stricken with paralysis.

It was not so much that for a time they did not know the worst, as it was that they would not think the worst. We are apt to say to the truth in such cases, "get thee behind me," far more determinately than to Satan. His wife and daughter sat there by the side of his bed for hours, and days, and weeks, knowing well that he would never rise from it again, and be as he had been—knowing this well, and refusing to believe it, and telling each other and themselves that it was not so.

Had he been weak, puny, ailing, had he been other than he was, in fact, a god of strength and courage to his daughter, she would have suffered less; she must have suffered less, for it is not in the heart of woman to lament in like degree the falling of a sapling as the shattering of an oak. Theo could not tend upon him with the unflagging, unceasing devotion of her mother. She had been so proud of him in his strength that it broke her down utterly to have to minister to his weakness.

Shall I linger over these scenes? they were simply heart-breaking, for as after a brief space there ceased to be hope, there soon also ceased to be anxiety. It was a dull, numbing heart-breaking time, nothing more.

There dawned a day at last when he could speak; but the bitter terror that altered speech created in their hearts! It was God's decree, and morning and night in the course of her prayers she said fervently, "Thy will be done." But "not in this way should he have died, not in this way," was her hourly cry.

This was the end of it all—of that which had commenced more than fifty years ago, when, a little midshipman of nine, he had first cocked his hat and drawn his dirk for the king—of that early promotion which made him a distinguished man while still a mere boy, promotion the fruit of a daring so winning, bright, and bold, that bring him what it would, none could be found to grudge it; the end of that restless, coura-geous spirit that lost all that early gain because, when blows were striking anywhere for that mythical liberty for which so many men have suffered, he carried his sword thither and drew it with effect, erring against the routine which commanded him to remain quiescent;—the end of a life that had risked itself freely on the chilly shores of North America—that had offer-ed itself up for the salvation of Greece—that had nearly ebbed away in floods from fearful wounds made by Mexican blades on Mexican plains—that had staked itself right willingly a thousand times, and never hesitated at placing itself where sharp, immediate payment of that stake might be claimed;—the end of a life that had been without fear, as all men could attest, and that if it had not been without reproach, was at least as free from it as the lives of men whose blood does not flow pale may be. This was the end, this was the end!

It was very sad! Even those who have never tingled to the tales told by the lips they love of such deeds, must feel that after them such an end was very sad. The poor child, his daughter, felt it to be cruelly, crushingly so, for she had fallen into the error of imagining that he had made himself famous by his sword, and that there was a twist in Nature's mind when she could bring such a man to such a pass as this.

He laid there for awhile scarcely living, yet not dying, they told then; and Theo sat by his bedside through long summer days and even-ings, watching the shipping on the river, and trying to interest him sometimes about the steamers and their destinations. But it was but a flaccid interest he took in these things. He rather liked to dwell in that past which had been in a measure glorious to him, than in these tame current days. Whenever he did speak of a future, it was of hers as Frank Burgoyne's wife.

It rejoiced her often to perceive how dear this thing was to him; how he comforted himself in it, and, by reason of his knowledge of it, resign-ed himself the more humbly to this sorrow of his own. She had never known before how he wearied over what would become of her when he was dead and no longer able to take care of her as he would have her cared for. How he had doubted and distrusted what the morrow might bring forth for his child in a way that was entirely foreign to the brave carelessness of his spirit. But she read all these truths clearly by the light of that reliance he displayed on Frank Burgoyne, and his satisfaction in her prospects.

These prospects were not brought before her too vividly just now, for she herself removed the onus that would otherwise have been on Mr. Burgoyne of coming down to Bretford whenever he was able to do so. "You see I must devote myself to my father while now I can," she had said to Frank, with a little gulp over the last three words; and Frank had responded, "well, then you see I had better not bother you by coming when I'm in town next: I'll write."

"You wouldn't bother me," she replied; "we both know very well that you wouldn't do that, but it must be dull for you to sit down here by yourself, and very sad to see me as I am now about papa."

"Well, I will try to content myself with writ-ing until your father is better, Theo," Frank said, and he looked as though he could content himself very easily with so doing, then he added, "Don't let Mr. Leigh imagine that I keep away on account of his illness; tell him we both thought it better till you had more time and were less tired. As it is, I feel that I'm in the way, and I can do no good."

"No, you can do no good," Theo answered sadly. "I'll tell him, but he doesn't heed much now."

With bitter, mute misery they marked that he heeded less and less as the days sped on. This withering foe that had come upon him while still in the pride of his manhood,—this blight that had blasted him in an instant,—seemed to lay deeper hold upon him day by day; and soon they knew that its progress might not be arrested,—that this first seizure required no assistance from a second edition of itself to prove fatal.

There, through those sultry July days, he laid,—the man whom I showed to you, when this story opened, erect and vigorous: an old sea-lion, murmuring occasionally little scraps of prayers that he had learnt in boyhood, and being very helpless and very patient always. They scarcely liked to tell him how old brother officers came about them, constantly tendering their heart-felt sympathy for that which Theo felt to be so bitingly hard—so void of mercy They scarcely liked to tell him for the fear they had of arousing an anxiety about him self which slept now. They did not quite realise that he had done with all hopes and fears for himself.

Currently, out in the world that knew of that blow which had fallen, speculations were rife as to who would succeed Mr. Leigh; whether his widow would make a successful claim for those arrears of half-pay that were due to him whether he had been provident enough to in sure his life for his daughter; and whether the man who would be appointed in his room woul have a large family, for "if so, these apartment would be cramped." These were the subject suggested to the minds of the passers-by, b the shaded windows of the house at the corne in which one of them lay dying.

Kneeling by his side one night, waiting ther in awe, Theo grew conscious of a desire tha her father had that she should pray for hi aloud; I mean, she was always praying for hi in her heart.

So she began the prayer of prayers in a low voice, and she saw him trying to follow the words that she accentuated in the steady voice that never failed her when she was near him.

He opened his eyes when she came to the place for forgiveness of our own sins, and his last words were:

"'*As* we forgive them that trespass against us.'"

As Theo rose and staggered away out of the room,—staggered under the first real blow that had been dealt her,—she uttered a passionate hope that "Frank would come and say something to her." She panted, she longed for kind, gentle, reassuring words. The very ground seemed shaken under her feet, and every impulse of her loving nature urged her to cling to Frank.

"If he would only come in; if he only knew, he would be here directly," she kept on sobbing to herself, as she sat in a darkened room, and listened with a painful earnestness to every slow footstep that passed to and fro in the house. She felt, with an intensity of feeling that was nearly sickening, what was being done in that other darkened chamber, in which the spirit had fled. Then soon there fell upon her ear the soul-subduing knell that told out the tale to all the place of one more comrade gone—of one of their band having received the last promotion.

While she was waiting for him thus eagerly, Frank was on his way to her. When he was about a hundred yards from the house he met Sydney Scott, and at the same moment the passing bell commenced its sad chime.

"That's poor Mr. Leigh," Sydney said, mournfully; "I would like to go to Theo, but I dare not;" and she shuddered, and then added, "besides, no doubt she doesn't want anybody just now."

So he did not go to the one who wearied for him just yet.

CHAPTER XXXVII.

FRANK'S SENTIMENTS.

IT was all over. The one who had fallen was buried, and his place in the ranks was filled up by an old brother-officer, who had been expectant of this good thing for years, and could not, therefore, affect aught but the most superficial sorrow at the loss which was his gain. The new appointment was an amiable, kind-hearted man, but he had a large family, and some members of the same demanded he be forthwith make a tour of investigation over the suite of apartments that had fallen to his share, and report to them without delay how the furniture was to be apportioned.

Death is sad enough, heaven knows, at any time, and under any conditions. But it is saddest when it falls in the midst of a but recently attained sunny spot, and when its effects are upon the "living left" immediately. There would have been woe and tribulation throughout the Leigh household whenever and however this .bolt had been let fly. But things had become so very bright to them just before it; and now, through it, things must of necessity be temporarily so very black.

It was in the order of things; nevertheless it was very annoying that the incomers should desire to have their carpets fitted to the rooms before the Leighs' carpets were removed from the floors. They (the Leighs) were only to sojourn in the place for six weeks after the date of the funeral. Truly there was no temptation to remain there longer; they had no desire to do so. Yet, for all this willingness to depart, the knowledge that they had to do it, weighed heavily upon the mother and daughter. Their sorrow was so very young,—so cruelly heavy a thing as yet. Time would lighten and render them less averse to the trouble of moving under it. But this was precisely what could not be granted them. Pity, friendly consideration, sympathy, assistance, if it were needful, in any small matter. But not time. Time was government property, and must not be wasted; moreover, the incomers were anxious to come in. Time, like a pitiless master, sped the six weeks away in most unseemly haste.

All Frank Burgoyne's best qualities came out and aired themselves at this period. He was considerate and most manfully tender to Theo, and Theo responded to him, as it was in her nature to respond to consideration and tenderness. She had entered into this compact at first out of a feverish desire to please her father, and make him feel that the world was not at all barren and hard for her, that her plan of life was not upset through Harold Ffrench. Having done this for her father's sake, she was soon repaid by coming to like Frank for his own; and now, in these latter days, the liking merged into something warmer, and Theo grew to love her future husband well.

But though all Frank's best qualities came out, they did so, it must be acknowledged, under circumstances so adverse to them that their flourishing at all was a marvel. Theo was much harassed and worried at this epoch about things that might not even be fully confided to Frank, and these things told upon her, and rendered her less pleasant to the eye than she had been formerly. Frank Burgoyne was not superhuman: he liked what was pleasant to the eye.

August, the month in which the marriage had been arranged to take place, had come and gone before those weary weeks of hopeless, helpless waiting were half over. It was October when the last barren honour of a military funeral was offered to Mr. Leigh, and in the same month they left the place to which they had come scarcely more than a year before with high hopes of various kinds.

It was a pleasant time of year. Heaths and commons look well in the autumn; one is apt to fall into the error of imagining at this season that they look well all the year round. Mrs. Leigh and her daughter, with the natural aversion of country people for closeness and thickly populated parts, eschewed London, and decided on settling themselves in a little house on the breezy brow of Hampstead Heath till such time as Theo should be married, and the mother be free to select her own residence.

It was an unfortunate settlement to have made as it turned out. "It's nice, and fresh, and quiet," Theo said to Frank Burgoyne, when she had acquainted him with their final decision as to their place of abode; "you didn't know where to advise us to live, Frank, but I think you'll like the place we've chosen."

"I dare say," Frank replied; "don't think much of the neighborhood as a rule, though."

"It's lovely about here, and we can have plenty of nice walks," Theo said.

Now "nice walks" did not enter into Frank's category of things pleasant. They were all very well when taken in an unpremeditated way, quite away in the country; but to lay oneself out in cold blood to take them in a suburb was a very different thing.

"Ah! ye-s-s; I wish you hadn't gone quite so far out of the way: it's a day's journey to get there."

"Is it very far out of the way?" Theo asked. She was hopelessly ignorant of localities and their respective worth. She did not know how inaccessible were all places beyond Mayfair and Belgravia to the Frank Burgoynes of this world.

"Is it very far out of the way? we seemed to get there very soon, I thought, and get the omnibus——"

"Omnibus!" Frank interrupted. "My dear Theo, your mother doesn't take you about in an omnibus, does she?"

"Of course she does," Theo replied.

"What on earth for?"

"Well, Frank," she said, with a laugh, "the sole carriage in our family is the box upon four wheels down at Hensley, you know."

"That's going from one extreme to another," Frank replied, in an annoyed tone.; "but there's something incongruous in your going about in an omnibus; I can't have it."

"Very well," Theo said; "it's rather far for a walk certainly, but if you object to the omnibus I shall have to trudge. I must go there frequently to see how they are getting on with the house before mamma goes in."

"You must take a cab, of course."

"I mustn't take a cab, of course," she said brightly; "don't mind such things, Frank," she added, suddenly and seriously. "I shall not be less worthy of better things, shall I, for having ridden in omnibuses?"

"Less worthy!—you're a darling girl; but you don't quite understand these things. Well, as the house is taken it's no use saying any more about it; it won't be for long."

Theo blushed. "It must be for some months, Frank."

"Perhaps you're right; for two or three months it may be; you'll be settled there soon now, won't you? by the time I come back you will be quite ready to receive me, and do the honours of Hampstead Heath as an inhabitant."

"Are you going away?" she asked, with a slight touch of disappointment in her tone; "it's so much to me to have you with me, Frank, that I'm afraid I'm getting selfish about it."

"Yes; didn't I tell you that I was going down into Norfolk for a week or ten days?" he replied, with a great assumption of carelessness.

"No; where?"

"To Galton's. Oh, yes, I must have told you, because he asked me long ago."

"I suppose you forgot it," she said, rather sadly.

"I suppose I did," he said quickly. "By the way, speaking of Galton, do you ever hear anything of Harold Ffrench now?"

She shook her head.

"I think, if you should chance to fall in with him again, it will be just as well to give him to understand clearly that you don't want to hold any communication with him; I think it will be just as well, don't you?"

"Perhaps it will be; I mean, it will be if you think so," Theo answered. She was beginning to feel far less interested in whether she saw or did not see Harold Ffrench, than in Frank's being fully satisfied and entirely pleased with her.

There was a pause after this, for Theo about this period was apt to be completely worn out in body very often, and so less lively in spirit than it behoves a girl to be in presence of her lover. Now, as regarded this particular of her fatigue, Frank was delightful: he never upbraided her for it by word or manner. He was sorry for it in a sympathising way whenever it chanced to come before his notice prominently; but he endured its existence with a good grace, and never reproached Theo for it by the display of any exuberant vitality on his own part.

So now, after Theo had agreed with him that it would be perhaps as well that, if she chanced to fall in with Harold Ffrench, she should make it apparent to him that what had been was not any more, or something to that effect, one of these customary calms befel them, and they sat for a space very silently. At last Theo spoke.

"When did you say you were going down to Norfolk, Frank?"

"Oh, in a day or two. I must go; it's a deuce of a bore, but I must go."

"Why is it a bore?" she asked simply; and here, be it remarked, that the pure and simple interrogation, when one is not prepared to give an equally pure and simple response, is about the most unpleasant form of question to which one can be subjected.

Frank shuffled.

"Because I would rather stay with you," he said; and Theo believed the assertion, finding it a pleasant one, after the manner of women.

"Never mind, Frank; it will be only for a week or ten days, you say. What a lot I shall have to do, while you're away killing partridges with that dear, good-natured Mr. Galton. My soul recoils," she continued, with a little hardly achieved laugh, "from the task of moving; the going out from here will bring back all things so vividly."

"Dear Theo," Frank said soothingly—and he was a capital comforter in this, that he never talked reason in a time of distress, by way of alleviating the latter.

"I am more than half glad after all that you will be out of it," she continued; "if you had stayed in town, you would have felt bound to come down and see me sometimes, through the turmoil; and I don't look at all well when I'm very dusty and my eyes are red. No, you'll find Mrs. Galton far pleasanter to look upon for the next ten or twelve days."

She said it carelessly enough, in her desire to reconcile herself aloud to this proposed absence of his. But he fancied he detected a hidden meaning in her words.

"Really, Theo, I don't think Mrs. Galton would thank you for making such a speech."

"O yes she would; she likes people to think and say that she's pleasant to look upon," Theo replied. "I have always thought it. I was completely carried, fascinated out of all judgment by her, the first time I saw her. I remember I called her 'charming,' and my poor father said she was as full of airs and graces and falsity as a performing monkey."

"A choice comparison."

"But then he didn't like her, you see, Frank; and he was half afraid that I was going to set her up as my model, and copy all her lights and shades (especially the latter), so he meant it as a warning."

"She has the best manner of any woman I know," Frank said decidedly; "any one might make her a model with advantage."

"You think I might, for instance?" Theo asked. It was scarcely a pleasant sound in her ears—this unconditioned praise of another woman's manner.

"I said, any one might," Frank Burgoyne replied. "I didn't mean you particularly, you little goose; there's a perfect repose about her that is as far removed as the north pole from the south from coldness or stupid indifference; it's wonderfully taking. A pity your friend, Sydney Scott, hasn't it."

"It wouldn't suit Sydney," Theo said, laughing; "fancy Sydney with Mrs. Galton's manner, and walk, and voice."

"They would be far more becoming in Sydney or any other woman than that assumption of boyish frankness and loudness in which Miss Scott indulges," Frank Burgoyne said severely.

"Oh, Frank, you've forgotten the nutting," Theo cried.

"No, I have not; I have not forgotten anything. She flirted furiously at me, if you mean that."

"And what did you do, sir?—one can't get up a flirtation unassisted."

"She always tired me, I know that," he replied; "she was well enough, but a little of her went a long way."

Theo was feeling rather warmly towards Sydney at this special juncture. The bright little blonde having nothing else on hand at the time, was being very friendly and devoted in numberless small and not easily to be recounted ways. She had volunteered her services on more than one shopping expedition, and she had approved herself great in the giving of advice relative to the most becoming way of having sable garments made up. "Black, dead black unrelieved, would make you look hideous, Theo, with your dark skin," she had said honestly. And as Theo had no overweening ambition to look hideous, she had availed herself of Sydney's instructions as to the "relief" of the aforesaid black.

"She not faultless, any more than any one else; but she's very nice and amusing, and good-hearted," Theo said earnestly. She was feeling very warmly towards Sydney, partly, it may be here admitted, because Frank Burgoyne was uttering speeches that savoured of disparagement of that young lady. Had his allusions to Sydney been more enthusiastic, Theo might perchance have remembered the nutting, and the wail for the absent violet bows, and sundry other things which she now elected to forget or magnanimously pass over. However, Frank's recollections of Sydney were not of an order to place Miss Scott in the worst light before his betrothed bride;

therefore female friendship reigned triumphant, as it is wont to do, of course; and Theo declared Sydney Scott to be "nice and amusing, and good-hearted, though not faultless."

"She's very brusque, if that is what you call frank; and she wouldn't hurt any one who didn't come in her light, which you may consider good-hearted," Frank replied. "That is my candid opinion of the young lady," he went on.

"Oh, Frank, it's an unjust one," Theo answered. Then she checked herself, remembering that after all Sydney Scott was not a point on which it was quite worth while to have a debate.

"I suppose you won't see much of each other when you go over to Hampstead," Frank inquired presently.

"I don't see why we shouldn't; in fact—well, to tell the truth, I have asked her to come and stay with me as soon as we're settled," Theo said, rather confusedly.

"Good Lord!" Frank groaned.

"What is the matter?"

"What can make you want to see more of that little mass of affectation?" he asked.

"I remember the time you didn't think her that," Theo said, trying a laugh, and failing. "Why did I ask her?—oh! because I shall be quite in a strange land, you know, and rather dull sometimes, I fancy; besides I like her. You surely have no serious objection to it, Frank?"

"Serious objection?—why should I?"

"That's precisely what I want to know."

"I only think she'll be a bore. Of course if she 'amuses you' (I must confess I can't imagine how) it's all right; she is just the mixture of giggling school-girl and sharp garrison-town hack that is most odious to me. But, if you like it——"

He did not say what might be expected to happen if Theo liked it. He paused on the speculation, and began a whistle under his breath, as it were—a whistle with no heart in it, but a great deal of ill-temper—a whistle of that soured, soundless character that is infinitely aggravating to listen to.

"Whatever she may be she isn't a bore," Theo argued.

"That's just as you take it; you must forgive me, Theo, if I don't congregate together with her at your new place at Highgate—Highbury—which is it?"

"It's neither," Theo replied laconically.

"Where is it then?"

"I had better not give you the address again till you are on the verge of visiting it," she replied; "you will forget it before occasion calls you that way, since your memory is so bad for that special quarter."

"Don't try to be sarcastic, dear," he replied with that big air of superiority of every sort to which a woman is tolerably sure to be subjected sooner or later when she ventures upon a verbal passage of arms with a man. "Don't try to be sarcastic, dear; that essaying to be it is one of your friend Sydney's most disagreeable habits. I should be sorry to think that you had caught it of her."

She was very tired. The only one who had been uniformly tender, considerate, and loving to her had been "gone away" such a very little time. She had been sorely buffeted. She was very tired!

"I won't try to be sarcastic, or anything else you don't like, Frank, really," she said, almost meekly; "only *don't* snub me for liking Sydney Scott, and sometimes wishing to see her, for I'm often lonely, you know."

"Lonely! when you have me!" The grand creature to whom she was engaged could scarcely realise the possibility of loneliness and himself revolving in the same orbit.

"Lonely! when you have me!"

"I haven't you always—or often even; I might as well bewail or behowl myself because you are going down to the Galtons, and ask how you can care for pointers and partridge-shooting when you can see me."

His fair Saxon beauty clouded over with a dark red flush.

"We are talking mere imbecilities now," he said coldly. Then, seeing that Theo's face fell, he added suddenly: "And it must be my fault that we are doing so, for you're a sensible dear girl."

Which afterthought was all very well in its way, but was utterly powerless to efface the impression made by the former part of his sentence.

"Come, Theo," he said, after a time, seeing that Theo still continued grave, "you're not going to be glum, are you?"

"No, certainly I'm not; but I am engaged to ask you to do something to-morrow night, and now I scarcely know how to do it."

"Never mind; tell me what it is."

"You won't like doing it, I'm sure now; but after all, I only engaged to ask you, and you can refuse."

"What is it?—to go and see that there are no leaks, or cockroaches, or other abominations at the new house? My dear Theo, you'll soon have a place of your own, a decent one too, by Jove! You'll never like this one, I'm persuaded, away on those wilds."

"It's not that, Frank," she said, half laughing, and more than half vexed; "it's not that at all; it's nothing half so bad in reality as you have imagined, so I have courage to ask; will you go with the Scotts to the ball to-morrow night?"

"No, why should I?"

"There's no reason why you should, of course; you may imagine that *I'm* not bent upon your going; only it was arranged that you should go, you know, before——"

She stopped suddenly, and Frank nodded his perfect appreciation of all she had said, and thorough appreciation of all she wanted, and found herself unable, to say.

"And now Sydney Scott seems to think it rather hard that you should be kept away, as she calls it, on my account; it's rather flattering to you, sir, for Sydney is at a premium here."

Frank Burgoyne smiled.

"Does she pretend to you that she cares for me to go? she doesn't mean it; it would be different if I were not done for."

"Really I don't think your being 'done for' makes the smallest difference in her wanting to dance with you."

"Those balls are awfully slow affairs, are they not?"

"I never found them slow," Theo answered candidly. In truth those balls had seemed dazzling scenes of delight to her, unhappy as she had been when she attended them.

"Ah! that was because you were fresh; I have heard that they are mere travesties of the military balls. However, as you have set your heart upon my going with your little friend, I'll do it."

"I think perhaps that Sydney's heart is more set upon your going than mine is, since I shall not be with you, Frank; but it's very good of you to say you'll go, very good indeed."

Frank looked as if he thought himself noble to a degree.

"I suppose there will be a whole army of Scotts, won't there? we shall go in procession."

"Oh, no: Sydney stands alone; only her father and mother will be there; here's the ticket."

Mr. Burgoyne took it with much unconcern.

"Need I write to old Scott, and express myself obliged for this?" he asked, "because I ain't obliged, you know. I hate anything of the kind."

"Well, as you like; it would be civil, but if you don't want to be that, I will tell Sydney to-night that your grace is going, and that she had better stand in a secluded corner and keep that portion of the British army there assembled at bay till you vouchsafe to arrive and lead her forth in the mazy dance."

He laughed. "You may tell her I'm going," he said. "I will just look in for an hour, and then come back here and talk to you, my darling." Which remark settled the subject.

CHAPTER XXXVIII.

THE BALL.

FRANK—a recruit for the overflowing ranks of the noble army of martyrs, came down the following night and exhibited himself to Theo's admiring gaze in glorious garb. That is to say his garb was not glorious by any means,—the dress of the day does not deserve this epithet,—but solemnly arrayed in slight mourning, as it is the custom of men to be when they are going to attend that most festive of all gatherings—a ball.

The ball-room was a long apartment, with stone walls and marble busts at the upper or honourable end. It struck a chill into Frank's heart as he entered it, partly by reason of these stone walls and partly because the light which pervaded it was of the dim religious order. A band was perilously perched in a little gallery (a temporary erection) behind and above the row of marble busts. And countless fair beings were the same—that is, perilously perched on benches on all sides of the room.

It was scarcely what one could have called a brilliant scene on the whole, but at least there was brilliancy in one portion of it, as soon as his entrance was marked. The spot of ground on which Miss Scott stood seemed positively radiant as that fair young being brought herself and her partner up abruptly at the sight of Frank, and welcomed him with a gracious smile, and a well gloved hand. She was incapable of speech by reason of having gallopped all her breath away.

"Shall I introduce you to a partner, Mr Burgoyne?" she asked, as soon as she had re covered herself in a measure.

"Thank you," he was about to add, "not just yet," but she nipped his refusal in the bud.

"There's Miss Clarissa Smith sitting down a

usual; look, shall I take you up to her?" She pointed as she spoke to a ·lady who had been young at some remote period.

"You're very good," Frank replied stiffily. "I think, if you'll excuse me, I will——"

"Or, see, if you don't like her there's her second sister. I wouldn't advise *her* for a round dance though," she continued, reflectively; "she has what we should call a gaudy action in a horse."

Frank tried to look disgusted with the manner adopted by his guide in this strange country, into which he had adventured himself. He tried to look disgusted, and he failed; more than that, he tried to feel disgusted, and not even in that could be quite succeed.

"There are four more Miss Smiths somewhere about the room," Sydney said cheerfully; "fancy coming to a ball with five of one's sisters!"

"I can't fancy it," Mr. Burgoyne replied.

"Will you take another turn, Miss Scott?" Sydney's partner, who had, like the far-famed Arab steed, been standing meekly by throughout this conversation, here ventured to suggest.

"Presently," Miss Scott replied; when she did take another turn she meant to take it on the arm of Mr. Frank Burgoyne, but she did not care to make her meaning manifest.

"The Miss Smiths being unpromising, as far as I can see, perhaps you will be good enough not to hand me over to one of them," Frank said.

"If you would rather not, I won't, certainly; but what is to be done?"

It was all plain sailing now. Frank's course was obvious.

"Nothing—unless you will take pity on me yourself."

Sydney showed signs of a readiness to desert at once. It .was useless the young ensign with whom she had been dancing assuming a look of humble trust that she would not leave him. It was useless his delivering himself of the hope that "she wouldn't spoil the best waltz of the evening in *that* way."

"Oh! you know everybody, and can find a partner directly," she said aloud; then she added in a whisper, "don't be disagreeable, Mr. Hargrave: what will Theo Leigh think of me if I don't try to make things pleasant to Mr. Burgoyne?"

Hargrave declined to see the force of this.

"I have no doubt that Theo Leigh would forgive you for not making such a tremendous fuss as all this about him," he said, rather sulkily; "let him stand in a corner if he can't find a partner. Our fellows never have much difficulty in getting one here though," he continued, with a small well-pleased laugh, that Sydney could have smothered, and was determined to punish him for.

"Your 'fellows' are more easily satisfied then, I conclude; come! it must be so," she added a trifle imperiously, "and I'll give you the next quadrille."

"So you really mean to throw me over?" Mr. Hargrave asked, to which Sydney replied, "Oh! not that certainly, but——" here she ceased all efforts at explanation, and went off with Frank Burgoyne.

When the dance was over Sydney made a fleeting allusion to her mamma.

"We can't work our way through that crowd, that is very clear," she began; "if we do, away will go the better part of my dress, and mamma is there."

"Never mind: she will know you can't be lost," he responded.

"Ah! but I must get to her presently, to introduce you."

Now Mr. Burgoyne had no marked inclination to be introduced to the parent-bird. Sydney was all very well, for an hour or two, he told himself, especially bedecked as she was on this occasion and brilliant from excitement. But a matured, expanded Sydney, from that he would abstain.

"Till I can pilot you in safety down to the dowager's divan you may as well. beguile the moments of waiting by telling me who's who in 18—."

"Shall I begin with the beauties or the peculiarities?" she asked.

"Begin with what you have most of," he replied.

"H'm, well! that's putting me in rather a difficult place. There are the six Miss Joneses, for instance——"

"You called them Smith just now," he interrupted.

"Ah! they were the Smiths, but there are six Joneses too; they run in half-dozens in these regions; that is Miss Jones passing along there in a blue dress and green wreath; sweet taste, isn't it?"

"Under which denomination do you place her? —beauty or peculiarity?"

"That is hard to say; she's the beauty of the family, for the others are ever so much uglier; some people ·out of her family may admire her too. I have no prejudice in favour of such an extreme length of nose myself."

At this moment Miss Jones came too near to be openly discussed. She was tall, fine, dark, flashing. Small wonder that Sydney had no prejudice in favour of Miss Jones' style of beauty. By her side the bright little blonde looked stumpy.

"Do you see those two Oakhursts, in their eternal black dresses?" Miss Jones asked of Sydney, as she came to a pause near her.

Sydney nodded. "Yes· they always look nice—not that I think them pretty," she replied.

"Nice, do you think they look? Well, now, I think them so dowdy-looking; black wants so much relief doesn't it?"

"Yes," Sydney assented carelessly. She wanted Miss Jones to ̇move on, and Miss Jones evidently had no desire to do so. Miss Jones was partnerless at the moment, and Frank Burgoyne looked·promising.

"Talking of black, I saw Theo Leigh to-day; *how* well it suits her! but then she's pretty in everything," Miss Jones remarked, rolling her big dark eyes round upon Frank. She had never been introduced to this gentleman, therefore it was quite allowable, she thought, to discuss the girl he was engaged to before him, and seem not to know him to be what he was.

Frank turned his head away, and looked and felt annoyed. Sydney replied curtly:

"Yes; she does. Oh! there's mamma."

"Wait one minute, Sydney," Miss Jones cried, and then she made a whispered communication

9

to Sydney, with many noddings of her head, and flutterings of her fan, and archings of her eyebrows, and rollings of her eyes. She was regarded as "a fine animated creature" by the members of her own family, and by very youthful marine officers generally. Small boys clothed in the uniform of that glorious corps, mentioned with pride the number of times in which they revolved round her in the mazy dance during the evening. She had a bounding way of taking the room at the first strain of waltz or gallop that caused their brains to whirl. "She was a fine creature, and could go the pace and no mistake," they said to one another as they wiped their brows when they had deposited her after a burst of the kind. Perhaps the secret of their adoration for her might be found in the fact of a progress with her never being wholly unmarked. When they lacked height, she had it. "She showed off well in a crowded room where little girls were lost, you know." Frank looked at the fine creature while she was making her whispered communication to Sydney, and he hated her. He hated her for her evolutions, after the manner of ungrateful men—though they were all gone through by her for the purpose of pleasing him. He hated her for calling the girl he was going to marry "Theo." He hated her for tapping Sydney Scott with her fan. "Why the deuce when women can't handle it better do they carry one at all?" he asked himself. He couldn't bear her blue dress and her green wreath. She looked to him like a woman who, when she had achieved an introduction to him for herself, would bring up her six sisters, and bid him stand and deliver himself up to one of them for a dance. In a word, he detested Miss Jones. He knew that if he urged a flight from her that he would be carried in procession, and shown to Mrs. Scott; but of two evils he favoured the unknown, and longed for the moment when dutiful scruples should again assail Sydney.

That moment came at last. "There's mamma making a dear old funny face at me," Sydney suddenly exclaimed, directing Frank's gaze as she spoke down along a vista that was bordered by beings with backs, and defenders of their country. Two sets of quadrilles had just been. And the onus was off Sydney of attending to any one save Frank for at least one dance more.

"Shall we go and see what she wants?" Frank asked, looking as he spoke at a wide old lady who was attired in what resembled silken bed-curtains, over which an arabesque pattern had been formed by an unsteady hand. Then his eye fell upon a something crimson with what looked like a shaving-brush stuck in at the top which surmounted Mrs. Scott's head, and he felt sorry that he had asked "shall we go and see what she wants?" "Why do British matrons wear turbans, and attempt to achieve a faint resemblance to the lusty Turk?" he groaned in spirit, as he led Miss Sydney up to her mamma.

Now Mrs. Scott had come to this hall fraught with the firm determination to render all honour unto Mr. Burgoyne. "I know what's due to the nobility—none better," she had said when Sydney had told her that Mr. Burgoyne was going to be there, and that they must all be civil to him. "I know what's due to the nobility—none better; it isn't they as give themselves most airs as has mixed with the best; before I married your father, Sydney, I sat down to dinner many a time with a lord's son." "

"Well, Mr. Burgoyne isn't a lord's son, and never mind telling him anything about those dinners before you married papa, mamma," Miss Sydney had replied. The mention of them was not, by any means agreeable to her, for she had gathered that the sole sprig of nobility who had partaken of her maternal grandfather's hospitality in those bygone days which Mrs. Scott recalled with unction, had been a naval cadet, the son of a lord mayor who had recklessly run up a long tailor's bill, and then affably dined with said tailor to decrease it. No wonder that Miss Sydney said:

"Never mind telling him anything about those dinners."

Mrs. Scott was absolutely basking in the refulgence of her own smiles when the pair came up to her. It had always appeared to her a most unjust dispensation of Providence that all the good that had come of that visit to Heusley, which her daughter had paid, should have fallen to Theo Leigh. The mother had some undefined feeling of Sydney having been wronged in the matter, for before the climax came, Sydney had communicated her belief in a widely different climax approaching. There had been a semi-tone of reproach in Mrs. Scott's salutation to her daughter on that daughter's return. "I never expected, after what you said, to see you come back as you went, Sydney; young men have no business to trifle with girls in that way, and if I were your father I should take the matter up. I'll be bound that's what Mr. Leigh went down for—to bring him to the point with Theo."

"I don't think that," Sydney had replied, "but I do think that Theo got him away just to spite me: I know he liked me best."

"To be sure he did," the fond parent replied with a touch of the true parental prejudice "and I have made no secret of what I think of their conduct in taking a young man by surprise, as one may say, before he knows his own mind; but they ain't married yet, and they've behaved as bad to you."

Which speech caused Sydney to regard herself as much wronged, and as being fully justified in doing anything. Nevertheless she practised the virtue of Christian forgiveness, and kept "very friendly," as has been seen, with Theo Leigh.

CHAPTER XXXIX.

KATE IMPROVES.

AFTER that sojourn at the Lowndes shooting box, John Galton and his wife returned to the Grange, and passed a very quiet time there together for some four or five months. As these were winter months it was really very dull even Miss Sarah could not feel much surprise at Kate finding it so. John Galton had a habit of going off several miles to the coast, and lurking about in holes in the marshes through cold winter nights with a long duck-gun, brace of big dogs, half Irish spaniel half retriever, and one of those rough beings only to be found on the coast, who are partly sailor, partly fisherman, and partly on the loose look-out for a night on the marshes with any gentlemen fond of wild-duck shooting and a position for many hours in a damp hole in the mud.

John Galton was a thorough sportsman, and as yet he had never had his ardour damped by ever so slight a touch of rheumatism. A mallard would repay him for any number of hours waiting, and a brace of snipes for any amount of wet. But Kate was very dull while he was away —so dull that she came at last to feel that there must have been something after all in this companionship which she missed.

At one period she took, as a sort of forlorn hope, to being very intimate with Miss Sarah. She would saunter down to Miss Sarah's cottage in the morning with little Katie and some cream or new eggs; and she would be made to repent having taken either of the latter, usually through a habit Miss Sarah had of accepting them with a grim allusion to the time when such goods from the Grange were hers of right in a measure, the time "before John married." "Well, John *is* married now, you see," Kate would reply as good-humouredly as she could, "and still you get the eggs and cream, so you've nothing to complain of." Upon which Miss Sarah would put her sister-in-law and her sister-in-law's good intentions to flight, by asking sharply: "Have I ever 'complained?' Don't I bear *poverty*, and *obscurity*, and *obloquy*, and *scorn* in silence, ow—a!" when Miss Sarah's lamentations reached this point there was nothing for it but flight, and Mrs. John Galton would be driven back to the desolate Grange, where the very watch-dogs hung their tails despondently because their master was absent.

But these visits of Kate were surely, though slowly, working upon the one to whom they were paid. The particles of real kindness that was in them might be infinitesimal, but the dose was constantly repeated, and so told at last, and met with its due reward. "John, I really think your wife is improving," Miss Sarah said to her brother on more than one occasion, "her conduct is much more like that of a respectable married woman than it used to be." Which meagre praise of the woman who was, despite her faults and follies, so unspeakably dear to him, John Galton had to accept and even to appear grateful for.

At length there came a break in the monotony which had hung over all things for so long a time. As a candid and honest historian I cannot say that the break was one whit more acceptable to any one of them than the monotony had been.

John Galton had departed one bitter winter's afternoon with his duck-gun and dogs for a night on the sands, leaving Kate rather more resigned to her approaching solitude than usual: she had just received a fine relay of new books. "Don't forget that we have to dine at that place to-morrow, John," his wife said to him as he was getting up into the trap; "that place" being the rectory, and to-morrow being the day of the first feast given within its walls by their new rector. "No, I won't," he replied; "I shall be back by twelve o'clock to-morrow: if you have nothing better to do, come along the road to meet me, will you?"

She promised him that she would do so, and then he drove off, and she went back to the cosiest corner of her drawing-room, and turned over the new books in pleasing uncertainty as to which of them she should first fall upon and devour.

The one she finally decided upon was that novel of Mr. David Linley's, which he had been compelled to go up to his publisher about while she was staying at Lowndes, and she began to read it with that pleasant clearness of vision for its faults and shortcomings which we are all apt to be endowed with while reading the work of an acquaintance. It is so nice to pick out errors of taste and grammar, and violations of the unities and propriety in the printed words of one whom we know. So Kate read away happily, and reviewed as she read far more severely than any of the literary journals had done.

She had the prospect of a long afternoon of uninterrupted bodily ease and mental relaxation before her. Instead of a dinner she had (after the manner of women when they are left to themselves) ordered tea at six. "Tea and something nice," she had said to John; and John, when giving the order to cook in the kitchen had added,—"which means that she'll trouble us for something else 'nice' at ten, interfering with one's supper-time."

John Galton had been gone an hour; it was now four, and so much of the wintry sky as she could see from her corner of the couch near the fire began to look dark. "He'll have a terrible night of it, poor old fellow!" she thought; "it *is* plucky though to go through so much hardship and find it all sport, *he'd* never do it"—she brought her hand down on the open page before her as she thought this of Li⬛ "He'd never do it; after all he was right⬛ough he did not mean me to think him so, when he said that the man who could do all such things was not so far behind the one who could only write about them."

Little Katie was stretched out on the rug before the fire with a Punch scrap-book and a tiny terrier puppy, and one or two other antidotes to dulness around and about her. The child had had more of her mother's companionship lately, and she seemed to love it so much that Kate unconsciously granted more and more of it daily to the innocent courtier. This latter was supremely happy just now, for she had been promised the exquisite bliss of having "tea with mamma;" moreover, the terrier puppy had been her "very own" but for two short hours. It was drear dull winter without, but in this room there was warmth and comfort of so perfect an order, that Kate's ardent prayer that she might have no interruption had been quite natural.

Before settling down thoroughly she had run over a list of possible callers, and she had given herself a good and sufficient reason after naming each one for that one not coming this day. "The Reynolds' have a child with the scarlet fever, so she'd never come near *my* child, and Mrs. Sparks wouldn't be unfeeling enough to leave her husband now he has sprained his ankle; Mrs. Williamson never calls when she *knows* it's getting time for her to have another dinner-party, stingy old thing; and as for the Caldwells, dunce as she is, she must surely know that I shall have quite enough of her to-morrow dining there." Then she thought favourably of one or two more acquaintances, who always got neuralgia if they came out in an easterly wind, and she blessed the wind for coming from the east this day, and went on with her book luxuriously.

Suddenly, in the midst of a chapter, the writing of which had made David Linley's hard old head ache even, he had so elaborated the intricacies of the situation in which everybody was plunged in it, suddenly, in the midst of this, there fell upon her ear the knell of parting peace, the sound of the hall-door bell, and the next minute Miss Sarah Galton came into the room.

She was not a pleasing interruption, undoubtedly. Even had she not been the interrupted lady's sister-in-law she could not have been deemed a pleasing interruption. As it was, Kate, watching her as she came forward in ungainly cloth buttoned boots, and barge-like goloshes, felt her to be unbearable.

The guise in which Miss Sarah Galton adventured forth in wintry weather, was comfortable, she asserted, but certainly it was not becoming. The sad-coloured bonnet which came "well-forward," as she phrased it, might be forgiven; indeed it had a distinctly marked purpose about it, and so far was estimable. It had been built to come well-forward, and it came well-forward, covering Miss Galton's ears from the cold blast, and saving those organs from many an ache. But the petticoat and dress that were short enough to be hideous from every point of view, and long enough to catch up and carry all extraneous matter in the shape of mud that might be in her path, were not things to be tolerantly looked upon.

"Such a walk as I have had," Miss Galton began breathlessly, sitting down opposite to Kate; "I thought I should never have got here: I tried the fields, and my goloshes were sucked off my feet several times."

"How very uncomfortable for you," Mrs. John Galton replied. She was marvelling much why Miss Galton had come at all, and why, of all ways, by the field-path.

"How very uncomfortable for you," Kate said, drowsily. Then she resigned herself, put her book down with ever so small a sigh, and added:

"You must stay to tea with me, Sarah. John is gone off for some duck-shooting, so I dined early with Katie, and ordered a heavy tea; you'll stay, won't you?"

Miss Galton looked sour. Heavy teas, any number of them and of any weight, could be hers in her own house. She had come up to her brother's to-day intending to have a good generous dinner at seven, and to see if the plate was in good order, and whether John's wife was a decent cook or not. She had another motive besides the anticipated dinner in coming, but the dinner had been a powerful one. So now, when Kate offered her the paltry substitute of a heavy tea, she looked grim, and replied:

"I suppose you're surprised to see me."

"Oh! no, I am not," Kate answered, though a little surprise might have been forgiven her, since Miss Galton had not been to the Grange for several months. "Oh! no I am not: I am very glad to see you now you are come; go up into my room, and take your things off; you'll find a fire there. Katie, go with your aunt."

Miss Galton looked more grim on the instant. "A fire in her bed-room, and coals such a price," she thought. Nevertheless she resolved to go up, and take off her boots by that fire in preference to going into a more inexpensively arranged chamber.

"Of course you wonder to see me," Miss Galton persisted. "I will tell you—dear, dear, how this wind affects my breath—what brought me; partly I was down in the village, and I thought I would just pass by the end of the station, and ask Mrs. Banham if she could let me have half-a-pint of cream on Friday night, for I have asked the Caldwells to tea, and while I can get it anyway I will not ask the clergyman I sit under to drink his tea without cream." Having said this with much severity, Miss Galton paused to gain breath, and mark whether or not Kate was withered.

But Kate was not withered by any means. Eventually she knew that the cream for Mrs. Caldwell's tea would go down to Miss Galton from her (Kate's) own dairy. She knew this, and was right willing that it should be so, and she knew that Miss Galton knew it also. So she declined to be withered, and only said:

"Oh! indeed; and then?"

"Then after I had heard from Mrs. Banham that Friday was just the very day of all that she would have the greatest difficulty, the *greatest difficulty*, in obliging me, I went on to the platform; I thought I would just go, just go on and see the three-o'clock train come in."

Miss Galton made another pause from lack of breath, and Kate suggested:

"Hadn't you better go up and take off your bonnet and wet boots?"

"In one minute, if you'll listen," Miss Galton replied severely. "Catherine, do keep that nasty dog away from me; of *all* the play things *in* the world to *give* a child, a filthy dog is the worst."

"He's a dear little, clean beauty, and he has only just left his mother," Katie the younger argued indignantly. She mentioned the latter fact as if it were something meritorious, something that redounded to puppy's credit vastly. Indeed, in a vague and undefined way she held that his having "only just left his mother" was puppy's chiefest trait. Others he might develope in time, but at present he had done nothing else worthy of record.

"Perhaps you had better take puppy into the nursery to tea, Katie," Mrs. Galton suggested.

"Oh, mamma! you promised I should stay here, and give him some cream out of my own saucer."

"Cream! for dogs!" Miss Galton ejaculated; "Do you know, little Miss, that your poor aunty only allows herself cream sometimes as a treat for her own tea."

"Oh! that's nonsense," Katie rejoined, emphatically. The plaint was intended to be very touching, but Katie looked at the respective parties, and was touched in the wrong direction. She was but a child! The puppy was so very pretty, and the poor old aunty was so very plain.

"Don't let me be the cause of my brother's child being banished, pray," Miss Sarah said, with some asperity.

"Very well; she shall stay here, since you

don't mind her," Mrs. Galton replied. "I wish you would go and take your things off, though, you would be so much more comfortable."

Mrs. Galton gave utterance to the wish as heartily as she could under the circumstances. She was not the sort of woman who takes a pride and pleasure in putting her own inclinations entirely out of court, but she did it on this occasion with a tolerable grace.

"Yes, I'll go," Miss Galton said, rising up, and marching in her muddy goloshes straight over a white Astracan rug; "but as I was saying, when I got on to the platform I stayed there, speaking now to one and now to another, as one *does*, you know, Kate."

"Yes," Kate assented, knowing well the while that she never did anything of the kind.

"And so I stayed there till the train passed —that is, it didn't pass as usual, it stopped, and one of the most extraordinary women I ever saw in my life got out."

"Ah! indeed?" Kate replied, seeing her sister-in-law waited for her to say something.

"Yes, one of the most extraordinary, I may say *the* most extraordinary; she had about a dozen yards of silk trailing behind her; and though she is quite old, old enough, at all events, to have known better, she had a little round cap of fur on her head that would suit that child."

"Who can she be?" Kate said, carelessly.

"That's what I wondered," Miss Galton snapped out; "when she had got herself and her maid, and all her boxes (she'd about a dozen of them), she began crying out in a cracked voice, 'could any one tell her the way to the Grange.'" The Grange, indeed! I told the station-man that we wanted no maniacs at the Grange, and that they had better keep her there till she was sent for; and then I thought I would walk across the field and tell you about it."

"Good gracious!" Kate exclaimed, rising up with a sickening feeling of some evil being about to crowd down upon her, "it must be my aunt, Lady Glaskill; I will send and see."

CHAPTER XL.

A TERRIBLE OLD LADY.

THE Caldwells, the people with whom the John Galtons were going to dine on the following day, had not been in the parish long; but, for all that short term of residence, locally they were large people.

Locally they were large, and religiously they were rigid. Mr. Caldwell had been in possession of a fair, not to say a fat, living for years before he had exchanged it for this Haversham rectorship; and, additionally, he had taken the precaution to ally himself unto a wealthy wife. Therefore had all things gone smoothly with him in the flesh, and in the spirit he was as unconditionally haughty and bigoted as any member of the priesthood he adorned.

From the day of his leaving college, nearly forty years before, up to this one of his introduction into my story, the Rev. Robert Caldwell's had been uninterruptedly a country life, and he had grown big and plethoric with the importance of it. His was no very uncommon character. He was arrogant, but he was also alive to the claims those who were in a worse plight than himself had on his humanity. He was intensely imbued with the letter of his profession; but, on the other hand, he had no small share of the best of its spirit. He was a staunch churchman, intolerant to aught that savoured of indifference to one of the smallest of his church's ordinances. He was not a bad country gentleman, having a fine taste in port wine and horseflesh. He was willing, nay anxious, that all good should be done to all men, but he desired that it should be done through that church of which he was a member alone. Not that he ever said this in so many bold, hard words, but he set his face steadfastly against any reform which it was proposed to make without the church's aid, guidance, or management.

Withal, he was a man much revered, for his life was a blameless one. He had married a wife, and brought up children, and sent these latter out into the world in unimpeachable case. His daughters had married, and married well—their husbands, though laymen, had plump livings in their gift; and his sons were well reputed in their respective dioceses, and were serving God with fair prospect of promotion. Altogether, the Caldwells were of good repute in the land, and their claims to consideration were not to be lightly regarded, even by their chief parishoners, the greatest landowner in the parish and his wife.

When Mrs. John Galton said in response to Miss Sarah's description of the person who was at the station making inquiries for the Grange, "It must be Aunt Glaskill," a qualm seized her heart, and dragged it down to low depths. To her husband and to Miss Sarah (who adored them), and to herself, Kate was wont to laugh at and deride the Caldwells—to call him a narrow-minded churchman who knew nothing of the world, whose whole soul was in matters parochial; and to regard Mrs. Caldwell as a woman without an individuality, merely as "the wife" of a recognized institution, who was a dull but necessary evil.

But despite this scoffing habit of hers, their respectability had impressed itself upon her, and she acknowledged to herself that it would be too terrible to shock them by introducing such an auxiliary as Lady Glaskill, and that Lady Glaskill would probably definitely refuse to be left behind. Here, down in the country, things stood out before Mrs. Galton with clearer outlines, and in truer colours. Lady Glaskill's much-bespattered old banner would not float out bravely in this atmosphere.

The certain conviction that it was Lady Glaskill—the dread truth, that she (Kate) was about to be infested with that most volatile and incessant of old women, smote her in such a way on the first mention of the stranger at the station, that she never questioned the probability of it for an instant. "It's Aunt Glaskill, and what shall I do with her at the Caldwells' to-morrow—ruddled!" she said to herself. And then she added aloud, "I think I had better have the waggonnette, and go down to the station and see."

"It's a sight that I should keep away from as long as possible if *I* were in *your* place," Miss Sarah replied grimly.

"But you're not in my mamma's place—you're not a married woman," Katie replied, with a child's odiously prompt partisanship.

"Don't be pert, miss," Miss Sarah retorted, with red spots on either cheek, and a gleam of angry light in her eyes, as if Katie's assertion that she was "not a married woman," had been a charge of an iniquitous, or at least compromising, nature. "Don't be pert, miss; I should send my little girls to bed for such speeches as that."

Now Katie was at the age when bed and all mention of it is loathed and abhorred by daylight.

"But you haven't any little girls, and you've no gentleman either, Aunt Sarah," Miss Katie retorted triumphantly; and Miss Galton felt herself worsted in the war of words.

Kate, in utter disregard of the altercation, commenced—"Will you excuse me? will you mind waiting here alone while I go——"

"On a wild-goose chase," Miss Galton struck in sharply. "I must say it will be the most ridiculous thing on your part, Kate, to go up and look after some mad woman, merely because you have an eccentric relative of your own. Of course none of your friends would have the bad taste to come to your husband's—to my brother's place in such a way."

"One never knows what one's friends will have the bad taste to do," Kate replied; "it's from no——"

She stopped; she was about to say that it was from no excess of anxiety to welcome Lady Glaskill that this journey in search of her to the station should be made. But she stopped, remembering that saying as to stale fish and the inability of crying it.

"Then, if you are going, I will say good-by to you," Miss Sarah said sharply, as Kate rang the bell and ordered the waggonnette, "I didn't come up here to sit alone."

"I will be back very soon, or—come with me?" Kate pleaded. Odd as it appeared, even to herself, she felt a desire to cling to something undeniable, something tangible, and true, and respectable—something that, however disagreeable it might be, could not compromise her husband now. The dread of her aunt, and of those ways of the world of which her aunt was a representative, was upon her strongly. No one could have sheltered under the wall of Lady Glaskill's reputation; it was a tottering structure, full of holes; and who knew this better than her niece?

So now that niece asked pleadingly that her disliked sister-in-law would stand by her in the meeting with the inevitable guest.

Miss Galton relaxed at the appeal, and was moderately merciful.

"I don't mind going; but as for its being Lady Glaskill, that's absurd," she said; "I have always understood that your aunt was a woman of fashion and position?"

"So she is," Kate said desperately. Lady Glaskill had been one of her highest trump cards, and she had been played with fell effect for the neighbourhood very often. The assertions of years may not be lightly contradicted in a moment; so now Kate said with desperation, "So she is."

"Then don't go, for this old harridan is

neither," Miss Galton said ruthlessly. Then for the first time Kate quailed before John's sister; Lady Glaskill was an old harridan; no one deemed her such more entirely than did her affectionate niece.

"At any rate the drive will do us no harm; I'll have my hat and cloak on in an instant;" so saying, Mrs. Galton ran from the room to prepare for the drive.

The waggonnette was at the door when Mrs. Galton came down, and Miss Sarah was standing at the hall steps ready to get in. This waggonnette was another of Kate's iniquities in Miss Galton's eyes, for in it Mrs. John drove a pair of wicked-looking chestnuts, and she drove them herself.

"Will you be warm enough?" Miss Galton asked as Kate came up in a black velvet bonnet and coat. Then Kate lifted up a corner of the latter, showing that it was lined with fur, and said, "Oh yes," cheerily enough, as Miss Galton mentally appraised the cost of it.

The drive to the station was a very short one, but during it Miss Galton found occasion to shriek thrice, and to give numberless other indescribable indications of woe. The chestnuts had good mouths, and Kate had good hands; naturally the corners were turned without any waste of space. "I'm no coward, and I'm convinced that I shall not die before my time," Miss Galton observed to Mr. Caldwell, in relation to this drive, when he drank tea with her on Friday, "but I do say that it's tempting Providence for a woman to take the reins in her hands, and to drive like Jehu the son of Nimshi, in the way Mrs. John Galton does."

To which Mr. Caldwell replied in general terms, that he was averse to reckless driving where he himself was concerned, but that, as regarded other people, he couldn't undertake to say: it was between themselves and their consciences.

Kate's conscience on this occasion did cause her driving to resemble that of the scriptural person afterwards alluded to by her sister-in-law. It reminded her that Lady Glaskill was her relative, and it told her distinctly that Lady Glaskill was a very unfit inmate for Haversham Grange. She remembered Lady Glaskill's sharp practices, and Lady Glaskill's double dealings, and Lady Glaskill's direful inability to discern right from wrong. She remembered Lady Glaskill's wicked old leers, and her horrible old stories, and her fearsome old jests. She remembered Lady Glaskill as a ghastly old occupant of a tawdry hardly won and held booth in Vanity Fair; and she trembled at the thought of meeting her at the station when she should arrive there.

It was evident at the first glance, on reaching this station, that something unusual had happened there. Kate drew up at the little door through which you came off the road on to the platform, and one of the porters came up to her with a respectful finger to his cap, and what she instantly construed into a disrespectful grin on his face.

"Is there any one here for the Grange, Hodgson?" she asked.

"There's a lady here as says she's for the Grange," the man replied; "but, bless you,—beg pardon, mum,—she's got twelve boxes, and a little dawg with a pink wrap on, and two cages with white cats in 'em, and a maid with paint enough on her cheeks to do the station-wall up smart for a year."

Miss Galton, sitting behind in the legitimate-for-feminine-occupation part of the vehicle, laughed hysterically. Hodgson had been a gardener at the Grange in John Galton's bachelor days; but his horticultural labours there had come to an untimely end in consequence of Mrs. John having discovered, shortly after the commencement of her reign, that the reason the best roses and finest branches of grapes did not grace her table was, that Hodgson drove a thriving trade in them on his own account. This discovery led to Hodgson's dismissal—his abrupt, not to say ignominious, dismissal; and Hodgson, being but human, never forgave the one by whom that ignominy was brought about. It was pleasant to him now to be insolent under the veil of ignorance.

"I will go and see," Kate said, getting out of the waggonnette; "at any rate, I shall like to see the cats; you won't get out, Sarah?"

"No." Sarah said she would not get out, and then Kate walked through the little door on to the platform alone.

Mrs. Galton did not say "Be still, my heart," as she walked along with that organ thumping vehemently; nor did she cry "Oh! my prophetic soul, my aunt!" as all her fears were verified, and the vision of Lady Glaskill in the flesh dawned upon her.

In the flesh; no, scarcely that; her withered old bones were decked in nothing so congruous as flesh. She really was terrible to behold; in her trailing silken garment, in her girlishly-cut paletot, in her small turban hat bound with fur. She was terrible to behold; and Kate, her niece and former disciple, felt her to be terrible.

Lady Glaskill was standing amidst her boxes haranguing an audience composed of all the porters and idle boys about the place, when Kate entered. The dear old lady had one hand on a cage, in which a bundle of something white was crouching, and she was redeeming the time and distinguishing herself by making these ignorant natives acquainted with the manners and habits of Persian cats.

"My dear child, my precious Kate!" Lady Glaskill cried effusively, ambling up to her niece as actively as her weak tottering legs would carry her. Then, before Kate could ward off the demonstration, the lean arms wound themselves round Mrs. John Galton's neck, and Mrs. John Galton was identified at once and for ever in the local mind with this terrible old woman.

"I could not credit that it was you, aunt; pray come away now," Kate said quietly, as soon as she could disentangle herself from her relative's caresses; then she added, "why didn't you send up to me at once, instead of staying down amongst the people?"

Lady Glaskill turned and waggled her head at her late audience, and kissed her wizened hand to them.

"The dear creatures," she said, "I told them about my cats, and made myself at home with them at once."

"Well, I wish you hadn't," Kate said a little coldly, as her aunt executed a little skip before passing through the door.

"Such freshness, such enthusiasm!" Lady Glaskill cried, when she had been twisted up into the waggonnette opposite to Miss Sarah. "Where are my boxes and my maid?" she continued, suddenly, in quite a different tone of voice.

"They shall be sent for; are you ready?"

Lady Glaskill was a very old woman. Indeed, no man now living could remember the day when she was young. She was a very old woman, and she was liable to exhaustion, especially after such feats of oratory and skipping as she had just performed on the platform. She was worn out and weak and old; and, now that the small excitement of making the vulgar herd believe her to be a gay, volatile, reckless, inspired young creature was over, she relapsed straightway into old-womanhood, and whimpered for her maid.

"She must come with me, Kate,"—she whined—"Hall must come with me, or I'm lost."

Which was true in one sense. No one but Hall knew exactly where to look for what there was left of Lady Glaskill amidst the millinery and paint. Hall put up the superstructure on the rotten old foundation, therefore Hall was essential for the nightly razing of the ruin that took place.

"Let her come, Kate," Miss Galton said, sharply. It was the first time Miss Galton had opened her lips since Lady Glaskill had been hoisted up into the waggonnette, and now she opened them with a snap that made her ladyship start and shiver. "Let her come, Kate; and then she can keep her ladyship from tumbling out of her seat when you turn the corners."

By the time Hall came to them, Lady Glaskill had recovered herself in a measure. She had got her gold-rimmed eye-glass up, and through it she was rapturously surveying a puddle, and a couple of pigs wallowing in the same. Presently she addressed Miss Galton.

"This is all very pretty and fresh; those creatures in the foreground,"—she smiled by way of finishing her speech, and made little movements towards the pigs with her hand.

"What?" Miss Galton asked sharply.

"Those creatures in the foreground," Lady Glaskill squeaked; but before she could get out the rest of her sentence and say how much she wished she had pencil and paper, in order just to dash down a few of these sights as they struck her first,—before she could say this, or Miss Galton could interrupt her by declaring them to be "not creatures, but pigs,"—Kate was up on the box of the waggonnette bidding them sit steady, as she was about to start.

When they reached the Grange, Lady Glaskill requested that she might be left alone in her own room with Hall for an hour; "then you can come to me, my dear, and I'll tell you the cause of this freak of mine," she said condescendingly. To which arrangement Kate—who was sick to the heart of her aunt's customs, if not indeed of her aunt—assented.

Before the expiration of the hour, Lady Glaskill's boxes and cats and dog—this latter an Italian greyhound, whose constitution had been seriously undermined in his youth—had all arrived. The boxes were many, as has been seen, and they were also heavy. Their number and weight were ominous to the last degree, as was Miss Galton's dark glance at them, when she at length went up stairs to remove the unbecoming bonnet.

"Between these two, what a night I shall have!" Kate thought to herself, as she stood with her hands clasped before the fire; "and I had intended being so cozy and happy; oh dear! Aunt Glaskill sits upon my chest like a gnawing anxiety; what can have brought her?"

Soon after this the hour expired, and as Mrs. Galton went along to the interview she prayed heartily that a freak might carry those boxes and their owner away from her habitation without delay.

Lady Glaskill was seated on a low chair before a Psyche when her niece came into her room; a fire was burning brightly in the grate, and there was an odour as of strong coffee and hot toast in the apartment. These creature comforts had done much to restore Lady Glaskill. She was no longer the rickety old woman ready to whimper and to whine of the waggonnette. She was a gorgeous being, strong in the strength that emanates from Bond Street—hedight in those special gems which render one beautiful for ever.

Lady Glaskill was seated before the glass, and this is what she saw. A slim form with skirts of apple-green moire antique, with fair shoulders rising very much out of the bodice, with golden hair rippling down in masses over a white brow and blooming cheeks; a figure with airs of grace and beauty, and, above all, youth that was passing pleasant to look upon. This was what Lady Glaskill saw.

But Kate saw something widely different. A decrepid old woman dressed like a girl, with hard, bony, unwomanly shoulders, displayed in a hard, bold, unwomanly manner; with the ghastly pallor of her withered cheeks brought into hideous relief by the rose-tints from the rougé-pot, and the golden sheen of the false glittering hair. This was what Kate saw, and her vision was the clearer of the two.

"I'm quite myself again now," Lady Glaskill said as Kate came on into the room.

"It's a pity you took all this trouble to dress to-night, aunt; I am alone, and I dined early," Mrs. Galton said, sitting down on a chair by the side of the dressing-table. Then she marked for the first time that Lady Glaskill seemed much aged, much shaken, since their last meeting in town, and her heart softened a little towards her unwelcome guest.

"You may go now, Hall," Lady Glaskill said when Hall had clasped a broad bracelet round one bony brown wrist; and as Hall went out of the room, Lady Glaskill, by a skilful backward movement, propelled herself out of the blaze of the lights on the table and said,

"My dear Kate, I have been infamously treated,—infamously; it has nearly killed me."

"What has happened, aunt?" Do what she would, Mrs. Galton could not succeed in infusing the least warmth into her inquiry, or even the least interest.

"Why, some men—some impertinent tradesmen," Lady Glaskill commenced, shaking her head vehemently, "sent me in bills that I must have paid over and over again, and as my funds were low, having had heavy pulls upon them, I naturally refused to pay them; when what do the insolent creatures do," Lady Glaskill continued, "but threaten to seize my things. How-

ever, Hall was invaluable: we managed to pack them all up, and get them away to her sister's (a most excellent person, the widow of a dissenting minister) in the night. In the morning I sent round the key of the house to the landlord with my compliments, got my few worldly goods together, and came off to one who, well I know —" Lady Glaskill choked herself at this juncture, and embraced her niece.

"But this is terrible," Mrs. Galton said, as soon as surprise and Lady Glaskill's lean arms would allow her to speak. And, indeed, it was terrible,—very terrible,—this possibility that Lady Glaskill, who had come to the Grange in her distress, might elect to remain there in her distress.

"But this is terrible!"

"It might have been worse," Lady Glaskill cried philosophically. She was a merry-hearted old sinner. She was quite ready to rest and be thankful in this haven into which fortune's gales had blown her. "It might have been that I should have been left without a thing," Lady Glaskill proceeded animatedly; "as it is, I have left nothing behind me but the key of the house, which, not being there any longer, I don't want. It's all for the best, I believe; I remembered how solitary you were, and I came down to you."

"Thank you, aunt," Mrs. Galton replied dryly.

"Don't mention it, my dear. Who's that woman in a poke bonnet and short petticoats?"

"My husband's sister."

"Ah! odd a woman at her time of life shouldn't know how to dress herself. Well, my dear, I like this room very much; with this, and the dressing-room and the room beyond, Hall and I shall do very well, and not incommode you, I trust. How pleased your rough diamond of a husband will be to see me, won't he?"

"I don't know," Kate replied vaguely. She was thinking "Should she ever be such an old woman as this one before her," and was shuddering to the bottom of her soul at the possibility. Then, as Lady Glaskill rose to her feet and pushed the golden locks back from her powdered brow with her trembling fingers, Kate vowed that never another grain of golddust should defile her hair. As she looked, Lady Glaskill's head began to shake at its image in the glass, for in fact her ladyship was slightly palsied now; but the gallant old worldling laughed merrily and explained,

"That she always had been so full of life and motion."

It was not a pleasant evening that which Mrs. Galton passed by her own fireside. It was her earnest desire, above all things, now to keep the peace; and between the two women, her guests, she had rather a hard time of it. It was her earnest desire to keep the peace now; war, declared and decided, might be inevitable; but until it did break out, there should be no unseemly brawling within her husband's walls. That at least she owed him, and that tribute she would pay. As she glanced from one to the other that night, Miss Sarah's austerity and unpleasantness were less patent to her than usual; but she felt a sick sinking within her whenever her glance fell upon her aunt: for that aged whited sepulchre was a very good representative of the gang to which she (Kate) had ardently desired to belong.

It cooled all such ardour now to look upon Lady Glaskill. She was a terrible specimen of that to which a worldly, weak, vain, incorrigibly vain woman may come. She was an animate bundle of falsity. There was nothing reverend about her old age; she was a pretentious old stucco sham. Kate recoiled from her,—from her, and from that of which she was a type,—as she sat and believed in herself over the fire.

Shall I tell of that which was uncemented and put to bed at night? Of the miserable old palsied frame, surmounted by the shaking head which was crowned by just a few stiff bristling hairs? Shall I tell of the rounded proportions, and of that which "formed the waist" coming away? Of the shedding of the golden tresses, and of the pearly teeth? Shall I tell of the snarls at the maid, of the snarls tempered by servility, for Hall was her "best friend," she told herself? In asking I have told, however; so I will leave Lady Glaskill to her text, and end my chapter.

<hr>

CHAPTER XLI.

THE CALDWELLS' DINNER-PARTY.

LADY GLASKILL did not get up to breakfast on the following morning. It took some time to put her together, she being a composite structure, and Hall was averse to early rising. Consequently the little bit that was real of Lady Glaskill remained in bed till a late hour; and Kate was left to think calmly over what she could do with it.

It was with a wonderful sense of relief that Mrs. Galton got out of the house, and went along the road to meet her husband. Lady Glaskill's leers, and Lady Glaskill's loose stories (these latter were always given in French, being absolutely untranslatable), and Lady Glaskill's allusions,—all these had been very terrible to Mrs. Galton the night before. In her own thoughtless girlhood she had heard them often, and thought nothing of them, or rather had only accredited her aunt with a certain vivacious daring of a pardonable nature for telling them at all. Nor had they occurred to her as offensive when she last met Lady Glaskill in town; for Lady Glaskill was only one of many there, and passed comparatively unnoticed in the crowd. But here there was no crowd. Lady Glaskill would be a prominent feature in the social landscape.

Mrs. John Galton's cheeks burnt as she walked along. She could not forget that at one time she had thought and uttered fine things of her aunt; she could not forget that she had hoped and even essayed to emulate her. Her ladyship's saloons had been regarded by Kate as desirable dazzling halls of delight in which to display herself; and now the truth struck her that the glitter and the brilliancy had been of a Brummagem order. Lady Glaskill had always avowed that she cared for nothing more so long as the "best men congregated at her house." Undoubtedly, however it might have been about the men, the best women never passed her portals. Those who had done so had come

and gone like fleeting shadows, leaving no mark upon others who met them casually. But Kate's memory reproduced them as they had been, and she felt that they had not been fitting in all respects. And she shook her head sadly over the impossibility of mentioning any one of them with pride and satisfaction.

She met her husband about the place and time he had mentioned; and such a feeling of security, such a sense of safety, came over her as she caught sight of his florid, open, honest face, she almost sprang into the trap as he pulled up to greet her, and her hand went out eagerly and clasped the one of his that was engaged with the reins.

"Take care you don't give him a chuck, dear," he said, as the horse threw up his head.

"No, I won't," she replied, removing her hand; "but I'm so glad to see you, I hardly know how to express it; I have such a piece of news for you."

Her tone was the tone of weariness and annoyance. Lady Glaskill, and her conversation and her boxes, weighed heavily on Kate's mind.

"There's nothing the matter with the child?" he asked eagerly, with a paling face and a gulp of agitation.

"No, she's quite well, it's——"

"Is it that bay colt, then?"

"No, John, no; everything is right at home, dear; but Lady Glaskill has come down. What are we to do?"

"Come down, has she?"

"Yes; what are we to do?"

"Make her as comfortable as we can. What has brought her?"

Then Kate poured out the whole story, and trimmed it with the tale of her own discomfiture.

"I see her exactly as what she is, and I am heartily ashamed of her," Mrs. Galton wound up with. "She must have altered immensely; she surely used not to be such a burlesque of old age as she is now."

Then Mrs. Galton remembered some of the speeches she had been wont to make, during the years of her married life, relative to the social power and social charm, and social success of her aunt, Lady Glaskill. She remembered how only last year she had declared that Lady Glaskill's countenance in years to come would be a fine thing for little Katie. She remembered all these things now, and wondered whether her husband remembered them too, and would tell her of them.

But John Galton was made of very different stuff. It never came into his big, generous mind to recall a foolish speech for the sake of confusing and discomfiting the utterer of it: more especially when, as in this case, the utterer of the folly was very dear to him. He did remember those speeches, but he only felt that it was a very happy thing that his wife had got over the habit of thought which dictated them. He never for an instant thought of raking them up and reminding her of them to her present abasement. Which course of conduct on his part made her feel the full force of her folly far more than any taunts or sneering allusions could have done. It did something else also: it made her heart throb in proud acknowledgment of the nobleness, the manliness, the great loving trustfulness of her husband.

John Galton made no immediate answer to that remark of his wife's, that her aunt could not formerly have been such a "burlesque of old age as she was now." At last he said, looking at her very kindly:

"You must remember her age, even if she forgets it, Kate dear; don't let her see that she's not welcome to you."

"I could bear it for myself, but she'll be such a bore to you, John; it's evidently her present intention to remain with us till she is tired of it; and she does not tire in a hurry of good quarters."

"You have stood being bored very often for me and through me," he replied heartily, pulling up at the door. "Come, let us make the best of it," he continued, lifting her out of the trap, and following her into the house; "let us make the best of it, and a fresh compact: whenever I feel bored I'll come to you for rest; and you'll do the same by me, won't you, Kate?"

"Ah! that I will," she said, in a low voice; and he felt in that moment that the heart of his wife was entirely his own.

"All right," he cried aloud; "we'll bear Lady Glaskill together very well, I have no doubt. I have brought you home half a dozen snipes and a brace of mallard, Kate."

"We will send the snipes up to the Caldwells at once," she said, laughing; "they'll accept them, perhaps, as a set-off against Lady Glaskill."

Then Katie came to them with a pitiful tale of one of the Persian cats out on parole having scratched the terrier puppy "on his little soft nose;" and so the time passed till luncheon was ready.

Lady Glaskill was rebuilt and ready for luncheon when Kate at last went into her room to see after her. She was at her usual shrine, surveying herself with a ghastly satisfaction, when Kate entered the room, but the hour being early there were no bare shoulders.

"My husband is come home; will you come down to luncheon, aunt?" Kate commenced.

Lady Glaskill rose up and patted Kate on the cheek with a weird finger.

"You have been using bad powder, child; you have made your skin quite coarse," she said, as Kate drew her face quickly away from the caress; "I have some that's excellent, 'imperceptible efflorescence;' I will give you a little."

"I shall never use another grain, thank you," Kate replied tartly. Innocent powder began to assume a hideous aspect in her eyes, now that she saw it lying in furrows on Lady Glaskill's cheeks.

"Highty tighty!" Lady Glaskill cried, causing her garments to sweep and surge about her in a way that partially concealed her hobbling gait. "Highty tighty! how virtuous we're become, to be sure."

John Galton was waiting for them at the bottom of the stairs.

"How d'ye do? Take my arm, Lady Glaskill, you'll get along quicker," he said kindly to his guest, giving his wife's hand a squeeze as she passed him. On which invitation Lady Glaskill put her hand on his arm with a little pat, and tried to trip by his side, and nearly tumbled in the attempt.

"And what are we going to do to-night?" Lady Glaskill asked, when she had made a very good luncheon, and had had all her pets brought in in procession and fed before her. "What are we going to do to-night? Is that very strange person who was here in a poke bonnet yesterday coming again?"

"We are going out to dinner to-day," Kate replied hurriedly. "I am sorry it should have happened so, but you must excuse us; dinnerparties in the country are made up a long time beforehand, you know."

"Oh! my dear, don't apologise," Lady Glaskill replied affably. "I shall be enchanted to join your rustic revels."

"It's not a rustic revel," Kate replied, in a vexed tone, while John Galton suffered from suppressed laughter just out of range of Lady Glaskill's vision: "it's rather a heavy affair,—a state dinner at a clergyman's house. You wouldn't care to go to it."

Lady Glaskill nodded her head with a halfhilarious, half-involuntary motion:

"My dear, the manners of such people will amuse me much."

A cold horror crept over Kate. She pictured her aunt feeling and betraying her "amusement" at the "manners" of the best that the neighbourhood held. They were sure to be such orthodox, well-bred, coldly correct, unassailable-inevery-way people, who would assemble at the Caldwells'. The Caldwells themselves were all these things. They were all "country people," or, at least, they were all connected with country-people; and when they went to London, right people—people who had local habitations and names. Whereas the majority of the frequenters of Lady Glaskill's saloons had had neither worth mentioning congregated about them. The Caldwell dinner might be dull; it was almost sure to be so, in fact; but it would be a thing to be mentioned with safety; and Kate was beginning to yearn toward all things in the naming of which there was no danger.

"You surely will like to stay at home and rest to-night, aunt," Kate pleaded.

"My dear! at my age! Time enough to talk of resting after a railway journey when I'm many years older."

"Then don't you think it would be pleasanter to be introduced to all these people at our house first? We'll have a dinner directly; won't we, John?"

But Lady Glaskill would not hear of this plan. She would go with them "to their nice quiet party," she said, wafting out of the room airily on Hall's arm; and so Kate was fain to give up the contest.

"I'd do anything almost to prevent her going up with us to-night, John," Mrs. Galton said in a vexed tone as soon as they were alone.

"Never mind, she's a woman of the world, and is used to swells," he replied.

"But not to respectable swells, that's a fact."

"She has always been in good society."

"All surface society, and she has tossed about on the top of it; the people she knew in London came in and went out, and made no more account of her than they did of her door-mat. I see it all now. And when the London season is over, she hunts about from one spa or one watering place to another, and just circulates amongst the riff-raff. However, there is nothing for it."

Kate was right in this, at least. There was nothing for it; for Lady Glaskill had a desire to extend her experience, and glean some notion of what good, solid, best-class country society was. Her view was right: she never had been in it. It would be as much a strange land to her as the dubious soil she had stood upon all her life would have been to the Caldwells and others of that ilk.

Hall had a busy afternoon; but by seven o'clock, the hour at which they were to start from the Grange, Lady Glaskill was completed. The pink silk skirt puffed with tulle looked very young, certainly; but that—in consequence of the large opera cloak Lady Glaskill had over her shoulders, and the wide hood enveloping her head—was the worst Kate saw till they reached the Caldwells'.

But when they reached the rectory, and Mrs. Caldwell's maid came forward to rid them of their wraps, Lady Glaskill stood confessed before her niece a terror and a shame.

Such old women are seen sometimes in some London drawing-rooms—old women with lemon-coloured bare necks, and roses on their wizened brows; but they pass away from the mind as does some hideously vivid dream: it shocks us, but it is gone. They sit mumbling to themselves or to their duplicates in corners, or they shake their fans bewitchingly at men young enough to be their grandsons; and they go away and are not missed. But in the country such a spectacle is rare, and is much talked about and commented on in the absence of better conversational matter.

Lady Glaskill's dress left off too far from her shoulders, and her blooming face and golden hair commanded immediate attention to her, and all that concerned her, the instant she entered. There were several stately ladies present—ladies in black velvet, in ruby velvet, and decorous lace that mounted to their chins; lace of price, lace from lace looms, lace to which the heart of Mrs. Bury Pallisser—matchless historian of the fabric!—would have seriously inclined. And over and upon their velvets and laces, diamonds flashed—diamonds that might not have been worth a prince's ransom (unless he were a very small prince), but that were of worth nevertheless. Yet the instant the shaking figure that Hall had erected in the course of the afternoon came into the room, the velvets and laces and diamonds of price were absolutely overlooked, and the common gaze was concentrated on Lady Glaskill.

Things were always done well at the Caldwells'. There was no need on the occasion of extra festivity in their house to seek extraneous assistance. There was no halting on the part of the dinner between the kitchen and the dining-room. All things were done decently and in order there, and punctuality was as well regarded as any of the other virtues. The Caldwell arrangements were always well conceived and well carried out; and if the admirable rotation in which one wine succeeded another at his table, was owing to the Rev. Robert supervising the bottles pretty sharply, and spending

a happy hour in his cellar before the guests came, who was the wiser for it? Or, if any one was the wiser, did that detract from the merit of the wines? Things were always well done at the Caldwells'. Whatever the effort there was never the least appearance of it, or the smallest possible flaw in the apparently perfect arrangements.

But to-day these arrangements received a shock. Lady Glaskill's appearance was as the bursting of a bombshell among them. When Kate found that her aunt's resolve was unalterable, she had sent up to the rectory to announce the unexpected advent, and request permission to bring it? Of course this permission was granted. But equally of course did the granters quake to their foundation when the result of that permission ambled into the room.

Her appearance was as the bursting of a bombshell among them; but, for all that, she was the widow of a baronet, and entitled to receive consideration as such. There were present two Honourable Mrs. Somethings, but they were young though honourable matrons; and Lady Glaskill was the widow of a baronet and very aged, despite that rich bloom and those golden tresses. Mr. Caldwell was placed on the horns of a dilemma; but he was a gentleman; so, though his soul revolted when those horns pulled him into action, he offered his arm to the rickety skeleton in pink silk.

Lady Glaskill got on very well, that is to say, very quietly, during dinner; so quietly that Kate was beginning to hope that, for this evening at least, her aunt was going to evade all opportunities of distinguishing herself. Bounded, as Lady Glaskil was, on the one side by her host, and on the other by a young man who officiated as Mr. Caldwell's curate, she was kept in place —kept down in a measure. Mr. Caldwell took care to honour himself by honouring all who sat at his table. But he honoured them after their kind. So now, when he had seen that Lady Glaskill's material wants were well supplied, he left the charge of her mental refection to his curate.

On the whole, this curate catered for her very well and very willingly. He talked London to the old worldling, and the old worldling, debating on the instant that he knew little or nothing practically of that of which he talked, delighted in him forthwith to an amazing extent. He, too, in common with the rest of mankind, had his hopes and ambitions. There hovered before his mental vision a velvet-cushioned shrine, yclept "pulpit" in the vulgar tongue, of which he should be the presiding deity. And before this shrine ladies, chiefly of the old and wealthy class, should congregate largely; and he should show them safe and pleasant paths to Paradise, and they should hang upon his words, and make him handsome presents, not of the worsted-work slippers and cheap flower-basket order, but presents of a rich, endearing, substantial, expensive nature, worthy of the acceptance of a son of the Church. This was his vision of the future, when he should have shaken off the trammels that were upon him here as Mr. Caldwell's curate. This was his vision of the future, and Lady Glaskill was like a little bit of it let into the present for his encouragement—for she was evidently wicked

enough and worldly enough to fire any man of
his stamp with the desire to save her soul—and
he took the wealth for granted, unwisely.

He was a young man, and an earnest one.
Ready for any amount of work, no matter how
uncongenial, provided it would put him up
another round or so on the ladder he was
mounting. Young, and earnest, and fair, with
a pale early crop of whiskers,—six hairs to
either cheek—and a pensive nose. But he
went to his work—the labour his rector had
apportioned to him on this occasion—like a
man. Lady Glaskill was not at all the type of
venerable dame he had honoured and revered
in theory, but he deemed her a very fair specimen of that which he might be called upon (did
things go well with him) to regenerate in the
future. Therefore he took to his task like a
man, and cracked *bon-bons* and ecclesiastical
jokes with her in the most gallant manner, and
tried not to blush when she told him a purely
Parisian story in an accent that scarcely matched
it—a story with plenty of "point" to it, undoubtedly with a point so sharp indeed that one
possessed of the smallest amount of decent
feeling could not fail to be wounded by it. But
she told this story of hers in the lowest voice
she found herself capable of sustaining for any
length of time, therefore Kate was unconscious
of it, and happy in that unconsciousness.

But later, when the ladies were back in the
drawing-room alone, Kate was not so happy.
The strings of Lady Glaskill's tongue had been
untied by sundry goblets full of divers kinds of
sparkling wine, and Lady Glaskill's tongue was
an unruly member. She spoke freely of one or
two things about which it would have been but
prudent to have kept silence. She spoke freely,
very freely, and the heart of Kate, her niece,
went low as she listened and looked round on the
audience of stately ladies in gloom and rich lace.

Lady Glaskill had deposited her draperies and
what there was of herself on a couch by the fire,
and the heat was pleasant to her—and so was
the glimpse of herself which she caught in a mir-
ror. Vain as her ladyship was, she had not that
trick of sensitiveness which leads its possessor to
take offence or see neglect too quickly, so now
she did not perceive that the others held aloof
from her, and that even Mrs. Caldwell abstained
from her as much as it beseemed a hostess to abstain.

Kate, however, saw it all; and Kate winced
under it, and hardly knew whom to blame in her
annoyance. Lady Glaskill might be objection-
able, but all the same Lady Glaskill was her aunt;
therefore Mrs. Galton resolved that some of these
stately ladies should "pay," in vulgar parlance,
for this holding aloof in the future.

It was but passive misery that Mrs. Galton endured while the ladies were alone, but as soon as
the men struggled in, in that sheepfaced manner
in which men do struggle into a drawing-room
after having stayed as long as possible over their
wine, passive misery went by, and active anguish
took its place. Lady Glaskill saw an opportunity for making a sensation, and Lady Glaskill
seized it.

She frisked about from her recumbent position
on the couch, and sat up in one corner of it, patting the vacant space by her side with her hand,
and smiling an alluring smile to the one who

had catered for her mentally at dinner, in indication of her desire that he should occupy the said
vacant space. Now Mrs. Caldwell's drawing-
room was not strewn with couches. The one on
which Lady Glaskill had deposited herself was
the softest of the two that graced the apartment.
The other was beautiful to behold, but it had a
rigid back, and was not affected a second time by
any one. Therefore when Glaskill patted the
couch and looked alluringly at the curate, Mrs.
Caldwell opened her eyes at him, and coaxed her
brows to express a hope that he was not going to
be so very presumptuous.

But he was young and brave—or shall he be
termed rash, rather? He thought of the prospec-
tive metropolitan congregation, and took Lady
Glaskill as the type of it, in a way that rendered
him careless as to what the former queen of his
soul, Mrs. Caldwell (whose sway was sometimes
a little severe over those helpless ones, her husband's curates), thought of his occupying her
most comfortable couch. He suffered himself to
be lured on to the extreme edge of it by the aged
charmer whose state seemed to promise such an
extensive field for exploits in his warfare with
the world, the flesh, and the devil. And as soon
as Lady Glaskill saw that inclination had conquered duty in him, she became excited, and consequently, her niece perceived, dangerous.

"Don't let us be late to-night, John," Kate
whispered to her husband. "The flood-gates of
Aunt Glaskill's speech are loosed."

"I will go when you like,"—he replied, as the
evening was seeming all its length to him, though
he was too broadly good-natured to admit even to
himself that it was dull,—"I will go when you
like; but Lady Glaskill seems all right."

"I don't know about that; she was wanting
that man to get up a game of three-card loo
just now; that won't do here, I'm very sure."

At this juncture Lady Glaskill's voice rose
shrilly above others in the room, and fell distinctly on the ears of both husband and wife.

"We were all as pleasantly occupied as possible in saying and hearing all the naughty
things that were said of each other and the rest
of the world, when the husband, a man from the
country, came in; and anything more like a
fool than he looked when he sat down at his
own table and none of his wife's guests knew
him, I never saw." Her ladyship laughed
hysterically here, and her chief auditor—her
fellow-occupant of the couch—shuffled uneasily
on the latter, and against his conscience said—
"It must have been very funny."

"The woman—I forget her name, but she
was a dear friend of mine," Lady Glaskill proceeded, "had run tremendously in debt for new
furniture, or else some man had given it to her,
I forget which—but there, it's of no consequence," she added abruptly. Her memory was
very apt to play her tricks—to utterly forsake
her at some moments and flash back half-truth
upon her at others. A something came across
her now and told her that it would have been
wiser far on her part to have refrained from
telling the capital story of the husband who had
arrived suddenly and found his wife in the midst
of revelry of which he knew nothing, and surrounded by friends who knew nothing of him.

John Galton had thrown his head up and
listened, not eagerly, but with a certain scorn-

ful attention, when her ladyship's tones first fell upon his ear. He knew well what incident she was narrating to these people, down among whom he was a great man, and his wife was above suspicion. He knew what incident she was narrating; it had been painful enough to him, God knows, for the slightest allusion to it to recall it to his mind. But well as he remembered it, and the bitter smarting that, for all his generous trust in Kate, it had caused him, there was no anger in the look he turned upon his wife presently. She, poor sinner, was almost visibly trembling in an agony of dread as to what Lady Glaskill might say next. Do not make a mistake, and deem Kate Galton a more erring woman than she has been openly shown to be in these pages. She had no dread, no carking fear of anything fresh coming to her husband's knowledge. But she did, by reason of her recently awakened love for him, shrink in her soul at the idea of Lady Glaskill making it patent to these people with whom he stood so high, that John Galton had been the husband who was kept in the dark and slighted by his wife's friends. That was her sole dread; but it was bitter enough and heavy enough to have expiated worse sins than hers had been. Lady Glaskill's allusions aroused fears in Kate's breast that had long slumbered, or rather that had never been properly awakened in it before. That furniture! It was rare and costly, that she knew—rare and costly, and very beautiful. But it was unpaid for up to the present date,· which was a slight drawback to the pleasure of possessing property which had been warehoused ever since she left London.

Mrs. Galton sat and· trembled. Six months ago she would have cared nothing for all this. She would have told John Galton that the furniture had been ordered certainly, and never paid for; that it had unquestionably not been a necessity. Still, that it had seemed good to her to have it, and he was always so indulgent that she felt sure, &c., &c. In fact, she would have put forth all her powers and have humbugged him out of his forgiveness and his money. This she would have done unscrupulously six months ago, but things were altered now. She had lately come to have a far warmer regard for her husband, consequently she had also a far more just appreciation of his good opinion. It pained her, it was grievous to her now, to think that he might with justice look upon her as a woman who had been careless, reckless, and extravagant, for the sake of making a show and a sensation in society, from which she would willingly have excluded him; society which was not absolutely above suspicion. The thought that he might come to estimate her thus was grievous to her. She little knew that John Galton would have counted himself a happy man just then, could he have felt sure that one suggestion Lady Glaskill had thrown out was entirely without foundation; and that his wife had in truth only ran him in debt to an upholsterer. He had never refused to give her money during the whole of her wedded career; more than this, he had never inquired into her expenditure of it. He remembered and feared that it had been no dread of a remonstrance which had prevented her sending in the bills to him; and she remembered it also, and took shame to herself for that

brief fling of extravagance—that short term of utter carelessness—that thoughtless, unnecessary strain which would be felt eventually through her on that generous spirit. "They would do for the Grange, and make the old place sweet," she said to herself; "only it's full already, and new things are not wanted. Oh dear! I wish I had screwed and paid for them out of my housekeeping and pin-money." She little knew how happy John Galton would count himself, in that they were to be paid for still; but she did know herself to be the sort of woman who never can screw a surplus penny out of her pin-money. Therefore, when the Caldwell conviviality came to an end, and Mr. Shalders (the aspiring curate) had aided in hoisting Lady Glaskill into the carriage, Kate sat in absolute, miserable, anxious silence, till they reached the Grange.

CHAPTER XLII.

AN EARNEST SHEPHERD.

THAT night, long before Hall had cracked away the shell and put the withered old kernel to bed, John Galton and his wife had come to an understanding.

Kate did not lack courage. With all her frivolity, all her vanity, all her natural longings for excitement, all her weaknesses, she was no coward. True she would often evade a danger, wriggle out of the way of an unpleasantness; but it was from no fear of the danger or unpleasantness; it was solely to exercise her skill that she did it. Or rather that she had done it; for now she was more desirous of bearing all the ills that might be consequent on her own acts, of bearing them entirely by herself—she was, in fact, a better woman than when I first introduced her into these pages.

Her reformation had been wrought by no very extraordinary means, nor perhaps, broadly speaking, was it a very wonderful reformation. She had never been a wrong-doer of a very marked order. Nor will she probably ever be a well-doer of a very marked order. To the end of her life she will most likely be addicted to excitements that do not lie legitimately in those paths of life which she is destined to pursue. To the end of her life she will be afflicted with a desire for admiration which is not always hers to command. She will never be a perfect woman, nor a specimen matron, but she will lead a guileless life enough, for every particle of good within her her husband has vitalized so successfully that it will only die when she herself does.

She came up to the encounter bravely and honestly enough that night after returning from the Caldwells'. The encounter promised to be a severe one, she thought; for John had scarcely spoken at all since Lady Glaskill had thrown the glove down and forced Kate to defend it. The encounter promised to be a severe one; there would be a sharp tussle, she knew, with her own pride; and she feared even a sharper one with her husband's just wrath.

She was resolved upon one thing—to make no little tricks of motherhood or domesticity her allies in this battle which her own errors of the past forced her to fight. She would not take her husband to the bedside of their sleeping child, and there make her confession and win his forgiveness. The trick was one that she would have tried a short time since, but she swore before God this night, that henceforth there should be no shadow of turning, no tinge of acting in her dealings with this honest, loyal man who had married her. "It shall be all fair and above board," she said to herself, and she meant it.

She ran up stairs before him and went into his dressing-room, and stood there leaning against the chimney-board till he came into the room. He had been hoping so earnestly, praying so fervently, that she would speak to him, and tell him whatever there might be to be told without his asking her, that the tears came into his eyes when he saw her there, evidently prepared to speak.

"John," she began, directly he came up to her, "you knew—I saw that you knew it—that Lady Glaskill meant you and me?"

"Yes, I knew it," he said.

"I was going to tell you that I had forgotten to speak to you about that furniture, but I will tell no lies on the subject; I have not forgotten it. I've avoided it."

"Why have you avoided it?" He asked this with a falter in his voice; he saw that she was straining to speak the truth, let the truth be as hard as it might be to speak, and he sickened at the thought of that which he might have to bear.

"Why have you avoided it?"

"Ah! why, indeed; you may well ask me, generous, lavish as you are with your money to me. I may well be ashamed of having hesitated to tell you I wanted more; I gratified my whim without counting the cost; can you forgive me?"

She put her hand out to him as she spoke, and the dew came upon his brow. He could not ask her "Had these things been given her?" but he very much feared it.

"What's the cost?" he asked, in a thick voice.

"I don't know;" then a blush came upon her cheek as she repeated "I don't know—I don't know, really; I'm afraid that I've run dreadfully in debt, John; but the truth is I don't know how much, for I tore up the bills when they sent them in without looking at them; the sight of the sum that would have to be paid would have bored me, so I tore them up."

He saw that she was speaking the truth, and nothing but it; and it was such an immense relief to him.

"Thank God!" he began. "I mean—then why shouldn't I say what I *do* mean?" he continued, taking his wife round the waist and drawing her up close to him. "Never mind the debt, you foolish girl." ("If I win that, there would be more excuse for her," she thought.) "What a brute I must have shown myself, that you dared not tell me before!"

"Then you are not angry?" she asked, with a great sob of relief.

"No; and you in turn tell me that in future you'll take me into your confidence in preference to Lady Glaskill."

And so they settled it.

After this the weeks rolled on, winter and spring passed away, and summer was over the land, and still Lady Glaskill made no sign of moving. She had established herself in the best suite of rooms at the Grange, and she had caused it to be distinctly understood that the one-horse brougham, which hitherto had been only used for night-work, should be held sacred to her sole and whole use. There had been more than one passage of arms between Lady Glaskill and Miss Sarah. Miss Sarah had reproved her sister-in-law's aunt for being a whited sepulchre, "and other offensive things," Lady Glaskill said, in the course of her complaint to Kate; and Lady Glaskill had wept and gnashed her last new set of teeth at Miss Sarah, and been generally, unavailing in her wrath. But, despite the weeping and gnashing of teeth, she had held her ground at the Grange, and so even Miss Sarah was made to feel that her attacks had been futile.

But after her last round with Miss Sarah, Lady Glaskill refused to join the family circle promiscuously. "I will come down when I'm protected by society, but when you're alone I'm liable to that woman in a poke-bonnet, and she shatters me," Lady Glaskill said to her niece. So it came to pass that Lady Glaskill spent much of her time in her own sitting-room, in the ante-room to which her prodigious chests were piled one on top of the other; and here Mr. Shalders called upon her often, and brought her the best of tracts.

"If Aunt Glaskill were younger and richer, and Mr. Shalders older and poorer, I should really think he was making up to her, John," Kate would say sometimes; "as it is, I can only think that he is, as Mr. Caldwell says, 'wonderfully zealous.'"

"What is he supposed to be doing?" John Galton asked, laughing.

"Bringing Lady Glaskill to see the error of her ways," Kate replied.

"Well, rather he than me, that's all I have to say about it," John Galton replied, carelessly. It struck him as rather pitiable, but nothing more, that Mr. Shalders should have nothing better to do on so many days of the week than to sit in a stifling room and talk to a stupid old woman.

"I have been so extremely fortunate, as I have secured—and secured, I may say, for a comparatively small stipend—the services of one of the most earnest men in the church," Mr. Caldwell remarked one day, when Mr. Galton made some allusion to Mr. Shalders's devotion to the very unpromising in appearance cause of Lady Glaskill's salvation. "He is indefatigable—not only on behalf of your aunt, Mrs. Galton—" (and here Mr. Caldwell looked as though he believed it quite possible that Lady Glaskill should take all the time of the most earnest and best of men)—"he is indefatigable, not only on behalf of your aunt, Mrs. Galton, but on behalf of many another lost sinner amongst our pauper population."

"Very good of him," Kate replied; "but, if it's just the same to you, Mr. Caldwell, I would rather that, before me, at least, my poor old aunt should not be included in the category of lost sinners. She has her good points. I have known her to do many a generous deed; and though she hasn't exactly blushed to find it fame, she has not blazoned it herself."

"We will hope the best for her. Shalders is

most indefatigable in his endeavours to bring her to a right frame of mind—a frame of mind befitting her age," Mr. Caldwell replied, solemnly, and Kate restrained her inclination to say, "Oh, you righteous in your own conceit," and only uttered aloud her hopes that Mr. Shalders' disinterested efforts might meet with their due reward.

Doubtless Mr. Shalders was earnest, indefatigable, disinterested; on the face of it he was unceasing. Through the winter and spring months the Grange avenue gates opened to and closed behind him daily. Lady Glaskill called him a "good young man—a dear, good young man," and declared him to be her sole comfort. He read to her long windy extracts from long windy discourses, in which a few originally good ideas were smothered beneath superfluous words. He talked to her over her five o'clock tea before dinner, in a way that made her feel that it was just as easy and pleasant to be pious when you were in the country, and there were no card parties going, as it was to be wicked and worldly. Above all, he listened to her; listened with keen interest, and laughed at her old stories, and seemed to like the flavour she imparted to them. He "was a very clever man," Lady Glaskill told her niece, "and if he were ever given his chance, he would be a shining light," she added. And Kate said, "Oh! would he?" and did not care much about it.

The tendrils of Lady Glaskill's tough old heart went out and wound themselves around him. He was the sort of man to win his way eventually with worn-out women, for he had a subservient manner at command, which they mistook for reverentialness, and a certain vivacity, a way of saying things in a cheerful strain, as if (the Lord willing) he too could joke within bounds, which they mistook for wit. He could bow his head and press his lips on the fattest or the most withered hand without the slightest sign of nausea. He practised this legitimate mark of affection on Lady Glaskill, and Lady Glaskill looked upon it as a very proper and becoming outlet and escape-valve for those holy enthusiasms of his which he assured her he felt in the society of the chosen. It was pleasant to her to feel that he believed her to be a chosen vessel; pleasant also to be the recipient of the osculatory sign of his belief.

He wrote notes for her ladyship, and got her to go to church on sacrament Sundays, by inducing Mr. Caldwell to drop the sermon on those occasions. He ran errands for her all over the Grange, rendering himself like unto a tame dog in her service. He told Mrs. Galton, with touching fervour, that he was "but an instrument," and led her to believe that her aunt was coming back to the fold from which she had strayed at some very remote period at a hand center. "I am only glad that her eccentricities have taken that form," Mrs. Galton said, in reply; and to her husband she added, "it's a harmless way of passing her time—which is more than can be said of any of her previous occupations, I fancy."

So the months passed on uneventfully, and summer came again, and John Galton asked Frank Burgoyne down to stay at the Grange, as has been told. "If he comes, I shall ask Theo Leigh down too," Kate said to her husband,

while it was still uncertain whether Frank would come or not; to which John Galton, who knew that his wife could not have been blind to Frank's hopeless passion for her, replied, "It would be better, perhaps."

But before anything was finally decided upon, Lady Glaskill declared that she must go up to town to "see about her dividends;" and when John Galton offered to save her all trouble, she snapped out an abrupt refusal. It happened, fortunately, that when Lady Glaskill's intention was made manifest, Mr. Shalders found that business which needed his presence in London would call him thither about the same time as her ladyship.

"So, if you could travel up together, and see after aunt a little, I should be infinitely obliged to you," Kate said to him; and he promised that he would go up with and see after Lady Glaskill; in fact, as Hall observed, "he was quite conformable to the plan."

Fortunately for Mr. Shalders, who accompanied her, Lady Glaskill did not put him to the test by wearing her velvet cap with the fur border. It was warm weather, so she spared his feelings, and abstained from the cap. But she wore a sweet simple bonnet, that would have been juvenile on a head that had seen but eighteen summers—a girlish, airy nothing, tied under her chin with tulle. Mr. Shalders bore the bonnet like a man, however. The last that was seen of him from the Haversham platform was the curve of his reverend back as he leant across and essayed to adjust the unadjustable railway-carriage blinds, in order that the sun might not disport too fiercely on the deftly prepared cheeks and brow which the before-mentioned tulle shaded.

"It's quite a relief to be quit for a time of poor Aunt Glaskill and her boxes," Kate said to her husband that night, when they were seated at dinner.

"I daresay. Rum freak, though, to lug her boxes up with her if she means coming back, which I suppose she does."

"Yes," Kate replied. "Really, that Shalders is good-natured, John. What trouble he gave himself about seeing them all put into the van, to be sure. He carries what Mr. Caldwell calls his 'earnestness' into everything."

CHAPTER XLIII.

SYDNEY SCOTT'S GAIN.

MEANWHILE the arrangements in that little house on Hampstead Heath were all perfected, thanks to Theo. Everything had devolved upon her since the day of her father's death—the ordering and managing of all things fell upon her, and she bore up under the unaccustomed burden stoutly. Mrs. Leigh had not loudly lamented, or openly bewailed, the real loss which she had sustained. But she had suffered horribly in a gentle, uncomplaining secrecy, and she had just sunk under it into a state of lethargy that was hopeless enough. She never worried, she never planned, she never interfered. She simply took no heed of aught that transpired. Accordingly, as I said before, everything had devolved upon Theo.

It was weary work, tedious uncongenial work, that going constantly to the little house, at Hampstead, and seeing things gradually right themselves. Theo, after Frank had graciously disapproved of the locality, had not had much heart in her work. True, it was to be her home for some time to come, and the place in which we are going to dwell must always command a certain amount of interest. But it was not going to be her permanent tent. Good and dutiful, unselfish and affectionate, painstaking and untiring, as Theo was, she could not forget that her own tent was to be pitched in a very different position.

Nevertheless, all unaided as she was, this young girl, cast at twenty on her own resources to stand or fall as the case may be, without any apparent let or hindrance from anybody, with no one to counsel, no one to assist, no one to control her, nevertheless she laboured unceasingly, and managed very well. No matter through what trouble of mind and body, through what perplexity and doubt, it was consummated; the house was habitable at last, the arrangements were all perfected, and it was Theo's work entirely.

They had been busy, bustling, unpleasant weeks. All the bore of furnishing, and none of the bliss, had been hers. She was not free to exercise her taste; bare necessities, absolute requirements, these were all that common sense told her she might get. Carpets and chairs and tables, that were good and substantial, and were warranted to wear well. Prudence held her rigorously to the purchase of those, and such as these alone, and bade her turn away from the tempting array of pretty things which were on view in every shop she entered. It was very hard work, for she was young and possessed of taste, and also of a feeling that the absolutely unadorned paths of life are scarcely worth pursuing. It was very hard to pass the adornments on every side, and know that she must pass them as though they had not been.

By way of improving the aspect of things, Frank, with a masculine disregard for the great grinding god necessity, suggested all manner of ways of relieving her which were not practicable.

"Awfully you bother yourself when there's no occasion for it, Theo," he would say, whenever Theo seemed less fresh than he deemed fitting; "why not put the whole thing into Jackson & Graham's hands, and let them do it."

"They'd charge more for looking at it than the whole house must cost, Frank," she replied; and then Frank, with a gleam of something like sympathy for the high-hearted, uncomplaining way in which she went on doing what she did not like, told her—

"Never to mind; she should have it all her own way at Maddington by-and-by." "By-and-by" meaning whenever Lord Lesborough should be good enough to die out of his grandson's way.

After the ball, Frank had inclined ever so much more kindly towards Theo's friend, Miss Scott. He cemented a fresh friendship with the bright little blonde, who never had anything in her head save the desire to make herself agreeable to the one present. She was always ready to walk, to talk, to do anything, in fact; and Theo very often in the evening was too tired to do anything more laborious than sit still and listen. When the Leighs migrated to Hampstead, Frank declared that to be an admirable plan which had once been frowned at by him.

"It will do you good to have Sydney Scott with you when you're settled, Theo," he said; and Theo agreed with him—

"As I can't have you always," she replied.

"I suppose you will quite desert Bretford when Theo is gone," Sydney Scott said to him one day; and he tried to slip away from under the weight of the full meaning of that speech, as men are apt to do when such speeches are made to them. It was not pleasant to him, even though he meant to marry her, to have every one thrusting that intention of his forward. Perhaps Sydney had not calculated on the effect of her speech—perhaps she had done so. Who can tell? She was believed by every one, herself included, to be a guileless, undesigning little thing. But the heart is deceitful above all things, and desperately wicked.

"I don't know why you should suppose anything of the sort," he replied, rather coldly.

"Oh, I didn't know; I fancied she wouldn't like you to come; but you won't quite cut me, will you?"

"No;" he promised her that he would not.

"We have all three been so happy lately," Miss Sydney went on rather plaintively. As Theo's contribution towards the happiness pervading their gatherings lately had consisted of lying down on a sofa and being very silent, it was generous on Miss Scott's part to include her at all.

"We have all three been very happy lately. Oh! dear; I shall miss you, and that's the truth; I hope Theo will let you come sometimes."

After this it was very natural, considering what Frank was, that Bretford should see him frequently. He gave up his contemplated visit to Haversham Grange, simply because his desire to see the mistress of it was fast fading away. He gave up the contemplated visit because it no longer had any charms for him; but not the less on account of that reason did he make a great merit of his abnegation to Theo, and hurl it at her whenever she suffered him to perceive that she thought he might find his way to Hampstead a little oftener.

"My dear girl, you surely wouldn't have me give up everything, would you?"

"No, decidedly not, Frank, but——"

"Didn't I give up going into Norfolk because I thought you would be dull without me, in this beastly, inaccessible spot you have put yourself in? What more can a fellow do?"

Miss Scott was held by all her acquaintances, herself included, to be guileless, undesigning, open as the day. She most probably was all of these things—in a measure. Who can exactly tell where she left off being them? Who, indeed, can tell whether she did leave off being them, or whether her acts and their results were as void of all calculation as they appeared to be? Who can tell anything about anybody, if it comes to that?

Sydney Scott was a pretty, naturally clever, observant girl, gifted with the great grace of making the most of herself in every way. She had the trick of seeming, not only frank and cordial, but well-bred, which she was not. At least her breeding, such as it was, did not come by inheritance, for the parent birds were unconditionally vulgar, and Miss Scott saw that they were so, and Miss Scott was heartily ashamed of them.

Her father was the more endurable of the two to her; that is to say, she could explain him away, as it were. "He went to sea when he was very young, and when the service was a very rough school, you know," she would say, when circumstances over which she had no control forced her papa to the front. But with regard to her mother, no such explanation could be offered. Mrs. Scott was a vulgar old woman, and her daughter saw that she was so, and didn't like it.

Sydney was naturally a sharp, clever girl, and as she was thrown more and more in contact with people possessed even of superficial refinement, she sharpened herself still more, and refined herself—refined herself, that is to say, quite enough for the society in which she was thrown not to find her wanting. When she had done this, those speeches of her mamma's about "knowing well what was due to the nobility," and the like, grated upon her irritable young nerves, and made her long for a fling in the world "quite free from mamma."

It was the old story of the new generation outstripping the old. They had themselves aided in making her unsuited to themselves. In her own outspoken way she had explained the whole case to Theo in a moment of confidence, and this was what she had said, "I pass muster very well, you see, Theo, and mamma *does not;* now is it undutiful of me to wish to keep her quietly at home, where she isn't laughed at?"

Theo declined to give an opinion. The position was a delicate one; but as Miss Leigh had never been placed in it herself with respect to her own parents, she perhaps failed to appreciate the full force of the unpleasantness that had been an incubus on Sydney since the day "distinctions" had first dawned upon her.

Theoretically she would have scorned the idea of aiming at a bird that had fallen already to her friend's gun; but Frank Burgoyne was "very nice," and it was very pleasant to have him at the house when her mamma would refrain from lavishing her was's and were's in the wrong places upon her. It was very pleasant to have him there, and to remember that he had liked her very much, and that he wasn't married to Theo yet, and that he would be Lord Lesborough.

Mr. Burgoyne was a great deal up in town now, though his grandfather was rapidly declining. At last Mr. Burgoyne received a letter from Ethel that made him feel that it would not do for him to dally any longer. Lord Lesborough desired to see his grandson married immediately: Lord Lesborough made it a special request that the days of Theo Leigh's mourning for her father should be shortened—brought to a termination by her marriage with his heir.

Frank Burgoyne had not been near Theo for ten days when he received this communication. Hampstead was a long way off. Her selection of Hampstead as a place of residence was the cause of all the mischief that might ensue he told himself. He felt righteously angry with Theo for having gone to Hampstead when he had protested against her doing so. He felt righteously angry with Linley for having hurried him into a

declaration before he was quite sure that he wished to make it. He felt angry with his grandfather for so unreasonably trying to precipitate matters. Above all, he felt angry with himself.

He was unstable as water. The curse of being so was upon him, and he knew it. He vacillated for an hour between his inclination to carry the contents of that letter to Sydney Scott, and hear what she would say, and his knowledge that it behoved him to go to Theo. He was unstable as water. Finally he went down to Bretford, and as soon as she caught sight of him, the sharp little blonde saw that a climax of some sort or other was coming.

She flushed brilliantly with the hope that the coming climax might be favourable to herself, and checked all compunction within her breast with the reflection that, "if she chose, she might charge Theo with treachery, since she had confided to Theo her belief in Frank Burgoyne's love and admiration for herself, and Theo had listened." She flushed brilliantly, and she checked all compunctious scruples. In fact, she looked very pretty, and ready to do and dare anything.

"Papa and mamma wanted me to go with them to hear the band play," she said, while she was shaking hands with him, "but I wouldn't. I thought you might come possibly."

One disposed to censure Miss Scott, might have thought that it was scarcely in the order of things that she should stay in alone, avowedly with the hope of having an interview with a man who was engaged to her friend. It was a dangerous piece of flattery; but Frank liked being flattered, and was not at all disposed either to censure Miss Scott or lament the absence of her mamma.

He just gave the small white hand a tiny pressure before he released it, and said,

"I'm very glad of that. I want to tell you something."

At once there flashed through her mind a vision of that which he had to tell her, and she resolved upon making a bold play to be Lady Lesborough. She interlaced her delicate rounded fingers within each other almost convulsively, and her large grey eyes dilated, and the corners of her flexible mouth went down, as she exclaimed,

"Don't tell me—and yet do; you're ordered over the precipice?"

"Yes, but I'm not over it yet," he said, placing his hand down upon hers, as they still clasped each other. Then she knew that the game was her own. She knew that she had won. She knew that this man was ready to jilt Theo Leigh at a word from her—at less even—at a look, a sigh! She knew this as she stood silent and motionless for a few seconds, excusing herself to herself, and declaring to herself simultaneously that no excuses were needed.

"No, you're not over it yet, certainly," she replied, slowly; "have you come to tell me that you're ready to go over it, though? because, if you have," and here she began to speak very fast, "say it at once."

"I didn't come to tell you that," he said, "I came to tell you—" and then he paused, for he was not quite sure of what he had come to tell her.

She gave what he fancied to be a gasp of

10

profound emotion; in reality it was only a bit of excited breath-catching. The game was not quite her own yet. She was horribly afraid of losing it.

A word might make, or a word mar her. She saw that. She recognised fully that it was upon the cards still that she might lose, and with such great gains in view, to lose would be so very ignominious. A word might make or mar her. She called silence, and sweet looks, and a half-stifled sigh to her aid, the guileless little creature, as skilfully as the most designing woman could have done.

He never thought for an instant of what Theo Leigh would suffer. He only felt that this "dear little thing" before him, with the clasped hands, and the big grey eyes, and the drooping corners to the usually joyous mouth, was "feeling awfully cut-up" at the prospect of his marriage with another girl. It would not be a good thing to do, but other men had done it before. "By Jove!" (with a sudden flash of memory) "another man had done it to Theo Leigh herself. It would not be a good thing to do, but——"

"God! I can't stand it!" he cried, drawing Sydney nearer. "Believe me I was let into that affair, Sydney, and I mean to get out of it, if you'll reward me for the bother it will give me."

So, on Sydney promising both to forgive and to reward him, he determined upon his perfidy to Theo, and justified his determination in the manliest, most honourable manner, by declaring that he "wasn't the first fellow who had served her so." This was quite natural—in fact, this was inevitable. The thing he was going to do was so very mean and low, that only on the meanest, lowest grounds could it be justified.

CHAPTER XLIV.

THEO LEIGH'S LOSS.

THE arrangements were all perfected in that little house at Hampstead. The place was very habitable, and would have been notwithstanding very dull to dwell in, had not hope perpetually told a flattering tale to Theo. This region, that was rather bleak, truth to tell, in this autumn weather, in which she knew no one (for the beautiful metropolitan custom of fighting shy of, and greatly distrusting, all new arrivals, holds good in the suburbs): this region, I say, would have been dull and unendurable to her, had she looked upon it as other than a waiting-place on her road to the joyous goal that was before her.

To those of my readers who hold that the "first" is the only true love, the statement that Theo Leigh loved Frank Burgoyne very fondly, very warmly, very *well*, will seem either wrong or ridiculous? Nevertheless it is a fact, that she did so love him, aye, though she had no more utterly forgotten Harold Ffrench than one human being can utterly forget another who has been near and dear, and much spoken about.

She did not utterly forget Harold Ffrench. She was neither weak-minded, nor false-hearted. She did not forget Harold Ffrench: but, remembering him only made her think the more fondly and constantly of Frank Burgoyne—of

the man who was aware of her youthful weakness, and who loved her in spite of it.

Hampstead was out of the way, was inaccessible from the Frank Burgoyne starting-point clearly. At least she tried to think that it was Hampstead's inaccessibility alone which made Frank keep away so much.

They were dull days, if the truth be told—those earlier days of Theo Leigh's residence in the little house on the Heath, the fitting up of which she had superintended with much weariness of spirit. They were dull days, very dull days: but then you see she had such bright things in store.

In the meantime, before these bright things were realised, she tried hardly to get back all those outward and visible signs of youth and happiness which had been bruised and banished. Frank Burgoyne's bride should go to him with roses on her cheeks, and brightness in her eyes, and the rich dew of health on her lips. So Theo went out bravely on that broad Heath whereon she felt so friendless, and sought for these fitting ornaments round about the region of Jack Straw's Castle and the Spaniards: sought for and found them, too, and rejoiced over her renovation with a girl's natural vanity.

Life went at a very sober pace in that little house on the Heath. The greatest excitement ever got up within its walls was on the rare occasions of Theo confidently expecting Frank, and making preparations towards his advent—which seldom took place. She did not make preparations after the manner of her estimable aunt, Mrs. Vaughan. She did not bustle and fuss furiously, and endeavour to keep the fact of doing these things in the background. She brought all her preparations, and all the joy she had in making them, forward frankly; she revelled in displaying them, and the grace with which they were made, to Frank, their good and proper cause.

With the exception of these occasions, life was very monotonous in Theo's home. That old hearty communion that had never failed, that had always been so pleasant let all else be miserable as it might,—this was a thing of the past. The strangest thing in her strange home was the want of her father's presence, and her father's friendship. The saddest thing in it was the thought that her father could never rejoice in her achievement of that destiny, the mere promise of which had been so prized by him. She gauged the joy he would have had in her triumphs by the proud trustful love she bore him,—and I think the gauge was a true one.

For all this want, though, the girl was very happy. She was only a woman, and the prospect of being a titled one was not unpleasant to her. Besides, as I have said before, she loved Frank for that generosity of his which made him apparently utterly ignore all that had gone before. She loved him with a hearty grateful love, than which there could be nothing better or more complete.

In the earlier days of their engagement it had been settled that she should be married in August. But her father's death had intervened, and from that other delaying causes had sprung. So that now, though it was late in September, she was still Miss Leigh, and still uncertain of how long she was to remain Miss Leigh.

Nevertheless though her marriage was thus indefinitely deferred, she looked upon it as a thing that would in the order of events come off very soon. Accordingly, being only flesh and blood of the middle class, she felt it behoved her to see about the buying and making of the purple and fine linen usual on such occasions. Moreover, being only of the middle class, as has been said before, she gave much thought to the matter. Travelled arduously eastward ho ! on more than one occasion, beguiled by an advertisement setting forth in large letters, with many notes of admiration appended thereunto, the miserable onus that was on certain firms of being cleared out, no matter how alarming the sacrifice, before a certain date.

Poor Theo ! There was no one to do it for her, gentle Mrs. Leigh having subsided into nothingness. There was no one to do it for her, and it had to be done ; consequently Theo did it herself. it was not pleasant for the girl who had never been about in the world before, to be abroad on her own responsibility now, bargaining with extortionate tradesman, and seeing cabmen, who were lambs when she entered their equipages, develop into roaring lions when she got out, and mildly and tremulously questioned the justice of the eighteen pence they put on for Hampstead Hill.

It was not pleasant for her to do these things. It was not seemly that the future Lady Lesborough should have done them. But unfortunately the prospect of being Lady Lesborough did not fill her purse ; and with this debased generation the proudest pretensions and the most profound belief in good things being in store for one, go for nothing if the purse be empty. Accordingly Theo did things that were neither quite pleasant nor quite seemly,—did them and suffered for them, as people do and suffer in this everyday commonplace world in which we everyday commonplace ones do dwell.

An obliging uncle had died when Theo was three years old, leaving her a small legacy—a sum of 150*l.*, into possession of which she was to come when she was either married or had attained the age of twenty-one. She was twenty-one now, and she was about to fulfil the other condition. Consequently the money was hers.

The money was hers to do as she pleased with ; and when it was first given over to her in the shape of a bundle of semi-transparent notes that crackled under her hand, reminding her of the well-cooked skin of pork,—when it was first given over in this wealthy-sounding way, she deemed it an all-sufficient, not to say fabulous, sum. But after a day or two it dwindled.

It dwindled in a surprising, not to say a shocking way, after the manner of money. Now the manner of money was new to Theo, and that way it had, of going fast and leaving no trace behind, was quite a new feature in finance to her. It was startling at first to find how small the amount of change was out of a five-pound note, when the price of the article to be paid for was four pounds nineteen and sixpence. This was very startling at first : but she got used to it after a time, and pocketed her sixpence with gratitude.

Aunt Libby had undertaken to give her the dress of dresses—the bridal robe and veil, and Aunt Libby's ideas on the subject of these things were of the most enlarged order.

" You may go to a guinea a yard, my dear," the old lady had said to her niece, when the auspicious engagement with the heir of Maddington was first made known to her. Accordingly Theo " went to a guinea a yard," and ordered home what she deemed a sufficient quantity of a white material with forked lightning and splashes like big tears upon it, known to the initiated as " moire antique, best quality."

There was great pleasure in getting these dresses : great pleasure in marvelling how she would look in them,—or rather, how Frank would think she looked in them. The solitary little figure in black grew very bright within as she toiled about from shop to shop ; the girl with so little money to spend in reality, spent it with a joyous lavishness over such things as misled the sellers of the same with the notion that the stock of crisp notes was large. But it was such solitary pleasure ! \ She went about this pleasantest task that had fallen to her share yet in the world, alone !

Alone, quite alone ! It was very improper, of course ; and not at all the sort of thing that those parents who have the wherewithal to mount outward guard over their daughters can credit is ever done by gentlewomen. It is very improper ; but all must allow that it is one of those improprieties which are not committed by preference. On the whole, Theo would rather have rolled about in a snug brougham, and had an intelligent footman follow her out of the shops with the packages.

However, she had no brougham and no footman, so perforce she was compelled either to walk upon the earth or to take a cab in her journeyings hither and thither, or (more terrible still) to get into one of those dismal swamps—an omnibus.

One day, after a severe morning of purchasing, and feeling guilty of extravagance, and yet being sure she could not do without the things,—after many hours of disturbance of spirit, she had practised a small economy, and gone down from the select region of West-End shops to Hampstead in an omnibus. At the foot of the hill her spirit of endurance broke down, and she crept out in the lame dilapidated way in which people do creep out of an omnibus after a lengthened indulgence in its delights—crept out, resolving to walk up the hill home, and so freshen herself for that visit from Frank which she confidently expected that evening.

That hill ! that terror and trial to the tried legs of man or beast. It is a hill to be thought of with the darkest hatred, if you have ever attempted to drive a lazy, self-willed, fatigued horse up it. A sanguine feeling is yours at the foot of it, perhaps. You imagine that your skilful hand will administer a flick on that precise portion of the quadruped you are driving which will ensure his pulling up well at once. You try the skilful flick, and it has just no effect whatever. He flags, and the traces slacken, and his head goes down, and so do your hopes, and pedestrians pass you, and time grows weary and you grow old, and still that hill stretches its miserable length before you. You can't hit your horse as it is in your usually kind heart to hit him, or you would be had up under Mr.

Martin's act. You don't like to weep and gnash your teeth for fear of being seized and immured by some myrmidon from a lunatic asylum. One may make ghastly efforts to while away the time by making intelligent remarks to one's companion, but this is a miserable device for the concealment of anxious misery, and is warranted to fail. It does not even impose upon oneself, —the most easily deceived of all one's acquaintances. The only thing to be done is to meekly resign oneself to melancholy, or to pretend to be looking for Clarkson Stanfield's house.

Up this hill Theo Leigh walked on a clear September afternoon, with the double conviction on her mind that Frank would come and cheer her up in the evening, and that she had spent nearly all her money, and would have to severely limit herself as to gloves, in order not to have to encroach upon that magnificent sum which Government awarded her mamma as compensation for the loss of a husband. "I must have a lot to start with," Theo thought, "And I had better get them all dark, though Frank unfortunately only likes me to wear lemon-colour and silver-grey. I'll write to Sydney, and ask her to get me a lot at the same place she gets hers from —at wholesale price, I think she says,—and I had better fix a day for her to come over and stay with me."

She quickened her pace as she said this, in order to get home, and write, and cause a letter to be posted before five o'clock. As she panted up the last bend of the hill she heard her name spoken in a voice that she knew well and remembered kindly, and looking up she saw Harold Ffrench.

She saw him such an altered man, such a grey-haired elderly man, that the blood leapt into her face with surprise. Great as was the inward alteration which had been wrought in herself during the last few months, the outward alteration in this man was still greater; and it is the outward alteration that we are apt to mark and lament.

There was no confusion in her soul nor constraint in her mind at this abrupt meeting with and recognition of him. Consequently there was no confusion or constraint in her manner. "I am very glad to see you again, Mr. Ffrench," she said, forgetting Frank's recently avowed feelings on the subject. "I am very glad to see you again;—but—have you been ill?"

Something seemed to jar upon his heart as she spoke. It was a cordial, kind, lady-like greeting, that which she awarded him. It should in honour have been no more than these things. Nevertheless it jarred upon him that it was no more.

"No, I have not been ill;" he replied, "but I have been worried and anxious during the last few hours."

"Won't you come back and see mamma?" she asked. "We live near here."

"I know;—I have just seen Mrs. Leigh," he replied hurriedly; "the fact is, I came up from Maddington this morning; Lord Lesborough is much worse, and wants his grandson."

"Is Frank gone down?" Theo asked quickly.

"No; we telegraphed for him, and no notice was taken, so I came up; he has not been at his place for a day or two, and I fancied he might be here, therefore I took the liberty of calling at your house."

He attempted to say this in a stiff conventional tone. Theo, in her frank indifference to him, and through her equally frank display of interest for Mr. Burgoyne, seemed so very far removed from him.

She marked his tone, and fathomed the spirit that dictated it. "Ah! don't speak to me in that way," she cried, "but tell me what you will do about finding Frank; I can't say where he is."

"I have left a note at his rooms," he replied.

"And is Lord Lesborough really ill — dying?"

"I fear he is."

"Poor Frank! How he'll feel it if he should be too late to see his grandfather," she said, earnestly. "I half fancied that he was at Maddington, as I haven't seen him for several——"

She stopped, blushing, as the remembrance flashed across her mind that Harold Ffrench might think that Frank was neglecting her, as she herself occasionally was afraid he was. The pause and the blush told him more than the completed sentence would have done, and he felt that the one who had deprived him of this jewel was not wearing it proudly by any means. It was hard for him to walk calmly along by her side and feel this; so he stopped and said good-by to her, and she went on quickly to her own home, with footsteps rendered fleet by the thought that she had "so much to tell Frank" —"so much" that she now felt would not be quite pleasant to him to hear, and that would oppress her with a sense of concealment, till he had heard. "He's sure to say Mr. Ffrench interferes unnecessarily," she thought, "and to rage against poor Miss Burgoyne for having dispatched such an envoy in search of him; anyway, I could not help meeting him on the hill."

As soon as the door of the little house was opened to her she asked,

"Is Mr. Burgoyne here?"

"No, miss; and your ma's——"

"Are any of my things come home?" Theo interrupted.

The servant shook her head, and resumed the broken thread of her discourse.

"And your ma's up in her room, taking on about something, miss."

"Poor mamma!" Theo thought, as she plodded wearily upstairs. All the fleetness was fled from her footsteps now that she learnt that neither of the expected arrivals were here before her.

Mrs. Leigh was sitting in an easy chair in a corner of the room, over which a shade hung, when her daughter entered.

"I'm home again, mamma, you see," Theo commenced, in bright accents. She never used the tone dolorous when people were in grief. It never improved their case one whit she had discovered; indeed, it usually had the contrary effect of plunging them into still deeper gloom.

Mrs. Leigh looked up with a start, and Theo's quick eyes read wistfulness in her mother's gaze,—such wistfulness as she had never seen in it before.

"My dear, are you very tired?"

"No, mother," Theo said, in more subdued

tones than those she had first used. Then she went and knelt down by her mother's feet, and Mrs. Leigh drew the head crowned with its wavy masses of brown hair down upon her lap.

Tired! No, she was not tired; but as she felt her mother's hand press closer, tremblingly, amidst those waves of hair, a feeling oppressed her that was not fatigue—a feeling of desperate helplessness, a very faintness of despair. She strove to break the spell of sorrow that was creeping over her.

"Mother, poor mother, you have been alone again, and are feeling dull," she said, fondly pressing her lips upon the hand she had caught and prisoned as it wandered over her head.

"No, my dear, not dull, but——"

"Ah! you've heard the bad news from Maddington," Theo cried, with a sudden recollection of Lord Lesborough's extreme case. "I met Mr. Ffrench, and he told me. He wanted Frank. I hope Frank will come to-night," she continued, hopefully.

Then the dull lethargy of sorrow that had been Mrs. Leigh's portion since her husband's death dissolved suddenly, and she threw her arms closely, tenderly, pityingly, round her daughter's neck, as she sobbed out,—

"Poor child! my own poor child! He will never come again."

"Mother! Mother!"

The girl was on her feet in an instant. She had started erect with fatal suddenness, as it is the wont of those who are shot through the heart to do.

"He's alive!" Mrs. Leigh cried eagerly. She had read aright the generous anguish that was Theo Leigh's first pang. Her daughter's first thought was of death, not desertion. As I said once before, Theo Leigh never believed people to be baser than they were.

"Then he has left me too," Theo wailed. "Mother, dearest, don't look at me in that way. I shall not die, though I have so little to live for."

<hr>

CHAPTER XLV.

LATE REMORSE.

When Frank Burgoyne had done the deed—had spoken the few words which made manifest that which was within his vacillating heart to Sydney,—he felt cast down and sorry. There was none of successful love's elation in his soul or on his brow. He knew that he had done a mean thing. He also knew that the girl for whom he had done it would no more have the power to make him feel all things to be well lost in winning her than any other woman had had the power to hold him heretofore.

He also felt—and in feeling this there was much natural soreness—that this change he had made, which could not be concealed an hour longer than necessary in honour, would not only damage him with his grandfather, but sorely distress the latter. He would now for a certainty deem his grandson capable of all the Hugo iniquities; and Frank acknowledged to himself that he would be deemed so not altogether unjustly.

It was made patent to him at once that the fetters he had himself adopted in such awkward, un-seemly haste would be riveted fast and sure. It was made patent to him at once that Sydney was a young lady of immense determination. It was made patent to him at once that he had been egregiously mistaken in imagining it to be feasible to play with fire without burning his fingers.

That first interview of his with the parent Scotts was an awful ordeal, a memorable misery. He would have given much to evade it, but his days of evading aught that Sydney desired should be faced, were over. As soon as those sensations set in, to which allusion was made at the commencement of this chapter—as soon that is, as the small excitement consequent on a verbal declaration of a change of faith, had faded away, and he began to feel cast down and sorry, he proposed "going away."

He proposed this in a half-guilty way—in a way that plainly showed that he felt his proposition would be opposed, and Sydney opposed it promptly.

"Go away! Why?" she asked. "No, Frank, do stay and see papa now; you ought to stay and see papa."

"I will write him a line to-night," he said, hesitatingly.

"That won't do at all," she replied, resolutely; "They're very particular, and they're very fond of me. Your going away won't look well to them."

"But Sydney——" he began, taking her hand caressingly.

"But Frank," she interrupted, quickly, "if, after all, you can't face it, how can you think of leaving me to face it alone?"

"There's nothing for you to face."

"Oh, isn't there? Oh, isn't there, indeed?! 'Nothing for me to face!' If you think so lightly of me as that, I wonder you could ask me to marry you. I have feeling; I feel very much, though I always keep up before people."

She became transparent under the eyes as she spoke, after the manner of blondes who restrain their briny tears, and she was very fair.

"My dear Sydney, it's no question of——"

"It's just a question of straightforwardness of speaking, it seems to me," she interrupted. "Papa would think me a sneak if I kept anything from him, and I can tell you I am not going to be the one to speak of our engagement first, so you must stay."

"Our engagement!" the phrase caused him to feel how thoroughly he was "in for it" here, before he was "out of it" in another quarter.

It was hard to say which of these twain, who were about to become one flesh, according to Miss Sydney's ordination, would have triumphed, had not Mr. and Mrs. Scott providentially returned at this juncture. They had timed their absence well.

As she entered the room Mrs. Scott became conscious of having that special sanguine hue over her face which bespeaks intense excitement, and it did not seem according to the fitness of things in her estimation that other than the cool and collected side of the family should be shown to Mr. Burgoyne just yet. She therefore endeavoured to explain her red cheeks away—much to Sydney's horror.

"This autumn 'eat is that trying when one is weak and given to flushing, that you'd scarcely believe, Mr. Burgoyne," she said in a voice that was far lower pitched than her natural one, in order to express that delicacy and fatigue for which the occasion called.

Frank looked at her by way of reply—looked at her distastefully, and thought "It's devilish seldom *she* shall see the inside of my house, if I have to marry her daughter.

"Then, mamma, go and cool yourself, do," Sydney struck in promptly, "and Frank will—won't you, Frank?"

She did not say what Frank would do. But he knew what she meant, and he said, "Yes," with external composure and an internal groan. He knew well that the aforesaid precipitate declaration of a change of faith would have to be repeated in due form to Mr. Scott, and he began to wish that he had not made it at all.

It was an ugly leap truly: but Sydney, the weaker vessel, had gone at a similar one so valiantly that he could not baulk it for very shame. It was not that he feared that there would be any difficulties thrown in his way on the Scott side; on the contrary, he knew that it would all be rendered offensively easy to him, as far as they were concerned; but the shadow of that letter which would have to be written to Theo's mother was looming over him already.

He was correct in his deductions as regarded one thing. It was all made easy for him as far as the Scotts were concerned; they were all that was tolerant to what was past, and most flatteringly anxious to smooth all obstructions in the future. Mr. Scott clapped him heartily on the back, and put on the last new uniform to sit down to dinner with Frank, the caged; for a promise to stay to dinner was wrung from him on the spot, as soon as ever he had spoken out what Mrs. Scott called "his most honourable intentions."

Sydney was the reverse of ill-natured; nevertheless she gave no very serious thought to what Theo would feel about it all. One allusion she did make to her former friend, her worsted rival, and, odd as it may appear, it was not a disparaging one.

"It will be only fair to let Theo know of this at once, Frank; you must promise me to do that."

She paused; but as he made no answer, she resumed quickly, "If you won't promise me, I tell you I'll make my mother write to hers at once; it would be too mean to keep her in the dark."

I do not think that he liked this first evening in the bosom of the family of his affianced. They tried to absorb him too entirely into themselves; to be hail-fellow-well-met with him; to be free and unembarrassed, and awfully intimate in a jocular way. Mrs. Scott leapt abruptly from the manner abject to the manner affectionate; and Mr. Scott mentioned so many things "by-the-way" to him that he could do when he took his seat in either House, that the last state of that man was infinitely worse than the first. Moreover, Sydney's habit of putting down both her parents alternately was confusing; this was a thing to grow, he felt; he might, in time, fall under that commanding young manner, which impressed the stranger as being so very fresh and frank. He had his gentlemanly well-bred instincts; blood always "tells" in some way or other; so, though he reminded himself that Sydney "ought not to forget what he had given up for her" (meaning the way he had risked his honour *in re* Theo Leigh), he never thought for an instant that Sydney ought to remember the great good a union with him would bring her.

He left at last, and walked up to town, revolving at his leisure the phrasing of that letter which should convey the sorry truth to Theo. "What will she think of me?" he thought. He had no fear of any outburst, any appeal. He knew the girl; he knew all her loving pride too well to dread that. But he could but reflect on what his sensations would be did she droop and fade, and *die* of this blow he was preparing to deal her.

It was but cowardly comfort, yet he hugged it to his soul as he walked along, this gallant young English gentleman, with the full supply of courageous cavalier blood in his veins: it was but cowardly comfort, yet it was the sole one left to him,—the thought that, let what would befall her, he would probably never know the fate of Theo Leigh.

He felt thoroughly ashamed of himself. But of idleness and a habit of giving way to the impulse of the moment, the mischief had been born. This trick he had taken up of loving and unloving, of wooing and leaving! He ceased to look upon it as a pretty pastime as he walked along alone; he saw it now as the low, dull, dastardly thing it was.

Ah! that seeing a thing as it is, and knowing that we have brought it on ourselves, and that there is no escape for us. "Lives there a man with soul so dead" as to have taken comfort in defeat and downfall from that sorry saying, "you have no one but yourself to blame for it?" There is bliss in blaming the whole world for the evil that overtakes us, but not in denouncing our own blunders and miscalculations. In this there is none, absolutely none—save in the case of a woman who loves the man who neglects her, and so excuses him by accusing herself.

Frank Burgoyne determined to write that letter to Theo's mother while the glow of the onus that was on him to write it at all was on him freshly. He thought first that he would make it very concise; but that seemed brutal. Then he thought that he would give a lengthy explanation; a summary of his own weaknesses, and of the trials to which they had been subjected. That, on reflection, seemed needlessly insulting, "By God! I don't know what to say for myself!" he said, at last, in the exasperation of his spirit. "I am a fool, a d—d fool! who has lost in the selfish game."

But, genuine as this statement was, powerful as it was in its simple truth, it would not do to write that, and that alone, to Theo's mother. It might be taken to have application to ever so many other things he felt, in this hour of his humiliation, and it behoved him to make his statement clear—all foul and base as it was—without needless delay.

There are many disagreeable duties to be performed in this world. Caligraphical exercises very frequently go against the grain. It is unpleasant to be compelled to write a cheque when your banking account is low. · It is odious to write a page and a-half of condolence to the bereaved with whom, in sober fact, you can't quite sympathise, having perhaps known but little, and that little but bad, of the deceased. It is not nice to be behind-hand with the last chapters of a novel announced as already in the press. But more repugnant to the spirit and taste than any one of these things is the knowledge that you yourself must write such a letter as will bruise another and blast yourself.

Such a letter Frank Burgoyne was in honour bound (such honour as was left to him) to write now. He had had previously no very overweening respect and esteem for Mrs. Leigh. He had merely regarded her as a nice, ladylike, excellent woman; but now the full force of her motherhood came upon him, and he flinched in his soul as he pictured her reading the letter which must be written. "By God! I'd rather cut my hand off than do it," he muttered, as he pulled a writing-table towards him after an hour's solitary reflection in the sitting-room he occupied at the hotel. Cutting his hand off, however, would have been a futile proceeding, void of all power to further those arrangements which he dared not suffer to stand still. Therefore he took up a pen instead, and wrote that letter, the contents of which came down upon Theo as a thunderbolt when she returned from her weary day's shopping.

It was a very lame performance. Looking back upon it in after years, when the bloom of time was upon it, he was fain to confess that it was a very lame performance indeed; yet he said all that there was to say,—all that he dared to say.

When he rose from the writing, when he had directed and sealed his letter, he felt that come what would of passion, of sober love, of joy in that love, and security in it, there would be a dimming shade cast over all by memory. He would never be quite to himself even what he had been before. The vagueness that would be over Theo Leigh's fate to him would be a depressing thing, or should that vagueness be dispersed, there might arise a more agonising certainty.

"Girls don't die of broken hearts in these days, thank the Lord!" he said to himself, after a time. But the very fact of his thanking the Lord that the probability was averted, proved that he feared the possibility of its arising. He was very miserable and very cast down, and later in the night he could but think of how all this would tell upon his prospects at Maddington. The title would be his for a surety, but—there was a lot of unentailed property.

───◆───

CHAPTER XLVI.

"ALL IN THE FAMILY."

THE letter was written: so far well. More than that, the letter was sent off: the statement it contained could never be recalled, never explained away, never softened.

The poor fellow who had penned it—for though he was young, healthy, handsome, and heir to a fine title and estate, he felt himself to be a very

poor fellow indeed in that hour—was profoundly miserable, more especially after he went to bed. His conscience had it all its own way with him as soon as ever he got his head upon his downy pillow. It made him feel very sick, and very desirous of sleeping away all his troubles, and very incapable of sleeping at all.

"There'll be the devil to pay, too, when they hear it at Maddington," he thought, and this, though a very minor evil, was quite enough to make the minutes he gave to reflecting upon it in the stilly night hot and unrefreshing. He had not reeked of this when he began flirting with these two girls. Of his own free will he had made the idle folly so very serious—of his own free will he had approved himself such a sneak.

If he could only get out of this second fix. He turned the possibility of doing so over and over in his mind, as the night faded away and the morning light crept into his room; and still he could find no loophole; still the impression deepened that there was no escape for him. He had gone into the Scotts' camp, and the Scotts had managed matters so that there was no getting out of their camp again.

But even though he could escape, what then? Of what avail, as far as Theo was concerned, would it be to free himself from Sydney? The letter which, when Theo read it, would make him seem so very mean a thing in her eyes, was written, was gone! He knew himself to have been a sneak in the transaction, and he knew that she would feel him to have been one.

Stormy sensations succeeded. He had been taken in, he had been induced to behave like a blackguard; the whole lot of them (he meant the Scotts) had traded on those finer instincts of his which made him gentle and gallant in his manner to women! He swore at his last betrothed and her family, as he thought of all these things, and there was more rage and fury in his heart against them than they deserved.

He knew himself now to have been a green foolish boy; and he was but this, for all that habit of his of seeming a man of the world. He had been David Linley's tool first, and since then he had been the tool of his own vanity.

Through the long hours of the night he gave himself up to a grim black view of the case; as the dawn crept on he began to be more hopeful —to think that he might drift out of it, and win a pardon from Theo before any one knew that he had contemplated this baseness towards her, even for an hour. But when the morning came, these latter hopes were crushed and killed at once and decidedly.

"There's a gentleman waiting for you in the coffee-room, sir," the man said, who brought in Mr. Burgoyne's hot water.

"What's his name?" Frank asked sleepily. He was much fatigued now with unwonted night thought; very gladly would he have turned his head on the pillow, and let the gentleman wait for yet another hour. But when he heard who it was, he knew that even so much respite from that family could not be granted.

"The gentleman said he wished to see you immediate, sir. Here's his card." The card was inscribed with the name of Mr. Scott, and when he read it Frank groaned, and said he would be down presently.

He went down presently, and found Mr. Scott,

Sydney's father, awaiting him in undress uniform. "What the devil *did* he come in that for?" the unfortunate Frank thought. "I must say that for Leigh, that he never forced the unwelcome truth down my throat that it was a fine thing to be a lieutenant in the Navy."

Mr. Leigh belonged to the past—to that past on which, all things considered, Frank ought not to have dwelt. What Mr. Leigh had done, and what Mr. Leigh had left undone, was of no moment whatever (or should have been of no moment) to Mr. Scott's future son-in-law. Mr. Leigh—grand dignified old gentleman that he had been—was of the past. It was with this very different sample of the service that Frank had to deal now.

He attempted to look surprised in a superior manner when he came into the room, and found Mr. Scott strutting about impatiently between the windows. Now, the strut was not a newly-acquired thing on the part of Mr. Scott. It had been his all his life. He had strutted out of his cradle under the grate when an infant. He had strutted on the quarter-deck when a man. The gait had done him some injury in the estimation of the many who judge by appearances, all his life long; but it had never been so offensively apparent to Frank Burgoyne as at this moment.

Accordingly, that young patrician, though he strove to look surprised in a superior manner only, looked disgusted at the mode of taking exercise affected by Mr. Scott, as well. Had Mr. Scott been a mere sea-bear, Frank could have stood him better. He would have laid all shortcomings to the score of the "service." But Mr. Scott was not a rough sea-bear; he was a pretentious under-bred old snob, and Frank saw him to be such.

"My dear boy, I thought I'd just give you a call as I was passing. I'm a-going on to see one of the 'Lords'—a most useful fellow for you to know, by-the-way; you had better come with me, and I'll introduce you."

Mr. Scott said this with affected carelessness; but Frank looked through that carelessness, and saw that his future father-in-law was bursting with impatience to be seen abroad in the best haunts he (Mr. Scott) knew with Lord Leasborough's heir. Frank saw the desire, and ill-temperedly resolved to defeat it.

"Rather early for a call, isn't it, unless you're very intimate with him?"

"Best friends in the world, my dear boy," (this form of address was perhaps the most obnoxious to Frank of any Mr. Scott could have selected). "Best friends in the world, my dear boy; his lordship has remarked to me more than once 'Scott, my dear fellow, you'd be in a devilishly different position if merit had its desert.'"

"Humph!" Frank grunted.

"You had much better come on to him with me, and I'll introduce you; splendid fellow for you to know; most influential man under the present administration."

"Perish the present administration; I don't care a damn for it," Frank replied sulkily, striking his hands in his pockets, and looking out of the window. "The old cad talks to me as if I were one of his own low-born whelps," he thought. Then he remembered that he had just asked one of the aforesaid to be his own wife, and he winced.

Mr. Scott's soul shivered at this blasphemous mention of one who was to him a demi-god. But he reminded himself that the speaker of that blasphemy was one of the denizens in that more perfect air in which his demi-god habitually dwelt out of office-hours. For all he knew to the contrary, this, his future son-in-law, might wing his flight more boldly in those regions than did the official! The thought was a proud one. It made Mr. Scott feel more affectionately towards Frank on the spot.

"His Lordship is very much bent on the extermination of some of our standing abuses: I should like to bring you together—you might promise him that when you take your seat you would ask a question on the mismanagement of——"

"Curse the mismanagement and the mismanagers; I don't care a damn about it." He glared out of the window savagely, and there was silence for a minute or two, till Frank felt ashamed of himself, then he asked, by way of apology,

"Any message from Sydney for me? You see I'm thinking more about her just now than about the blemishes in the decayed old system."

Sydney's father accepted the partially expressed apology with admirable promptitude. The strongest feeling within him at this epoch was, that it "was a mighty fine thing to be father-in-law to a very magnificent," *not* three-tailed bashaw, but that far finer thing, a rich young English gentleman, who would before long have a handsome handle to his name.

"Yes," he replied, diving into one of his pockets, "Sydney sent you this note, and she hopes—I mean, Mrs. Scott and I hope—that you will come down to-morrow and dine with us at seven; quite a plain family dinner, I assure you."

Mr. Scott spoke the last portion of his invitation in the impressive tones people are apt to use when endeavouring to persuade another to come and partake of a repast under their hospitable roof. Why on earth the assertion that it is a "mere quiet affair—quite a family dinner," should be looked upon by the majority of warm-hearted inviters as an irresistible inducement, I do not know. A family dinner, as far as my experience goes, is a thing to flee from, if you would not have melancholy claim you for his own. Others must feel the same as regards it, I am sure; yet the promise of it has a permanent place in the conventional formula man speaks when he asks his brother-man to come and feed with him.

There was no excuse for him; now, that is, that he could readily make. There was no escape for him; he was in the meshes; and any struggles he might make in the attempt to free himself from them would be not alone unbecoming and undignified, but futile. The reflection they would be this last kicked the beam in favour of his not making them. He felt himself to be a calf, but he reflected that the riotous calf is even more ridiculous than the meek one.

He promised therefore to go down to the little pleasant family gathering at Mr. Scott's on the following day; and when he had so promised, Mr. Scott, finding that the honour of strutting out in company with Lord Leasborough's heir could not be his, strutted away alone.

Frank Burgoyne sauntered back to his private room, where breakfast and the contributions of many posts were awaiting him, and as he sat himself down to paté and the perusal of those letters, he swore that he would never gratify old Scott's wild desire to show him off. "I'll marry the daughter,—I shall have to do that I suppose, and then I'll cut the whole connection," he muttered. "My God! fancy my being asked to go off and sue for the patronage of an intimate friend of that old fellow's." Then he fell upon the paté morosely, and found it lacking in flavour, and opened letter after letter with a lax interest until he came to one—a brief one—a sheet of note-paper, containing a few lines from Harold Ffrench, telling him of his grandfather's danger and approaching dissolution, and desiring his instant presence at Maddington. He put the letter down with a sigh of relief. He was not naturally cruel, or even callous, but the fear of the consequences of his own bad conduct was crushing out the best of his nature. Formerly, his first thought would have been to regret the demise of his kind-hearted, wrong-headed old grandfather; but now his first thought was that his change of faith would not change his prospects. He would be Lord Lesborough himself in a few days, perhaps in a few hours. Anyway, if the transition of his troth could be kept quiet for awhile, there would be no danger of his being cut off with the entailed property alone.

His first impulse was good enough, only he did not act on it. "I will go down to Maddington at once," he thought, as he laid the letter down. By the time he had finished breakfast, however, it had occurred to him that he could do no good by going down to Maddington at once. "A day—since his grandfather was so far gone already—could make no difference; if he could do any good, of course he would go without delay; but what good could he do? He would only create confusion; so he had better wait till to-morrow." Could it be that he was getting cowardly—this gallant-looking, brave-fronted, frank-eyed young fellow?

So he stayed in town, and strove to pass the time in such a way as to preclude thought, but this he could not manage. Ever and anon it would come upon him that he had done a base thing, without the faint excuse of its being very pleasant in the doing. The girl he had left had to the full as much charm for him as the one for whom he had left her. As much? Nay, more, he began to feel bitterly, and as he felt this he cursed that baneful habit of flirting which had wrecked him.

There was no comfort in his Club for him this day. He shrank away from all the men he knew, lest they should have heard of his grandfather's state, and should ask him "why he was not down at Maddington?" Under ordinary circumstances he would have been as quick with the tale and ready with the lie as the majority. But this was not an ordinary occasion; he felt himself to be equally unable to conceive a satisfactory fiction as to tell a shameful truth.

Finally, he bethought himself of going down to Bretford to see Sydney, this day, since he would be compelled to break his appointment with her on the morrow. Moodily he assured himself that he "should not see any fellow down there whom he knew"—none of his set congregated in those regions. With which complimentary reflection on the locality in which dwelt his future bride, he set off to visit her.

He got down to the Scotts' about five o'clock, and no sooner did he cross their threshold than it was made evident to him that his coming just then was very inopportune. A gabble as of Babel had smote upon his ears from the open drawing-room window as he passed it, the sound of many female voices in full cry over some recently started subject. But no sooner did he ring and give his name in a loud voice than a dead silence, a fearful calm, a terrible lull fell over all the house. Then whispers like zephyrs were heard—then breezy suggestions—then windy remonstrances; lastly, Sydney's voice rose clear and defiant above all others. "Nonsense, mamma," she said, "he's not to be kept dancing in the hall any longer, I can tell you;" and then the drawing-room door was thrown open, and Sydney, very becomingly arrayed in demi-toilette, came out determinately.

She was put out by something; perhaps it might be by his coming when she had not expected him. He did not care to fathom the cause, he was only conscious of being amused by the effect. Sydney was very bright in the eyes, and very flushed in the face, and very bustling in manner. He was very glad that he had come to-day, for he cared for no "calm of love" with her.

"Oh, Frank, it's you!" she began; "will you come into the dining-room for a minute?"

She half-opened the door of the empty dining-room as she spoke. Frank shook his head, negativing her proposition.

"No, no; you have some friends with you, I presume by all this" (he touched her diaphanous draperies as he spoke). "Why should I take you from them? I can't come to-morrow; so as you hadn't told me of your company, I thought I might come to-day."

"Why not to-morrow?—I must have you."

"You can't, unfortunately," he said coolly; "I'm off to Maddington; my grandfather is dying."

The spirit of exultation at the prospect before her leaped up within her in a flash.

"Dying! is he? Of course you will go; dear Frank, I'm so glad you came to-day. Company —it's no 'company;' but, come in."

She walked in before him willingly enough; she no longer sought to delay his entrance into the assemblage they were entertaining. She was oblivious of all things save that it was on the cards that she should soon be Lady Lesborough now.

It was a tolerably large party that upon which he entered; there were about a dozen or fourteen people seated round a table, on which a high tea was steaming. It was clearly no impromptu festivity; there was a look about all who were partaking of it of having come for the express purpose of partaking of it—a look of having been invited for that solemn end, together with a certain air of resolution not to be defrauded of an atom of it. There were several well-conducted young men at the table,—young men who sat straight on the extreme verge of their chairs, and made remarks to their immediate neighbours in still small voices; and interspersed amongst these there were several elderly ladies, who were one and all eating hot toast with a wealth of butter upon it, in white kid gloves, that didn't fit them. For one moment on his entrance Mrs. Scott almost took fire from excess of vexation; the next she spoke with the Brummagem hilarity and recklessness of despair.

"Law! how glad I am you're come, Mr. Burgoyne. Find him a chair, Scott, and make him comfortable; no ceremony you see—it's all in the family."

Then horror took the place amusement had held for a few minutes in Frank Burgoyne's heart, as Miss Scott introduced him separately and distinctly to each of the white-kidded ladies and well-conducted young men, and he found that they were one and all aunts and cousins of the bright-eyed young being who was attentively watching him through this ordeal, to see how he stood it.

It was simply awful to him. Had they been grossly vulgar he could have borne it better, he thought. Anything, in fact, would have been preferable to this atrocious under-breeding which kept them straight on the edges of their chairs, and suppressed and subdued their tones. From the moment of his appearance on the stage not one of them would eat a bit more toast, or do more than simperingly sip their tea. They were all in awe of him, that was evident; in awe of his position and future rank; but above all, in awe of that gentle breeding which was stranger than all else to them. I am ashamed to say that, for all his outward calmness, he was "cursing the lot" in his heart, as he glanced round the circle, and saw that the eyes of the whole party were fixed smilingly upon him, in a way he could have murdered them for.

CHAPTER XLVII.

NEMESIS.

"Is he alive still?" Frank Burgoyne asked eagerly of his aunt Ethel as he was embracing her immediately on his arrival at Maddington the following day.

"Yes, dear," she replied, through her tears, "and quite sensible, thank God! and oh! Frank, so anxious for you."

Frank Burgoyne was not bloodthirsty by nature, nor was he murderously inclined. Yet it is a fact that his heart sunk when he heard that Lord Lesborough was alive, and in full possession of his senses still. As he was going to die, it would have been so much more pleasant and convenient if he had done it already. His hanging on, if discoveries were made, would only complicate an already complicated position.

"Come up to papa at once—do, dear," Ethel pleaded, after a silence of a few minutes.

"I'm coming; hadn't you better go and tell him first?" he pleaded.

"No. I sent up word of your arrival the instant I saw you coming in. Oh! my dear boy, I am so glad you're here. Do come!"

"Ye-es, I'm coming. Is Ffrench with him?"

"No. Mr. Ffrench is in the oak parlour with Mr. Vaughan; the dear Vaughans, they are so kind. How's Theo?"

Frank started up.

"Come up with me, Ethel," he said, without noticing her inquiry; and then they went upstairs together, he almost seeming to seek support from her arm.

He had an invincible repugnance to going into the presence of the moribund. It was not the superstitious fear which sometimes seizes a woman in the immediate atmosphere of death. It was rather a weighty dread that the death would be delayed till his secret had transpired. He almost prayed that his grandfather would be past taking an interest in anything worldly; he had difficulty in checking an ardent hope that Lord Lesborough might be quite speechless and deaf.

But Lord Lesborough was neither. Frank could not control a little start of surprise when he came up to the bed, and saw so little that seemed to him to resemble death in the aspect of the composed old man who was stretched upon it. Then a spasm seized his heart. Supposing that composure should be marred and broken up by him before it was merged in the more complete and absolute composure of death. He could not trust himself to speak immediately on the birth of this reflection; so he contented himself with putting his hand on the pale one that was put out feebly to greet him.

"I'm glad you're come, my boy. I'm going fast,—going fast, Frank," Lord Lesborough muttered feebly; and then Ethel created a diversion by bursting out with a sob, for which one of the nurses in attendance instantly ejected her from the room.

"Don't say that, sir," Frank replied feebly.

"But it is so, my boy—my dear boy, it is so," and here Lord Lesborough's own voice broke with a sob, for life was sweet, was very sweet to the old man even yet. Presently he resumed in a calmer tone, "There's one thing I should have liked—to see you married before I go; but you'll not wait long before you marry and settle here, and be an honour to your name, will you Frank?"

"No," Frank said faintly; he felt that he was acting a lie by thus suffering the belief which dictated Lord Lesborough's words to remain undisturbed when foundation for it no longer existed. But "what could he do," he asked himself; "what could he do—now?"

"No, no, you'll not delay it long," Lord Lesborough repeated. "She's a dear good girl, Frank, a dear good girl; I wish she had come down to see me before I go," and when he said that Lord Lesborough began to cry again, and Frank tried to shuffle away from the side of the bed.

"I have left my black cabinet—that one that's filled with blue Sévres, to Theo, and many other things that Ffrench thought she would like for her own."

("How can a man on the brink of the grave think of blue earthenware?") Frank thought ("he can't be half as bad as they made out, wish I hadn't come.")

"Harold Ffrench is very thoughtful for Miss Leigh," he said aloud.

"He knows her and values her. You're not jealous, are you, boy?" the old man asked, as his grandson drew himself away, and sat down on a chair that was partially behind the curtain.

"Jealous! No, no, sir."

"I liked the little girl," Lord Lesborough went on dreamily; in truth he had thought but little, and cared less for Theo Leigh, till his favourite Harold had impressed the fact of her value upon him. "I liked the little girl; always liked her; I should like to do more for her; but it doesn't matter, she will share a very fair fortune with you, my boy, a very fair fortune indeed."

Could he sit there and hear this. Oh! for a tongue to tell the truth without a falter that might betoken fear. Such a tongue was not his, he knew: therefore he kept silent.

"All you have she'll share with you, and they all tell me that she richly deserves it. You have done well in your choice of a wife, my boy. God bless you and her."

After this Frank got himself away out of the room as fast as he could, and made his way to his own suite of apartments, from whence he dispatched a messenger for Ethel to come to him.

"I want you to come and bathe my head with eau-de-cologne, Ethel," he said, in his old half-imperious, spoiled-boy tone as soon as she came into the cosy den they called his study.

"Does it ache, dear?" she said, fondly putting away all thoughts of her own throbbing brows at once. Then he laid himself down upon a couch, and she bathed his forehead tenderly, and beguiled the time by thinking how handsome and good, and noble altogether he was.

"I hope you'll be able to see Mr. Vaughan before he goes, Frank?" she said softly at last, in a suggestive tone, "he wants to see you."

"He be damned," Frank returned morosely: "there, I beg your pardon, Ethel. Lord how my brain racks. I can't see old Vaughan, I tell you; what does he want to see me for?"

Frank spoke with such unwonted peevishness that Ethel stared. "Really Frank, I don't know what he wants to see you for; it's very natural that he should do so, isn't it? Theo is his niece, remember."

"What is that to me? There," catching her hand; "I didn't mean to be impatient; but I'm upset altogether; don't you worry me, there's a good girl. The two people in this world who bore me most nearly out of my mind are Vaughan and Harold Ffrench; I can't stand either of them now; you may make any excuse you think proper" (this was uttered after the magnificent manner of men who never deem it necessary to furnish those unfortunates whom they elect to the honourable post of their excusers, with fitting words) "you may make any excuse you think proper. Say I'm in my bed, or in my grave, or in the devil's own humour; anything will serve, so long as you keep them from me."

"Oh, Frank, Frank, what has come to you?" Ethel asked thoughtfully; "something has gone wrong with you; what is it?"

But he told her nothing had gone wrong with him; "he only needed a night's rest." Soon after this she left him, and for the remainder of that day he was spared all mention of Theo Leigh.

The morrow brought a little spurious strength to Lord Lesborough, and (more distracting still to Lord Lesborough's grandson) a letter from Sydney Scott, that got animadverted upon at the breakfast-table before it was handed to Frank by Ethel.

"Why, is that Miss Scott's writing—what can the little thing have to say to you, Frank?—nothing amiss with Theo, I hope?" Ethel asked eagerly, as Frank, after glancing at the letter, put it away in his pocket.

"No, nothing," he replied, and he looked up scowlingly at Harold Ffrench, who was watching him as he said it.

"She was a most charming little flirt, that Miss Scott," Ethel went on; "do you remember she even tried her hand on Mr. Linley, and he was very much at her feet for a time."

"Very much at her feet—might have been her grandfather!" Frank exclaimed.

"So he might; but all the same he was, and she liked it," Ethel replied. "He was, wasn't he, Mr. Ffrench?"

"Was he?" Harold Ffrench evidently was not thinking about whether the statement was correct or not. "Has anything been heard of Linley lately? Do you know where he is, Burgoyne?"

"Abroad—where, I can't tell exactly; somewhere on the Rhine I believe," Frank replied affably. He was uncommonly glad to change the subject from Miss Sydney Scott and her letter.

"If you come across his address I wish you would give it to me," Harold Ffrench said quietly; and Frank in all unsuspiciousness promised that he would do so.

Lord Lesborough continued better during the day. His medical attendants shook their heads with much sapience, and told everybody what everybody knew already, that his lordship had rallied wonderfully; "there was no saying now what turn the case might take," they added—a phrase which is frequently found to be soothing as well as safe.

Frank had paid his grandfather a visit after breakfast, and had been tortured by more allusions to Theo Leigh. When he came out of the sick room he felt much depressed and grieved in spirit. A longing for sympathy seized him, and he resolved upon making a confidante of Ethel —of Ethel, who had always "stood by him" since their babyhood.

"Come out in the grounds and have a turn with me, will you, Ethel?"

"Yes; you ought just to go and give Mrs. Vaughan a look, Frank."

"Oh, Mrs. Vaughan be —— Well, I won't say what, only don't make me go there."

"Very well," she replied simply, going away to get her hat and shawl; and he hoped the matter was ended, for already Frank, the vacillating, had begun to repent him of the but just formed determination to confide in Ethel.

When, however, they had been out in the grounds for a few minutes, Ethel resumed the subject.

"Frank, tell me. Why do you shun the Vaughans?"

"Oh!—I don't know."

"You do know, of course. But will you tell me?"

He walked a little faster, and made no answer.

"Something has gone wrong with Theo and you; tell me, Frank."

Still no answer.

"Have you found out that you were over hasty that night at Lowndes?"

"Yes, I have," he replied, suddenly.

"And broken it off? Oh, Frank, it will be an awful blow to papa, after things have gone so far —if he lives to know of it, that is," she added, mournfully,

The spirit of confidence was upon Frank now.

"That isn't all," he said, sadly. "I wish to heaven it was; but I'm in for another affair, Ethel. I'm——"

"Not engaged to any one else?" she cried out in her clear, ringing accents, dropping his arm, and looking at him fixedly.

The colour came into his face under her gaze.

"Don't tax a fellow with it as though it were a crime," he said, deprecatingly.

"A crime—it would be a crime, Frank. Tell me?—you're not guilty."

"Not guilty, but engaged again," he said, miserably; for again he felt himself to be a very poor fellow.

"I can't think it of you," she said, sorrowfully; "Indeed I can't. You must tell me all there is to tell now, Frank. You must, indeed; but, before you tell it to me, understand that I'll be no party to anything underhand. What there is to be known ought to be known at once, I think."

And then, though he dreaded nothing so much as its getting abroad, he felt himself drawn on to tell her the whole story.

She loved him very dearly, but he could wring no more from her than this—that she would not volunteer the tale to his grandfather.

"I won't go up and tell papa, unless anything is said that would make my holding my tongue appear like a belief in the marriage between Theo and you, Frank. In such a case I must speak, because it would be mean to be silent."

When she said that, Frank remembered how mean he had felt the night before in holding his peace; and so, though he was very wroth with her for entertaining such scruples, he could not doubt their being genuine and strong.

"Well, I can only hope that nothing will be said; but it will be like my cursed luck for it all to come out. Lord Lesborough will make the most of it, you may be sure."

He spoke in a bitter, sarcastic tone, and Ethel's heart bled for him, but still she could not side with him here.

"Don't sneer at papa, Frank," she said, mournfully. "You have behaved very badly. The only thing now is for you to bear the fruits of your fault like a man."

As ill-luck would have it, the subject was mooted by Lord Lesborough again that evening. Mooted in such a way that Frank could not evade it.

"And you hadn't the courage to avow your scoundrelism yesterday, when, sir, my fond folly made plans for your mutual happiness, as I thought," the old man said, choking with rage.

"If you think me a scoundrel, I had better not stay in your presence," Frank replied, turning away and walking out of the room. His heart was hardened against his grandfather, and

his grandfather's heart was hardened against him.

In the night Lord Lesborough altered his will, leaving the whole of the unentailed property to Harold Ffrench; and on the following morning Lord Lesborough died, and Frank was master of Maddington.

CHAPTER XLVIII (AND LAST).

A SOUND OF WEDDING-BELLS.

FOR a little time after the meaning of that letter had been made clear to her, Theo laid at her mother's feet with her head on her mother's lap, remained there powerless and motionless for the unexpectedness of the blow had struck her down completely. They were terrible thoughts that rolled through the girl's mind as she laid there; her soul was very dark, and there was none by to "quickly string" a harp whose chords might perchance tell a tale of brighter things. An hour before she had been rich in the anticipation of so much. She laid there prostrate now—a bankrupt in love, in hope, in happiness.

For about an hour she remained there on the ground, motionless in her misery. Then she rose to her feet, and her face, instead of being wan and pale, and worn, as her mother had anticipated seeing it, was flushed and hot. She looked at herself in the glass for a minute or two, pushing her hair back over her ears as she looked; and the action was so childish, and the face that gazed into the glass so young, that her mother could but sob over the many years of sorrow that were before her child. After looking at herself in silence for a few minutes, Theo retreated from the glass and rested against the side of the window, with her face buried in the curtains, and then she spoke:

"I mayn't be able to remember two things in a day or two that I ought to tell you at once, mother dear; one is, that I have bought my wedding-dress, and it must be got rid of—it will not be needed now; and the other is, that I am glad this didn't happen while my father was alive."

She did not say this calmly by any means; she said it with many sobs, and with a terrible quivering throughout her frame. Suddenly, and before her mother could frame a reply to her last speech, she changed her position. Her restlessness seemed to betoken bodily pain as well as mental; she went over and leant on the bed, with her face upon the pillow.

"It's very bad, very hard; do you think it has come to me because I was ready to love another man so soon after Mr. Ffrench? It couldn't be that. Or is God spiteful?"

"Theo, Theo, my child!"

Again Theo moved; this time it was away to the mantel-piece, against the cold marble of which she pressed her forehead.

"I can't think it's that, for he made me loving. What is it?—what is it?—why am I cursed?"

Again the hot tears poured themselves in a torrent from her eyes, as once more she moved back to the bed. Mrs. Leigh congratulated herself at sight of those tears. "She won't suffer so much if she can cry," she thought, in unconsciousness of the exquisite anguish tears caused one afflicted with such a temperament as Theo.

"I wonder what will become of me," she said presently; "it doesn't seem to matter a bit now, battered about as I have been; but perhaps I shall care again some day. What can become of me? Oh! all those things I've got! I'll lie down and think what I will do with them."

Then once more her hands went up to her head, and she sank down upon the floor wailing.

"I thought he loved me,—I was so sure of it."

They gathered her up, and carried her to her room, and laid her on her bed, where she lay tossing about and moaning for hours. In the middle of the night she woke, and told her mother, who was watching her with an anxiety that precluded all thoughts of fatigue, that she was "better now, and in no pain, only thirsty." After this the absence from pain and the thirst continued for four or five days, during which she got up and dressed as usual. But when she was up and dressed she would sit for hours doing nothing, and saying nothing, and looking very pale. At the end of that time the fever that was in her came out and showed itself, and soon she was shorn of her wavy tresses, and was lying perfectly helpless, and perfectly unconscious of her misery. And this lasted for weeks.

Meanwhile the old Lord Lesborough was buried, and the young Lord Lesborough had fairly taken possession of Maddington, to which place Mr. Scott came presently, in order to comfort his future son-in-law in his affliction, much to that unlucky one's chagrin. Miss Burgoyne and Ethel, together with their little sister, had decided upon living in London, so Frank was free to bring home his bride as soon as he pleased, a fact which Mr. Scott soon gave Lord Lesborough to understand he perceived.

Harold Ffrench had left for—none knew where. Before he left he had got Mr. Linley's current address from Lord Lesborough, to whom David Linley had written immediately on his accession to the title. Mr. Linley was living at a "sweet sequestered spot," so he described it, just free of the tourists' track, in a village whose very name was unknown to the frequenters of the Rhine. Here he was innocently, and he trusted profitably, employed in writing a novel, that, when it came out the following year, should win him that celebrity and fortune which had hitherto been denied to him. Harold Ffrench listened to these details with interest, and even jotted down the name of the village in his note-book.

It must be understood, before I proceed farther, that though Harold Ffrench was aware of the late Lord Lesborough having some cause of wrath against his grandson—some cause sufficiently strong to induce him to alter his will in favour of Harold Ffrench—Harold Ffrench had no suspicion of the real reason of that wrath, for the Burgoynes were so absorbed in their grief for their father, that no mention was made of Frank's shortcomings. Accordingly, when he left Maddington, Harold Ffrench still believed that Maddington was Theo's future home, and Lord Lesborough her future husband. Had he known the real state of the case, the end of this story might have been sunnier, perchance.

He went to London and saw his lawyer, and made a will, leaving not only all the property Lord Lesborough had left him, but all the property he had been possessed of before that, to Theo Leigh. "It shall all go back to them," he thought; "her husband shall not eventually be a poorer man through his grandfather's liking for me," and as he thought this an unwonted softness crept over him, and he went out to Hampstead, and just looked at the house where his jewel was, not trusting himself to see her again, in his blind ignorance of how matters were going within.

Well, the end must be told, and told quickly now, for very little space is left to me. It must be told: it is not bright, but "it boots not to delay," as Thomas Ingoldsby has it in that most perfect of mediæval poems, "As I lay a thinkygne," "It boots not to delay," "let that which must be done be done quickly."

I must drop all my characters for a space, leaving them planted on the board of life thus: Theo ill of a fever; Harold Ffrench on the eve of departure for the Continent in unconsciousness of every evil that had befallen her; Lord Lesborough in possession at Maddington; and Sydney Scott rather impatient than otherwise to become 'my Lady.' The subordinate characters in this quiet little drama, which has been played out before you, shall come out in a body at the end, and bow their acknowledgments to a discriminating public for a gracious hearing.

So for a space the curtain falls. It rises again some three months later in the year to the sound of wedding-bells.

They are ringing out merrily through the keen December air, foretelling all sorts of good things for the pair whose nuptials they are melodiously celebrating. The church in whose belfry they are hung is in the West-End district. Pausing on the threshold of that church, inquirers may hear the murmurs of a "double event."

A double event! Two pairs made happy on one day. Hail smiling morn, that sees this blessed quadrilateral. They have "no connection whatever," the fusty old pew-opener will tell anyone who will tip her sufficiently well to induce her to tell anything at all. Nor had they, in reality, any "connection whatever," save the connection formed all unconsciously to themselves in these pages.

The first pair, the pair to whom the pew-opener and her fellow-sycophants curtseyed the lowest, —the pair to whom the best-horsed carriages belonged,—the pair that called a hearty "God bless 'em" from the populace,—were Lord Lesborough and Sydney Scott. He made her a happy woman that morning, not perhaps with the best will in the world, for he hated her cousins, who required all sorts of good posts and lucrative appointments at his hands; but still with a sufficiently good grace to pass muster, and look all that was desirable in the eyes of the crowd.

Sydney was gorgeous,—as gorgeous as it was possible to be in white. She looked very happy and very plump, and very much as if all things had gone well with her in life, as she passed down the aisle under her title and lace veil. "Don't kiss me till I get home and take off my wreath, or you'll cram it, Frank," she said to him, as soon as they had seated themselves in the carriage; and he ceased from his demonstrations at once, in prompt recognition of her superior self-possession. Lady Lesborough made only one more important speech that day: it deserves to be noted down ere we take a last leave of her.

"Mamma, dear," she said, when she had made a very good breakfast, and was holding herself in readiness to take her husband away; "give the whole lot of them" (by the "whole lot of them" she meant all such as sat on the verge of their chairs and made timorous speeches)—"give the whole lot of them to understand that they keep clear of *me*. Frank shall provide for the boys, as far as getting them good berths goes; but I won't have them lumbering up my house."

The other pair whom God joined in such a way that no man could put them asunder, will, I fear, administer a slight shock when witnessed in this conjunction.

The bride quakes like an indifferently-made jelly as she comes down the church, leaning on the arm of the earnest young divine, Mr. Shalders, who has taken Lady Glaskill for better for worse in consideration of her dividends, the fabulous wealth in those boxes which she has never permitted him to open, and his own intense desire to have a London pulpit, and an impressionable female audience. He will have these things now, and Lady Glaskill, the wife of his evangelical bosom, will mutter and mouth full many an evening in silent solitude, while he is intoning prayers under a deftly adjusted light, pleasantly posed upon crimson velvet cushions.

As for John Galton and Kate, they are going on much as when we saw them last, with this difference, that Kate is in sorrow just now, in a very natural and legitimate sorrow, for one who had been very dear to her has come to an untimely end. The sorrow is so natural and legitimate, and Kate evinces it in such a thoroughly tender, womanly, open way, that even Miss Sarah cannot find it in her heart to deem her sister-in-law a flagrant offender for betraying it at all. And here, as a veracious chronicler, I must pause to observe that Miss Sarah is not one whit more agreeable generally than she was when she made her first appearance in these pages; but for all that Kate now prefers her to women of the "Aunt Glaskill" type.

This sorrow which has come upon Kate is one that the reader will have surmised already—Harold Ffrench's death. He had fallen in a duel which he had forced upon David Linley, who shot his old friend through the chest, and then fell down by his side sobbing over him and kissing him as a woman might have done.

As for Theo, she recovered from her fever to find herself an heiress, and a person of sufficient importance to make it well worth her while to struggle for life. She has not, as she once jestingly declared she would, taken a yearly ticket on the line that leads to Maddington; but she travels about perpetually, and is very contented in mind, and only altered for the better from the Theo we knew of yore in person. Perhaps being only a woman, and being convinced of the truth of that assertion that it "is not good to live alone," she may find a certain pleasure in the reflection that a woman's life is not over at her age. But in these pages we take leave of her as Theo Leigh.

Library Edition of Thackeray's Works.

VANITY FAIR: A Novel without a Hero. By WILLIAM MAKEPEACE THACKERAY. With Illustrations by the Author, and a Portrait on Steel, engraved by Halpin after Lawrence's Picture. A new and elegant Library Edition, in Three Volumes, Post 8vo, on Toned Paper, Cloth, $7 50.

"Vanity Fair" needs no recommendation. But this beautiful edition of it deserves special notice. The designs with which Thackeray illustrated his works, which are, so to speak, his own commentary upon them, and without which the story loses half its point—which illustrate Thackeray's character scarcely less than his pages—are admirably reproduced.—*North American Review.*

In the tenderness which presided over its preparation, in the profusion and beauty of its illustrations, in its elegant type and delicate cream-laid paper, we have evidences on the part of the publishers of a love and reverence for the writer which will find an echo in the hearts of his millions of admirers.—*New York Herald.*

Perfect in all those externals which are so pleasing to refined taste, and which make books as ornamental as they are useful. Paper, type, illustrations, and binding are all exquisite.—*Boston Traveller.*

This beautiful edition will receive a grateful and cordial welcome from every admirer of the great English master of fiction.—*New York Tribune.*

Nothing has been spared, in paper, type, and binding, to gratify the most fastidious taste.—*Boston Courier.*

The paper is rich, heavy, and exquisitely tinted. The type, marked with a racy dash of the antique, is the perfection of clearness. The illustrations are Thackeray's own, reproduced in the best style of engraving, and the binding faultless in taste.—*Buffalo Courier.*

American bookcraft has produced nothing more elegant or artistic.—*Albany Evening Journal.*

If there is such a thing as an art amounting to poesy in book-making, the enterprising publishers may certainly be said to have achieved it here. This edition is something of which our country may well be proud. We thank Messrs. Harper for having shown to the world that peace has here its triumphs as well as war. We feel gratified to think that America has anticipated Europe in embalming so fitly the memory of William Makepeace Thackeray.—*Detroit Free Press.*

"*Thackeray in Full Dress.*"—Fine feathers do not always make fine birds; but the finest birds do not disdain their fine feathers, and therefore Thackeray, if he were happily still living, with all his scorn of finery, would feel proud of the garb in which he is arrayed by Messrs. Harper & Brothers.—*Philadelphia Evening Bulletin.*

These volumes are almost perfect specimens of book-making. The type is clear, the paper beautiful, the binding tasteful, and the illustrations, by Thackeray's own hand, have never been better printed.—*N. Y. Evening Post.*

A most elegant edition of the works of this greatest master of English fiction of the present age. In every respect it is among the most beautiful issues of the American press.—*New York Daily Times.*

Thackeray deserves a lasting monument—not a mere bust in Westminster Abbey, the British Pantheon, but under the roof-tree of every educated family. We rejoice that Harper & Brothers have laid the first stone of the new and magnificent monument. It is indeed a reproduction, in such a superior style, as regards fine type, careful printing, tinted and hot-pressed paper, delicate yet firm binding, and careful engraving, that it can best be briefly described as an *edition de luxe.* A luxurious edition it is, worthy of the author, and lower in price than that originally issued by the author himself. It has never been surpassed in execution here or in England. It is superb in all respects.—*Philadelphia Press.*

The Harpers are embalming Thackeray. The odor of sweet spices seems to hang about this edition of the great satirist's works which these favorite publishers are now issuing, and the reverence of art for genius is made apparent in every detail. A more exquisite monument was never dedicated to an author's memory. Daintier volumes have seldom come from the press in any part of the world.—*New York Express.*

The volumes are faultless in every thing that pertains to their mechanical execution, and in some particulars are an advance on any thing yet attained in the art of book-making. They are just of the right size. The printing is of the best. The binding is exquisitely tasteful. It is so well done as to give us the beauty of appearance of cloth, with almost the substantial character of a firmer material. The outside appearance of the book is a real feast to the eye. Every thing about it combines the chaste and the elegant to a degree very seldom realized.—*Norfolk County Journal* (Roxbury).

The tributes paid to Thackeray, living and dead, by the great English nation, whose literature he heightened and adorned with the generous outpourings of his genius and tenderness of speech, have not had—no, not one—such solid worth and loving appreciation of the man and author as these American publishers have shown in this superb copy of his works. An earnest lover of rare books will finger these volumes with dainty touch—will turn the page more tenderly for looking again upon the tender face, which Lawrence has preserved to us—will find new beauties in them as he slowly and softly touches each golden-tinted leaf, eloquent with sweet fancies, humor most delicate, wit keen as the scimitar of Saladin, and pathos deep and true as the heart of the great humanitarian who sadly penned them. The etchings are Thackeray's own, and the hand that copied them here performed its task with very loving fidelity. We accept this tribute as the truest that has been ever paid to the great humorist, and we feel a pardonable pride that we owe it to the enterprise, taste, and liberality of American publishers.—*Philadelphia Legal Intelligencer.*

The binding is the perfection of beauty and neatness. The smallest amount of gold upon a ground of delicate green gives the sides the refreshing look of a meadow starred with a single buttercup.—*Indianapolis Journal.*

It is a matter of almost national congratulation that the first excellent, complete edition of Thackeray's works is to appear in America. No more appropriate testimony and monument of his genius could be than the edition that Messrs. Harper & Brothers have projected. It would seem that the most loving appreciation has presided over its preparation. Thackeray would like to have handled it, and we can not but think that his honest regard for this country would have been deepened by such a mark of appreciation. Surely no novel has ever been so typographically honored in this country. It is such an edition as every lover of handsome books will want, and every appreciator of Thackeray will have.—*Hartford Press.*

PUBLISHED BY HARPER & BROTHERS, NEW YORK.

Sent by Mail, postage free, on receipt of the price.